THE GYPSY LOVER

THE GYPSY LOVER

A Novel

Roger Ladd Memmott

Copyright ©2001 by Roger Ladd Memmott

Library of Congress Number: 00-192528
ISBN #: Hardcover 0-7388-4416-0
Softcover 0-7388-4417-9

All rights reserved. No part of this book may be reproduced or transmitted in any form or by any means, electronic or mechanical, including photocopying, recording, or by any information storage and retrieval system, without permission in writing from the copyright owner.

This is a work of fiction. Names, characters, places and incidents either are the product of the author's imagination or are used fictitiously, and any resemblance to any actual persons, living or dead, events, or locales is entirely coincidental.

This book was printed in the United States of America.

To order additional copies of this book, contact:
Xlibris Corporation
1-888-7-XLIBRIS
www.Xlibris.com/bookstore
Orders@Xlibris.com

A Gemstone Book
♦ SAN FRANCISCO, CA ♦

Publishing Services & Cataloging by
XLIBRIS CORPORATION
A Strategic Partner of Random House Ventures

This book is available and may be ordered
through all major bookstores and bookstore web sites
in hardback, paperback, and digital formats.

Orders may also be submitted directly to XLIBRIS CORPORATION, 436 Walnut Street,
11th Floor, Philadelphia, PA 19106 – Toll Free: 888.795.4247
www.xlibris.com/bookstore – Orders@Xlibris.com

For autographed copies, visit UNEXPECTED LIGHT
@ www.unexpectedlight.com/gypsy.html
(Standard orders may also be placed through UNEXPECTED LIGHT.)

COVER ART
Copyright © 2001 by Roger Ladd Memmott
Jacket Design: Aaron T. Memmott, MFA
Author's photo: Marrianne Memmott

THE GYPSY LOVER – A Novel
Copyright © 2001 by Roger Ladd Memmott
FIRST EDITION

All Rights Reserved
Printed in the United States of America

BOOKS BY ROGER LADD MEMMOTT

The Gypsy Lover
(novel)

Gardening Without Gloves
(short fiction)

Catharsis
(novella)

Praise for *The Gypsy Lover*

"I must tell you, it's worth it! *The Gypsy Lover* is a classic coming of age story . . . an artfully written novel that can be understood on many different levels; it is a book worth reading several times to capture the full flavor of its message of hope, healing and redemption."

—*Steeped in Thought Book News*

"Intoxicatingly poetic . . . by turns stunningly beautiful and prosaic, *The Gypsy Lover* is innovative, unequaled, and recommended."

—*Romance Reviews Today*

" . . . a real talent. *The Gypsy Lover* is a picaresque coming of age story, rich in plot, romance, tragedy, and theme. The prose, always evocative and graceful, engages the reader for its own sake together with a skillful modulation of atmosphere and suspense."

—*The Editorial Department*

" . . . intriguing . . . I found myself avidly reading page after page to see how it would end."

—*Kathy's Faves & Raves*

The Gypsy Lover is a well-developed story of one teenager's life . . . and a very good story about the Gypsy lifestyle.

—*Scribes World Reviews*

For
The Gypsies of My Youth
both real & unreal alike

For
Marrianne
heart & soul

For
Christian & Aaron
without whom…

Habent sua fata libelli

The Gypsy Lover is a work of fiction. If characters and events portrayed in the story bear resemblance to actual persons, places, or things, either living, dead, or yet to come into this world, it is coincidence of the highest order and beyond control.

ACKNOWLEDGEMENTS

"To a Sleeping Child"
Robert Herrick (Renaissance Poet 1591-1674)

"I See Not a Step Before Me" (Excerpt)
Mary Gardiner Brainard

I would also like to express appreciation to Renni and Ross Browne and to Peter Gelfan of The Editorial Department, especially to Peter whose editorial assistance and commentary on the manuscript was both insightful and instructive–and to Dan Stein and Oakley Hall who long ago imagined the possibility of fires unquenched.

A lexicon of Romany words and phrases may be found at the end of the book.

CONTENTS

~Prologue~The Voice 17

~1~ Before the Telling of It 23

~2~ How a Thing Comes to Mean 32

~3~ The Errant Heart 53

~4~ Dreams 65

~5~ A Dog's Life 76

~6~ Escape to the Pits 96

~7~ The Cowboy & the Gypsies 104

~8~ Coffins & Ghosts 117

~9~ Madness & Mayhem 134

~10~ Riddles & the Wandering Man 154

~11~ The Curse 170

~12~ The Fortune 183

~13~ Her Champion 198

~14~ Gates of Midnight 222

~15~ The Bujo 242

~16~ Tunnel of Love 256

~17~ The Revelation 272

~18~ The Wedding 288

~19~ Panic 312

~20~ A Sad & Joyful Exchange 325

Lexicon of Romany Words & Phrases 341

Publisher's Questions for Discussion 345

A Note About the Author 349

Whatever you claim is mine is yours;
whatever you claim is mine.

Yana Markovitch, Drabarni Extraordinaire

What lies behind us and what lies before us
are tiny matters compared to what lies within us.

Ralph Waldo Emerson

~Prologue~

The Voice

Think of me and remember . . .

*E*VAN—

The voice shrank inside him like some phantom whisper from another world, cold and without shadow or even light.

Evan—

And he knew whose voice it was.

> *I was of flesh and blood*
> *as other creatures be*
> *Yet neither flesh nor blood*
> *remains in me.*
> *My mother, black as ink,*
> *once rode on air*
> *Then, girlish, stood before you*
> *but was not there.*

He listened to the riddle and then to the sound of his own name, as one fretful and wearied by dreams. Yet awake, he struggled even against the strange reassurance when the voice came to him, came like some inner fire yet cold, owing more to the realm of fantasy than fact. For when it came, it came with the confusions of heartache and joy. It came whispering the everyday enigmas of disaster and love. It came upon labored wings with fleeting visions of the other world where spirits abound. It came bespeaking desire and fate, sighing his name . . . *Ev-a-a-an*. Whispering *Remember me*. And if he heard, he knew. And if he knew anything at all, he knew the meaning—the answer—could be found in a single word, a phrase at the most, hidden somewhere in the telling of it, for contend as he might, he could not forget.

*   *   *

"Come on, kid. You'll miss your plane."

The sheriff leaned toward him, a fleshy hand waving him through the terminal wing toward the security gate. Before they entered the metal detector, the sheriff turned around and said, "I guess I'd oughtn't let you have this back, but I don't always do what I ought. The department's got no claim to it now."

Evan unshouldered his bag and dumped it on the conveyer. He looked at the sheriff. Kentuckian, he'd bet, or maybe even deeper South than that, come North to sheriff across the river in Cincinnati.

"Go ahead."

Go ahead?

He looked at the sheriff's meaty palm and in it the bone-handled hunting knife that once belonged to his father. The police had found the knife within hours after he tried to get rid of it. They had held it as evidence until after the inquiry. Now here it was again, come full circle just like a prophecy in the words of a song. The sheriff held the knife toward him, inside a materials evidence bag that, for all intents and purposes, looked like a plastic ziplock sandwich bag. The cops hadn't even cleaned the thing; dried blood the color of rust smeared the handle and speckled the blade.

"You can't carry it on, of course."

No, he couldn't carry it on.

The sheriff turned and explained something to an airport security guard and the security guard looked at the knife and whistled. "This the kid in the papers?"

Evan walked through the scanner while the sheriff went around the gate in order to avoid triggering a beep. When they were on the plane, the sheriff handed the knife to the flight attendant and told her she could give it to "the kid" when they landed in Salt Lake City. "A family named Robbins will be there to meet him."

The flight attendant smiled kindly. "We'll take care of him." She reached up a little and patted his shoulder as though she were patting a dog. He didn't care. He could smell her perfume and she had nice legs.

In parting, the sheriff said, "Adios, kid. Don't take no wooden nickels and never pet a burning dog." He took off his hat and looked in the crown of it as if looking at something either humorous or obscene. "Adios," he said again, and then to the attendant, "You look after him now. He ain't quite to the center of hisself."

The stewardess led him to his seat and looked at him across her shoulder and smiled too brightly. She had the unmistakable hips of a girl, though she was older, of course, and her aroma was something wonderful. She took the satchel from him and put it in the overhead bin. It was the first time he had ever flown, and she leaned over to help him with his seat belt, her hair swept forward caressing his face. She adjusted the window shade and across the tip of the wing he could see a band of light brighter than the rest stretching along the horizon above and beneath the setting sun. She looked at him sympathetically and this time patted him on top of his head. She had such a nice aroma, something he had never smelled before, and he couldn't help wondering all the wonderful things there are to wonder about a beautiful woman who smiles too brightly.

When she left, he sat back, undid his seat belt, and took from his pocket a small heart-shaped stone. But for the defect, fine as a filament and just off center, it was smooth as glass, translucent with light. He held it and stroked it with his fingers and listened to the turbines whine.

The voice surprised him, trembling into his thoughts like the stone itself disturbing the flat surface of a pond, a watery rush across his eyes, and then all at once on pounding wings, close to his heart, whispering *think of me and remember*, and before they had taxied to the end of the runway, a thousand ragged images and painful desires came flooding back. Was it some confused notion, or the pitch of the engines, crying like a raven in the dark? *Think of me and remember.* Had he been able, he would have saved the voice. He looked toward the flare of the brightening sky as the sun softly sank. He would have saved them all if he could. But the voice was without timbre, and the single dark eye of the bird whose pounding wings beat deep in his head and then in his breast was blue and cast and there was no reflection in it and nothing of the world. It was a dream and a voice within, without triumph or defeat, without discovery or loss, without even some sad and joyful exchange. It was a voice beyond remnants of light, beyond motion and sound, the flat dull echo on the shore of an unknowable void, and it gripped him like the witness to certain inevitable truths he could never escape.

Evan—

Listening, he closed the window shade and shut his eyes and worked the warm surface of the stone between fingers and thumb. The plane bounced and picked up speed, rolling toward takeoff.

The sheriff hands me a knife in this grizzly looking bag and tells me to give it to the kid when we arrive in Salt Lake City. He tells me to look after him, as though I'm his mother or something, and I smile like an idiot and touch him and lead him to his seat. The funny thing is the way he looks back at me when I buckle him in. I've never in my life been looked at like that, and believe me I've felt the yearn of many a look. I patted the top of his head and hurried to the John to see if I had a button missing or a spot of something on my blouse or a makeup smudge. I think of it now, and it makes my stomach go small. I looked at myself in the mirror. I wondered if he had seen what I saw, leaning over him like that, and something inside me blossomed like fire. I flushed the toilet and shifted my breasts with my hands. I went back to the kitchen and took the knife out and looked at it. I didn't take it out of the bag. I motioned to Sheila and she went to the mike. I walked back down the aisle with the demonstration belt and oxygen mask. His eyes were closed and he looked older than I'd thought, not a kid so much. Sort of happy-sad. He was rubbing something in his hand. I wanted to touch him, his eyes, the shape of his mouth. After Salt Lake, I would probably never see him again. Sheila had started the spiel, and I couldn't get the belt to unbuckle. I felt like I was under some spell.

~ 1 ~

Before the Telling of It

. . . that the world might be according to his hope.

EVAN'S father was killed two months before he was born. It was in all the papers, about the train carrying propane, a seal from one of the tankers thrown two miles, killing him where he stood watering the hedges between the sidewalk and the street in front of the apartment building he lived in with his pregnant wife. Evan's mother died when he was seven. A rose killed her. It is a medical fact, recorded in the *Annals of Internal Medicine.* Nicked on the back of the hand by a thorn from one of her beloved long-stemmed reds, she died after a brief period of infection.

Evan remembered the hospital and the dark unfamiliar odors of her bed. She cried out but once: *Let me have my baby!* But Evan's head was already upon her breast when she said these words, and he listened quietly to the breath in her, to the whisper of a wail in that final rattling sigh: *I see her. There! Standing in the window.* Shortly afterward, the nurse came in and put her hand on his mother's wrist, the unbandaged one. She looked at the boy with shining eyes, so dark and glistening he could see in them a longing for the world's end. He looked toward the window, but there was nothing, not even a reflection against the black interior of the room.

Sometimes, the nurse said, cupping her hand beneath his jaw and turning his face toward her, *the only way to hang on to yourself is to leave everything else behind.*

Or had he read that in a book years later?

Before the death of his mother, his world was one of shadows that came and went, like images beyond some burnished gatelamp, somber and haunting as ghosts. At the time, he had little sense of those shadows or of the knowledge of what it meant to "leave everything else behind." But he had, and not knowing it made no difference, for memories and images that may or may not have been true—or at least accurate—were nevertheless his own, and he kept them inside himself, deep, like secrets he had swallowed with his mouth and that had gotten into the blood parts that washed through his veins. There, some remnant of his own dead sister lay feverish and red, but little more of her than a visit to the graveyard with a bouquet of roses and his mother softly singing,

> Here a sleeping child lies,
> Sung to sleep by lullabies.
> As you look, she will not stir
> The silent earth that covers her.

She lay steeped in his blood, nameless and effaced, this and the simple account of her death the year before he was born, having lived only a month or two. So beautiful and tiny and dark, but nothing of her standing in the window of a hospital as his mother lay dying.

And his father?

From the earliest days he could remember his father lingered inside his head or perhaps his heart, ghostly, cheerful, and dark. How easy it was for him to remember his mother and the sob in her throat whenever she spoke of his father. Her memories were always his own, and though troubled at times, without accusation or spite. She told him, he was certain she had, how his father had been a railroad engineer for the Union Pacific, usually on the Iron Mountain or Las Vegas run, and in his spare time, something of a poet. Hadn't his mother told him that, too—that his father had an artistic bent—or had he inoculated himself with the notion for immunity's sake, another secret steeped in the blood? Hadn't she told him how his father had been away two, three, four days at a time, and then maybe home for a week before being called out again? And now, these years later, remembering, how he would come home at two or three o'clock in the morning and crawl into bed with her, fresh and alert with the energy of the night, and how she would receive him warm and delicious with her own drowsiness, unable to tell where her sleep left off and his adoration began? Hadn't she told him that, how one such night she had lifted herself into the tender embrace of those arms all for the hope of a son?

O, what poetry! Every touch a sonnet! Hadn't she told him? Without a word of accusation or spite? Or had he read that in a book as well? Perhaps one of his father's books—the remembrance of a single line in one of the few published poems in newspapers and small press reviews, or that slim volume from some obscure press, but nothing earth shattering, nothing that might ripple the waters beyond the heart of his wife or his dead or unborn child. Nothing about the secrets, the slights, nothing about the dark little vagabond that some might think.

She told him, at least he thought he remembered her telling him, about dreams of his father's return at the moment of birth, as though he had been there, in the delivery room, was there, with Evan's first breath. Now, if he were to speak of his father, some undefined ambiguity of character the man must have possessed rottened certain hearts. It nagged and fascinated him at the same time, this secret of character that evil found so detestable. Perhaps it was some blessed insight into the world and its creatures at large, some quality approaching the divine, and he wondered what fraction of it imbued his own curious soul. Even though he knew his mother and father hardly at all, he supposed them the two most wonderful people in the world.

The nurse said, *You be good to him now.* And, at age seven, placing his hand in the damp palm of an aunt's, he came to know terror, not just in the simple fear of dark closets and dank fruit cellars, not in the reasonable contemplation of loss, but in the cruel exchange of a strop on the backs of his thighs, the welts so raw that blood leached through to the surface of his flesh, leaving a wafer of puss and scab.

He's my husband's brother's boy, that is to say half-brother. We got responsibilities to kin and expect to own up. Don't dawdle, now. It's late and we got to git.

Evan came to know her as Missy Begonia. From the landing outside his room at the top of the stairs, he would sometimes watch her through the stair rails in the kitchen below, weary with fascination and distaste, for she was a shrill piggish woman given to occasional fits, who lunged about with the over-stuffed look of someone ready to explode. Her lean-necked husband, whose red shock of hair and hooked nose gave him the uncanny resemblance to a rooster, always had a plug of tobacco in his jaw and a gob of spittle staining his chin. Evan soon concluded they were entirely brainless and evil only in the way that certain plants are poisonous.

From the time his mother died, the three of them lived on a potato farm at the center of the Mineral Range Valley, about two miles from the nearest town in Southern Utah. Because of the begonias she raised, Aunt Missy had gained a degree of notoriety throughout the valley. The blooms were perennial prize-winners, the biggest, most colorful begonias in the county, and she fussed and cooed over them as if they were children and could, in some queer way, return love in kind. "Mother Begonia," so to speak. The tuberous variety she raised were, in fact, rather pretty flowers—a bouquet looked like puffs of different colored smoke. But Missy remained lard-white. Still, her name was less a puzzle than her husband's. Since he looked more like a rooster than even a man, Evan could never figure out why they called him "Goose."

He told no one about the childhood beatings, neither his elementary nor Sunday School teachers, not even his friends. And then one day, Alta Mae Robbins' mother saw the backs of his legs at a swimming party, just a few welts and scars, mostly scabbed and healed over. He was teetering on the brink of a dive from the edge of the pool, when she called to him. He knew she was there, leaning back in a chaise longue, wearing a two-piece yellow swimsuit. He had noticed her earlier, and even before she called to him, he could feel her presence, wondering if she had noticed him. When he turned, she was balancing a glass of iced lemonade on her upper thigh, but she rose a little from the lounge and waved him over.

"Evan—Evan Adamson. My gosh, honey. Come here."

She was kind of skinny, and her tanned body glistened with oil, all up along her legs and across her stomach and the tops of her breasts. She had a narrow waist and unmistakable breasts haltered and slung in the yellow bikini top. She leaned on her elbow as Evan approached her, and her breasts up close were even more surprising than he'd thought. Alta Mae and her plump friend got out of the water and came and stood on the other side of the lounge, and looking at them he felt the rabbiting of his heart. In their one-piece suits, shiny and soaked through, they had hardly any breasts at all, arms clasped in shivering self-love, points of water dripping from eyelashes and chins—but still Evan could see an older Alta Mae in her mother, in the blue eyes, the damp, wheat-colored hair greased slick at the temples, and the little parentheses at the corners of her mouth. He remembered thinking even then that he could maybe sketch her like that, if only he could carry her away in his head, back to the dim light of his second story room. The arc of her jaw with a charcoal and the line of her nose smeared by his thumb. Her mouth was saying something or trying to; she was leaning toward him and her mouth went like a fish's, swallowing air in circular gasps.

"My gosh, Evan. Turn around," she finally said. "My gosh. Thomas, come here a second."

Alta Mae's father came from the patio, with a pair of hedge clippers in his hand. He was prematurely gray, wearing a kindly smile beneath his moustache, and his legs were alarmingly white beneath the hem of his shorts.

"Holy shit," he said.

"Daddy!" Alta Mae closed her eyes against the mortification in her voice.

He set aside the clippers and stooped up close to get a better look at the backs of Evan's calves. He whistled.

"Bobbed wire," Evan explained, looking across at Alta Mae, before he could even think.

"Barbed wire?"

He told them he had fallen into some barbed wire and the doctor had given him a tetanus shot and sulfathiazole.

"Well, you be careful in the water," Mrs. Robbins told him. She leaned toward him and pecked him on the forehead, and he felt the singe in his cheeks and glanced away from her bikini top to the fixed blue of her daughter's eyes. Mr. Robbins put a hand on his shoulder and squeezed in a friendly way and the sensation of it sank around him both hallowed and warm, each watching eye unknowing witness to something restored in his heart. Evan wondered about being part of their family, and briefly saw how it might be, where images of hope, fantasy, and expectation got hold of him and darkened all else, and he glanced from one to the other, father-mother-daughter, and wished that maybe he could have hugged one of them—Mrs. Robbins, he guessed.

Though it wasn't Mrs. Robbins he attempted to sketch. Time and again, in his room at the top of the stairs, he brought out his sketchpad and tried to get the line of her jaw and the shape of the breasts she didn't yet have, and the very thought of his trying was so warped and sometimes surreal, and, sketching, he often smudged the lines and burnished the charcoal to a sheen, either for longing or for spite.

He would tear the unfinished sketch from the pad and shred it with his hands and go to the window and look toward the mountains for release. There, gazing out over the roof of the back porch, he could see the nearby foothills and the trailing edge of the Rockies' granite-slabbed Mineral Range Mountains. How, so young, could he translate the world around him and those he knew to a smattering of his own fanciful thought? Shape every molecule and atom with a stroke of the brush? Pattern events with his mind? Every notion of it was in the flesh, fluid, and bone of him, that the world might be according to his hope. He tried to see himself smiling there, standing atop a peak, hands on his hips, where nothing could touch him—nothing—certainly not his aunt Missy and Uncle Goose. He tried to feel in himself a change, imagining swift green outfits woven from softened flax, a feathered cap. He imagined himself flying above the rooftops and sodden fields up into the foothills where he could live as a true member of the wild, where he could escape every last tatter of shame. And imagining, it was almost as if he had been born unparented, a product of himself.

But he never came by the swift green or feathered cap of a Peter Pan. Instead, he stubbed among the potato ruts and milked the cows. He cut the wood and slopped the pigs and grew into the additional chore of changing the morning and evening water in the potato fields—cousin to a begonia. At school he listened but didn't speak unless he was called on. The teacher moved him into a class with older children who stared at him and whispered when he answered the questions they could not. Miss Butler gave him an A on his mid-term and told him it was this "raw unadulterated bliss of pastoral living" that would shape him and speak to his nature and give him a muse, but even as much as Evan had himself taken to poetry by his sophomore year, he saw life on the farm as no more than a couplet without rhyme or reason, longed for by some would-be poet-teacher writing hackneyed verse.

Now, sometimes in the spring, he would ride the little appaloosa up above the pasture lands into the foothills, as high up as Rock Corral or Griffith Springs and from there, on a ridge above the cedars, he would look back over the expanse of the valley. Beyond the patchwork of fields and irrigation streams he could see the farmhouse, the barn and corrals and other outbuildings, and bordering the farmyard the dark earth of perfectly furrowed fields ready to plant. The Sevier River glinted back at him and wound its way like a loose snake from one end of the valley to the other. A few miles north of the river's southernmost bridge lay the old roundhouse and a scattered network of switchfrogs, semaphores, and glistening rails where the yellow diesels, with their red, white and blue shields and the words Union Pacific in red block letters along their sides, hostled back and forth, between the stockyards and the roundhouse, banging and coupling and uncoupling the cattle cars and flatbeds and switching them throughout the yard, from one track to another, back and forth, up and down, ceaselessly both night and day. On the sidetracks an inventory of boxcars from the great railroads of the nation stood idle: Union Pacific, Southern Pacific, Baltimore & Ohio, Rock Island, Norfolk & Western, Sante Fe, St. Louis Express, and others that only the ghost of his father might know. Further yet to the north by at least a quarter mile, the white adobe facade of the depot—with its arched porticoes, fluted columns, and green tile roof—stood with its back to the town, and on a bright, cloudless day, he could see the town clearly. He could see the peaked cauldron of the water tower glinting above the trees, the high school where it stood as prominent as the Parthenon of Athens on the highest knoll, and the huge earthen mounds of the potato pits with their tall wooden gates. And he would look beyond the town, toward the upper reaches of the valley, his eyes following some hotshot as it rode the distant diminishing rails to a vanishing point, disappearing with the subtle waves of heat into a watery blink. He would sit on the ridge, listening to the horse stamp and blow, yearn for his father, and consider the geography of his life.

He asks how me and Goose tied the knot, and I tell him. I tell him about Goose cut the eyes from a bull. Old Cow we called him cause he had balls size of an udder. A big reddish thing, and his eyes was red. I remember it on toward dark, and Goose, he's gone crossed the corral, just a hired man, to half-halter Bess. I up the fence as Old Cow gets the notion he'd rather Bess than Goose leading her out. I shout, "Goose," and Old Cow paws and lets swing them balls, and Goose, he lets go that rope and dodges without a backward glance. Old Cow thumps Bess and circles and Goose trying to make the fence. I seen him step to the side to grab a horn, Old Cow bellowing like a calf, slobber and snot. He come up from down under, hugging that horn. Old Cow plants them feet and slings him like a rag through manure and mud, Goose hanging tight, but I seen how he got to a pocket and bit the blade with his teeth. He gouged one eye and Old Cow stumbled and shit and threw blood and rammed Goose to the rails, and Goose gouged the other and let loose and rolled like a man on fire under the fence. Old Cow hollered and stamped and looked around with his nose and his ears, blind as he was. Next thing, Goose comes out the house with Pa's 30.06 and shoots that bull dead. Simple as that, I tell him. I tell him I says to myself, "any man with balls big as that bull's deserves a place in my bed. Yours should be so big someday." He just looks at me with them sissified eyes and asks how come we never had any kids.

~2~

How a Thing Comes to Mean

He had a curious sense of himself and the space he occupied.

"LOOKY here," said Goose. "You paint that shit?"

"He won a prize for it," laughed Missy. "Don't be hard on the boy."

Goose scratched back in the kitchen chair and spit a gob of sheer diarrhea in his picked-over salad dish. He pinched a pair of half-lenses from his shirt pocket and poked them on his nose and in doing it rolled the slop to the other side of his cheek. He snorted and swallowed. He tilted back in the chair and tipped the canvas this way and that, apparently to diminish a throw from the overhead light.

"Who's this in the background? This girl?"

"Why that's the little Robbins girl," Missy said. "See here?"

"Not it's not," said Evan.

"O, you bet it is," Missy said. "Look at that prissy little nose." She leaned across the table with a grunt and put her thumb on the paint. "Hair's a tad dark. Eyes, too."

"I don't get it," complained Goose, wiping his mouth. "This girl in the background and the ghost of hisself coming out of hisself all spooky around these flowers and fowl?"

"Them's begonias, ain't they, honey? And that'n's a rooster or duck."

"Hisself coming right out of his guts. You've no better time but to paint shit like this, I can find you something to do."

Evan snatched the painting from between his uncle's hands, and Missy's hand bounced up and struck the top of Goose's head who, in turn, smacked it away.

"Put your fat thumb out of my eye, old woman."

Missy smacked him again as Goose fended with an arm and struggled to re-right his chair, and Evan took to the stairs that led to his room. In growing older, the abuse of Missy and Goose had turned mostly to threats, and if not threats directed toward him, they instead tore at each other with a ceremonious brutality that was akin to a cockfight. Each of them promised the other with a variety of shameful deaths. Goose fought his wife the way a coward fights, with feet and fingers and teeth. She, in turn, fought back in a cartoonish feminine way—with rolling pins and frying pans, and occasionally a glass or plate would sail toward his head. At least that is how Evan sketched them, using a wide nib and diluting the ink. In reality, they scrapped, skirmished, and finally brawled, all the time groaning and cursing and spitting. This together with the cloistered sound of falling things, and flesh on unastonished flesh.

Evan watched the two of them, then watched himself, how he sometimes scurried, sometimes trudged, toward the refuge of Miss Butler's "raw, unadulterated bliss," abandoning himself to the nearby fields and streams, the rabbits and pheasants and ducks, getting it all down in a rush of chalky pastels between the distractions of school and chores, thieving back whatever time he might for a good book and bluegrass tunes on his harmonica. Gazing across the fields from a vantage point against some bloody evening sun, he watched the jokin jackhares scramble and check and scramble again, their bullet eyes never ablink. He would rather sketch one than shoot it, much to Goose's chagrin. He worked hard to get the attitude of a hawk taking wing, a fox on the sly. Even coyotes ranged in from time to time. And then one morning, with the coming of light at the world's most distant edge, the ugliest little mongrel bitch. He found her in the south field, hesitant at first to approach him, favoring her left front paw. He turned his baseball cap backwards on his head and kissed for her to come, at the same time placing his sketchpad and charcoal on a stump.

"C'mere, Bozo."

When he knelt, she laid her ears back and squirmed toward him, her lips furled in a ludicrous grin, and her tail whipping back and forth like a windshield wiper in a downpour. In this squirming, snarling fashion, she inched her way toward him until her head was in his lap. The head of a Golden Retriever, possibly, but skinny, with the markings of a coyote.

"You what?" said Goose, thumping the kitchen table with his hand.

"I want to keep her."

"What kind of name is that for a dawg?" said Missy.

"It's a goddamn clown's name," said Goose.

"That dog a clown dog? That dog jump through a hoop?"

"We're the ones jumpin through a goddamn hoop."

"What's a boy without a dog," said Missy. "Maybe it'll give him a sense of who he is." She leaned against the kitchen sink and wheezed. "Ain't Bozo the name of a boy clown? That'n's a bitch."

"She's a bitch damn right. Flea-ridden and vicious for all we know." Goose rolled a slop of juice in his cheek. He turned and spat in the sink. He wiped his chin with the back of his hand. "That miserable cur has pups on this farm'n I'll drown em ever goddamn one. Member old Buddy, how he got to the hens? Raised in a barnyard, too, but didn't I do him right slick?"

"Thanks." He didn't add, "for nothing."

"Don't thank me. It's your aunt who's give in."

Poor Bozo!

"The day you were born," said Evan, stooping and roughing-up her ears and looking at his uncle with a squint, "they should have put a bullet through your head or drowned you in a ditch."

Goose looked at Missy as if struggling to complete a thought and Evan stood up and grabbed an apple and took the dog outside, letting the door slam hard.

But wasn't it the wormy little mutt who turned his life around, set his head in the opposite direction, and spun him on a separate course? Until she came whimpering into the picture, life on the farm wasn't without its problems. A powder keg with a short fuse, maybe, but still unsparked. Instead of sugarplums, Evan dreamt of Cherry Bombs in Missy's mincemeat pies and sand in Goose's chewing tobacco. Goose hadn't locked him overnight in either a closet or the fruit cellar for a couple of years, and only seldom did Missy lay into his backside with a shaving strop. He figured it was because he was putting on some meat, shooting up in the space of a few months to nearly as big as Goose. Life had been reduced mostly to threats and fantasies. So it wasn't only the dog. It was time and circumstance. Missy and Goose had grown a little weary, it seemed, and even before Bozo came along, Evan had started developing a sense of himself. There was a shift in the way he saw things, a growing intolerance for two spooky creatures whose joint mentality was less than a slug's.

"Damned if he don't put away more'n the two of us combined," growled Goose, ladling gravy over his potatoes and meat and then slopping the corn. "Pass the horse shit."

Evan looked up.

"Radish, goddamnit. What do you think?"

"It's the hollow leg of a teenager," Missy griped. She pointed. "Them peas."

"I know it. Plus a head hard as them peaks to the east. Salt."

"What? You lay awake in bed at night feeling your bones grow?"

"Which bone you mean?" Goose gabbled like a hen. He troweled butter along the edge of a bun with his knife. "You can bet at his age he lays awake feeling a bone all right. Not long and he'll run smack into his nature, them hot little biddies chasing him around. It's all there if you look, in them eyes like his Pa's."

Evan waited until the conversation turned and then looked at himself in the back of his spoon. He widened and considered his eyes. After supper, he went to the bathroom and shut the door and locked it and studied his face in the mirror. True, he had to admit, in a convoluted way, but he was past humiliation. His body had already defined itself in dreams and admonitions—in spite of any likeness Goose might loathe.

Then, in the spring, Alta Mae Robbins and a couple of her friends sashayed through puberty and redoubled his fits. They got him up close to his nature and so lost in his dreams he thought he might come out the other side, and the oracular powers of his uncle drove him again to the bathroom for another wide-eyed search. He anguished and looked but found little more than himself lallygagging downtown after school with a bunch of other kids or sitting next to Alta Mae at church or in a booth at the Hong Kong Café, the both of them discussing affairs of the heart if not the head and sharing fries. At a table nearby, Owen Roberts and a couple of pimply-faced jocks, toked a joint and spiked their Cokes from an unlabeled fifth. Beyond them, in a booth against the wall, sat an old woman and a dark-eyed girl Evan had never seen but for an odd and unsettling glint of recognition as she glanced up from her plate from time to time. Her face was as if whittled from soap and clear as butterscotch scorched in a pan. The old woman had a face like the soft petrified bark of a tree if there was such a thing, which of course there wasn't.

"So tell me."

"Tell you?"

"It's not your fault, Evan. Any of it. And I'll tell you again—this assignment and such notions of fate . . ."

Alta Mae leaned across the table in her loose yellow dress and it was hard for him to keep his eyes on her face and he wondered if she knew how hard. He wondered, too, about Mason Talbot and the rumors about the two of them and whether she held an image of him yet in her head and, if so, what sort of image that might be. But now she was looking at Evan, searching.

There was a pinch of lipstick encircling the end of the straw in her glass and when she kissed and sucked at the straw the vacuum of it caved at her cheeks in a maddening way. She swallowed and for emphasis touched the back of his hand.

"Well?"

"Not me. Miss Butler."

"But you agree with her. Your own sense of loss, I mean, and such notions of guilt—the way you see yourself in terms of this assignment and all."

He shrugged.

"There. She's looking at you again."

"I don't think so."

"Gypsies, I bet." Her voice got husky and low. "So romantic, don't you think?"

"Just migrants. Late for planting, early for harvest."

"But look at that face. Checking you out." She clucked her tongue. "Those eyes, that hair, and looking at you like that."

"You're looking at me."

"She's got a face you could paint, all that glossy black hair." Alta Mae blushed, but didn't really. "I want," she said and cut herself off. "I want you to paint me someday." She glanced at him and then looked at the girl across the way, and he thought he knew what she meant. "Your art, the things you write, they give meaning, don't think they don't, to the world around you. What does Missy know anyway, your Uncle Goose? That's plain crap, no reason for stuff when it happens—one the epitome of chaos, the other despair."

"Tell it to Miss Butler."

"Well, yes. I see. Though not really. A person's attempt to find meaning in a supposedly meaningless world is meaning itself?"

"Something like that."

She leaned back and poked a fry in her mouth and chewed at the notion and swallowed and leaned and kissed at her drink. In leaning, a strap unlooped from her shoulder leaving a pale white line against the otherwise sunreddened flesh and she left it where it had fallen across her arm. He watched her and thought about his watching and the next thing he might say. He could see in her even then the possibilities, the early stirrings of life. She waited and smiled and fiddled with the straw in her drink, leaned forward now in a whisper and put a nugget in his head.

"Tell me," she said.

"Tell you?"

"Tell me about us, Einstein. This creepy assignment and our *raison d'être?*"

"Don't be cruel." The weight of her French was like gold tipping the scale in his gut. He groped around for the words to balance it, stole a blink at the dark-eyed girl, the strange familiarity of her fisted, masticating jaw. Stymied, he muttered something about the assignment, and half witless beneath the spell of those eyes bemoaned again both the source and meaning of dread.

"Look, Evan," and she took a tangent, as if to balance their struggle with some illumining gospel script, "but for the principle of opposition we couldn't freely choose."

"?"

"Become who we can." She looked at him and pursed her lips and looked away to the fingers of her hand pinching the straw in her drink and shrugged it all away, everything she might have intended.

Something spilled at the table nearby, and laughter. He followed the twist of Alta Mae's head as she glanced across her shoulder at Owen. Owen raised his eyebrows and nodded and made a kiss with his lips and dallied his tongue, and she looked back at Evan with a look that said a variety of things, none of them particularly pleasant, and tucked up her strap, the knit of her brow petitioning him.

"Losers."

He could see how the mascara she wore deepened the blue of her eyes and softened the way of her face and how the pouty red bow of her lips parted and touched and formed like a debatable kiss.

"So tell me, then."

"Tell you?"

"The assignment, Evan."

He could see the goose bumps on her forearms as she hugged and rubbed at herself and up toward her shoulders and on the flesh of her where in breathing she pressed and heaved above the scooped neckline of her dressfront and he could see there how the air conditioning, together with something he had said perhaps or the way he had said it, had done its work in a superior way.

"How a thing comes to mean, Evan. Miss Butler."

He searched her face now, and she looked back, searching his.

"When you say that such and such has happened, thus and thus is so. Or something like that. *The Red Badge of Courage.* You know? Fiction versus fact." She swirled the straw in her drink and the strap unloosened and drooped. She glanced up from her drink and caught him with the blue of her eyes and together they blushed. "Otherwise I couldn't make sense of it, and that's supposed to be the gist of the paper, too."

He looked at the Coca-Cola clock on the wall behind her: 4:21 and the sweep of its second hand moving the hour toward who knew what. A triangulation of shadows from the Venetian blind fell across the chipped Formica of the tabletop and stenciled the napkin holder and her hands and arms and the Naugahyde of the seatback where her body leaned away from the window side.

"Fiction is not fact," he heard himself quote, at the same time ketchup-dipping a fry and waving it around in a professorial way, "fiction is fact selected and understood; fiction is fact arranged and charged with purpose."

"Fiction sucks," she groaned, "and the rest of it too. And stop looking at her like that."

"Well, it's her theology just the same, Miss Butler's. You, I, and the rest of the planet live in a universe of fiction rather than fact, suck though it may." He put the fry in his mouth, chewed once and swallowed, took a gulp of his Coke. "The notion of any meaning we give a thing confuses the fact of the matter. That's her point, I think. We create a world in our history and heads far different than the world that was, the world that is—all arranged and charged with purpose. Ourselves little gods."

"O, and that's the paradox of truth, as she put it?" He liked the ironic twist of her mouth and her eyes flashing like that. "How a thing comes to mean?"

"Sure, how a thing comes to mean. Take Goose or that chick with the old lady in the booth. Not an iota of meaning except in the torment—"

Alta Mae cocked her head and leaned toward him without batting an eye, the abyss of her dressfront nothing but rapture and doom.

"—meaningless as the seal from a railroad tanker launched from a mile away. Meaningless as the scratch of a thorn."

"I didn't mean—"

"Take Owen, then. Thus and thus is so, even when it's not. History. Memory. Photographs. You smile for the camera to mask a heartache and what does history record? Not the heartache."

"Yes, well."

"But some things go beyond understanding," he told her, surprised at the conviction in his tone, at the same time stealing a felonious glance. "You see what they mean but can't get them right in your head."

"Yes, well." She grimaced and brushed at a fly as if brushing at her own frustration to see what he meant. "Regardless of whatever thorn in your side and life's abuse, you have to remember who you are."

"Who I am?"

"Who you can be."

He caught the girl in the booth, her unremembered face

querying his, then the promise of Alta Mae's. He knew what she was thinking and knew, too, that she was waiting for him to say and knew that in saying how her heart would lift and in lifting touch the very expression in her face and the lilt of her voice, and so then watching he said what he knew in her heart she wished him to say.

"You mean a product of him who made me?"

"A child of God, Evan. Whose very purpose, I think, lies in our freedom of choice."

Two girls, one a heartache away from memories unclaimed, those eyes. The other but notion and touch. "Listen. A kid walks into an ice-cream parlor with thirty flavors staring him in the face, and what choice does he have? This time it's the Bubble-Gum Goo or Kid's Krunch. He can't bring himself to sample the Chocolate Chip or Daiquiri Ice anymore than he can choose to change the color of his eyes or his mother's death or a heart gone bad. Even old Butler might say that choices lie less in the head than the heart."

"Well," and she pouted an enfeebling pout, "it's too abstract for me." He watched her shiver and rub at herself, caressing her shoulders and arms, and he couldn't help but see how thin and compliant the front of her dress now striped in sunshadows coming through the blind. "Something more on the order of a college prep class than sophomore lit." She looked at him and nothing in her face seemed to care.

"She just wants us to think."

"O? A penny for your thoughts, then." She looked at him and looked at him looking and looked at him, both of them this time refusing to blush. "If you dare. I'll be lucky to get a C on this thing." She pointed a finger, first at herself and then at him and then at herself. "Thus and thus is what?"

"You tell me."

"Tell you?" She searched his face and widened her eyes.

"Tell me," he said, and he leaned toward her, urged by some cloying scent. "Tell me some things."

She looked away and studied her drink.

"O, I could tell you, Evan Adamson. If only you would listen."

He waited, but she told him nothing, of course, except in the expression of her downcast eyes and the slouch of her shoulders and head.

"I'll tell you," he said, lowering his voice with an odd sense of conviction that even he couldn't name, and it was something true and ineffable beyond knowing or desire itself. "Ask me thirty years from now."

"O, won't we be a story then?"

"Won't we?

"And what will you remember more than my dress?"

"What will you remember more than the way that I look at you in it?"

The old woman wiped her mouth and made a ruckus getting up from the booth. The girl stood up, and a little moment in time seemed to score itself and fold back like the leaf of a book. Evan saw how the girl's hair fell across her shoulder and eclipsed her face, and for a moment she was all the mystery of a dim but undeniable dream.

Owen Roberts said in a loud voice, "Hey, do I know you?"

The girl stood next to the booth and slung her hair back and torched him with a glance. So far as Evan could tell, she wore no makeup and hadn't a blemish on her unspoiled face or at the pod of her throat or on her olive-skinned arms. She regarded Owen while the old woman rummaged for a tip.

"O, baby, if looks could kill. Is that a curse or something?"

Her eyes strayed to Evan, and in them the hint of a smile, some slight caress, acknowledgment, and in the twist of her head as she passed, and then she was gone. He wanted to look. She was slouched in a pair of Levis, shredded holes in the knees, a loose-fitting blouse, and he craved a single confirming glance, but the expression on Owen's face told him everything he needed to know. Even Alta Mae said "wow" with her eyes.

"Now what do you suppose that meant? That look? The way she looked at you like that?"

He shrugged, trying to make a fit inside his head.

"No. There was meaning in that look. Just a girl passing through and a world of meaning all in a glance. Spooky."

"Whatever," he said.

She didn't say anything further and they sat for a moment in silence. Except for the snickers from the table nearby, they were lost in an old Bobby Darin song playing on the jukebox, "Dream Lover." Evan watched the water beading on his glass where it sat on the table before him, half empty, half full. He manipulated a thought or two, tried remembering, but couldn't make the fit, and his thoughts and the lingering image of the dark-eyed girl fluttered away with a disquieting pang. When he looked at Alta Mae, she still hadn't tucked up her strap, and she looked at him and twirled the straw in her drink clicking the ice and looked at him and shifted her legs beneath the table bumping his knee and looked at him as though with a worry and a wish. Evan looked at her as well and looked at the untanned line on her shoulder and where she sat so loose in her dress and across her shoulder he looked at Owen and the boys who leaned their heads in toward the center of the table and whispered and laughed. For now, Mason Talbot and the possibility of his wandering hands was less than a dread. She was looking at *him*.

"So for my birthday," and her voice was a conversational sigh, "for my birthday in August, did I tell you? I asked Daddy I to get me a dog."

"?"

"A Black Lab, I think, and the Alves' expect Milly to litter about the first part of July."

"She's a good old girl."

"And bred at the Vet's. The Vet's own papered dog. But I just as soon have a mutt like Bozo. They can be smart as a purebred."

"More intelligent than most humans I know."

"Sure," she said and laughed. "Dogs are people, too."

Evan watched Owen, who looked back and lifted his glass in salute. He turned to the others and said something and they put their heads together and all laughed and then looked over at Alta Mae and then to Evan raised their glasses again in salute. One of them said something about breeding and wasn't talking about dogs when he said it and they all laughed again and Owen motioned Evan with his hand beneath the table so Alta Mae couldn't see and gave him a thumbs up sign with one hand and an okay sign with the other and then put his thumb's up thumb in the okay ring formed by his index finger and thumb and drove it back and forth like a piston. At sixteen, Owen was already beginning to bald and his face had aged like the moon at the end of a month.

Alta Mae glanced across her shoulder and Owen raised his hands, palms out, and widened his eyes in mock innocence, like a man caught in a holdup, but Evan couldn't help wondering if Alta Mae maybe had seen and then knew it for sure when she turned back to him with her face like it was.

"Please," she whispered. "Play me a tune. Those guys give me the creeps. Let's go sit on the library lawn and you can play me a tune."

She leaned across the table and touched him, her body both loose and compact in the loose yellow dress, and he could see how much like her mother she had become, how she had kind of popped out of herself in the last couple of months and how everything was there and in place as she slid across the seat and stretched a leg to stand.

"Bummer! Them legs for real?"

Evan leaned over the table and put his face in Owen's. "Tell you what. She had them lengthened last week and now they go all the way up."

"I don't doubt it."

"He ought to know," she said, "or hope to imagine." But in saying it, she blushed and pulled at her skirt.

"Well, look. Maybe you lovebirds heard the one about the

cowboy and the milkmaid." Owen studied her, his expression both brazen and crude, and ran his tongue between his lips to wet them. "Must be chilly in here." The others leered and wondered for a moment and then saw what he meant and nickered, tossing their heads. "Mason know the length of them legs?"

"Back off, Owen."

"That a threat?"

"A promise more like it."

"Now, country boy. At least have a drink before you go."

"Thanks, dude. We got a date."

"O, with destiny, I suppose." It was Stud who piped up. Like Owen, he had thrown decency to the wind and was looking hard at her breasts, his look a vague certainty of something they were meant for, all dazzled with purpose and prospects removed from biology and nurturing the young. "Damn," he said and repeated himself. He made an imaginary camera with his hands and clicked at her and smacked his lips and slobbered a little from the side of his mouth.

Alta Mae bent to fix a sandal strap then apparently thought better of it and wiggled and shuffled her foot and stood on one leg to force the fit and looked at each of them in turn until they lowered their eyes and then, sandal in place, she took his hand and pulled him between the tables and toward the door. A table wobbled when she bumped it with her hip and he watched her while she waited and warmed herself in a wedge of sunslant coming through the glasspaned door and rubbed her hip and looked back with disgust while he paid the cashier and then snatched him out the door with a giggle and a squint.

It was a short walk to the library, and once there she sat on the grass with her knees together and her legs to one side propping herself with an arm and twirling a length of grass in her teeth. No, no. She looked up and shaded her eyes from the sun and told him to sit. He turned his baseball cap around so the bill shaded his neck and sat, but slowly, looking at her all the time, his eyes fixed on the again fallen strap and the surprise of the partial sphere of her breast, and she produced a daisy and plucked its petals one by one and glanced up at him now and then from beneath her brow with a half smile fixed on her lips and he could see the blue in her eyes. He faked a little camera click with his hand in front of his face and it made her laugh. He watched her and scooted back against the city monument and took out his harmonica and watched how loose and compact she fit in her dress and how the sun astonished her hair and, watching, he rested an elbow on his raised knee and riffled off some bluegrass melody he had learned listening to tapes in his room at the top of the stairs. Self-taught, self-consoled, and forever surprising those who gave an ear. He was playing and watching her fingers so cruel and so kind, and she was everything he could possibly imagine. Everything he could possibly hope. As she plucked, her lips moved in silent adulation forming the words of the song, and he watched her as much as he could take her in and played, so far at the moment from worrying about how a thing comes to mean. He played and watched her and watched until Owen Roberts and his runted sidekick confused the issue and, like a recurring, unfinished dream, hoisted themselves up over the retaining wall from the sidewalk to the grass and stepped toward them with a dismal jaunt. It was only then that Evan noticed a kind of roostery look about the two and his nightmare was complete.

"Go ahead, country boy. Don't let us stop the serenade."

"And whatever else is under development here." Stud grinned at them all around and shouldered himself against the stone monument, the closed slit of his lipless mouth begging them to believe he knew more than they might think. An irksome silence, and Owen gave his buddy a look to wipe away that grin in an otherwise deadpan face.

"She's just sizing up his dumbstick, talking about old lady Butler's bullshit in class and doing it like dogs. What d'you think, Stud?"

"Like goats in rut. That's what I think."

THE GYPSY LOVER ·47·

"Maybe they'll have that drink with us now."

"What did I say before?" Evan started to get up.

"Don't bother, farm boy. Just a snort."

"You got wax in your ears?"

"Whip his ass," said Stud.

"One snort."

"What don't you understand?"

"Watch it. Farm boy's getting ready to rumble."

"Whip his ass," said Stud.

"In your dreams."

"Wait. Not on my dress, please!"

Alta Mae scrabbled to all fours and then to her knees, brushing at the front of herself, and he could see how it was before it happened. He had barely given it a thought, and before she rose to her feet, the harmonica was in his fist but undamaged. He felt the pain of it grooved there, and the pain of it again, and he watched as the bottle went sailing up over the monument in an arc and sort of drug itself back sloshing a piss-colored rain. It turned once and in turning startled the sun and then smashed against stone.

"Get up, *dude.*"

"No, Evan. Leave him. You broke his nose, I think."

"Get up. Tell her you're sorry."

"It'll wash. Come on, Evan. You broke his nose, I think."

"Say you're sorry, city boy. Get him up, Stud, and his sorry ass for home."

She gripped his harmonica-gripped fist and leaned into him— her shallow whispering breath—all the while the both of them watching the bloodied mess crab about and cup its hands beneath a weeping nose.

"I know your aunt Missy will have a fit," she whispered, "but the dance tonight. If you can get away, I'll be ready by eight."

Not an iota of sense, and so far removed from worrying about how a thing comes to mean. Under the Goose Man's tutelage, he had learned to out-box everybody in his gym class and even in the class above, and his own blood didn't frighten him. He could take a punch across the jaw without changing expressions. But he wondered at the use in it, bloodying somebody's nose or fattening a lip. He got so he didn't much like fighting kids either with or without a cause. Though it was nice to know that he could, and it seemed to give his gym coach a curious sense of pleasure to watch him addle their brains.

"That's right. Now take it inside. That's it. That's it. Give him the left. That's right. Bam. Bam. Bam."

He became both envied and enviable, a little threatening to have as a friend, the reserved thoughtful type of whose mood you could never be certain, and when he spoke, it could well be in the form of a clever put-down, a new catchphrase. You might think for a moment you were close to him and then suddenly be stung, not with a fist but with a word, and you had to grin and bear it. *Bam. Bam. Bam.* Or so he wrote in his journal, with a twist and a slant all his own. He wrote how he had stored up all his observations and emotions for a purpose, how he liked being a spy, as though he were in another country, recording within himself in some mysterious chamber on some personal film the most significant events. In his journal, he could write and edit as he pleased, twist meaning into every meaningless phrase.

And even as he wrote, adventure loomed before him, always with a stab of surprise: the soft shadow of Alta Mae behind the gym after a track meet, her wet mouth experimenting with his, the thrill of her breasts flattening against his chest. Certainly something to write about, something to consider, something to revise, how a thing comes to mean. He wrote her name in his journal, in his most careful hand, and sketched her from the bust up using as much negative space as possible, and then he wrote the names of her mother and father and brother, as if the blank page were expecting it, as if her name and aspect alone were but a part of the greater whole, and now, surrounded by the names of her family, was complete.

The Robbins family had a BMW and a new Range Rover and a pool, of course, and on Sundays went to church like they didn't mean maybe. Missy, on the other hand, was a self-proclaimed reprobate, one who, to hear her tell it, had once had the spirit then woke one morning to find she had misplaced it. Whether she ever searched for it as fervently as she might have searched for a misplaced set of car keys was unlikely and open to debate. Evan could see the difference as clear as an absence of light on the one hand and a radiance on the other, Missy's embedded scowl compared to Alta Mae's bright smile. Goose, as far as Evan could tell, had simply forever been without, and it was difficult to comprehend whether having lost or never having so as to lose was the greater cause for wretchedness and despair. So Evan went to Sunday School with renewed interest and then to early morning Seminary—though less for the sake of his soul than for Alta Mae who was there saving him a seat. She smiled brightly and whispered good morning and flashed her eyes and uncrossed her legs, and Evan breathed the scent of her, confused all the more about an absence of fate and how a thing comes to mean. The teacher taught something about agency and freedom of choice, and while this was all well and good, Evan couldn't help but remember his mother and think of his father, disturbed by his own quandary, whatever that might be, whether in the guise of adoration or truth, and how the pain of it nuzzled inside him, such a pleasant and disquieting fear, knowing that it might one day awake all refreshed and with a disturbing range of expectation and desire. Presently, though, it all came down to an early morning greeting and the names he had written in his book; it came down to that inexplicable thrill of Doublemint breath and the notion of adventure behind the gym.

"You cop a feel?"

Allen Dreyfus was walking beside him on the way to the bus stop, smoking a butt.

"That's for me to know and for you to worry about."

Lightening sparked to the east, and Evan looked at the

gathering clouds and felt the first few drops of rain. Something watery and electric shivered his flesh.

"If I was you, I'd worry about Mason Talbot's quarterback hands."

"Mason?"

"You don't think he's put it in the end zone of half the county?"

"O, you bet. Including the school nurse and a Holstein or two."

"Well, look at her."

"I do."

"Sweetest orgasm I ever seen waiting to happen."

"What?"

"Yummy as her mummy."

Before Evan could slug him, Allen staggered out of range, his shoulders convulsed and bouncing like an ape's. He took a drag and squinted against the smoke as it came back in his eyes. He put his ear to the soft rumble of thunder and then his face to the rain. "If I get the old man's car this weekend we could maybe take her and Alison down to the river and look at the moon."

"The moon in the sky?"

Allen chuckled, paused, then chuckled again as though he liked the sound in his throat. "See if that halo's for real, and whatever else. Me, I'm about due to get a hand up Alison's blouse."

"Dream on, Sherlock." Evan cleared his sinuses with a snort, rolled the gob to the front of his tongue, and hacked. Let Allen and Owen and the rest of the world think what they liked, so casually and cautiously worrying about how a thing comes to mean.

That afternoon, Evan sat by the window in his room watching the lightening and the rain. He sat and sketched that sodden land in broad strokes, the hint of a ghosted express coiling its way along the prairie floor and up toward the foot of glistering crags now lost in their ascent among clouds that roiled back between the peaks, the wires of light, but he could not sketch how that panorama so vast and contained sparked within some reclusive nerve, nor the droning of his flesh nor the soothing of his bones, for in spite of any weather either without or within he was beginning to have a curious sense of himself and the space he occupied as if by some divine token his very spirit had been made radiant, and he by no means ordinary, all so familiar and yet unknown. And for the first time, as the rain lifted and the granite peaks of the Mineral Range Mountains came into view, he had a clear vision of life and the possibilities beyond. He had only to unfocus his eyes to see. The glistening rails looped beneath and around the base of those peaks like filaments lighting a way—where beyond, the valley streams fed into the river and the river into the multi-faceted wonders of a glimmering sea.

He hits me the first time and then hits me again before I open my eyes. Bam, bam. What a chickenshit, and Stud dancing around like a old woman with nary a wit. Skunked or not, to get knocked on my ass and them eyes agog. She looks at me like I'm some kind of bug squalling round in the grass. Blood everywhere, but some things hurt more than a smack. I shoulda beat the shit out of him a year ago when I had him in size. Knock that grin right off his jaw. Think he'd care? Spit teeth. Puke snot. Center of the universe, he thinks. Straight A's. Old Butler's pet. She orgasms every time he waves a hand in class. He pipes up and the whole class turns around like it's Einstein sitting there. Alta Mae, she nods till her neck would break and gets all fidgety, bouncing in her seat. It's a sight, them tits ajiggle. If she's not putting it to him, I'm a horse's ass. Miss Goody Two-Shoes. You can tell by the way they walk. They walk down the hallway and you can tell, tell by the walk, the way a girl walks. What you look for is "loose." Give me half the length of the cafeteria, 20 feet, a dozen steps, and I'd bet the old man's 4-Runner on it. I can tell every time.

~ 3 ~

The Errant Heart

Afraid of crisis beyond his ability, he held himself in.

AGAIN, but with changed meaning, he watched Gypsy car nivals and migrant workers—from Mexican wetbacks to California Gypsies and other nomadic tribes—wander into the southern part of the state to harvest potato crops. They came into the valley about the first part of August, petitioning for work, setting up their carnivals, and selling their wares. More often than not, Evan worked the rows of Goose's potato fields with Spanish in his right ear and the peculiar, enchanting dialect of Romany in his left. Caravans pulled into the yard and little sunblackened children poured out. After them came women dressed in pleated ankle-length skirts and sleeveless blouses, men bold enough to wear neck scarves and single earrings. Of all the wanderers, the Gypsies were the most interesting, the most mysterious, perhaps because they kept largely to themselves. Besides laboring in the fields, the Gypsies sought other chores, such as body and fender work or fence mending. Among them were tinkers who fixed kitchen utensils, sharpened knives. The women pandered a variety of dressmaking material, baskets, and hand wrought jewelry. Then, of course, there were the fortunetellers.

Missy Begonia once had her palm read then spit on it

afterward to cleanse it of the Gypsy's Curse. If she bought any cloth or had her knives sharpened, she always spit on the thing three times for good luck. And more than once, she left Evan with the warning to keep clear of them: "They're filthy, Evan, and carry disease. They don't like nothing better than little tow-headed boys what'll snatch you up in a minute and cut your heart out to eat it cold." She was forever saying things to embarrass him, sometimes in front of a friend, once within the hearing of Alta Mae. Even the summer before he turned sixteen, she still talked to him as though he were a twelve-year-old. She would sit at the table or in front of the TV eating her pickled pig's feet and pork cracklings and say to Uncle Goose: "Maybe we'd ought to sell him to the Gypsies, since his britches is getting too tight. Your not old enough yet, Evan, I can't whip you with Goose's strop." Then she would turn to Uncle Goose who hadn't heard a word, and absorbed in some sit-com or pay-per-view boxing match, didn't give a tinker's damn. "Goose?"

"Sit on it, Fatty!"

She would respond with a grunt and a rumble, and Goose might hold his breath until the air cleared or gasp a few times. Then he'd roll his chaw and spit absently on the floor. Even in company. Evan saw more than one gob lay like an oyster in the carpet for over a day—unless Bozo got to it. And Missy, she would grab her heart, shrieking something incoherent and garbled.

"Dog shit," she'd say. "I'll cut you," she'd say. "Dog shit for brains. Nip 'em like buds."

"You and your blubber, you will. Not before I bloody your nose."

It went like that—until one day Evan found himself astonished by his own lack of amazement. They were unreal, simple-minded parodies of their own worst selves, and the reality of those parodies, together with his own growing indifference, all at once horrified him. He saw himself as worse than a parody, terrified by the dreadful image of himself standing beside their bed like some bewildered weirdo watching them sleep. On the moonlit wall, the premeditation of a shadow raising its arm.

It was this memory that he gouged from his mind when, toward the end of that summer's harvesting, he came home with a knot in his throat. The sun was setting on a gray day, tinting mauve the undersides of clouds that hung beyond the deserted fields where a single dark bird slanted above the trees. He boxed his charcoal and hoisted his easel and moving against the lengthening shadow of his stride marveled at how the setting sun seemed to portend more than just the close of day. Someone has died, he consciously told himself. Or is about to.

At the yard he paused and looked back across the field, a solitary witness to some fiery paw come from below to grasp that sorrowful blaze and drag it mute and howling from the sky. He watched for a while the waning struggle there and then turned, as he knew he must, and undid the gatelatch and swung open the gate and closed it behind him. He looked at the house, how it loomed against an absence of light, even the windowpanes dulled to that sheen from the West. A few hens scattered and flapped and settled and pecked a final series of pecks before going to roost. He edged his way between the coop and the old stone well and in a half circle around the big rooster Goose loved so much. Uncle Buck. Even in the dying light, he could see the menace of Uncle's spurs and a glint in that wicked eye. The bird strutted and shook its comb and opened its yellow beak as though to express itself in some garbled birdtalk. But it was a silent warning. Uncle cocked its head to be sure and hopped with a flap to the well's cobbled rim. It shook its feathers and fluffed itself and made to crow but didn't. There had been an unspoken truce between them since the day Goose brought the rooster home— as long as they kept a respectful distance. Evan fended with his easel as if to swat the thing then drew back and started up the path, but backward, half-stumbling, his eye on the bird and muttering an oath. He trusted the treachery of Owen Roberts more than he trusted that bird.

Before he made the house, the dog waddled up all a-whimper, her belly slung nearly to the ground with the weight of a summer romance. She was a leggy, mustard-colored bitch with black freckles speckling her jaws and the underside of her gut, and Evan wondered what new marks her litter might bear. She whined and yipped and swatted her tail from side to side, and when she swatted, her whole hindquarters wagged, but she was too miserable with the weight of her pups to jump on him. He should have reached down and scratched her ears, he knew, said something sweet to her, and let her lick the salt from his hand. But the night was falling down from the east and the darkness that passed over the farm came in a sudden breath of cold and stillness and passed on, as if the darkness had a soul itself that filled him with some resentment deeper even than his increasing conviction of neglect.

All he needed was to walk into the kitchen, the air rife with tension and an odor of rancid meat. They'd been in the thick of it already and supper wasn't even on—for Evan at least. Aunt Missy sat at the table hogging calf brains and kidneys, grunting pig sounds into her plate. Her face and knuckles glistened with grease.

Uncle Goose turned on Evan, seeking new blood to let. He stood in the light of the open refrigerator door, swigging a bottle of *Coors.*

"You see to the south five where Johnny's got them Gypsies running the rows?"

"I saw to it."

"Don't get snide with me, that tone of voice. You best put it all behind you, son, that scowl and whatever expectations and come to a conclusion fast. This farm's the only place you'll ever know, all you got in the world, where someday by my good graces you might stake your claim. Otherwise, what you gonna do with your life? Be an ar-teest like your Pa never could? You ain't gonna amount to squat."

He took another swig and foam seeped up out of the neck of the bottle and oozed down the side and over his hand, dripping on the kitchen linoleum. When he saw the dog skulking from around the corner, his boot lashed out. He missed and the mutt went for him with a snarl and a snap. He booted again and this time caught her beneath the snout. She scrabbled away, rolled on her back, and yowled.

"Goddamnit," cried Evan. "Dogs are people, too."

"Dogs are people, too? Holy apple shit. Dogs are people, too? I ain't telling you again. That bitch has pups on this farm, they're goners. Dogs are people, too." His face was the color of a glowing coal. He palmed back the rag of his hair and the gesture was like wafting a flame, as if that alone would either fan it to a blaze or, in fanning it, douse it or at least keep it slicked down like a dandy's, but it sprung back up in the spires and spikes of his own unwitting disgust. "By Gawd, I'll drown 'em in the crick, if I won't. Dogs are people, too."

By "crick" he meant the ditch that irrigated the potato fields. He was so stupid, Evan thought, he didn't know the difference between a creek, a ditch, and a canal. He would spit in a river and call it a lake.

"Hear?"

Goose glowered and Evan felt his hands become fists.

"C'mon, then, you little bastard. If there's a God, by God, I'll rip your head off and spit down the hole before you see another day. May he strike me dead if not." With one hand, the rooster man hitched up his pants the way they do in cartoons. He snorted and grinned, squaring himself in front of his nephew, and Evan nearly took a stance himself.

"Give me a year." His voice cracked with the embarrassment of adolescence and rage. "If tobacco and booze haven't killed you by then, I might oblige."

"Sure, now—" Goose barked and threw back his head and took a manly swig of the beer. He leaned toward Evan, grinding his teeth and jutting out his spittle-stained chin.

Perhaps there was something in the tone of Evan's newfound voice or the expression on his face that brought Goose up short.

His rooster eyes and weak jaw worried themselves, trembled either with abating rage or amazed curiosity that a boy should call his bluff. He blew air through his nostrils and attempted a casual laugh and turned and waved Evan away with his open hand.

Pumped up a little, Evan glared in disgust at his aunt. If he had known a spell he would have cast it. Her face was the size and shape of a huge greased cantaloupe, bobby pins pinning her hair in ringlets close to her head. Her little pig's eyes roamed from his chin to his ears as though she were searching the prairie for a familiar watering hole. Her tongue reached out and touched tentatively the kidney held to her lips on the tines of her fork. It occurred to Evan that she was looking at a stranger.

A silence of diminished rage washed through the kitchen and Evan tested both of them further by sounding his lips in a kiss as he mounted the stairs to his room. On the landing at the top of the stairs, he paused and held the dog and together they listened to the shuffling below.

"I dunno what's got into that boy. Who does he think he is?"

"I know what's got into him," said Goose. "It's the ghost of his old man. I seen it in them girly eyes of his. Dogs are people, too. All summer long, him sniffing around that little blonde Robbins clit and he's turned inside out."

"I know it. And him not old enough yet to drive let alone date. I told him. I told him. Didn't I tell him?"

"Got to the point he wants to make all his own decisions, and he's been reading them damn novels again—and *poetry*. For all his book learning, he ain't gonna amount to squat. And look at them pictures he draws. What? Gives him a sense of hisself, that's what." His voice fell to a murmur. "A false sense. Just like his Pa."

Evan had never been able to understand Goose's resentment toward his father, but even more than that, he had never been able to understand why people who didn't like books hated people who did, unless they admired their own ignorance. Perhaps they mistrusted themselves. Once possessed by the written word, you were assured that there was nothing that people could not know and therefore nothing that you could not know. Crack the pages of a book and your imagination could soar. Your heart could escape. You could live and love and die in the pages of a book.

One charmed and miserable day winters past, when the world outside was awhirl in white, Evan found the courage (or, perhaps, he was driven) to do what he had procrastinated for so many years. He bundled himself against the cold and climbed above the din. In the attic, he found the trunks that had been left by his mother. He opened them, one by one, and rummaged through the odds and ends: old letters and clothes, a scrap book with paper hearts glued around the edge, photograph albums and other loose pictures—one of a wartime bride and her gray-clad uniformed groom, something of his mother in their eyes, all weepy and curiously Teutonic, faded with age amid flowers and . . . and . . . heartache or joy; one of himself standing between his mother and a man in front of the Elephant House at the Zoo. He remembered something about the man and closed the trunk. Why dig up recrimination and mistakes? How could you fault the fiction when it remedied fact? He loved his mother and knew which memories to preserve. And his father. When he opened the third trunk, he found volume after volume of his father's musty books. He found some of the small press publications his mother had told him about and a slim volume of poetry entitled *Riding the Absolute.* The book had his father's name embossed in red foil on the cover, with an expressionistic drawing of a voluptuous nude. Evan took off his glove and touched the cold foil with his fingers, his own name dulled by a frosty plume of breath. When he opened the cover, the spine cracked, but he sat right there in the cold attic and read it through, reading as if the words were his own, his mouth forming shapes in a sort of twilit *deja vu.* In the weeks following, he read almost everything he found in the trunks and grew even more earnest in his trips to the library.

Now, almost sixteen, he had finished *Poems of Robert Frost, Huckleberry Finn,* and even portions of Twain's *The Damned Human Race,* a tattered copy annotated in his father's hand with apparent relish. He had read most of Robert Cormier's and S.E. Hinton's books, even labored over the dark mystery of sin in Hawthorne and looked forward to *Lord of the Flies* and *The Catcher in the Rye.* He found *David Copperfield* and *Bleak House* a little too weepy for his own tastes, regardless of Miss Butler's adulation, and though names like Dostoyevsky and Kafka fascinated him, he grappled with only portions of their language and their worlds. He liked especially the nature of Emerson and the inexplicable attitudes of men found in such histories as the witchcraft trials of Salem and the chronicles of Joan of Arc.

It was there in the attic, when that year's thaw had begun and buds were all asprout with allergens and hope, when rivulets of sweat found their way beneath his matted arms and along his ribs, that he discovered a dog-eared copy of *Fanny Hill.* O, surprise. He brought the book down to his room where he kept it hidden along with his journal behind the bookcase. She was something to make you grimace, Fanny Hill, and he couldn't quite get her fixed in his head. Occasionally, he would take the book from its hiding place and read a passage just to feel his heart cramp.

More tormenting than *Fanny Hill* were the magazines he found tucked away in the bottom drawer of Goose's bureau: half a dozen *Playboys* and other monthlies with poses of naked women in them. It was as if, lost in his reveries of Alta Mae, her yellow dress and shadowed breath behind the gym, the spring weather had brought forth the world in a daze. There was one magazine in particular, the centerfold a dead ringer for Alta Mae. She called herself "Sindy," and he couldn't help going back to her picture time after time. The woman was kneeling on a bed with a pink satin bedspread and sort of hugging a big lacy pillow. Her hair was done up like Alta Mae sometimes did hers, and though she was more womanish here and there, there was still a youthfulness about her eyes and mouth. He would open the magazine, the pages all soft and curled back from Goose's thumb, and there she'd be, gazing back at him, her inexplicable breasts and a too-coy smile, just the two of them in the dark little universe of Goose and Missy's bedroom, the texture of her skin smooth as ink and leaping right off the page. He would look at her face and look at her breasts and his insides would crawl around, worrying him about the possibility of Mason Talbot and Alta Mae. But whose were the rumors? Whose were the little fictions of desire in another boy's heart? When he pondered the woman named Sindy, he could easily imagine himself with Alta Mae—at least the spirit of Alta Mae—in his bedroom at the top of the stairs and remember her encouraging whispers behind the gym. Though, unlike Sindy, Alta Mae was always haloed against some artificial light, angelic in her expression and wearing a negligée of white. He would think of Mason Talbot and look at the Alta Mae of the magazine, and she would be kneeling on his bed in his room at the top of the stairs, waiting for *him* (not Mason), both of them glancing and trembling and hardly able to breathe, his own cruel heart like a fist thudding beneath his ribs. It took all the energy he could muster to close her up and shove her back in the drawer.

And it nagged him.

He was not quite used to himself, regardless of what Uncle Goose or Missy might think. His own nature, even his body, felt slouchy and uncomfortable at times. Too many books, Goose might say. But it was all in the process of becoming. In his journal, he used the word "vicarious" and copied the fragment of something his father had written on the flyleaf of a book entitled "The Wandering Heart," perhaps the germ of an unwritten poem, confident that between the lines lay meaning he would someday be able to grasp:

> *. . . while planets continue to spin, even the earth on which*
> *we stand, and stars ignite in the void and we wheel like*

castaways riding the absolute, rough riders ahorse, galloping
into that absence from which all began ...

Now, wincing at the touch of Goose's gnarled finger on a sore spot, Evan closed the door to his room and stared at the tattered, dog-eared variety of books that lined the dim uneven shelves next to his bed. If wishes were horses, maybe his books could spirit him away. A few thousand horses in those big yellow turbines pulling their load along the glistening tracks...charging into that absence from which all began. Wish, *wish* . . . said all the books he'd read.

He felt miserable with the weight of himself. He didn't want to undress beneath the naked bulb, so in the screened light he helped Bozo onto the bed and undressed in the dark. Still, he could see the walls covered with floral paper faded to the hues of old wedding bouquets. On the wall above the headboard he stared at the shadowed outline of his parents' portrait. Even in darkness his father's face clarified identifiable as his own: blond, slightly wavy, all-too-shaggy hair, seagreen eyes, and what Uncle Goose referred to as the expression of an idiot. Was it truly his face, the face of his father? Some castaway riding the absolute . . . galloping into that absence where dreams of adventure wore him thin. But where? Neither in this room nor in the space beyond. Nothing to curl the lip. Nothing to lighten the heart. Nothing to give an indication of how much longer, how much longer he had in this room. How much longer turning spuds with a hand spade? Suffering the silly abuse of a nasty uncle and a nattering aunt?

He sat down on the bed, too weary and depressed to feel hungry and too indifferent to go to the bathroom. He picked up his harmonica from the nightstand and put it to his lips, but he didn't feel like playing a note and laid it back down. Light had fallen from the sky, his eyes now adjusted to the dark. The dog lay at the foot of the bed, her rubber-cleated teats splayed to one side. Before him, reflected in the mirror of the vanity, he could see his own dark image watching from a separate world. It was not the face of an adult. It was not the face of a child. Then whose? He sat with his shoulders slumped under the weight of the room, under the curious press of himself, the utter, hopeless, thwarting that was his blood and bones and flesh. Afraid of a crisis beyond his ability, he held himself in, his body and breath absolutely still in the passing and fading whine and rumble of a plane overhead.

Some time passed before he threw back the covers and arranged himself with reluctant effort in the lumpy terrain of the mattress. Below, he could hear the querulous voices of Missy and Goose. The terrible act of stealing into their bedroom in the middle of the night as they slept again shuddered his flesh. Briefly, Alta Mae crossed his mind; in the floating shadows behind the gymnasium he saw her face and remembered her lips and the press of her breasts. Then, as usual, his thoughts drifted to the last few years before his mother died. He remembered himself as a child—or thought he did. Remembered her bathing him and feeding him and getting him ready for school as all the millions of other mothers normally do for their children. In contrast to the cold, unadorned room in which he lay—carpetless and with plaster flaking from the ceiling and chipping from the walls behind peeling wallpaper—he recalled the snug little bedroom she used to spend hours vacuuming and tidying for his benefit. He loved it especially in the evenings when she tucked him in his bed and told him stories—or even better when she told him about his father. The bedside lamp was turned low, and he could breathe her wonderful smell of roses, and wonderful it was to lie there snug and warm in bed in his little room. Most wonderful of all was the feeling that when he went to sleep, his mother would still be there, as close as her room across the hall—within range of a whisper.

He was always tucked back in himself like a leaf folded against the wind. I think of him like that and abhor the lot given him for my roses and thorns. That's the way I think of him, even now, reassured by the possibilities of another world. Folded against the wind and tucked back from the rain. So worried about adventure and how a thing comes to mean. If I could reach down and touch him, I would. I would, if I could reach down my hand. In spite of ancestry and guilt, if I could tell him one thing, I would tell him how a thing comes to mean. If I could sing for him, I would sing from afar. I would sing the lullaby, "O, here a sleeping child lies," for if we believed in anything together at all, we believed in the sister he might have had.

~4~

Dreams

. . . something was fumbling along through the trees.

"IT'S them dreams," Aunt Missy complained. And Goose, disgusted, with that far away look in his eye, ducked his head in agreement. Stories and poems and music, sketching and dreams, whatever you wanted to call his artistic bent, were responsible for the collision course, for the disaster, he was fast becoming, zinging toward with lightening speed. At least, to hear Missy or Goose tell it. But what about now? Was he dreaming? He was dreaming, and he knew he was. It all came around together in a confusing but reasonable way, more memory than dream. He could feel himself lying deep and exhausted in his bed, Missy and Goose just down the hall, and yet he could see his mother from a top angle down and a little of himself beneath her, much younger now, before he had even a sense of this or that or the immense and unfortunate possibilities that lay before him. Here, now, with the squirm of the dog against his feet, and yet in another bed, his mother leaned toward him.

Here, now, though in another time and place, wind gusted about the eaves of the house, and the sudden sound of blown water dashed over the panes like gravel. Rain thrummed on the roof. From a corner, where the ceiling and walls came together,

Evan watched as his mother turned the lamp down low. Then, by the magic of dreams, he was looking up at her. The weight of her settling on the bed beside him tipped him toward her. Her scrubbed face shone in the dim light and her breath, scented with the peppermint of Colgate, drifted into his nostrils. Two yellow barrettes held her hair in "bird's-wings" back from her forehead. Her eyes were clear as the sky after a good rain. Beneath the peppermint odor he detected the more subtle scent of "rose soap" with which she always lotioned her hands. With a handkerchief she dabbed at her eyes.

"As the twig is bent, so grows the tree." She put her mouth gently against his forehead and, even dreaming, he was sure he could feel her trembling breath and the pressure of her lips. "How much like your papa you are."

Dreamily, he touched the nearly invisible down on her naked arm and, knowing he shouldn't, let his fingers caress the silky stuff of her nightgown where it fell loosely in folds across her breasts. He felt the slight trembling of his limbs and saw the cowboys and Indians on his pajama top gallop all over his arms.

The windowpanes chattered with windswept rain.

" . . . nor did I know my own papa," she whispered, remembering. He followed the direction of her gaze toward the tapping pane but careful, careful, not knowing what he might encounter there, his eyes just a squint and all at once the shrinking of his flesh. No, no. He looked at the wad of nightgown in his fist. She was simply thinking out loud—or, possibly, by another trick of the dream, he was inside her head, wondering about any number of things as she spoke not of her papa but of his, a father who could somehow hear her "grumbling on the other side of a solid wall," or if she were happy, could hear her *not* thinking ill. Such a papa to be proud of, now in the sky or somewhere invisible, like a shadow against the windowpane, there, where the lamplight folded back to catch the dark.

Tap, tap.

She took his hand away and held it in her lap and again

blotted her eyes. "Sometimes," she said with a hush and a pause, surveying the room, listening. "Sometimes I think I can almost hear him now, your father. Forever listening to everything I do and no place to hide." She took his hand from her lap and placed it under the covers—plucked a piece of lint from his hair.

"But how can you hear someone listening?"

He was proud of the thought, so deep at the center of this debatable dream, though in dreams he was assured of the possibility of the wondrous and the odd. Her mouth opened, revealing the edges of her perfect white teeth, but when she spoke, it was in the voice of a child. He was listening to himself, so adult, his voice in her mouth.

"How? Why, you pay attention. It's as simple as that. Now say your prayers, my love. Pray for knowledge and truth. Your papa did. I'm sure he did. I'm sure he did. Your daddy had a kind of Second Sight he couldn't shake. A tender nature. It was no fault of his, something he couldn't shake. And he took it with him every time he made a run to Las Vegas or Iron Mountain, every time he wrote a poem. He knew things close to the heart, things more of the heart than the head. How can you fault that, a sensitive heart? But he never touched her, that little vagabond, like some might think. So tender and thoughtful of others. So filled with desire. So hungry for love. And he hears us, too—hears our every thought. Like shadow, like sun. What we do and what we think. And watches over us. But if he touched her, he never said. He never said. And who am I to say? Say your prayers and then listen, my love. Always listen and watch. And promise me. You must promise."

He looked for meaning but could see only himself in the dark center of her eye. Could she see her own face in his?

"Promise never to hurt the one you come to love. You must promise."

"Why would I hurt you?"

"No, no. The one you love. Your heart's desire. You'll know. Now promise."

"Yes."

"What you fail to see with your eyes, let your heart believe."

He swallowed and something went through him warm as soup, surprising his chest. Had she said what he thought? Or, at the center of dreaming, had he thought what she said?

"Here's one for the night." Her own voice rose in her throat, and she leaned over and pecked him on the cheek, and then matter-of-factly without an iota of self-pity: "And here's one for the sister you might have had."

"Sung to sleep by lullabies?"

"As you look, she will not stir."

At that moment his father's death or the prospect of his father, or God, or whomever, listening and watching was less troublesome than the idea of a sister stealing his mother's affections. But hadn't he promised? He held it hard in his mind for a while, and it was like putting his finger into an electrical socket just to feel the jolt. He knew what that felt like.

"Here a sleeping child lies . . ."

But his beautiful mother was looking at something far away, something beyond the room, deep inside herself. She seemed to have a notion, an idea, that the more she struggled to grasp slipped further away. "Never," she said. "Not once." She was beautiful and yet in years to come, except for the photographs, or such deep and exhausted dreams, Evan would not be able to remember her face. But her voice would linger in his head like the uneven patter of rain that night, distracting him again and again from his most intimate thoughts: how his father who had never touched another must have touched her in order to bring him into the world, how he must have held her in his arms, kissing her face all over, realizing in their embrace a sense of his own immortality. Evan would come to wish that his father's touch could restore the dead and that the railroad cars carrying propane had never passed that day and that his mother's fateful rose . . .

O, how deeply in love they must have been, his parents.

Perhaps they were even still. For he had heard late at night in the darkness of his room unworldly sounds, and he had seen with unfocused eyes hard evidence of the world beyond: unburnished shadows struggling in the lamplight beyond the drawn curtain of his door, which, like a glowing scrim, revealed the celebrants of some sacred passion coming and going with a sudden embrace or a terrifying moan.

She introduced him once to a man who stayed for dinner and on a separate occasion took them to the zoo. But he knew when he awoke in the night and saw the shadows behind the drawn curtain of his bedroom door that it was his father come back to console her, the shadow of him moving upon her and uttering whispers in her hair.

O, Rose, Rose, my lovely Rose.

Now, heavy with sleep in his bed at the top of the stairs, her voice came back to him from that night when she spoke to him of his father who had never touched but her—all for the want of a daughter, all for the want of a son—or perhaps it was from many nights over a period of time, all strung together and compressed in his mind into that single most meaningful night, when the rain begged the two of them to come to the window and peer into the dark. With their faces to the window each saw his own slender resemblance to the other in the reflecting dark of the glass: her arm draped about his shoulders, his head pressed against the contour of her breast. Were they but ghosts come out of the night to torment and chide? Beyond the windowpane they stood in midair, and he watched her lips move only slightly as she murmured, to the effect, "Can we ever really know?" And then she turned to him and tipped his face up between her hands and recited for him with a certain pleasant melancholy a piece of her favorite poem:

> *I see not a step before me*
> *as I tread on another year,*
> *But I've left the past in God's keeping—*

the future his mercy shall clear,
And what looks dark in the distance
may brighten as I draw near.

They moved away from the window, and she lay with him on his bed where they held one another and talked and caressed as rain beat steadily above. Mother and son in a forgiving embrace. Even as she wept, she told him about his father, how he loved to hunt—and to travel, and to write. Anything to remove himself from his stepbrother and the man's misguided wife. Anything to remove her from the possibility of hurt and the misdeeds of a rash and unforgivable act. For the commitment to love should be greater and is more important than love itself. Didn't she say? Didn't she say? *Promise. Now promise me. Promise me, now.* How once, in proving the theory to mutual satisfaction and before Evan was born, they had traveled coast to coast—like Gypsies—sleeping in the back of a camper, roach infested motels, and sleeping bags on hot summer nights . . . *should be greater . . . and more important.* Hadn't she said? Such was their commitment to love, in spite of the rumors, in spite of the odds.

Not long after that trip, his father had died. Then seven years later, his mother. He could see yet an image of himself standing by the open grave as her coffin was lowered into the earth and feel the damp press of Missy's palm in his own. From dream to nightmare, without so much as a breath, the big, scary woman stooped as best she could and whispered kindly that he had three minutes now to finish his blubbering. At home there would be no more of that. So he stood at the edge of the universe feeling the wind sting his eyes as this foul-smelling woman and a man named Goose hefted wreath and bouquet from graveside to car. They left only an arrangement of chrysanthemums, or maybe it was begonias, and squeezed him into the back seat amid petals and stems and thorns for the long ride home. Perhaps it was the intermingling reek of death in a single bouquet, but before they hit the driveway his stomach cramped and he spewed great gobs

THE GYPSY LOVER ·71·

of his lunch on the back seat and floor of the car. When he tried
to get his breath, he couldn't but cry.

"Git him to the top of the stairs," said Goose.

And then . . .

"Didn't I tell you?" Missy snapped the strop across the small
trembling legs, bared from ankles to hips, as Goose stood looking on. "Pipe down, now." The second and third times, he heard
it cut the air before it struck and when it struck, the blaze of it
went all up through his intestines, into his lungs, and out the
back of his head like a wrong-way claw.

"Beat the snot out of him," said Goose. "That's it. That's it.
Give him one for his Pa!" The rooster man swung open the closet
door and held out his hand to show Evan the key.

More in dreams than awake he was to learn that his wailing
fell on deaf ears. How long they left him in the closet each time,
he had no idea. It was simply to wait, his ears full of the pounding of the fight beyond the door. They yelled back and forth and
struggled in the slop of it like incubus and succubus and flung
things with a clatter or a smash and the sound of it rose and fell
in waves, grunting hoglike sounds, not theirs but his, rooting
out a place to sleep . . . his own undulant breath and the smell of
mothballs and wool, once his own urine and puke, both damp-
ness and stench black as the all night sky.

It may have been that first night in the closet, curled wood-
enly on the hardwood floor, or shortly thereafter, or even later,
that he had a dream. He dreamt of a woman—a girl, really (decidedly not his mother)—who came up out of a river with no
one around to watch but him. She came up out of the river
shedding water like an earthbound fowl. Behind her, he could
see the mass of a barge making its way effortlessly up stream to
some scheduled point. In passing, the vessel darkened her features, but he could see the nakedness of her all the same, glistening and damp, as much adolescent as adult. He looked for a sign,
some acknowledgment in her face, but her face was blank, just
empty and unexpressive and deep. It was as though she had been

birthed from within, like an infant from the world of itself, and when he looked, the river behind her closed solid as flesh as though she had emerged from a wound. In the same dream, he saw a man sitting alone on a curb—just a man (decidedly not his father)—who had wandered into the street out of nowhere and sat himself down on the curb. From a second story window, the rivergirl looked out at the man sitting in the street below. She drew the window curtain back as if expecting to see something and looked out at the man. From a point of view a little above her head, or perhaps through her eyes, Evan, too, could see the man and the street and the buildings behind him that lined the opposite side. The street was empty, except for the man on the curb, and the man looked back. His eyes were huge and black, like moons on a stormy night. But black. When he looked again, he saw the rivergirl standing in the street. She wore her hair loose and shiny and dark, and she stood naked in the street, a little pregnant, perhaps. She had fastened a rose in her hair, behind her ear, and she turned with a smile and a glance and motioned and gave Evan her hand. Was he naked as well? He tried to see through the eyes of the man on the curb. He tried to see her nakedness, but it fell away from him even as he tried. Her nakedness and his. "You promised," she said. She took his hand and laid it over her breast and pressed it there and closed her eyes. He knew then how the world lay in the palm of his hand and in the tightening of the bud and in the beat of the heart. She opened her eyes and pressed his hand to her belly and some fear inside her rose in his breast and all around them like invisible steam. "You promised," she said. She let loose of his hand and crossed the street, the two of them together, Evan inside somehow but a little way back, and the man stood up. He came toward them, one eye so blue it was black. The man said, from somewhere inside him, as if to demand, though he couldn't be sure, and the rivergirl searched about their nakedness, searched high and low, but couldn't find a thing, and then she found a thing from out of her mouth she gave to the man. The man studied and turned his hands all around it and held it near, as one might hold secrets or truth, and Evan could feel it in his hands, in the hands of the man, and thought maybe it was small and heartshaped, like the breast of a dove, like crystal or hewn stone or the hardness of life. The man held and turned it loose in his hands and opened his hands with an upward sweep. When he opened his hands, a birdthing rose shining into the sky, bright and soft as the girl's hair or sound, even, and the faint and familiar scent of bittersweet roses and mint. He dreamt that buildings dissolved into trees and him among shade and some wavering light watching a child come up from the water and now through the trees, up to the rivergirl and touch her and, lo, he was beholding himself.

It started to rain.

Within the diamond haze of the rain, far away, something was fumbling along through the trees. Evan saw it, and it came up from the river and he watched until his watching grew tired. Together, they watched. It was as though some creature had stepped from mirage onto the wet grassy field. Darkness and shadow came up from the river, came close, stopped, forever dry in the steady downpour of rain, and held toward Evan a hand. He moved toward it like a promise. In the clasp of that shadow he could feel the beat of a heart. But whose? She leaned toward him a shadow no more, not the dark-eyed girl but his mother, and held him and set him on the grass and held him for a long time, whispering, *What you fail to see with your eyes, let your heart believe.* Over and over, *What you fail to see with your eyes, let your heart believe.* Again and again. She stepped toward the man, and for an instant Evan thought it was himself all grown up. He watched the two of them, his mother and the man, as they wandered away from him, hand in hand, never looking round, diminishing with the distance, stepping from earth back into mirage, from blurred human form to the same dark creature dissolving into the diamond haze of rain.

Only he and the dark-eyed beauty remained, only Evan and

the withering rain, he and the everlasting image of expectation, squeezing away the last few rays of sun into a pallid gray light.

Now ghosts float about him and dreams express themselves as vague premonitions of things to come. Evan turns each memory in his mind like delicate glass, thinking: *Yes, I see what it means, but somehow I can't get it right in my head.* It is the voice of some whispering ghost, reminding him again and again that there will always be that in this world which goes beyond understanding and speaks to the heart in a more meaningful way.

What do you say to the gist of yourself? I would tell him, if I could, to let his dreams buoy him up. I know you, my son, how you long to paint the cold, dark place within. How you long to paint the sludge at the bottom of a river or a lake or some secluded, camouflaged, watery hole. How, as poets affirm, you long to make the colors of your palette dance around the rim of the heart's abyss. How you long to throw stones in it, holler until your lungs collapse, measure it, and not fall in. I know you, my son. I would tell you, if I could, that it's all a matter of dreams. I would tell you to believe, as children believe, that if the truth were known, you might have a better glimpse of yourself. But would you, could you, believe, even hearing it whispered from beyond, the very worst of your father? For though truth may long for expression, the palette of memory keeps those around you both safe and close to the heart. What more in truth than that?

~ 5 ~

A Dog's Life

When he spoke, he did not speak loud.

A scent of nightrain cleansed the air and came through the open window on a blaze of sun. Evan opened his eyes in a squint. From her place at the foot of the bed, the dog raised her head. Together, they listened for signs of stirring below. Bozo lowered her ears and Evan shrank deeper under the quilts until the springs beneath the mattress groaned and finally grew still. In waking a second time he dreamt he was standing in some swampy wood. A solitary bird slanted dark above the trees, and the sun smashed itself cold along earth's rim. He glanced back at the sinking tragedy of a split-second mistake, though look as he might he could but feel the sense of it within—the muck of it ebb to his knees, the tops of his thighs, his waist. He studied the sun through a watery glare, saw the ghosted remains of some girl looking back at him with ardor and wit. If he had dreamt otherwise or more, he couldn't recall.

He opened his eyes to another sun, the wedge of it on his bedspread and up on his clock in a spire. Strange that Goose hadn't stumped up the stairs in a rant or Missy squawked from below. He threw back the covers and sat up. He yawned and the dog put her head up and looked at him and yawned. She panted and smiled in the way that only dogs are capable and pawed the edge of the mattress and laid back her ears and put her chin on her paws. Evan clucked at her and smoothed back her coat, let her lick the salt from his hand. Her tongue was dry and her breath hot and odorous and she had a moist, dirty smell about her, but Evan petted her for a while and submitted to her tender licks. He petted her and whispered to her like a lover might and then he reached beneath her distended gut, arms in wood carrying fashion, and hefted her down. The dog looked up at him in a sort of stupid beguiling way, her lips curled back in an unwitting leer. She thumped her tail and sneezed.

Evan grabbed underwear from the bureau and a clean pair of Levis from the closet. He went down the hall to the bathroom, sneezing all the way. He showered, brushed his teeth, and took a long time to comb his hair. A couple of pimples had come to a head during the night. He leaned toward himself in the mirror, tongue plugged in cheek, and squeezed the whiteheads until the cores popped out, speckling the glass. He double-checked the growth on his upper lip, blinked at his father's eyes.

When he stepped from the bathroom onto the landing at the top of the stairs, he heard the grunt of Missy below. She heaved herself about the kitchen and rattled the pans and opened the cupboards and shut the fridge and snorted and wheezed. He was about to descend the stairs when he thought he heard the doorbell ring. The kitchen door opened onto a wooden porch with a balustrade and columns at the back of the house, and due to the configuration of the driveway, visitors were inclined to call there. The doorbell rang again before Missy could throw back the latch and open the door. Evan grabbed Bozo by the collar and gave her a shake.

"Why, Alta Mae!"

The old woman chirped like a bobolink, though few understood the warning.

Evan stepped back up and squatted, at the same time yanking the dog and struggling to get a glimpse of Alta Mae. He could tell she was out of breath. She muttered something formal with Evan's name at the center, something about the carnival.

"Why, Alta Mae. Ain't that just like your Ma, send a invite to Evan. Allus thinking on others, ain't she?"

Alta Mae tried to catch her breath and muttered between gasps, something about Allen driving, and a whole slew of kids going together, something about—

He heard the cluck of Missy's tongue, and felt his heart lump in his throat.

"Now, Alta Mae. Shame! You ain't sixteen yourself. Though like as not it matters since your looking more and more like a growed-up girl each and ever day." Missy ratcheted her tongue and, to Evan, it sounded like the cock of a pistol's hammer. He gave the dog a shake and held her and tried to get a look between the balusters. Through the curtained pane of the open door, he could see the shadow of his aunt, her fat finger wagging in the poor girl's face. "You oughtn't start dating afore your sixteen, young lady, you'll find trouble in your lap, you get my drift."

Alta Mae sucked for breath. She tried to say, and Evan longed for her to find the words. He could see but that shadow behind the pane and the shadow had taken a stance. Hand on a hip, head cocked, invisible eye the size of an egg in that bowling ball head. They stood below him conjoined and at odds, like two mismatched conspirators troubling both his and the world's design, the one so beatific in the hush of her voice and the other like some horror come from beneath.

His name again and something about meeting her there.

"Why, Alta Mae. Ain't you the little sneak? I'll tell your Mama, that's what."

"Oh, Missy," she said, raising her voice. "You don't understand. Daddy's in the truck right there."

"I unnerstand, all right. And I don't need to talk to your Pa. You're filling out right smart, titties and all. Git along now. And don't come around no more tempting my boy."

Something . . . something . . . lost in the mortification of that husky little voice, with Evan's name at the center. " . . . maybe you could—"

"And maybe I couldn't. Now you skedaddle. And cover up your tummy. Hear? I got breakfast on."

"Tell him I'll see him in church on Sunday—"

"Church? Church? And you in that outfit? Jezebel herself, if ever I breathed a day."

The door rasped against the linoleum and shut like a fist.

When Evan hit the bottom of the stairs, a scent familiar and kind lingered and mingled with the smell of bacon grease, and something rose and caught in his throat deep as a groan.

"Well, ain't you the Rip Van Winkle. Mr. King Farouk."

He forced himself to the window and swiped back the curtain just in time to see Alta Mae climb into her father's truck. She did a little hop across one of last night's rain puddles, the water already being sopped by the sun. The little blonde was wearing a pair of cutoffs, sandals, and a half-buttoned blouse that was knotted at the bottom, exposing her midriff. The jiggle of her hop played low in his gut. How soft she looked! And he remembered how soft she had felt behind the gymnasium. And once when they'd found themselves alone beneath the yellow glow of a bug lamp in the school parking lot waiting for their rides. It was after the sophomore dance, and waiting there she took his hand and said something about friendship and drew him back toward the shadow and reached up and kissed him just a peck and then slid her mouth around all soft, her body soft and loose and a matter of concern beneath the jacket she wore, breathing, "O, my."

He considered briefly the possibilities of Alta Mae beside him in Allen's car, and a wave of disappointment splashed next to his heart, slid down heavy somewhere deep and lay like a stone. He thought again of her mouth, and the way she pressed against him. For a girl touched by the spirit, she nevertheless seemed to know the size and shape of her breasts and the nuances of making her mouth perform. Besides his mother, she was the only girl he had ever kissed, and remembering, he could almost taste the breath of her. He had never kissed Missy Begonia in his life, except on the ass ten times a day.

"The little bitch make a mess in your bed?"

Evan let the curtain fall back and glanced at the dog. He looked at his aunt, but she was flipping the bacon with a spatula, and he hardly saw her at all. "Bitch?" he said with a tone. "Takes one to know one." He said it before he thought it. He could feel the movement of his own breathing and the tremor of his body beneath his shirt. He glanced around the kitchen, from cupboards to counters to table to floor, all about him and his very life like some vague and unaccountable dream. He looked back out the window, and for a moment the only sound was bacon sizzling in the pan. He understood the meaning of gloom.

"What?" he heard her say, but she didn't look at him.

He turned from the window, the sound of rubber pinching gravel as the truck pulled down the drive. A taste rose in his throat, and it was vinegary as his suddenly bitter-thick heart. He looked at the clock above the sink. Uncle Goose must have left for the fields over an hour ago.

"Sing," he said, and the sound of his voice seemed to come from afar.

"What?"

"Sing, fat lady."

"What?"

"You might as well sing, because it's all over but the shouting."

She stood with her back to him, between table and stove, hair still done up in last night's bobbypins, a flowered nightgown huge as a truck tarp draping her hulk. He could see the backs of her ears get pink. He watched, and it seemed to take forever for her to turn, and he stood in the center of the kitchen, his arms at his sides like sticks. Bacon fat smeared her mouth; she shook the spatula in her fist. He didn't know what, but something struck him as funny, and when he started to say, the words wouldn't come. He chuckled and wheezed.

"Sing, old lady." He heard his voice crack. He looked around to see who had laughed and realized he had. "Ha-ha. Why do you hate my father so?" It seemed like a fair and reasonable question at the moment, long overdue for the asking, as if an answer might clarify the settling murk, explain a thing or two, and get to the bottom of malice and spite.

"You," she said. "Who do you think you are?"

"Who am I?" He tried a number of beginnings, groped for the words with his thickening tongue. He chuckled, wheezed, knew with a stab the meaning of hysteria and self-abuse. "Not me," he said, without raising his voice. "You." He told her to look in the mirror. "Though I don't suppose there's one in this house big enough you could see more than one tit at a time." He called her pathetic. "You and that gob of spit chicken shit husband of yours. Not me. You. Take a look in the hall mirror and tell me why you hate my father so."

"What, then? Pathetic, am I? Chicken shit? Go on, then. If you dare."

"A big pathetic tub of lard—"

"TUB A LARD?" She spit a fine mist, then gobs of something reeking and green. "TUB A LARD?" She heaved her frame around the table, her right hand above her head, wielding the spatula like a sword. "Tub a lar-r-rrd." She sang like a soprano struggling to hit one slippery note an octave up. Howled. Certainly more howl than song—a finale, no matter how you looked at it, with all but descending curtain and thunderous applause. She opened her mouth in an aria, sang, "*You-o-o-o!* Tub a lard, am I? *You-o-o-o.*"

She lunged for him and he grabbed both her wrists.

"Leggo, now. I'll strop you, don't think I won't."

She was big and powerful and mad, but Evan felt the potato fields in his arms, the woodpile in his back, and he had her thick, flabby wrists in his hands so tight her fingers were turning blue. She used her right hand like a flipper, trying to whack him with the spatula.

"Leggo, now. What's got into you?"

They did a grotesque dance around the kitchen, catapulting from refrigerator to table and back again. First Missy led, then Evan. Bozo danced her own weird jig and scrabbled into a corner. She set about serenading the kitchen ceiling, yipping like a coyote searching for an unlit moon and hitting more than once that greasy note Missy had failed. Evan yipped, too. He barked, then snarled, then growled, at the same time choking his stomach back down his throat. Chairs tumbled over. Plates and glasses slid off the table and smashed to the floor. Forks and spoons. Milk spewed beneath their feet. Smoke billowed from the frying pan, smogging the kitchen. Her frame rolled in a mad ballet and Evan held fast, gasping for air.

"Out changing your water. Goose." She lolled her head, the green spittle bubbling in the corners of her mouth and frothing her chin.

"My water? I wouldn't claim anything on this hell-hole."

Bozo went round and around, the ragged end of her tail whipping about like a flame at the end of an unruly fuse. She got between their legs again, took a snap at the fat lady, and tried skedaddling here and there, but not before Missy kicked her in the head. She reeled away, yelping.

"Why do you hate my parents so?" He asked it, and asked it again, though not with a shout. This time her eyes went blank then all at once expressive, with a certain hint of injury. Possibilities tottered. A thought rushed into words, formed around what he knew—or hoped—would be a hurtful core. "How come you and Uncle Goose never had any kids of your own?"

"You!"

"How come?"

"You little pip squeak. Do you think I could? Goose, that is." She lunged with her gut, the madder it seemed for his having asked, for her having said.

But having said, there was clarification. In the midst of all the smoke and turmoil, there was enlightenment. The threads of malice that had forever crept toward him for having been born of worthy parents were now explained in the simple-minded envy of those who couldn't toward those who could, of those who hadn't toward those who had—centered as a reminder to such inability and loss in "them girly eyes" of his.

"I can tell you about your Pa, I can. A thing or two. And your Ma so prissy in her blue and white, hair tied back—them icy German eyes and Aryan hair. She put her face to the pillow and wept more than once for his doing."

"Liar!"

"Him and that Vegas showgirl, little vagabond from who knew where."

"You lie."

And he knew she did. For spite and ruin she would have him by the throat in a stranglehold if she could. The memory of his father, no matter how ragged around the edges, was inviolate and steeped in his blood, and neither evil incarnate nor she could wash it black. Not with a word, not with a lie. Nothing she told him held any weight or bearing—not now—not since her having said and in saying clarified the malice in her heart. Her mouth opened and closed, and she continued to blab on ears gone deaf. He was too occupied with slinging the weight of her and with the taste of his own venomous phlegm to hear her garbled shriek. That taste washed through his mouth and with it a thing or two about Leila, Missy's sister, edged to the tip of his tongue. Leila and Goose, bragged on by the rooster man himself. In times past, Leila and Goose in the loft. After all, Evan knew things, some things that would shake the very foundation of the house beyond their own mad dance. But when Missy ripped, he swallowed the cruelty back, and it went down his esophagus like a flame.

"You old bat," was all he could think to say, as he swung her around.

Missy ripped and her hide spilled out of the nightgown. The sight terrified them both. She was rolls and folds and tucks and dreary speckled flesh. Every jounce rocked the house and slopped the more of her than even untold stories or imagination could bear. Evan gaped and fought past the sympathy in his heart.

"Goose!"

Missy waltzed him back against the stove and butted him with her gut. He swung away, wrenching her arms. Then he saw himself—the two of them—as if from a point outside his head, from the ceiling light fixture. He watched their own absurd twists and turns, that lunge, this lurch, a mad pirouette, knowing full well—for the rage of the beast within his grip—that he could never let go. They did the plod and stomp. He started to laugh all over again, in little coyote barks. Missy's eyes widened; the blood came into her head until Evan thought it would explode, spattering the kitchen, the dog, him, with blood, bone, and brain. His eyes burned, teared. What brain? He laughed until his ribs ached. His heart sank, and laughing, he bawled like a maniac.

"Okay. Stop," he shouted. "Stop and I'll let go."

But he knew she wouldn't stop—*couldn't*. Blood was in her ears. Her eyes egged white with heartache and rage. She could neither hear nor see. So deaf and blind and dumb.

He loosened the fingers of his hands around her wrists, but the doughy flab clung to him. Finally, out of desperation—or a sense of the absurd—he flung her hands back toward her head. The spatula went flying and they were free. At least he was. Detached, she continued to flail, totter, and tip. She swung around on one foot, sloshing spilled milk, the momentum of her own bulk throwing her to the floor like a collapsing tent. Before she could reclaim herself Evan was gone—Bozo yowling at his heels— the windowpane of the back door rattling in its frame.

He never thought twice about going back to the house, helping clean up the mess, and apologizing. A tub of lard's got no brain. It worried him that he, himself, had been so well greased over the years that if he slipped on a banana peel he would slide all the way into the next county. Like detestable Uncle and Aunt, like nephew, he thought with a sense of doom. Even weeks later, sometimes in the middle of the night, he would awake to find himself giggling through his tears. In his journal, he would write about a sense of regret, but never shame. He would come to write about falling into the cogs of some great machine, unable to do little more than ride the mechanism to the end for which it was set. He would write, in the soft press of his lead: "O, why did you leave me?" and then turn the pencil over and scrub it away. He would jot from memory the closing lines from one of this father's poems:

> *. . . these are visions of becoming*
> *when the light begins to fail.*
> *These are the desperate moves*
> *of a guitar player whose fingers know*
> *emptiness & what it means to play*
> *from a room the size of a wound.*

He ran from the kitchen into the barn and hoisted himself up the ladder two rungs at a time and into the loft. There, in the flat, sharp shadows, he dumped himself into a pile of straw. Before he could shift onto his back, he heard an agitated gabble. Uncle buck fluffed himself and cocked his head at an angle beyond severe and fixed Evan with a shining black eye. Insult to injury. The bird took a step back and scratched at the straw.

"How'd you get up here?"

Evan glanced at the yellow spurs long as his thumb, the black ruffled feathers shining blue-green like oil on water. The yellow beak opened and closed. Something empty and decisive filled the loft. Uncle launched with a flap, twisting in air to arrive spurs first. Evan threw up a hand to cover his face and was cut across the wrist by a spur. Then again, and he flailed like a blind man in a room full of bats. He scrabbled around in the straw on hands and knees while the bird ripped the air with its wings. The broken light was shattered further in a blaze of dust and feathers and straw. Somehow, he got hold of a crosstie fallen from the rafters. He feinted left then right. When Uncle flapped again, he had the tie on his shoulder and brought it around like a slugger in a ballpark. A little inside and high, but the blow knocked the bird from the loft. Evan drew a breath. The thump below was followed by an unbirdly squawk, and he scrambled to the edge of the loft and looked over the rail. He couldn't see the bird at first in the shadows below; then he saw the struggle of it, the flop and the twist, a contending wing, but still it didn't right itself.

He took another breath, the scent of dung and hay afflicting his lungs. His eyes blurred and the clot in his chest worked its way up in his throat. He puked a little over the rail and wiped the puke from his mouth with his sleeve. He shut his eyes against the sudden vanishing ghosts of Leila and the rooster man up in the loft, then glanced around in a daze. An old bridle tangled in a pair of traces hung from a peg by its bit. He checked the gash on the underside of his wrist and wiped the blood on his pantleg. He lay back and shut his eyes, holding tight his wrist. Still, his heart would not quit. It whacked at the underside of his ribs like hammer blows from inside. His face felt tight from the paste of bacon smoke and tears.

All the while, he lay in the loft holding his wrist while bars of sunlight sliced through gaps in the siding, and the morning got up on the legs of an old man, his own rubbery bones, and meandered toward noon. He could see it in the angle of light shifting over the straw according to the throw of the sun and feel it in the rising heat from below. In time a crucifix of light fell across his breast either to bless or condemn him, but which he couldn't be sure. He rolled his head back against the slats and pondered the fragments of light and remembered the dream he'd had last night, just snatches and snippets, and how within the dream he'd dreamt. No, no. Not the darkeyed girl but Leila scrambling up the ladder and into the loft on a hot summer's day, Goose close behind. Certainly reminiscent of the story of his father and the bohemian showgirl—but nothing to it—or Goose would have said, and not having said, Goose made the story his own. What greater proof was needed to dismiss the lies of his aunt and memory's abuse?

Evan looked at the bridle hanging from the peg, the way the reins twisted and looped and hung like a noose. Something encouraging in that. Not unlike Goose strangling himself on debatable stories and disastrous jokes: how clever at getting away with some slight malice or unplanned injury. Together, they would ride the truck along the canal, Evan at the wheel, Goose with a chaw. From one field to another, they would jounce along, checking the crops and routing the water, Goose letting loose. He especially liked to tell of how he had romanced Missy's sister in years gone by. How, just a hired man before their parents passed away, he took to Leila, "a little saucer-eyed filly, wild and unbroke," and how they would go up into the barn loft on a hot summer's day and diddle themselves stupid. He told of how this went on for nearly a year, day in and day out, until they found the little thing all maimed and torn to pieces, lying in a heap in the hogs' crib as though the pigs "had somehow got a sniff of her when she was in the midst of her slopping and et her up like silage." Who else could he turn to but Missy, and wait for her folks to pass?

Evan loosened the hold on his wrist, just enough to feel the pain of his pulse. How, he wondered, is it possible to forget the things you remember? And where, on a hot summer's day? Right here among the rancid straw and chicken shit? Up against the broken slats where the loft opened onto the derrick above the hogs' crib below? He could see how the dress had slipped from her shoulder, head twisted in a gasp to greet the man behind. And Goose . . . his little saucer-eyed filly, all wild and unbroke, tackle from a singletree wrapped in her hair. Evan could see it for what it might have been, the slip, the shove, the inadvertent fall. All from a man who, on another ride around the fields, told with relish how he'd once got a wrong number and the party hung up on him like the anonymous asshole he was, and how he'd phoned the man back and called him the same and a thing or two more. How he called the fellow every day for a week or so to tell him he was a sonofabitch until one day he got the wife, and how he laid into her about the s-o-b she was married to who was sleeping with her brother's wife. He hadn't known from Adam whether she had a brother or not and just took a shot at it and hit the bull's eye. The woman said, "Marla?" like maybe she'd expected something all along, and Goose said, "One and the same." He could only wonder how it went from there, but the wondering was enough to satisfy his penchant for revenge. Some luck for a man who'd gotten a wrong number in the first place, something about turning opportunity to advantage, especially if the advantage maligned or undid another, no matter how inadvertent or by chance.

He looked back over the rail, relieved to find Uncle Buck still there, a dither of unruly feathers lying in a huff. When he sat back, he shut his eyes, shut them against a large history map of the United States studded with arrows and pins. Nebraska, he thought, but couldn't remember the shape of the state. Wyoming, Missouri, Ohio, perhaps. He didn't think of anything to the West. Not even the Las Vegas run. But in his mind, he could see the empty glistening rails running East. He considered direction and what to leave behind. And then he thought of how good the hurt in his wrist felt and mousey Miss Butler's obsession with "pleasing pains," the "agony of joy," and whether he would die of an infection as his mother had. If he were to die, that would fix them, that would fix them, and he applied pressure to his wrist, feeling the welt of coagulated blood. But how to forget the things you remember? And what to leave behind? Alta Mae pressed up close to him behind the gym? Alta Mae whose hot hard mouth pulled at his: *O, Evan, touch me if you want.* Did she say that?

No, no.

Our salvation. Where do we come from? Why are we here?

Sitting up close to Alta Mae in a central pew, that was the

image—something to get hold of, rock solid, for insurance sake if nothing else, like iron.

He looked at the noose.

And Jesus said.

But as for Missy and Goose, forgive them? They knew what they'd done, all right.

For a while Evan dozed, simmering in his own fluid, while flies darted among light rays stabbing between slats. Once, the sound of his mother's voice rang in his head as clear as if she had been standing at the foot of the ladder calling his name, and his own voice startled him.

"What?"

Flies jabbed past and the stench of dung rose with the heat. He thought he heard the rustle of clothing, footsteps, beneath the loft; a shadow, like the wave of a hand, passed among light rays. Something womanly, sweet. It was nothing, of course. A swallow? The dog? His head was thick with the heat. Outside he could hear the faint drone of tractors, hardly audible above the hum in his ears, and the distant sob of a train. Wyoming? Ohio? Everything about him was damp, sweat stung his eyes. He wiped his face with the tail of his shirt and scrambled to the wall fronting the house and peered between the slats. Missy Begonia labored among her namesakes, pruning back the overgrowth with a pair of short and powerful scissors. She wore a straw sun hat and heavy leather gloves to protect her hands while she worked. Her gestures were exaggerated and a little vindictive, while at the same time surprisingly gentle. He watched her for a while and watched the securely defined silhouette of the dog beneath the foundation of the porch. When at last Missy pulled off her gloves and dropped the scissors into her apron pocket, he climbed down from the loft.

Uncle Buck lay at the foot of the ladder, still alive but badly hurt, dying he'd bet. Evan positioned the heel of his boot over the top of Uncle's head, and the bird thrashed as though tethered by an invisible thread. Crueler to, or not to? To leave the thing in its agony or to finish it off? The contemplation of such questions had the animal rights troops, the medical profession, big government, and half the rest of the world in a stew. He did what he thought best and ducked out of the barn.

For a while he wandered the creeks, cut through the marshes, and followed the roads. A carload of Gypsies passed him once, heading toward the fields. The dust from their tires billowed upward in feathery plumes and the blue sky was momentarily obscured by a brown haze through which the sun shone dully like the lid of a tin can. An hour later he found himself standing at the edge of one of the last fields being harvested. He might as well have been standing at the edge of the universe, watching from a separate world. It was all so familiar and yet vague. In a day or so the ground would be free to re-plow and prepare for next spring's planting.

Uncle Goose was nowhere in sight—probably finishing up the west acres over a mile away. Evan considered grabbing a bucket and an armload of gunnysacks to work a couple of rows. Instead, he kept his distance, watching the stooped forms inch across the field in an uneven line, like a wave, their progress measured by the squat, upright sacks they left behind. Women and men squatted, stood, crouched, sat, knelt. There was a continuous thumping in the buckets.

The foreman patrolled the rows, fists tucked inside the mammoth bib of his overalls, yelling: "Trim those eyes!"

Had Evan waved his arms, would anyone have seen or paid attention? He drew a sharp wedge of air through his lungs. He held his hand in front of his face and made sure his fingers worked. The sun lounged in the sky and distance was obscured by failing light. His eyes lost their focus and closed; he saw himself, a vision of himself, far away working the rows. It was not so bad in the fields—although he would rather be in his room with *Don Quixote* in his lap. You simply worked the rows, grabbing each individual potato plant in one hand and with the other chopping your hand spade through the roots to sever the outlying tubers. The ground was kept moist and the tubers already plowed came up easily, shedding dirt. You trimmed the eyes and tossed each potato into the bottomless bucket hooping your sack. The spades were sharp as the blade of an ax and if you weren't careful and held the plant stalk too close to the ground you could easily mistake your fingers as part of the system and slice off a thumb. One summer, a big Mexican working next to him did just that. He had been fluctuating between Spanish and English, using four-letter words ten to the sentence all day long, cursing first the heat and then, if the sun went behind a cloud, the shade, telling over and over the raunchiest jokes. When he stopped, the silence brought a dozen heads around. He was examining the severed forefinger of a leather glove, beads of sweat rinsing his eyes and face. Someone gasped and they all waited, expecting a stream of the foulest words in two languages to erupt from his mouth. A little pig-tailed girl with eyes as black as ash blew an inadvertent spit bubble and stared. She blew a spit bubble and shivered her leg and gaped for all as the big Mexican stood watching the bright arterial blood pump from his ruined hand. When he spoke, he did not speak loud.

"Aw, shucks," he said.

Evan opened his eyes and the image vanished, but standing there he wondered if, in the same circumstances—separate, alone—his father would have smiled.

Now, making his way back across the fields, a sense of purpose struck him. It was nothing definite and without explanation turned him in the direction of the farm. Before he had gone ten feet, he saw Uncle Goose about a hundred yards away. The man was a jagged silhouette against the sky, and seeing him there Evan felt the cogs of that great machine churn in his gut. The sun was in its cradle, the sky bleached to an almost colorless lavender except for an orange glow above the distant mountains. A shadow passed overhead and Evan saw that it was a blackbird winging toward the sun. He felt the breeze tousle his hair. He felt a sense of momentum, as though pushed from behind.

Goose stooped, then stood, then stooped—now hunkering on the other side of the irrigation ditch near the water gate. In the road behind him, the truck stood idling, its door wide open. He must be out changing the water, closing this gate and preparing to open another farther up the field. No, no. Evan screwed up his eyes against the light. The man was beating clothes against one of those old fashioned washboards. No, no. Missy had an automatic washer and why would Goose be washing clothes in a muddy ditch? Evan shook his head: the afternoon sun must have gotten inside and addled his brain. He plodded across the rows, drawing closer, potato plants lashing the legs of his jeans. The evening sun flared over the ground before him and mourning doves rose out of the cottontails by ones and by pairs and whistled away with thin calls. The rooster man was less silhouette now, in some sort of buzzard's hunch, intent on his work; in the sun's final rays, his hair blazed darkly. Evan crossed another row about to call out when Goose leapt to his feet.

"I told you—" His mouth opened to a large O and squawked shut and he strangely whimpered, or so Evan thought. An open shoebox stood on end at his feet. As Evan crossed toward him, the rooster man shrugged and reached about with one hand to find himself and took out his pizzle and leaked a broad stream into the waters of the ditch, as if oblivious to the world at large and in benediction of some closing scene. He shook himself off and zipped his pants with a singlehanded yank, and as he did, something inside Evan's head doubled back on fast wind. Sure enough, Goose's other hand came alive, something in his fist squirmed and squeezed back in his fingers like an animal trying to back down a hole, and Evan broke toward the rooster man, stumbling over plants and furrows.

"Here, now!"

Evan vaulted the ditch that lay between them. If Goose hadn't wheeled away in his own cowardly fashion, shaking empty his hand, the momentum of Evan's body would have sent him sprawling backward into the ditch.

Evan scooped up the live cold thing and stuffed it damp and mewling inside his shirt. "How many?" he said. His eyes blurred. He felt, for a moment, all the rage it must take to kill a man. And then he was watching himself as though on a screen, each movement slowed and perfectly timed. His arm came around and his shoulder dipped forward catching his bewildered uncle square in the gut. Goose tripped backward, his long arms flailing, teetering briefly on the bank. A puzzled expression drew his face into a knot, then surprise. He was lost, backpedaling down the bank, arms rowing, hands clutching, such a look of disbelief on his face that Evan nearly laughed as he cried. "How many?" Goose smacked the water hard, holding up one hand with five fingers splayed.

Evan flew up the path into the yard, clutching beneath his shirt the squirming pup. The gate slapped back against the post, and he took the porch steps in a leap. The back door stood open, and he slammed through the screen into a kitchen spick-and-span.

There, Missy sat at the table grunting into her plate. She glanced up, and a stupid expression washed through her eyes. An odor of pine nuts roasting in the oven choked the air. By morning both she and Uncle Goose would be rancid.

"Ask me where's the dog," she said. She had the gristle of a pig's foot caught between her teeth and was busily digging it out with the tine of a fork. "Ask me now where's your little bitch."

"What?"

"Go on, you little pip squeak, ask me."

She was looking at the shotgun where it stood out of place between the doorjamb and the sink. She looked back at Evan, and Evan felt the cogs of the great machine grinding away. He felt the blow of a fist hard in his gut. He felt something move as if his guts had come undone, and he held tight to the only thing left. He might have cursed. Or wept. He might have turned the table upside down in her lap. Or rushed outside like some deranged being and thrown himself through her begonia patch. He might have turned on Goose who stomped in behind him squeaking like a sponge, Goose who had gone about the business as uncaring as an old woman beating her laundry against a rock.

"Naught but malice in your heart," Missy said. "The way you done that bird."

He looked all around him, around the kitchen, with unfocused eyes. He looked from Missy to Goose, but nothing was there. He looked from his unsevered thumb to the gash on his wrist, and holding the live thing beneath his shirt went quietly up the stairs to his room.

I'da never took him in but to teach him a thing or two about the ways of the world. Not for money, marbles, or chalk, not for Goose's notion to get his hands on that tidy sum miss prissy'd put away in the bank. It was enough, the touch of the strop blistering them Pinocchio legs of his like the master's wrath, and still I don't think he learned a whit. He come to us like a pup snatched from the teat before it got its fill. Not a grateful bone beneath his flesh—sass me, do Uncle Buck that way, Goose half drowned, and runs off in the night. He's growed up in spite of it all, like a product of hisself. Now, he want to spoon that little Robbins piece like Goose used to me. It don't matter what you do. You work, you slave. That prissy mama, she didn't but sissyfy the nature of the boy, and I could tell you a thing about his Pa, them lingering doubts, though some things is better left unsaid. The imagination takes care of such in ways the truth never will.

~6~

Escape to the Pits

*Along the muddy banks of the river,
red-winged blackbirds sang in the cattails.*

HE shut the door to his room at the top of the stairs and wedged the back of a chair beneath the knob. First he took from beneath his shirt the whimpering mass of hair and guts and bones and wiped a smear of afterbirth from its eyes. He sleeked back its coat and the coat shone like dull copper in the weak overhead glare. He wrapped the animal in an old T-shirt and laid it on the bed as though he were laying a fragment of mosaic in place. There was blood. Not from the pup but from his wrist. He smeared it on his pillow and across the ragged edge of the bedspread. He got a strip of gauze and Merthiolate from his drawer and dressed the wound by wrapping the bandage around and around and fastened it with a butterfly clip. If he were meant to die, at least Missy and Goose wouldn't have the satisfaction of his groans.

From beneath the bed he took his backpack, zipped it open, and carefully placed inside a few essentials: underwear, socks, shirts, jeans, an extra pair of shoes, the sketchbook and journal he kept hidden behind the bookcase, *Fanny Hill*. He looked at the book, a Signet Classic, the dog-eared cover curled tight like the bud of a rose, the faded image of some girlish form bursting a bodice of old, skirts hiked to the thigh. He remembered something someone told him once, *Sometimes the only way to hang on to yourself is to leave everything else behind.*

He stuffed the book in the bag as vision narrowed and felt the spite of his doing it rise in his throat. He would hide in one of the potato pits close to the railroad tracks and wait for an early morning freight. Right out of a dozen books he'd read. He could nearly see the words on the page, the irrefutable image of such heroes standing at the mouth of a tunnel, refusing to look left or right, awaiting the train. How each stood alone, peering into that maw of darkness, a pin of light at the end, though nothing in sight. Now, the storybook walls of some such tunnel swallowing those vanishing tracks held his vision firm. He had a slight headache and tried to loosen the knitted flesh across his brow by opening his eyes wide and forcing a yawn to crack his ears. Still, the walls of the tunnel narrowed and he found himself hardly able to blink. Then he remembered something else. From the wall above the head of his bed he lifted down the photograph of his parents and cushioned it between his shirt and pants. He threw in the bone-handled hunting knife sheathed in its scabbard. Then he made a mistake. He dug the knife from the bag and, unsheathing the blade, felt the contour of the handle, how it fit his palm so slick. He saw how his own name had been burned into the scabbard so many years before, and he massaged the handle and jabbed the blade into the mattress, hard. His mouth grew watery with the taste in his throat, and he knew there was no turning back. Something like jell spilled along his spine and oozed beneath his flesh, and he saw himself at their bedside, alone in the darkness listening to them breathe, his own emaciated shadow thrown by the moon against the wall, and the image plucked at him and shivered its way up into his shoulders and down through his legs. He muttered a little, but nothing even he could understand.

He glanced around the dimly lit room, unsure of the shadows, feeling perhaps watched, and busied himself with the gym bag. He re-sheathed the knife and tossed it in, considered the irony of taking the old boy-scout compass. He found a flashlight in the top bureau drawer and with it the battered harmonica his father once played; from the closet a sweater, a jacket, and there in the pocket the only other memento he had of his parents: a pair of wire-rimmed spectacles that had belonged to his father. He liked the feel of them on his face and the way the slight magnification resolved words on a page. Again, from the back of the vanity he took his life's savings: nine twenties, three tens, a single, and seventy-nine cents in change. This he stuffed in a pocket.

He zipped the bag closed, then opened it again, still unforgetting. Some of the library books on the top shelf were more than five weeks overdue. He read silently a few of the spines and wondered if he would have chosen differently had his reading belonged to other books. Or were the books he read simply a product and reflection of himself? He shrugged, gathering up the slim volume of poetry his father had published, that and a worn copy of *Where the Red Fern Grows* and Wood's *Masters of American Literature.*

Once he heard Missy lay into Goose from below; she had a voice like a lunch whistle. "If you had the balls—" he heard. "Goose!"

He put his Giant's cap on and twisted it backwards on his head and listened for the sound of either of them laboring up the stairs toward his door. Their voices fell to a low pitch, rose, fell again to a low sustained mumble. He stuffed the mewling pup, still bundled, inside his shirt, scooped up the gym bag, and ducked through the window onto the roof above the back porch. In another minute he was on the ground, out of the yard, and hugging the banks of the Sevier River, winding toward town.

He picked his way along the river bank, committed to little more than putting time between then and now, distance between there and here. Dark clouds extended to the horizon. Along the muddy banks of the river, redwing blackbirds sang in the cattails.

Once, he passed a dirt turnoff used by lovers and fishermen, but it was too late for fishermen and too early for lovers. In the distance he could see the lights of the carnival shimmering against the jagged clouds. He thought of Alta Mae and thought again of her damp mouth behind the school gym while waiting for the bus. *Touch me, Evan.* Something in his stomach felt tight, one appetite or another, and he realized he hadn't eaten since yesterday noon. The smell of wood smoke and meat grilling on an open flame wafted across the water and brought his sense of hunger home.

On the other side of the river a Gypsy band had thrown up their tents. Passing, he crouched low. They were not the carnival Gypsies but migrants from Central California. The light from their campfire shimmered on the water and their jabber floated across to him on the still night air, harmonious and happy. Of course, Evan knew that Gypsies weren't for real. Nothing about them. Neither the stories nor the dreams. They were but figments of expectation and fear, just shadows moving between wonder and awe.

He stumbled along the riverbank, once nearly losing his footing and getting wet. Now and then he looked back over his shoulder, but no one was following. The sky darkened, the melodic strains of a meadowlark diminished and ceased; a mallard swam back to the shore, climbed up the bank and huddled in the reeds. The lights of a farm came on in the blue distance where wisps of tule fog lay on the barren muddy fields. A wind came with the darkness, rattling dry leaves, and a low, honking flight of geese passed overhead. Evan stopped and put on his jacket, shifting the bundle beneath his shirt. He took off his cap and raked his fingers through his hair.

In the river where the water eddied back and flattened smooth as the surface of polished glass, an unfamiliar face looked up at him. On second glance he saw that it was his own ghostly image: all-too-shaggy hair and girlish eyes, mouth screwed to the side, a little silly with curiosity and poise. He threw a pebble at his eye and watched his face come apart; then he continued along the riverbank and up through the mud. To the north, all the sky had darkened and the fields and foothills on the other side of the river as far as the eye could see had turned a neuter gray.

He broke away from the river and followed the tracks. Eventually, the tracks switched back close to the water and over a bridge. Beyond the bridge and about a quarter of a mile from town, lay the dark whaleback humps of the potato pits. They were three earthen mounds, fashioned out of the side of a hill, each of them high, wide, and deep enough to accommodate an eighteen-wheel tractor-trailer for loading. Their huge doublewing doors would be locked by now, but he could climb up the terraced berm to the sodden roof and slip through an airvent that dropped like a chimney through the roof to the rafters. Then it was nothing to shinny the rafters to an angle beam and climb to the potato cribs on either side of the pit. The thought of a raw potato for supper made his stomach leap.

The wind whipped the night into an unseasonable chill and buffeted his ears. He had just set foot on the bridge when a light rain began to fall, pocking the surface of the river. He thought he heard sobbing that seemed to come from across the water, but it could have been anything, anyone, even a she-cat making her yearning known. Once, glancing into the water, he imagined he saw another face, all blurry, looking up, maybe dead or inexplicably alive, but this time it wasn't his. Rather feminine, grave. And the sobbing rose again, breathing, he thought, his very name. He paused for a moment to listen then looked again for the face in the water, saw only the concentric ripples left by the rain, and continued across the bridge. He chided himself against the sudden chill. He had ghoulish thoughts sometimes.

The warm sprinkle came and went, came and went. He turned up the collar of his coat and hurried for the cavernous pits. In a few minutes he was through the airvent and inside. In the darkness of the rafters he laid his head against the backpack and breathed the coarse damp smell of potatoes all around. It was pitch black, and he nearly lost his grip climbing through the airvent. Now, trying to hang onto the bag and be careful of the pup beneath his shirt, it was close to impossible to shinny along the rafter to an angle beam.

He lay there, trembling with hunger, the air moist and close with the smell of raw earth and potatoes. The railroad yards were close by and every so often he could hear the slam of a boxcar or an engine hostling back and forth. The wind lifted and howled through the airvent. Evan decided to lie there for a while, then he would climb back out the vent and—rain or no rain—watch for the early morning freight train. He jockeyed the puppy around and snuggled up the best he could on the rafter beam.

Evan woke with a start. Beneath and in front of him a wedge of light sliced through a gap in the doors. Beyond the doors the engine of an automobile growled and sputtered. Before he had time to adjust himself on the beam, the lightwedge shifted and broadened; the huge log doors were swinging inward.

He could make out the image of a man and what appeared to be a boy, about his size and age, wearing a baseball cap. Each of them stood by a door, pale shapes in the flat yellow beam of a single headlight. A gust of wind swept through the doors and pelted them with rain. The man beckoned to the vehicle with his arm, and a dilapidated camper pickup lurched forward and groaned into the pit. The camper unit was an old one that sat in the bed of the pickup with overhangs on either side of the truck bed and above the cab. It was all painted with shadows and light, replete with a confusion of colorful images and emaciated scenes.

"Okay, *mamo,* shut her off."

The engine gurgled and choked, died. The man and the boy each shouldered a door, swinging them slowly closed.

"So where's the fire, then?" An old woman climbed down from the cab.

They busied themselves in and out of the weak yellow light, the old woman erecting a little cast iron tripod beneath which a small cauldron hung and a fire was soon sawing in the draft. The boy killed the truck lights and lighted a lantern, and they all sat close to the fire while the old woman appeared to scrub, peel, and slice various objects and throw them into the pot.

Smoke wafted up past the beams toward the airvent and after it the aroma of succulent stew. Evan couldn't tell if the whimpering came from his stomach or the pup.

To get a better look—or whiff—he knelt upright on the beam and swinging his leg around kneed the backpack into space. Time froze. The figures around the fire leaned in and mumbled and joked. Firelight gleamed on their faces. The odor from below brought tears to Evan's eyes. That icy patch of time began to thaw and lose its sway while the world entire ceased to breathe then drew a gasp. The bag hung just out of reach. He groped, losing then saving himself, sucked in his breath. He watched as the thing dove toward the little party of three like a bomb.

Though each of us could mend our course and lengthen our stride, what choice did he have but to light out on his own? Then, again, as I told him, if the only way to hang on sometimes is to leave everything else behind, might we still have the power within to let ourselves go, relax any grip? But there is one thing, and perhaps his father imbued him with the gene of it by gathering his mother into those arms months before deciding to water the hedges that day, and that is this: There is always the possibility, the intimation, that there may reside within us other than who we are. Who then wouldn't tell him to open the closet door, the dank fruit cellar of youth, and let whatever remains inside out? Who wouldn't tell him that he could be surprised by a rush of liberation and even joy, that he might soon learn that the way through his anger and damage and grief is the way to the truth?

~7~

The Cowboy & the Gypsies

He longed . . . for swarthy skin, dark eyes, and black wavy hair.

THREE faces blinked up at him.

"Who's this—?" The man stood up.

It was difficult for Evan to tell whether or not they could see him in the shadows of the rafters. The old woman craned her neck forward, squinting.

"You coming down then?" The man stepped toward the bag where it had fallen, prodded it cautiously with the toe of his boot. As he turned his head the firelight caught the gold in his ear, and Evan knew they were Gypsies.

"It's just a kid," the old woman told them. *"Raklo."* Her face bobbed from side to side, eyes pinched nearly shut. She wore a headscarf, a fringed, delicately embroidered shawl, and a bright red ankle-length skirt.

"You should might as well come down, kid. Ain't I got your bag?" The man picked up the backpack and held it above his head, grinning a broad-toothed grin.

Something soft as a prayer, smooth as a curse, fell away in the pit of Evan's gut, and the wind played the airvent like a cathedral tune. He could see the three of them watching as he eased along the rafter to an angle beam. He tucked his shirt around the dog, swung down to the gate of a crib, and jumped to the ground. He retucked his shirt and hitched up his pants. He hacked phlegm, spit, took a deep breath, spit again, and stepped into the light. Like a Gypsy, he would lie through his teeth.

"What you doing here, kid?"

Evan looked at the man.

"Smart kid." The man grinned that same broad-toothed grin, not too threatening, and glanced at the old woman and then at the other one—not a boy, Evan could see, but a girl. She sat on her haunches in front of the fire, elbows on her knees, hands dangling between splayed legs. Her jeans fit more like a boy's than a girl's. In place of a jacket to ward of the rain and the wind, she wore a loose-fitting shirt draped over a blouse, but it was hardly damp. She studied Evan with big dark eyes—almost purple looking eyes, like moons on a night when there's going to be a storm. But dark.

"We been hired as security," the man lied. "Ain't we keeping guard against potato thieves?"

He tossed his head back and laughed, just as you would expect a Gypsy to laugh. He was a little off balance. His left arm appeared to be longer than his right, and he stood on an angle to one side. He was as swarthy and creased as you would expect a Gypsy to be, with the same black eyes of the girl, yet a little florid in the jowls, the chest. He wore a close-cropped mustache and sideburns. A black felt hat with a flat brim sat square on his head, and from the hatband jutted a small green feather. Beneath the hat his hair was black and tousled, and, in spite of his laugh, he had a wild-eyed tragic look. You had only to look at him to know how dreadful it all was, and yet he threw his head back and laughed in a condescending, sometimes jovial, way. Like Uncle Goose, he had the trace of a paunch, squeezed and bagged by his belt.

"You're not with the carnival." Evan said it with a tone of accusation and looked at the girl.

"What? Ain't she the fat lady? Ain't I the freak?"

"Why aren't you with the tribe camped down by the river?"

The dark eyes went flat and the man limped toward Evan. "I ask the questions." His voice was too loud and there was nothing funny in it this time.

"Come on." The old woman waved her hand at the two of them. "Bring him here, Nikki. Be nice to him. Maybe he'll talk. You want to talk, kid? You hungry?" She gestured toward the pot suspended above the fire.

Her kindness surprised him. Working beside them in the potato fields, he had come to know that Gypsies seldom broke bread with *gaje*—their word for outsiders, non-Gypsies—and with her invitation, the notion of her invitation, he felt the flesh around his jaw go slack.

"Come on, kid. Sit down here." The old woman patted the blanket she sat on, indicating a place beside her. "You maybe got some funny notions about us." She smiled a sly smile, as though reading his mind. "Sit."

The girl took off her baseball cap and shook out a tangle of dark pretty hair. She looked at Evan from beneath heavy-lidded eyes, her face tipped toward the fire. She had dense black lashes, and the shadows of the fire played against her swarthy skin and shone wet upon her black thick hair. "What's that? You try to kill yourself?" She pointed toward his bandaged wrist, toward the spot of blood on the underside, then as quickly lost interest. "What you got in there?" She nodded at the bulge in his shirt.

"This?" He glanced from his wrist to his waist. He undid a button and withdrew the bundle. He knelt on the blanket beside the old woman and glanced up at the man for approval. The man gestured almost imperceptibly and Evan spread open the bundle before them. The old woman looked blankly at the girl.

The girl reached out and poked it with a long brown finger. "It's dead."

Evan looked at the dog and poked it himself. He poked it and groomed back its coat. The little body was all saggy and limp, somewhat caved in on itself around the guts. He looked at the man, then at the old woman, then at the girl. Something weak got down inside him and sapped at his bones. He tried to contain himself, but the more he tried the more difficult it became, and all at once he felt his insides come apart like a window smashed by a rock. His eyes burned and he ducked his head. The old woman placed a hand on his arm. She said nothing. The man hunkered and flipped the T-shirt back around the dog and took it away. Now something went through him like a wedge. He blinked fast and chewed the inside of his cheek, then shuddered and reclaimed his breath.

When he looked up, he found the girl studying him curiously. Her black eyes didn't move. *"Gajo,"* she said in a husky voice. "Go dig yourself a well before we all float away. Maybe try to kill yourself all over again. Ain't nothing in this world worth your tears."

"Armanda." The old woman turned a shallow eye to her, softly trilling the "r" in her name. "Can't you see?"

"Sorry, *mamio.*" She stood up and slapped the dirt from her behind. "Look." She stooped and brought her head up close to Evan's, showing him her unblemished face. "Nothing personal, understand?"

He started to say something clever, something like, *Hope your I.Q.'s as big as your mouth,* but it was more juvenile than clever, and the man stepped back out of the darkness, chuckling, and said to him instead: "The heart ain't so hard as the head."

"She's a good girl, my Armanda—so to speak. Come. We wash first."

He stood up and the girl stood her ground, forcing him to sidle around her as he stood. She smiled a bit, at least he thought she did, and watched him go. The old woman led him behind the camper into the shadows where they both scrubbed their hands in a porcelain basin with a strange rose-smelling soap. She drew up the flame in a lantern and he could see how the sides of the truck groaned with a tableau of images, both bright and fading, some in bas relief, carved and painted by the hand of some artisan with a New Age flair. The images were all garish and ugly and in a wicked sort of way beautiful as a gnarled root rotting with age. Here an apostle, or perhaps the Savior himself, haloed with face screwed up in anguish, searching for meaning in the rafters above. There, a whirling Gypsy girl, red skirts flaring, her body lithe as a snake's, hands at arms length clasped in a nave above her head. Some old hag chuckling over a gazing ball. Death in the form of a skeleton with scepter and scythe. The fool in his conical cap with drooping bells. Some woman-like bird with a raven's head. An armored knight with leveled lance, galloping toward an invisible foe. The sun. The moon. Stars. A face without eyes. Another without lips. One without ears. The camper was a study in rugged and colorful finesse with countless stories to tell. And to complete the image, hanging by the back door, a slab of salt-cured pork, a bag of jerky, some garlic bulbs (to ward off vampires?), and a variety of other spices and herbs.

"I didn't try to kill myself," he explained with some urgency, toweling his hands. "It's not what you think."

"Nor is it ever. Come."

She led him back to the fire and, sitting, patted the blanket once again. A demon rose in his throat and he knew he must be half possessed or losing his mind altogether. Otherwise, why this sudden emotion and desire to explain himself? He looked at her. Such a handsome old crone, she was gnarled in all the right places. Nubby and pinched. Even a wart or some other disgusting growth lay like a slug at the side of her nose. She was a squat woman with a disturbing way of reaching forward her neck like a menace, and he was drawn to her. "Eat and you will feel better. Maybe talk some. Coffee?"

"Thanks, I don't drink it."

The old woman looked at him and stirred the steaming pot and ladled a stewy-looking paste into a wooden bowl and told the girl to get him a soda.

"Here, kid. Eat."

"My name's Evan."

"Cowboy," said the girl. "You're a cowboy. Mud and dung all over your boots. I don't give a shit what you say. And that's what I'm calling you."

Evan looked at the old woman who shut and opened her eyes wearily and shrugged her shoulders. "Eat, Evan."

The man called Nikki chuckled sadly, at the same time ladling himself a bowl full of stew. He took off his jacket and sat down across from Evan and crossed his legs in the fashion of a Buddhist Monk. He thumbed back his hat and blew on the stew to cool it, and then he used his hand, dipping into the stew and licking his fingers. From time to time fireglow sparked the small gold ring in his ear.

"You eat, Armanda." The old woman shoved a bowl toward the girl who had wandered aimlessly about for a minute then returned, whistling, to the fire.

"*Mamio* wants meat on my bones. Fatten 'em up for the kill."

"Eat!"

Evan picked at the lumps with his spoon. He stirred the heat up from the bottom of the bowl and, as they watched him, tasted the stew. It was hot with spices and pasty and surprisingly good.

"What is this?"

The girl shrugged; her shoulders moved loosely beneath the frail white blouse. "Potatoes."

"Cut me up in pieces," droned the old woman mysteriously, "and bury me alive; the old ones will live and the young ones die."

"That's backwards, *mamio*."

Evan chewed slowly, his mouth genuinely amazed. "It doesn't taste like potatoes."

"What is and what isn't is less than can be."

"*Mamio*—grandma—adds things. Makes it different than it seems."

The old woman dished up a separate bowl and set it aside,

together with a napkin, spoon, and a cup of wine, as though expecting someone else to momentarily step out of the shadows. The girl tore a chunk of bread from the loaf and placed it next to the bowl. Evan looked at each of them in turn, but no one spoke, and he kept to himself. They ate in silence. A sorrowful wind breathed through the airvent, and beating wings sounded in the darkness of the rafters. Evan thought for a moment he heard someone crying again, as down by the river. Sobs both womanly and soft. But it was only the wind, the wind, a sorrowful wind, and the rustle of wings in the dark.

The smoke of the fire drifted toward them, then away. The girl—Armanda—ate her stew with her fingers like the man. She swept the dark glossy hair from her face and behind a shoulder, where it fell to the middle of her back. She tilted her head and sampled the stew. Both she and the old woman wore Gypsy-like earrings: she, large golden hoops that pierced the ear directly without dangling; the old woman, ruby colored stones dangling from delicate chains. The old woman leaned toward the fire and stoked it with the serving spoon. She wore a massive necklace of gold balls that otherwise hung to her waist but now swung out and threw back the flames; at the end depended a gold coin the size of a silver dollar. She wore both gold and silver bracelets. The girl wore only an ankle chain and a loose gold bracelet on her left wrist. The neck of her blouse fell open around her own surprisingly slender brown throat, and as she leaned in toward the fire Evan could see the shadows of her breasts playing beneath.

"How old are you, kid?" The man unrolled a pack of cigarettes from the sleeve of his shirt and tapped one out.

"Sixteen," he lied

"Armanda, she's sixteen."

"Almost seventeen," said the girl.

"You want to talk now? Here." The old woman took the bowl from his lap and set it aside and then took his right hand between both of hers. She spread his fingers and studied the open palm. "You're a runaway," she said.

Evan snatched back his hand.

"Look here. In the old woman's eye. Yana knows." She leaned toward him. She had the face of a toad. "Yana knows more than you think. A runaway who's come now to seal our fate."

"O, *mamio.*"

Evan looked at her, anuran in feature according to the lines of her face, salient as a poisonous frog but ancient-eyed. He wanted to say, but didn't, how psychic powers and second sight were hardly necessary to peg him for a runaway. But to seal their fate? He looked at her and felt the blood drain from his face and stupidly wondered should he close his eyes would they cut his heart out to eat it cold. In those sunken eyes he saw a hint of the eyes of the girl, and he felt the tug of that face in his heart. Perhaps because Aunt Missy had warned, *Never trust a Gypsy,* he let them in—a little weak, desirous, and spellbound. Just generalizations at first and then particulars by degrees. He told them of his father's death, his mother's. The loss of a sister, too, before he was born. He told them about Missy and the strop. When he tried to hold back it was useless, and he found himself bemoaning the loss of his dog. It sounded queer in the telling, simple-minded even, somehow removed from the fact, especially as he went on to confess the spite of a rooster with the intelligence to lurk in ambush up in the loft. He told them one thing or another, and thought once to have revealed too much. And he almost told how he had stolen into his aunt and uncle's room in the middle of the night and stood at their bedside watching them sleep. He altered the details somewhat, padding the story here and trimming events there, but he was merciless when it came to the characters of Missy and Goose, tender toward the memory of his parents, and before he finished they had the gist of the truth.

The old woman made a sour face at the whole thing and spat. *"Gaje!"*

"What?"

The girl looked away darkly. "I know this cowboy," she said. "I seen him before."

The man chewed his potatoes.

Evan studied them, each in turn. He didn't like the way he felt—sour as dirt and acid mixed, the grit and sting of it now searing his throat and up through the flesh of his jaw. He looked at the old woman, wondering, but she dropped her head and refused even the glint of an eye. The shun made him feel as if, by telling his tale, he had stolen something from their race, or perhaps, in some strange way, compromised himself and sullied his own. Such horrors recounted embarrassed him more than he'd thought. He felt shameful, belonging to such a despicable breed whose name was so easily spat with italic disdain—*gaje!* Although it wouldn't have made any difference in the end, he longed at the moment for swarthy skin, dark eyes, and black wavy hair. Who then would he be? How would he come to conclusions? What decisions would he make? But each of them remained silent. He had bared his soul to them, and now they were mute. *Marime.* He had heard the word before and now uttered it beneath his breath—outcast, polluted. *Gaje* were *marime* unless concessions were made, and not one of them—neither the lunatic, the tramp, nor the witch—would pull him back into the circle of an eye. Such was the scourge of Missy and Goose, time to dust off his shoes and hit the road. Why had he ever thought—

He stood up. "I got a train to catch."

All three of them stared at the fire. The man appeared to be listening to some distant strain, and Evan, too, thought he heard that weeping and a rustle of wings. He could see that a cold scum now encrusted the stew in the still untouched bowl where it had been placed between the old woman and the girl, an expected guest perhaps delayed or sidetracked altogether. But the bread had been torn, leaving crumbs, and a closer look revealed the cup was empty of wine. But who? When? The man sat too far away. Of course, Evan had been less than attentive in telling his tale and had certainly been oblivious to that extra place setting in the heat of his telling. He looked at each of them in turn, but not one looked back.

"Thanks for the stew. Wherever you're going I hope you have good luck. Can I have my bag, now." He picked up the backpack and shouldered the harness. "So long."

He started past the pickup and into the shadows toward the big log doors. The earth trembled and boxcars banged in the yard outside. Behind him he heard whispering, then the voice of the old woman, emphatically: *"No!"*

"Who's *phuro*, here, *mamo*? Who's in charge? Sonia tells me—"

"Sonia! Don't give me Sonia! Maybe she tells you wrong."

"Hey, kid. How much money you got? Any?"

"Papa!"

"Nikki, Nikki. I seen it in his palm. The possibility and potential, though I wouldn't say but you struck out my eyes."

Evan turned around. In the firelight they appeared as shadowy images from another world, moving far off behind a veil. "What did you see?"

But the man was insistent.

"You want my money?"

"O, don't think that. I just worry about you."

The girl stood up and came toward him. He watched her fingers nibble at the buttons of her blouse, one then two, and how she reached a hand inside. "Watch out for Gypsies, Cowboy."

"You," the old woman hissed toward her granddaughter, "watch out for *gajo!*"

Evan watched in a stupor as the girl floated toward him, dreary as a phantom amid shadows and light, a hand working at her breast. He watched and as he watched, he failed to understand why the one who had befriended and consoled him in the first place, she who had taken him behind the truck to cleanse himself, who had begged him to talk, now acted so hostile. He had a sudden impulse to rush to the light and examine the troubling chart of his palm as if he might find all the answers and the world at large contained therein. But he could trace those creases one by one, inspect his very bones, and it wouldn't do much to dispel his "funny notions" about them. The old woman reached out her neck as if to strike, then pulled it back.

The girl moved closer to him, black almost, with the fire at her back. She held the bowls she had gathered from the supper in her left hand, reaching into her blouse with her right, passing him on his right next to the pickup. He could smell her hair as she passed, breathing, "Be careful of the choices you make, Cowboy, if choices you have." She was so close that their shadows, to the old woman and the man, must have momentarily merged, slipped together as one.

"I know you," she whispered. "I seen you before."

"You've never seen me."

"O, yes. I've seen you in nightmares and dreams, now come to seal our fate."

There was a cool, mint scent to her hair and he breathed deep without thinking. For an instant she was inside him, and he held her, filled with possibilities, more than possibilities, a remnant of hope, her scent familiar and unknown. At the same time something poked into the palm of his hand, his surprised fingers curling around it as she passed.

"I'll let these bowls soak awhile," she called back, holding the supper things above her head.

"How much?" the man repeated.

"Enough."

"Now—" The man changed the tone of his voice so that it almost sang. "—I was just saying to Nikolai—" He pointed with both of his thumbs at his chest. "—maybe we can give this kid a lift. Save him grief and risk of hopping a freight. Not to dissuade him, of course. Surely a kid like this can think for himself. So I say to myself, Nikolai, what's this kid to you? But maybe he's got some bucks and could do with a lift—to our mutual satisfaction. See? How much dough you got?"

"I'll take the train, thanks." Evan was fumbling with the thing in his hand, holding it away from the light. It was paper, all twisted and crisp.

"Goddamit," said Nikolai. "How much?"

He jammed the wad in his pocket, pretending to grope around, and pulled it back out. He held it up close so he could unfold the bill and see it in the dim light. "Fifty?"

"Hell!" The man yawned, stretched, and stood. He chuckled gravely. "Where you going with Fifty bucks?"

"I can work."

"Yah! You got muscles, eh? Lessee."

Evan met him halfway between the pickup and the dwindling fire. The man limped slightly, tilted a little to one side, his right shoulder higher than his left. The old woman disappeared with the girl, and Evan could hear their hushed voices bickering on the other side of the truck. Evan opened his hand and showed Nikolai the wadded bill.

"Okay. You get fifty dollars worth of space from here." He snapped his fingers and held toward Evan an open palm.

As Evan gave him the money, Nikolai grinned and, reaching toward him in a friendly gesture, cupped with his hand and shook gently the back of his neck.

"You're adopted, kid."

It's true. He never polished an apple for me, never required reproach. His was but a wanting to know. And that's enough for any teacher worth her slate. "Throw away your expectations," I told him, "and seek the truth." For years he had been living in some shadowed corner of himself, and I remember the first time he poked his nose out, got the scent of some scrap I'd thrown. After that, he was forever bedeviling the class with his own magical thought: How can the world exist except in my head? He grasped easily the notion that there is more truth in the legends of Robin Hood and Camelot than in any historical account. When you understand that, it's only surviving desire that counts. I've seen his paintings, so perfectly skewed in his attempt to shape the world anew, as if every stroke of the brush were an irrevocable choice.

~ 8 ~

Coffins & Ghosts

She spoke somberly . . .

ALTHOUGH Evan understood Gypsies to be a peculiar people, he soon learned to be unamazed. When he and the girl, Armanda, crawled into the camper that night to sleep, he himself felt like a ghost in the dim lantern light. And then she went so far as to put a hand on his arm, her warm fingers icing his heart, and he knew for a certainty that his heart beat louder than it had earlier that morning as he lay in the loft of the barn. He could hear the beating of it up in his ears, as if the tympanum would burst, and feel it in his throat. The force of pounding blood restricted his breathing as if every breath he drew was sucked through a sieve. All for a miserable Gypsy girl packed to her eyeballs with insults and scorn—yet who, by pressing the fifty-dollar bill in his hand, and now by her hand on his arm, expressed a wanting of him impossible to fathom. When she looked at him, whom did she see? And what? When she looked at him, he could hardly look back, his cold heart suddenly afire. If cold hands, warm heart, as the adage went, then the notion of warm hands, cold heart, squeezed air from his lungs. But such breathless amazement would not hold up for long. He had crossed a threshold—or was crossing—slipping one leg at a time, then torso and arms and shoulders and head, into a world that explained itself in likely but unimaginable terms.

O, he remembered the stories of Gypsy brothers and sisters and even cousins sleeping and bathing together until they were nearly adults, but his "funny notions" had hardly prepared him for this. His sense of discomfort must have flashed around him like a beacon, for the girl reclaimed her advantage, and reaffirming the pressure of her fingers on his forearm, batted one of her long eyelashes at him. How her dark eyes shone, and he knew that it was more in the light of his uneasiness than in the light of the kerosene lantern hanging outside the door.

"Don't worry," she whispered. "We sleep with our clothes on. I won't even unbutton my blouse unless you ask me nice."

"Nikolai!" The old woman grieved. "Have you no shame?"

"Crawl in with them, *mamo*."

"With *raklo? Gajo?*"

"Armanda's eyes are *gaji!* She bleeds *gaji*—my Sonia's blood. And you, old woman, who saw it yourself in the map of his palm, how can we forestall it?"

"But he should maybe prove his self," she hissed. "First a riddle, perhaps some ability to see."

"Bah! I see it in the eyes of my darling, some ability to see. Riddles mean nothing, but dreams of the heart and a spot of her mother's blood—"

The old woman stood at the back of the truck wringing her hands while the man leaned through the door socking a pillow into shape. He handed it to Evan. It was a big feather pillow with the same sweet scent he had smelled in the hair of the girl when she passed in the dark to give him the bill. He breathed again the unnamed possibility of her and something beyond, so familiar and unknown. A mix of aromas to keep him both grateful and confused. After all, it was one thing to offer *gaje* a meal when in need, but quite another to give him a bed. Such was the old woman's lament.

And he nearly protested himself. Though, faced with the

alternative of who knew what, he thought better of it. A few hundred miles in any direction away from Missy and Goose would be worth a single night of sarcasm and sleep. Still, the dark girl's willingness to crawl into the camper next to him was complicated by his inability to make sense of the mad Gypsy's charity in the face of the old woman's distress.

"Nikki," she wailed theatrically. "You bring us only trouble."

"I bring us peace, *mamo*. For Sonia, I bring us peace. Have good night, *gajo*."

"Evan."

"Come then, my darling. Give us kisses, your *papo*."

Armanda, the girl, leaned first toward her father then away from Evan toward the face of her grandmother who, regardless of her despair, pressed her cheek against her granddaughter's and to Evan's surprise, with an affectionate hand, squeezed gently her breasts. As she leaned back, Nikolai shut them in.

"Sleep tight, Cowboy."

Evan crawled around what seemed a chest or trunk of some sort and dumped himself on one of the two small cots on either side of the camper. The darkness was cramped, the two of them wedged and split by the cumbersome box. He felt like a dope—that was the nearest he could come to it in his mind—like a dope without bones, as if his shoulders were melting into his arms, his arms into his hands. Rubbery. In the darkness, illuminated only by the lantern, which shone dimly through the window of the door and through the small porthole windows on either side of the camper above the cots, he could feel her dark eyes upon him. They sat in a knuckleheaded silence marked only by the squabble outside.

Outside, Nikolai and the old woman were going at it hammer and tongs. The old woman complained in garbled terms how Nikolai was going to be the ruination of everything sacred. She whined something about letting the spirits rest, and he came back at her with a hex on somebody's clan . . . "them salamanders!" Back and forth, back and forth, in whispers and shouts. Something about reclaiming the damned. Something about letting her go. Something about a ceremony. The old woman complained about a wedding . . . that it would be ruined. She feared something about "this business of rummaging among the dead" and he returned "for my Sonia's sake?" . . . back and forth, back and forth, until finally their voices receded, one after the other, fell to a vague muttering at odds, little profanities, a jumbled curse. It was a stand off, of sorts. Then silence. The cab door slammed shut and Evan raised his face to the porthole window to see the man spreading a bedroll next to the remaining embers of the fire.

"Don't it bother you, eavesdropping like that?"

So, she had been watching him, watching all the while as he struggled to hear the conversation outside the truck. His eyes were adjusting to the dark, and he could see her across from him, thought he could, on the other side of the chest, in silhouette. In the darkness he was getting his lungs back. She sat across from him, some half essence, like a memory only partially there, except for the sound of her breathing. And, too, he could see more clearly the chest.

"What is this?" He ran his fingers across the surface, so smooth and cold, and rapped his knuckles against the lid.

"Do you believe in ghosts? So what."

"A coffin?"

"The man who made it did not want it," she sang mysteriously. "The man who bought it did not use it. The man who used it did not know it."

He jerked his hand back as though from a flame. A kind of breathlessness shut his throat. But he was grateful. Grateful for the dark. Grateful that she couldn't see his face clearly. At least he couldn't see hers. He tried to get the bones back in his arms, shore himself up. "A coffin?" He wheezed through his nose. "Whose is it?"

In the darkness he could feel the weight of her shrug. She shifted around on the bunk and arranged herself with a creak and a groan, sang in the night:

> *My mother said, I never should*
> *play with Gypsies in the wood.*

"*Whose?*"

"I don't know. How should I know. Papa will take care of it. Be thankful it's not yours."

"Isn't it illegal or something to drag a coffin around the country?" A battery of questions came into his head, and he fired them off as though her barbs and verbal abuse had given him the right. "Where you taking it? Is somebody in it?"

All he got for an answer was the wind in the airvent and the stench of potatoes all around. From one nut house to another. Not in a million years could he have guessed such a night, and now this buzz in his head. From Goose in the ditch to sleeping with ghouls, but nothing more puzzling than the dark girl herself.

"Why did you stick that fifty-dollar bill in my hand?"

He listened to the sound of her breathing for a long time before she answered him. The inside of the camper smelled of garlic and turpentine and the faint odor of her. "You're a cowboy," she finally said, as if that meant something. And then to clarify, "I seen you in dreams, just the outline and the possibilities so vague."

Evan could not see her clearly, but he could see the contour of her jaw, softened by the dim lantern light as it spread through the porthole. "Yana . . . ask her. She'd tell you I'm odd." She continued in a whisper, "Yana—the old woman—is my grandmother, Papa's *mamo*. She worries will I turn out okay. She worries this and a little bit of that. Odd, my giving you the money, not to say how you come in my dreams. Just something odd."

Evan scrutinized the coffin in a gauzian blur. "Is there a body in this thing?"

"I hope so. Was last time I looked." A beam of light splashed from her hand across the coppery surface. She did something with the latch and heaved open the lid. An odor of sulfur and formaldehyde swept through the camper. She held the flashlight in his eyes for a moment longer than necessary, then dipped it behind the lid. There lay the ashen features of a corpse, tousled hair, head slumped sideways against the satin pillow: forty, maybe fifty, years old, nose mashed across the face like a squatting frog, sparsely stubbled chin. One eye was open a slit and the jaw slack so that the mouth made a curious hole. Scattered around the head and torso in wrinkled and wadded bills of various denominations must have been hundreds, maybe thousands, of dollars. The lid started to fall away before Evan realized his own hand had shoved it closed. The girl laughed and snapped off the light, sang:

> *If I was to be so badly done for,*
> *I wonder what I was begun for?*

"Who is it?"

"Somebody."

"Where you taking him?"

"Somewhere." He heard her yawn with apparent boredom. "Go to sleep, Cowboy. You're just along for the ride. Remember? You live in a different world. You and your suicide heart."

"A rooster did that."

"Sure. Whatever you say, Cowboy. Got in a fight with a rooster."

He muttered something unintelligible to even himself, at the same time touching his wrist. He wondered if she meant to tease or to provoke or if she had just taken pity more on her own refusal to believe anything he told her than on the possibility that he *had* slashed a wrist. *Gypsies.* Aunt Missy's disdain rang in his head, and he wondered again were he to close his eyes would they cut his heart out to eat it cold. Certainly, a death less profane than by the infection from the spur of that miserable bird.

For a long time he lay awake in a half-puzzled stupor, worried sick about what he'd gotten himself into, worrying and listening to the old woman knock about in the cab trying to get comfortable, wondering now and then whether the coffin lid was securely latched. Tired as he was, he could hardly get his eyes to close. The mad Gypsy must be crazy, roaming about the country with a corpse in his truck, but even that was less puzzling than the inexplicable wit of this sixteen year old girl whose breathing rustled the otherwise still night and sparked his imagination like rock against flint. Who were these people? All mystery and riddles. Wanderers more of the imagination than even the earth. Wanderers more of the heart than the head. What would his father have called them? Migrants of the soul?

He lay there for a time, all rubbery and deboned, his flesh like an itch. Without listening, he listened. At first he thought she was weeping and almost wondered aloud. *Are you crying?* he thought to say, but it was not her, she who had scorned his own bitter tears, she who had told him to go dig a well "before we all float away." No. Certainly not her. Rather, the sound was coming from beyond, and perhaps not sound at all, but coming from within as much as without, a sighing of grief low as the wind in the vent, sighing from the darkness of the rafters, from the darkness of the potato cribs, and close as the cot on which the mad girl lay.

Coming from nowhere at all.

Are you weeping? he thought to say. But, no. Not weeping so much. Not now. Rather like a flood, seeping up and over and gabbling about the truck, less weeping than speech, a swirl of watery voices that fought for exchange. It was as if those images and scenes on the outside of the camper had in darkness come softly to life.

Or could it be the man in the coffin?

He listened. He dug at the flesh of his throat.

"What?" The hush of her voice in the dark.

He may as well have been dreaming, such was the struggle, for a cacophony of voices swirled and rose, aggrieved as lunatics disturbed. And they seemed a little spiteful, a little sullen, a little queer, even as he chuckled sadly at the unfortunate demeanor of life.

"What is it?" she asked.

Just murmurs at first, less telling than tempting the possibilities at hand. Were they speaking to him? Softly, softly his name, but garbled, couched in the promise of something hopeful and bright. No, no. A shadow passed, and he nearly pulled himself up to the window.

"I wouldn't," said a voice in his head.

And then a grunt of admonition and dread. Without listening, he listened, the voices themselves all tangled and webbed between the love and the hate of something unnamed, so defiant on the one hand and obsessed on the other. He listened and as he listened the whole of the evening came back with a yearn. He longed to repeat himself with this brood, seek the unclaimed. He pressed tight his eyes then opened them again with a developing thought. Yes, yes. He had it now, by a thread. Something . . . something . . . but the whispering grew faint, the voices gathered themselves into a hard desperate knot, and only the weeping remained. Not weeping, but wind in the airvent.

"What is it?" she asked.

A murmur from nowhere, soft as a breath, and he blinked his eyes as though looking for a glimmer in the dark, and waited, but no whisper came. He felt his original sense of amazement already beginning to slough off, grow dull around the edges, when out of the darkness, her wee voice sang:

> *My mother said I never should*
> *play with Gypsies in the wood.*

He gave back a mirthless snort.

"Go to sleep, Cowboy Evan. Fretting never did a body good. And you fret about things you don't understand. Might as well fret about doom and the world's end. Might as well fret about shadows of the soul or some sad and joyful exchange to right every wrong. Go to sleep."

"Look. I haven't got a clue what you're talking about, your riddles. My day's been pulled inside out, and the only thing I've got to show for it is you and your simple-minded jokes."

"Me? You've got me? And I've got you, babe." She sang it in the style of the old Sonny and Cher song. "*Babam, babam, de babam.*"

"Now what?"

"Baby, baby, oh baby."

"What's that supposed to mean? *'Babam, babam, de babam.'* Can't you say anything without it ricocheting off this dead man and glancing between the walls? If you want to tell me something, tell me straight out. Like why your father took me in—I mean, in the camper like this. With you."

"If I had a nickel for every question you asked, I'd be rich. What you gonna do to me I can't maim you for life? He wanted fifty bucks, that's all. And it was your choice, anyway."

"?"

"You think you're worth more than fifty bucks?"

"?"

"Call it pride. Call it pity. Call it love."

"?"

"All father's love their daughter's, don't they? Mine loves me with a passion."

He opened his mouth but nothing was there.

"O, I know what you're thinking. I make about as much sense as a tornado. But we don't hate you. We don't even know you."

"Except in your nightmares and dreams."

"Look, Cowboy, dreams are the unrealized alternatives of

life. If such had happened in place of so, we'd be dreaming so and telling our grandkids such."

"Another riddle," and he laughed a laugh of dismissal in the saying of it.

He was vaguely aware that the day had crept up on him with all the force of a dynamite blast and now this strange girl was a victim of his fallout. "You're so full of Gypsy arrogance. So full of contempt. You and your Gypsy secrets, all crammed up in there where most of us have a brain—" Then he started to apologize but lost his train of thought and, rummaging, said in a kinder tone: "You an only child or is there more like you to worry about?"

"One of a kind, thank you, but for the stillbirth of my brother a year after I was born." Her words hung above the coffin like something tangible and harsh. "Tell me, *raklo*, you carry that big chip on your shoulder for the fun of it? Or you just like the weight?"

"My shoulder?"

"You heard what I said."

"Come over here and knock it off, sister."

"Sure."

She thumped around in the darkness, and he worried she might get up to meet the challenge, throw herself across the coffin like some nightthing with claws. He waited, trying to make out the shape of her, relieved as she worked out her comfort and propped herself on an elbow, sang:

> *'Tis the gift to be simple,*
> *'Tis the gift to be free,*
> *'Tis the gift to come down*
> *Where we ought to be . . .*

She called him by his name and then said Cowboy, her voice but a whimper, a sob, and he could hardly make her out, the very thought of her now ghostly and dim.

"What?"

"I said, you leaving a girl friend behind?"

Now what sort of question was that? So chummy in tone and out of the dark? Whatever pops into her thick little skull? He listened to the chatter of rain and wind shivering in the air vent and heard the boxcars coupling in the yard. How they seethed, shuddered, and groaned, and he knew she was setting him up— but with what thrift and design?

"I thought so. She a nubile thing? Blue eyes? Blonde? Nice boobs and a cute little tush? A cheerleader, I bet, since you're kind of a jock."

"I'm not a jock."

"You ever made it with her?"

"?"

"Done it, Cowboy. Jumped in the saddle. Mounted up. Rode the range, so to speak." She breathed the words for him. "Made the little filly whinny and buck." And in breathing, she held him at bay, steeped in a cargo of silence. "What do you know about Gypsies, anyway?"

He leaned forward and graveled his voice with a low-throated laugh. "For one thing, they try too hard to be tough. I could say a thing or two about your cute little tush—"

"You think so?"

"—so don't try to shock me. You don't even know me, who I am or where I come from, regardless of what I told you or me stalking your dreams. Tell me about you, tough girl. Mounting up. Riding the range."

"I'm pledged," she said.

"What?"

"On virtue of blood."

He didn't say anything at first, and then he said in confusion, dismay, "Forget about it . . . pledged."

"What? You don't wanna talk about it now? What do you know about Gypsies, anyway?"

"What do you know about *gaje?*"

In darkness, she hissed. "My mama was *gaje!* I've been to *gaje* schools. I *know gaje.* You tell me about Gypsies."

She said it with a fury that flashed through the caravan and seethed in the dark. True, she spoke as though she had been to better-than-average schools, although there were occasional hints of Romany inflection or a throwback to poor grammar in her speech, and she became almost hysterical when she mentioned her mother.

"Look," he said, searching for ground. "Are you *marime?* Outcast? Is that it? Is that why you aren't traveling with the band camped down by the river? On virtue of blood? Because your mother wasn't a Gypsy?"

"Mother of God," she whispered, "and the Savior, too." Her voice crescendoed in a breathless groan. "That's the kind of notion that makes me piss myself."

"Piss away," he said, listening to his own dry voice in the dark. "But I've been around Gypsies, pledged they may be. My father wrote a book about them."

"A book?"

"Well, a poem or two."

"Listen, *raklo.* I've read the books, and they tell you nothing about the soul."

"The soul?" He struggled for a glimpse of her. "I can tell you about the soul. What's your name again? Armanda? That's the blood of it. I've worked beside them in the potato fields and read about them in novels. All the men are named Luigi and all the women Zelda. Such wildly passionate women. Their heaving bosoms and unquenchable thirst for a roll in the hay. And the men, aren't they basically good-natured knaves in baggy pants and boots ready to break into song at the first screech of a violin? *Gyp-sy.* Listen to the sound of that word. The romance, the mystery. I know all about you and your Papa and *mamio.* Lost wanderers from another age. Migrants of the soul. Swindlers, cutthroats, and thieves. Of whom everything and nothing can be expected—"

"Pretty impressed with yourself, aren't you, Cowboy? All pumped up, and my blood like a flame. But you might as well slit the other wrist. You might as well lay the blade against your throat, because you never know when you'll be in need of them you've despised."

His tongue was weighted with unfinished words, and he swallowed to clear his throat.

"Listen, Cowboy. You want to know things? I'll tell you about Gypsies. That tribe camped down by the river? They're not of our *vitsa*—"

"Vit-sa?"

"Our family. We're *Kashtare Rom*. They're *Kuneshti*. The carnival people are mostly *Kuneshti*, too. *Papo* once worked as a knife-thrower in a carnival, but that was for a short time only. The *Kuneshti* have no background for honesty." She sounded as if she were repeating by rote the complaints of her elders. She said in a voice of gloom, rapping on the coffin lid: "That's *Kuneshti*. They are not so pure."

"Pure?"

"Expect everything of the Gypsy. Expect nothing."

She spoke so somberly for the next few minutes that he kept the wisecracks to himself. He felt a little sorry for her and ashamed of himself for it. Nikolai had taken the lantern from the back of the truck and the two of them now lay in darkness so thick that he could sense only the vague outline of her. Then she said something sarcastic and before long they were again trading insults back and forth across the coffin. Beneath the smell of turpentine and garlic an odor of potatoes wafted through an open vent. Windblown rain continued to pelt the sodden roof of the potato pit and a switch engine revved and hostled in the yards. Evan listened to the engine coupling and uncoupling the boxcars as if moving from one lover to the next, and as he listened he hoped for a whispering voice. How maybe she had gotten her period, for that would explain a thing or two. The boxcars clattered and she said something stupid and giggled, and the switch engine growled, backing away, and she grew somber and spoke with the tone of someone gown old.

As she talked, the nature of sarcasm between them diminished. She must have been possessed by the same demons that urged him to explain earlier, because she began telling him things, jabbered a little mindlessly, he thought, about Gypsy customs and the world of *gaje*. It was as if she had fallen under a spell of her own. She told him a number of unhappy and troubling things, things that compounded his confusion and confirmed a suspicion or two, and as she spoke, her words painted for him a vivid and continuous dream, and he could see in a glimpse, this snippet or snatch. How, for instance, in the fifth grade, she had stood outside the classroom door each morning as the other children filed in. How, as they seated themselves with a giggle, the teacher combed and parted her hair inspecting her head for lice. She had never had lice in her life and was far cleaner than the dirty-necked little tramp she sat behind.

He asked, and she told him how, in the cities, her father moved from one job to another, from body and fender work, say, to pumping gas, but was always discovered and let go as a result of his swarthy looks, partial accent, and semi-literate ways. He asked, and she told him how, when her mother was alive, they had lived between two worlds, Gypsy and *gaje*. He asked, and she described her mother to him, so bright, beautiful, and talented, and told him how certain Gypsy women hated her for it. He asked, and she told him how, in the community of Gypsies—*kumpania*, she said, rounding the word in her mouth— her mother was tolerated but never completely accepted as a *gaji romni,* or non-Gypsy wife.

Marime, he thought to say. Outcast. But instead he asked, and she told him how, only a year ago, they had spotted the little growth, like a dark, irregular mole, on the back of her mother's neck. In less than six weeks she was dead. Since then the three of them had traveled from one *kumpania* to another, from New Jersey to Florida to California, picking up relatives here and shedding them there. For all she cared, it might as well be Uncle John in the coffin; they would soon dump him as they had the rest. But she had no Uncle John. She had only Yana, the old woman, and Papa and the road, their little *tséra*—house on wheels. Without his asking, she even went so far as to conjure their reasons for wandering the roads from one end of the country to the other: something about Yana's health, the inability of schools to keep track of a roving sixteen-year-old truant, migrant season, her father's love for her mother—and for her, of course—and a dozen other little secrets, reasons she said he would never understand, couldn't, all according to a pledge and the virtue of her blood. According to some pledge she'd made, in spite of an empty heart. He struggled to see her, just a hint, and she betrayed herself, at least he thought she did, and spoke a little madly even of the restless spirit of her mother wafting about the highways, her father in hot pursuit.

"You mean a ghost?"

My mother said I never should . . .

"Do you believe that? Like some ghost, your mother's spirit flitting about the countryside?" He remembered the extra bowl of stew prepared at supper. Goulash for a ghost? His own fanciful thinking couldn't hold a candle to this kind of stuff.

"Let me tell you why you are here, Cowboy."

"You read it in this morning's tea leaves?"

"You're here because Papa seeks peace for both the living and the dead."

"Is that another riddle or something?"

"I'm thinking maybe Mama guided you to us. Or maybe she guided us to you—into this potato pit. Our destinies cross, come together, so-to-speak, to our mutual satisfaction, maybe, as *papo* said." She paused as if summoning a thought. "We didn't plan to be here, you know, and then the rain."

"That's serendipity," Evan told her, "an accident of sorts—"

"Accident?"

But she had grown weary and it came through in her tone. "The whole world's an accident, just chance," she said, unphilosophically. "You come to us unawares, our destinies entwined." And she added with a mumble, "To seal our fate, perhaps."

"What's that supposed to mean?"

"Whatever you want it to mean, Cowboy. I'm tired now. Sing to me, Cowboy, a cowgirl song. Something sweet and homey with a clippity-clop in your voice."

But the joking had worn itself thin, failing at last to relieve his discomfort over coffins and riddles and goulash and ghosts—and Gypsy girls, too. He lay back on the cot and turned his face into the pillowed scent of her hair. He felt foolish and beside himself. But why should he feel silly? Hadn't ghosts plagued him in one way or another most of his life? Though he had never seen one in the form of a blackbird.

"Sometimes a raven," she said, sleepily, as if plucking his thoughts. "Sometimes in dreams. And if *o Del,* if God, is kind enough and her spirit refuses to rest, it is possible that through some sad and joyful exchange she can return in the form of a beautiful woman." She said it hopefully, without belief.

Evan was about to comment then changed his mind. He gathered his backpack from the floor, zipped it open, and rummaged for the harmonica. When he began to play, she didn't say anything, just listened, and he thought once, between bars, he heard her softly hum. He played first a sorrowful rendition of "Red River Valley" and then a heartfelt version of "Aura Lee." When he finished, the strange (not so unpleasant, really)—undeniably beautiful—creature across from him had finally grown still, and in spite of himself, he felt eerie, two uncertain voices and the soft strains of a debatable song now hushed in the dark.

The world we live in. Who wouldn't run off with the Gypsies given a chance? He listens to my jokes and laughs, and I look at him and think what a jackass. Not him, me. And her, the way she looks at him, just a fantasy to those on the outside looking in. I mean she has this face like it's something to make you weep. And the way she sits, the way she stands. Walks. I've heard Owen on that subject, and Mason, too. The way she walks. Deep down, if I get honest with myself, I know Mason Talbot's just talk, those quarterback's hands, her so unspoiled and ripe that every mind in town runs amuck. The world we live in. Every time I toke a weed or take a drink or try the goods with Alison, every time I make some pitiful joke, I think why not him? I think why not her? He's got nothing but that uncle, his aunt, been raised by two cards short of a deck. He's got nothing and still, one way or another, for the most part, he's been hammered straight and could knock his pick in the school for a loop, you name who. So why not him? I mean this story instead of that, what I'm trying to say. Who cares the truth? The world we live in. You figure it out.

~ 9 ~

Madness & Mayhem

A shadowy image passed like the wave of a hand before the windshield ...

EVAN slept fitfully, dreamt.

Dreaming, he saw her come down out of the mountain astride a gold palomino, bareback, the granite peaks of the Mineral Range towering behind.

O, cowgirl, she.

She was riding fast in an effort to beat the rainsquall building to the east, the dark clouds looming above. As she rode, her black hair tangled and lashed about her throat and the lightning lit mutely the black clouds beneath and she continued to ride fast and low, galloping toward him but unseeing, blind even to the first sting of rain that blew on the wind and into the foothills, blew beyond the bleached churning river, finally seizing her up and shrouding her figure against that landscape of dreams— dream rider astride some magical pony riding a dream.

Even as he dreamt, he knew but it was a dream central to the imaginings of men, steeped in that universal consciousness both primordial and innate to which each has claim, and he awoke beneath the dark shell of the camper, hot and perspiring, unknowing what he had dreamt. He pressed his knuckles hard against his eyes. The cot jounced and his feet stubbed some cushiony thing. He pushed himself up, groping for the porthole. The sky was still black but lighted now by a half moon. And the moon, too, was in motion, ringed and sailing between a silvery mass of shredded clouds. Below and in the distance a few lights spotted the horizon, and there, for an instant, lightning stood in ragged chains, silent, the rough-sawn mountains trembling blue and barren out of the void. He wondered how long they had been moving and in what direction. The pickup rattled and bumped and his feet stubbed against the thing at the foot of the cot.

He yawned until his ears cracked, felt something ugly drop away in the pit of his gut. What did it matter where he was, where he was headed, or who was taking him? A corpse is a corpse, dead or alive. And he knew zombies. Missy and Goose had been brain-dead for years. He looked at the gob of the moon up there, like phlegm, and something queer pushed his insides around.

He leaned on an elbow and looked over the top of the coffin. The Gypsy girl lay on her side with her face to the wall, her knees tucked in a prenatal position. He raised himself up to watch her sleep, and the dim rise and fall of her hips and waist seemed pleasantly reassuring. In better light he would maybe sketch her like that, her broad shoulders and the curve of her spine, those hips. Only then did he remember his dream of her and the black clouds towering above, how she was no more than a shadow behind a curtain of rain, and he could feel that rain in his veins, not rain but the sear of adrenaline from the last two days coursing his limbs. The fluid leached through his flesh in the form of sweat and burned beneath his arms. His stomach fluttered and he felt as if he were about to shed skin. He spoke to himself in little phrases, meaningless and uncertain: O, cowgirl, she. Wondered how the speed and grace of a galloping horse in a dream could indicate longing and eagerness for change, the two of them now like castaways riding the absolute. How the rain and lightening and this rough rider ahorse, galloping into that absence from which all began, might bode the wonders of expectation or desire for . . . for what he couldn't tell, and the bleached churning river left him suddenly cold and without a clue to any of it at all, just the confused riddle of his own empty dreams.

It was the pillowsweet scent of her mixed with the smell of garlic that got to him, and the potatoes he had for supper boiled in his gut. He lay back and closed his eyes. Dog shit for brains. He wondered if they had discovered he was gone . . . and wondering, saw again the great girth of her like a decaying whale lounging beneath the covers, intermittently wheezing and breaking wind, poor Goose groaning like a sleepless bear, saw the shadow of himself thrown back against the wall and struggling to breathe, his uplifted arm drawn to a point.

He clawed his fingers through his sweaty hair. His face was wet, his insides so pushed around there was nothing left. He was afraid the girl would awaken and say something cruel. There was something evil and brainless going on in his life, but that was beside the point: he needed to blow his nose. He wiped his face with his shirtsleeve and snorted in a crack where the bunk hinged to the wall of the camper. Snot and sweat and tears.

He pulled himself up and then out of himself the very idea that even murder could compare to the misdeeds of Missy and Goose. He laid a hand on the coffin and tried to remember the images painted on the sides of the camper—the dancing Gypsy with her arms held high, the armored knight ahorse with charging lance—as though he could find meaning in a mix of images that meant nothing at all, or in the murmur of an unknown voice.

Then again, what if?

What if he and the Gypsy girl were only pawns with little control in some larger scheme? The one driven by destiny, the other by fate? Wouldn't Miss Butler get a kick out of that? What if? His eyes grew heavy with the thought, and the truck jostled and bounced. He started to doze when out leapt the image of some wraithlike presence hovering above the cot. His eyes opened and he was back in the camper, the product of a spent, bewildered laugh. He heaved himself up to the window again. Stars paled and shone between rags of clouds, the sky had turned a deep clear blue. A car came from behind and passed the camper on the left. They were riding the freeway, looping the perimeter of some town, rattling past dark houses, gas stations, neon lit motels, and the high vague smokestacks of some dozing factory, past a drive-in movie, its great screen white and luminescent in the approaching dawn. Near a red and white Dr. Pepper billboard, the truck turned off the freeway, lurched down the exit ramp, and picked up a highway moving into the country. The trellised structures of electrical towers laced the highway for a mile or two then broke away abruptly, the more distant diminishing in size.

He lay back, feeling flushed and still slightly ill. The girl sighed and rolled on her back and thumped around on her cot trying to get comfortable. It was close and warm inside the camper, and she kneeled up and popped open a vent, letting in a stream of cool air. She flopped back onto her stomach, her face toward Evan, a hand dangling above the floor, between coffin and cot.

Evan lay quietly for a while trying to sleep, but it was a lost cause. He lunged over on his side facing the center of the camper, better able to distinguish images in the gathering light. He had bolstered his head on the pillow in order to see the sleepy-eyed creature on the other side of the coffin. She opened her eyes and reached a hand over, her fingers hovering above the coffin lid, as though she could hardly make a fist. She groaned into a corner of her pillow.

"You awake?"

She had a pretty mouth, even squashed against the pillow, and her teeth were square and white. "It was getting hot in here," he said. "The air feels good."

"Where are we?"

"I dunno. Where we going?"

"I dunno," she said, the words pushed with fatigue through

half of her mouth and dulled by her pillow, "but I got to get there fast. My teeth are floating."

"Maybe I ought to rap out an S.O.S. on the back of the cab."

She said nothing, and he listened to the whine of tires upon asphalt and something clattering against the wall.

"You play from the heart," she slurred, remembering. "With soul. And it gets down inside you, like somebody who's been there and returned, come back with more than just luck."

"Somebody who's been there—?"

"Love me tender." Her voice was a drowsy breath. "Never let me go."

"Thanks, I think."

But she was asleep again, at least her eyes were closed and the rhythm of sleep was in her breathing—a ripple so wee and so far it somehow studied his bones.

Evan lay watching her, and then following the light as it clarified this object and that within the limits of their little room. Above his head, against the back of the cab, a tiny kitchen with a sink, hotplate, and cupboards. A fridge the size of an apple crate. Walls slung with odd tapestries and mottled drapes, the floor laid with a thick, colorless shag. At the head of Armanda's cot pieces of luggage stacked on an old steamer trunk, the trunk faced with latches, the corners of hammered copper. Hanging from a leather thong, a Ouija board and its heart-shaped pointer clicking against the wall. And there at his feet a patchwork carpetbag laid open at the top, intercut and sewn in primitive fashion with cured animal skins and rawhide. He could see how it was scarred from such travels and the years of it and he could only imagine that inside of it nestled all the accouterments of Gypsydom, including old accounts and ledgerbooks and albums of genealogy and such history of the past their ancestors had followed and perhaps even a reckoning of the cost of that history. A ball the size of a honeydew melon crested the lip of the opening, and

Evan saw that it was glass. He pulled his foot back, afraid he might disturb the thing and witness the future come pouring out.

The girl's breathing had grown shallow, and he stretched his legs to avoid the old valise and nudged onto his back. He felt the lids of his eyes grow heavy and blinked them shut then open. Voices, he thought. But, no. Nothing but the sound of rubber against rock and the weight of his own desperate bones. And now in the light, on the wall above his cot, he could see the photographs, half a dozen clippings, and pictures all cockeyed in gaudy gilded frames. He propped himself to see. Two were of Gypsies lying in their open coffins like sleeping ghouls. He raised himself up and studied the picture of a gravestone inscribed with a name and a birth date, but no date of death.

YANA MARKOVITCH
BORN
YANA O SPIROSKO/SALLOWAY
[AUGUST 12, 1931]
MARRIED
WENDELL MARKOVITCH
[JUNE 1, 1945]
DIED
[   ]

Beneath the picture of the gravestone, on a fabricated mantel, stood some sort of shrinething containing pictures and statues of saints, a resurrection plant (like the one Missy kept on her grandmother's organ), candles, and a bottle labeled "Holy Water." Evan lay back against the scent of her and wondered absently what kept the bottle and saintly statues in place, why they hadn't bounced off the shelf during the night, ceramic Saints to pray for and baptize him against all possibility of pain. He gazed sleepily at the stuff above him and contemplated the lesser miracles that kept his feet to the ground and overhead bottles of "Holy

Water" secure in their place, and he saw himself dropping away, down into a labyrinth of twists and turns, and then a long passageway extending before him. He began to jog and then to run and as he ran he saw that he was leaving behind little pieces of himself, like outgrown clothing, until he felt transparent, weightless, and at last without fear.

"Hey, wake up!"

Someone was pounding on the door. He summoned his joints and opened his eyes and raised himself, half blind in the light, and glanced across the coffin at the opposite cot, blanket in a heap. He glanced toward the door. She was banging on the screen with the butt of her hand, peering in at him with a wild-eyed grin.

"Wake up," she shouted. "You'll miss the race."

"What race?"

"The *human* race!" she cried. "Ha ha."

Evan waved her away and flopped back down.

"Come on, Cowboy. Breakfast's on."

She opened the screen and climbed in, pulling it shut behind her. "Think they've missed you yet?"

"What time is it?"

"Time to rise and shine. Think they've called out the dogs?"

Evan sat up and raked his fingers through his hair. "Who wound you up?"

"If looks could kill," she sassed.

He glanced around for a mirror. "I don't know what makes you tick," he said. "But I hope it's a bomb." He scrubbed his scalp with his fingers. He scraped his teeth with his tongue, a taste there sour as the inside of a Hungarian wrestler's jock strap. Dog shit for brains. "Does this sink work?" He crawled around the coffin, lurched to the sink and tried the tap. The faucet slobbered a bit. He hacked, spit, and splashed water on his face.

"Don't nobody spit in that sink, Cowboy. That sink's for washing dishes."

He looked at those big playful eyes glazed by a serious caul, and then he looked at the sink. She shook the hair from her face and ducked back through the screen. He spit again in the sink and took the comb from his hip pocket and ran it through his hair and jammed it back in his pocket and followed her into the sharp morning sun.

The truck was parked beneath ponderous oaks beside a creek, and he could see from the texture of the water that it was lazy and not very deep. In the fashion of a lean-to, they had rolled out a canopy from the driver's topside of the camper, and the canopy had been stretched taut between tent poles and tethered and staked to the ground. An aroma of clean damp earth, wood smoke, and frying pork greeted him. Beyond the edge of the canopy, the old woman hunkered beside a fire, turning meat in a skillet. Her back was toward him, but Evan stretched and called out. She labored over the skillet and laid the back of her hand against a coffee pot, snatched it back. Evan ducked beneath the canopy and circled the fire until he stood in front of her. He called her by name, thinking she might be a little deaf, but she looked through him, beyond him, until he almost looked around for himself.

Armanda came up from the creek, laughing. "You're not in the world yet, as far as *mamio's* concerned." She stopped and unbuckled her belt and hitched up her pants and tucked in her blouse and re-cinched her belt. She was taller than he remembered from last night.

"The Cowboy washed already, *mamio*—sort of. You can say good morning to him. He's clean." She looked at him from head to foot, batting her heavy-lidded eyes, and curling the tip of her tongue against her teeth. "Aren't you?"

"You got no shame, Armanda. In *pants!*"

The night before, she had confided to Evan—or perhaps he had dreamt it, or been told in some other context, or even read it somewhere, but he had some notion, the possibility of her confidence, her trust, both vague and specific, but as real to him in his memory and mind as if she had whispered it the night before, told him in a tone of anger and disdain—of how, when she became a woman and according to custom, the old woman had slapped her twice across the face and told her that she must never again pass in front of the elders or show her legs, that she must develop a sense of shame in her behavior toward men. She must wear only the Gypsy garb, consisting of a separate top and long skirts. She must never again sleep with the children and her clothes must be washed separately from theirs, with the clothes of the women. She must wash the upper and lower portions of her body separately, reserving special soaps and towels for the upper body and certain ones for the lower body, and she must stay close to her parents and help more with the daily household chores. He could hear even now the hush of her breath and he was certain of the voice and the tone and the plea that rang in his head. Wasn't she her mother's daughter, as well?

Now, even as Evan remembered this, Armanda stooped to roll up a cuff, and the old woman gave him a squint. Hers was the face of a wizened hag that some thankless artisan had carved out of a dried apple. She poked her neck forward as if to bite him, showing her mottled teeth. It was only a grimace—gas, he supposed. She dished him a plate of spiced ham, potatoes, and eggs, and handing it to him, grunted with disgust.

"C'mon, *mamio*. Papa told you that if you came with us, you would have to put some of your Gypsy behind you . . . for my sake. Let this cowboy alone."

Nikolai sidled up, bent over the old woman as she poured him a cup of coffee, and reached his hand inside her blouse. "Show some respect, my daughter."

"Tell her to be kind then."

"And last night, were you so kind?"

She sort of rolled her shoulders and flipped her head so that her long hair danced. "I feel better this morning," she drawled. "Me and this cowboy got to be right good chums last night. And I'm still intact. No blood, *mamio*. You'll be happy to know we kept the dead between us."

THE GYPSY LOVER ·143·

Nikolai produced a pack of cigarettes from the old woman's bra, tapped one free, and returned the pack from where it came. Yana went about her duties so casually that Evan wondered if anything had happened. Nikolai took the steaming cup of coffee and sipped it gingerly. He lit the cigarette and smoked.

Evan sat down on a log, jabbed a chunk of ham with his fork and stuffed it in his mouth.

"Want a smoke?"

When he looked up, the dark girl wrinkled her eyebrows and winked. She arched her back, emphasizing the fulness of her breasts beneath her shirt. He felt the blood rush to his cheeks and stuffed a gob of eggs in his mouth. "The coffin," he said at a loss. "What about the coffin?" She looked at him with steady unblinking eyes, and he thought of the possibility of a pack of Camels right next to another fifty-dollar bill. He could tell that beneath her baggy clothes she had the breasts and hips of a dream, and by the look in her eyes he could see that she could tell he could tell. "What about that coffin?" he asked, keeping an unsteady gaze on the top button of her blouse, trying again to get his head clear. But he may as well have been mute or they without ears.

He and Armanda rode with Nikolai in the cab, while Yana grumbled and knocked about in the camper. They were headed east, toward afternoon the sun at their backs. The morning camp, he learned, had been an old Gypsy caravan stop a couple of miles south of the highway and east of Grand Junction, Colorado. Now they were halfway across the Rockies, on Highway Six, heading for Denver. The road angled and wound, rising past the Colorado then descending only to rise again. At ten thousand feet the air grew crisp, the sky a clever blue. Once pinetree-shaggy cliffs grew rocky and bald, and the little pickup clattered and whined, straining against its lower gears.

"Be careful, *papo*."

The shadowy stroke of a wing, nearly indistinguishable,

transparent, passed like the wave of a hand before the windshield, and heavenward they rose. For a moment Nikolai's driving became more intense. A blue Cadillac passed on the left, cutting close to the front of the truck. Nikolai hammered the accelerator, double clutched, and geared down until the truck groaned and jerked. Except for the glistening Cadillac in front of them, he might have strained the engine beyond itself and thrown a rod. The car seemed to be having trouble of some sort. It swerved into the oncoming lane then back. The driver appeared to be drunk. Nikolai hit the brake once to avoid a rear-end collision. When they reached the summit and started down, the Cadillac balked and wove and forced Nikolai to hit the brakes again.

Armanda jounced against Evan. They both gazed out the window where the edge of the road dropped away into a steep ravine. Nikolai threw the steering wheel from left to right as if he were a rodeo champ throwing a steer, not an ounce of consideration for Yana flopping around in the back.

"Papa!"

Once, when the brake lights flared ahead, Nikolai gunned it, and before the driver of the Cadillac could re-accelerate, gave him a nudge. Armanda clutched Evan's leg and then his arm, her mouth clamped tight. He felt the terror in her grip equal to his own.

"Ain't that Charlie himself?" shouted Nikolai. "Him and Carla his cow. Them pissants! Follow me around the country, will they?"

He geared down and put his foot on the brake, allowing the Cadillac to chauffeur them off road to a scenic overlook.

"Daddy, you're not stopping."

"Ain't I? Evan, you get ready."

The tone of voice rang too familiar. It could have been Goose intoning his own malice and delight. Both were scoundrels in their own way, though Evan would sooner Goose hang for it than Nikolai whose indignation seemed at least . . . what? Pure?

Nikolai double-clutched and geared to low and the truck

clamored to a stop behind the Cadillac. The turnout ovaled toward a precipice along whose edge ran a waist-high fieldstone wall. There, a meridian divided the overlook, spaced by a loamy area between some pine trees where a water fountain stood next to a topographical map. The map was riveted beneath a thick sheet of plexiglass and framed with brass and wood. Beneath the map a single blackbird patrolled like a guard.

Nothing happened for a moment, then the car door flopped open and out stepped a paunchy one-eyed Gypsy man.

"Where is it then, Markovitch?"

Armanda's father grabbed a tire iron from beneath the seat and flew out into the man's face. He waved the iron around the man's head while a large cow-faced woman unpacked herself from the car.

"You want to mess with Markovitch, Charlie? Don't you better think twice, Charlie, before you stop me like this."

"What's you done with my brother, Markovitch? You got him in the back there?" The man flapped an arm in desperation as though he expected to get airborne. "God will punish you, Markovitch."

"And who's my Angels of Death, Charlie? You and Groucho, that salamander?"

The big cow-faced woman had finally pried herself from the car and now leaned for support against the stone barricade overlooking a still life of the Rockies. She was struggling to get her breath, dressed in some rag-tag Gypsy garb that looked as though she had grabbed it in flight from a burning building that very morning. She was big, but Missy would have made two of her.

Nikolai limped in frantic circles, brandished the tire iron, and raved. "You still unhappily married, Charlie? You better had taken your queen and gone back to the carny. This won't never do, you chasing me around like this. Haven't they dishonored me and won't grant me a *kris*—even a trial to save my Sonia's good name—and don't I spit on them, now? Don't I spit on you, Charlie?" He feinted like a boxer then stumped past the

Gypsy's blind side to the car, swung the tire iron and bounced it off the windshield. He swung again and the glass came apart intact, smashed like the pattern of light through a prism.

"You sonuvabitch."

"Yeah?" He limped around to the front of the car. "You hadn't ought not to be up here on this cold mountain, Charlie. Alone with your Carla. Something might could happen, maybe." He smashed one headlight, shook the tire iron in the Gypsy's good eye, then smashed the other.

"This is a brand new car, you bastard!"

"Yeah? Where'd you steal it from?"

"Nikki!" Yana came screaming from the back of the camper. She threw up her hands like a character in a comic strip and wailed in despair.

The cow-faced Carla was huffing and puffing, leaning so heavily against the fieldstone wall that Evan thought it might give way. He had this image of the wall collapsing and her rolling like a boulder into the shaggy glen below. The blackbird, unruffled by the commotion, strutted across the dirt and hopped up on the wall within arm's length of the big panting woman.

"Evan—" Nikolai waved the tire iron at him, signaling in the gesture what he intended.

"Not me," said Evan, nevertheless climbing down from the cab. In a sense, he had already made his choice, if choices he had, for he felt a peculiar helplessness, as though moved by forces not of his own will. He knelt beside each tire in turn, closing his ears to everything but the hissing air while Nikolai kept Charlie at bay with the tire iron. Kneeling, Evan couldn't see the activity on the other side of the car, but he could see the truck, and for the first time he realized that the tableau of images painted on the visible side appeared different than those he had seen in the dim light of the potato pit the night before. In place of the lance-bearing knight and the Gypsy girl all decked in gold, he saw an open coffin being dragged up a hill, and this scene was overwatched by a black, hookbeaked bird roosting in a leafless tree. A sequential panel delineated the image of some mad Gypsy dancing on a grave. Too, there was a fat woman partially sketched. Then again he couldn't remember for certain which side of the camper he had studied last night, and his arm was growing heavy. His head was filled with noise, but from nothing external, neither from unworldly voices nor from the bickering across the way. He moved from one tire to another and, finally, on the fourth tire, he grew impatient pressing the valve stem with a stick. He unsnapped his knife from the scabbard on his belt, and gripping the bone handle, drove and sliced and screwed the blade into the sidewall. A little puff of air puckered the slit, bulged, and wheezed out in a final rubbery breath. When Evan stood up, the car was resting on its rims.

"You sonuvabitch," said the one-eyed man. "You little twerp," he said to Evan. "Who is this kid, anyway? Who does he think he is? You can't do this. We'll get you—"

Nikolai hefted the tire iron. "You and what dwarf?"

"Where you going, Markovitch? You can't leave us here like this. We got no food. We'll freeze. Carla's asthma—"

"You got legs, Charlie. See if they work."

The man lunged for Nikolai in a single-eyed rage, but Nikolai backed away, threatening him with the tire iron. "You got any brains, Charlie, or do I clout you to see?"

The fat lady opened up. "God in heaven look down and swallow up this man. Ain't he thief and fiend?" She wheezed and cursed, about to double over in agony, though her gut wouldn't bear the crease. "He steals our Knobby and pukes on death. Charlie," she hollered, "if life don't mean nothing then here's an end to it!"

"Carla, blossom—" Charlie closed his blind eye and reached for her while she labored to throw a leg across the barricade. The blackbird, still unruffled, flapped its wings, hopped once, and hammered its beak three or four times into the fleshy web between Carla's fingers. Charlie swatted at the bird and it flew off, squawking.

"I'm a goner," the big woman puffed, flailing her bloodied hand, still trying to get a leg over the wall.

"Don't try your stuff on me!" cried Nikolai. "Ain't I on to you long ago?"

"She's gonna jump, Markovitch. Her noodle's boiled!"

"You better save her then, or kiss her ass as she waves goodbye. Ain't I good as gone? C'mon troops." He shooed his hand at some invisible or imaginary shape as though he were shooing a pesky fly. Then he extended the gesture and shooed his little brood of onlookers, speechless, back into the truck.

The one-eyed man and his suicidal wife clasped hands across the barricade and watched their ploy collapse.

"I'll get to Cincinnati, Markovitch. Don't think I won't. By the time that little half-breed whore's got wed, don't think I won't. Me or Groucho will. You'll pay, don't think you won't. I got a gun, too—"

"Na phir pala manda! Pala ma phiresa, opre potjinesa. Believe me, you'll pay!"

The truck lurched forward and Armanda caught herself with a hand on Evan's knee. Yana thumped in the back. Nikolai made a fist and extended his middle finger, shaking it out the window as he drove away. "Pissants! That takes the cake. Half-breed whore, he says. I should oughta slit his throat." Nikolai mumbled something to himself, and Evan waited for a word of explanation, some hint of purpose to such rage. He got nothing—only the troubled realization that he, not Nikolai, was responsible for stranding some crazed Gypsy named Charlie and his overstuffed wife in the top of the Rocky Mountains.

"You think maybe we owe you?" Now it was Armanda reading his mind. "I think Cowboy Evan's confused, *papo.*"

"Ain't we all."

She leaned her body up against his as they went around a curve. But that was it. Nothing more. A world of meaning could someday open before him, bleak as pitch, but for now even their destination remained a mystery, unless "Cincinnati" meant something. When the curves came, Armanda leaned close, and he contented himself with her half-angry stories of life in and out of the *kumpania* or on the road, of Gypsy customs and rites, Nikolai occasionally spicing up her already detailed and hardly believable narrative. She said little about her mother, and Nikolai, too, when the wrong question was asked, grew preoccupied with his driving. Sometimes they spoke in half-sentences, riddles, usually in English, salted with an occasional Romany word or phrase.

"*Lungo dromesa ïas.*"

Evan caught something about the basement in a cathedral overlooking the Ohio River and heard the word "*daro*" repeated half a dozen times by Nikolai. He had a confused notion . . . but before he could examine it, the conversation came full circle. They wanted to know about his experiences on the farm, more about what he remembered of his parents. Armanda expressed a fascination for his Aunt Missy and Uncle Goose, though she seemed equally dumbfounded by their antics. She could more easily accept a corpse, a coffin, and ghosts than the two miserable cartoons Evan described. He told them again about the mad dance in the kitchen and knocking Uncle Goose in the ditch; it didn't take much to exaggerate their features, their antics, their lack of intelligence. Nikolai snorted and coughed, shook his fist, and threw back his head and howled. Armanda wondered whether they might have dredged the river by now, looking for Evan's body. Did he think they had put out an All Points Bulletin?

After a while, when the conversation lagged, she slumped down in the seat and put her head against Nikolai's shoulder. Evan dozed too and when he awoke found himself jammed against the door, the weight of the Gypsy girl pressed sleepily against him. She was clean smelling and softer than he'd thought, and it was all so familiar that for a fleeting moment he could almost tell what was going to happen next.

Golden, Colorado came at them out of the trees, and then a sign:

BUFFALO BILL'S GRAVE 3 MILES AHEAD
CHEVRON—ARCO—SHELL

Nikolai took the first exit and pulled into the Shell station. He got out and checked the oil, battery, and belts while the attendant pumped gas. Armanda awoke all at once, pushed Evan out of the truck, and hurried him past the restrooms to a telephone booth. From a little open window in the ladies room, they could hear Yana cursing *gaje* toilets—filth and disease. Armanda pulled Evan into the booth and closed the door, dampening noise from the world outside.

She ran her body up against his, giggled unlike the girl of last night, and searching for coins, battered him with an arsenal of elbows and knees. She was about five feet six or seven and he was four or five inches taller—just tall enough to put his nose in her bittersweet hair and surprise himself up close at the size and shape of her eyes.

"What's this all about?"

She fidgeted and wormed her hips against his, finally found and plugged a quarter in the slot. All of a sudden she was screaming at the operator to put through an emergency call to the sheriff back home. She cocked the phone away from her ear and tipped Evan's head down so he could share the receiver. When the county sheriff picked up, she made her voice husky and boyish, said she'd witnessed a drowning and wondered if they had found the body. Evan's face was up close to hers and when she talked into the receiver, her breath got in his lungs. Her story was the gloomy reality of having witnessed a murder, or the possibility of one—last night. Yes, coming back from the carnival, she couldn't be sure but—what?—she wanted no part of it if something sorry had happened. Nope. Just a worried Gypsy girl. No names. Half way across the country by now. Yep . . . coming back from the carnival. It was dark, before it started to rain . . . close to the riverbank, across from the Gypsy camp . . . not just some horrid Gypsy girl being ravished down by the river . . . she had seen that more times than she cared to remember behind the Ring Toss booth . . . but this . . . hurrying back to the Gypsy camp before the rain started to fall . . . this big overweight woman with a head like a cannonball, and a man who looked like he came from a henhouse. (There was a needle of saliva at the corner of her mouth and when she spoke it sprayed against his lips.) What? No. Arguing . . . doing something with a third party, there in the water . . . some sort of struggle . . . all this splashing and thrashing . . . and then like a log floating in the river. Like a log . . . and bubbles . . . loops and loops of waves rippling out into the river . . . just the two of them, now . . . the rooster-looking man and this fat woman trundling up the bank . . . bickering . . . something about geese . . . and that funny-looking log spinning away down river, arms and legs, branches, maybe . . . but she wasn't sure . . . maybe fifty yards away, or less . . . didn't occur to her until this morning . . . didn't want to poke her nose in. What? No. She only saw what she saw, and that's that . . . didn't want to muddle the facts. Just some Gypsies, maybe, or drunk Mexicans. What? A missing persons' report? Somebody from the community? A teenage boy? Blond? About six feet, hundred and seventy pounds? Could be. Then, again, now that he'd mentioned it—pretty blue eyes? Square jaw? Pecs like Achilles? Lips to die for? Sorry, got to run now. What? Just doing her duty . . . didn't want to meddle or misconstrue . . . but that log, arms and legs, branches, maybe . . . thought the sheriff's department ought to be informed . . . like a murder she'd once seen on TV . . . Bye, now.

She put the phone gently in its cradle.

"You're kidding," he said. *Lips to die for?* "That was cruel."

"Wasn't it? I suppose you'll never forgive me."

"Never," he said. "It makes me want to kiss you."

She wedged him up against the door, pinning his arms.

"What are we talking about here? Your pretty mouth or the wickedness of my Gypsy ways?"

"You tell me."

She studied him, every word a breath. "The evidence is only hearsay, of course, circumstantial, at best. Except for this half-witted phone call and the missing body, they won't have much to go on, but the cops might put those two lunatics through the least unpleasant rigmarole they deserve." Her face came up close. "Cowboy?"

"What?"

She swallowed whatever she had in mind, said instead, "Lemme outta here, Cowboy. My teeth are floating." She squeezed by, startling his flesh with the unfettered softness of her own.

They was on a cross-country with designs on my bud from the start and some scheme to bilk the goods out of that Walcott tribe in the East, but to come across them there in the Rockies was I dreaming or what, a dream become a nightmare turned inside out, that's what. I knew he had Knobby there, in the back, I'd of put a dollar on it. Not something you'd put past a Markovitch. Steals a man's bud right out of the morgue. Carla says force them off the road, and I think maybe I can dicker with him, until out steps this other pair of hands. Some kid, a goddamn stray they picked up from god knows where. He comes out with this dog-assed look on his face like he doesn't know from shit, and I think about the gun in the trunk. But Markovitch, he's got that tire iron and waving it in my eye. I think, if only I had that gun. The kid's screwing a knife in my tires, and Markovitch is going from one headlight to the other, from the windshield to the hood. A brand new car, goddamnit. Who did he think he was? A brand new car, and in five minutes looks like it's hit by a Mack. Carla, she wants to cast herself over the edge for sympathy and doom. Blackbirds all over the place. I close my good eye to see, and the old bitch, she comes lolling out of the back where I know they got Knobby crammed, and the half-breed looking like maybe she's going to curse the rest of us right there. I know it was Knobby died under the hand of a curse, and whose else? Tell you what, curse or no, I'd of fucked her mother myself stretched in her coffin to wipe that look off her face.

~10~

Riddles & the Wandering Man

When first she appears she seems mysterious . . .

IN order to get the coffin through the camper door, they had to tilt it up on its side.

"Heave!" cried Nikolai, equal to the director of an insane asylum. "That Knobby, he's a heavy bugger."

Evan wondered how Nikolai and the two women had ever gotten it into the camper in the first place. He helped the lopsided Gypsy lug the miserable thing up on its side, then boosted it toward Nikolai who stood outside at the head, guiding it through the door. They had it half-in, half-out while Armanda and Yana stood a little ways off chattering instructions. When the lid was through the door, it came unlatched with a pop, and the chattering stopped. The entire group may as well have been star gazing or deaf and dumb people in a library or pretending they were posts in a fence or something. Each of them watched as the corpse hinged upright at the waist, rolled to the side, and thumped stiffly against the lid. A few of the wrinkled bills fluttered to the ground. Evan felt a little sick to his stomach, but like the rest of them, he just stood there, leaning over the coffin, his head poking out of the camper door.

If the thing had opened its mouth and said "Howdy-do," not one of them would have been surprised. But this was no resurrection, and if it had been it would have been short lived, for Nikolai threw up his hands, cursed, and tore into the body like a man robbed of his wits. He ripped at satin and lace. He grabbed fistfuls of money.

Yana lunged forward, horrified. "Nikki! You don't steal from the dead."

"He steals from me, don't he? Even my life."

Arms flailed back at him and he damned its soul. These were death throes. He groped and grabbed for the money and stuffed it in his pockets. He snatched a bottle of Vodka from the coffin. The women moved closer and he slugged the corpse. Evan thought he was going to climb in with it before he punched it again and finally wrestled it back into its bed and closed the lid.

Nikolai was furious, a little humiliated by the looks of it.

They hefted the coffin the rest of the way from the truck and without a word dragged it up a slope away from camp. Evan thought of a hundred things he might have said but kept to himself. Even Armanda hadn't so much as cracked a grin, and now she stood watching the two of them lug the thing up the slope, as somber in expression as the bewitched captive of an ancient troll. Evan looked around, impressed by the medieval complexion of the ground whereon he stood, how like an illustration in some fairy book—an uncanny repeat of the caravan stop they had eaten breakfast in that morning. As far as he could tell, unless they had crossed into some fourth dimension (which seemed as possible as anything else he had experienced over the last two days), they were still in Colorado, just off Interstate 70 outside of Burlington. The same small brook, or what appeared to be the same small brook, babbled across the meadow, dropped toward the campsite and passed beneath overhanging maple trees. The only difference was the split rail fence dividing the pasture. It wasn't much of a fence, but it was quaint, dipping across the brook and rambling away up a knoll. On the other side of the fence an old Hereford watched with disinterest, chewing her cud. They dragged the coffin up the knoll, and the cow turned away and plodded across the brook.

Armanda came up the hill carrying a pick-ax in one hand and a shovel in the other. Evan felt a little queasy over the whole lousy business, but when Armanda handed him the shovel he just held it for a moment then turned and kicked it into the earth as Nikolai swung the pick. The earth was damp and easy to turn. They worked together without talking. As they worked, the affliction in Evan's stomach dissolved, but it seemed very unreal to be digging in the earth just then, as though his hands weren't his own. All across the meadow, tiny white flowers poked their heads up though the grass and clumps of purple violets dotted the incline. There was hardly a breeze and Evan looked up once in a while to gaze across the pasture where a line of spruce broke against the foothills. Nikolai was content to dig a shallow grave so the whole job took less than an hour and they hardly worked up a sweat.

"See that? The more you take away the larger it becomes."

Evan rested on the handle of the shovel while Nikolai shaped the corners of the grave with the pick. He looked out across the pasture, remembering another time when he had stood beside an open grave. There had been a wind and the smell of blown flowers and the hot press of Aunt Missy's hand. In comparison, this evening was relatively calm with a smell of fresh dung—Evan's preference to Missy's B.O. and stomach breath. He felt the warmth of the declining sun in his hair and filled his lungs with the rustic breeze.

"Tired, Cowboy?"

Armanda sat in the dirt a few yards away. Her legs were crossed Buddhist style and she was absently pulling grass while watching them work. From somewhere, perhaps down by the brook, she had plucked a wild rose and fastened it in her hair. It was big and white and lopsided just above her ear, but she was all the more beautiful for it, if not a little sad.

Evan acknowledged her with a scant toss of his head and watched her and wondered how she felt about all of this; he wondered whether she had the same sense of unreality as he, or if she even allowed herself to feel. He kept his eye on her and wondered about the corpse and decided that this meadow was an acceptable and rather pleasant place to be buried. The who and the why and the where were none of his business, he guessed, and it didn't make any difference, anyway, as long as they hadn't killed the flat-faced man lying in the coffin.

By the time the two of them got the coffin into the grave, it was pretty well battered. The lid had gotten sprung in the process so that it wouldn't close properly. Nikolai took out a handkerchief and toweled the back of his neck. He stood there for a while without ceremony. Evan muttered a couple of lines, in the way of last rites:

> *. . . and what looks dark in the distance*
> *may brighten as I draw near.*

Armanda considered the words and then she contemplated him as one might contemplate a beetle in a jar.

"Won't they look all around the country?" chuckled Nikolai. He blinked his eyes kind of fast so that in the gathering dusk he appeared to have an uncontrollable tick. "Not in a thousand years will they find him here. Not in a million." He cursed and spit into the grave, chuckled miserably.

Evan looked at the gob, gleaming like an oyster atop the lid, and wondered about the fate of the one-eyed Gypsy man and his cow-faced wife. Surely, they would be able to hitchhike their way out of the mountains. What then? Track Nikolai to the ends of the earth? Nikolai himself could very well be running from something, roaming about the country, hiding out. From whom? Another Gypsy band? The *Kuneshti?* The law? What about his own part in all of this—deflating the tires, burying the coffin? Could Charlie and who else—this Groucho—be far behind?

What if they caught up? Most horrible thought: what would Nikolai do? And how did Cincinnati and the cathedral overlooking the Ohio figure into it? And this garble about being pledged by virtue of blood? He wondered about all the possibilities; he wondered about fate and expectation and then confused himself and wondered about the farmer who might plow his land come spring.

Armanda opened her mouth as if about to say something then closed it.

"He won't plow this field," said Nikolai. He shoved a bootful of earth into the grave, the damp sod thumping on the coffin lid. Evan put the shovel to work, scoop after scoop. Between shovelfuls Nikolai stepped in and out of the grave, stamping firm the earth. He stamped his feet and swung his hips, a little off balance and girlish, stomping in and out and whirling to the inaudible beat of some mad dance.

When he stopped he was out of breath, grinning, but it was a cold, untelling grin. He threw off his hat and wiped his forearm across his furrowed brow. He shouted to Armanda to turn her face and tottered about spraddle-legged and released himself and urinated a broad endless stream across the mound, weaving in the loose splashing sod some private and indistinguishable design, railing at both heaven and hell, and calling forth angels and fiends to sanctify the curse. When he ceased, it was as if the firmaments, both above and below, clashed with a sudden ringing absence of sound. Satisfied, he turned with a tidy dip and tucked himself away. He paused to admire his fancywork and stepped to the side.

"So then," he breathed heavily, nodding toward Evan's waist. "You know about the knives?" He was referring to the bone-handled hunting knife strapped to Evan's belt.

"This?"

"Lessee."

Nikolai roped an arm about Evan's shoulders and turned him from the grave. He handed Armanda the pick and shovel, and she followed them back down the hill. Evan unsnapped the scabbard and handed Nikolai the knife. Nikolai hefted its weight, feeling the balance between the blade and the handle, nodded surprised approval. When they reached the bottom of the slope, Nikolai limped away two or three steps and stood by himself. In a singular, fluid motion, he brought the knife back past his ear and flung it hard into the trunk of a maple tree. He limped over to the tree, pulled out the knife and wiped the blade on his trousers, came back and threw it again. He did this several times, not only sticking it in the tree each time but sticking it within an inch of the same spot.

Knife-handler extraordinaire. But when Evan asked him, Nikolai didn't want to talk about it, except to frown and say, "*Kuneshti!* Here, my darling."

Armanda went to the tree and stood with her back to the trunk like an obedient daughter. She touched the middle of her breast, off-center to the left, "Put it here, *papo*, in my heart, next to the pain." She didn't close her eyes or look away or even blink.

Before Evan could protest, Nikolai threw. The blade bit the trunk of the tree, chipping bark, not an inch from her throat. Armanda reached back, gripped the handle, and without turning around, yanked the blade from the tree. She held the knife by the blade and lobbed it back to Nikolai who caught it by the handle.

"Here." He handed Evan the knife, blinking his eyes in that same nervous twitch. "Go ahead. But not to fling." He put his hand on Evan's. "Like this." He gestured a slight flick of the wrist, starting from just behind the ear.

Armanda was still standing with her back to the tree. "C'mon, Cowboy. You put it in my heart, where the pain is. Don't miss."

"Darling, move."

Armanda obeyed, and Evan threw the knife. He watched as it left his hand, flopping end over end, caught the edge of the tree about where her shoulder had been, a little lower maybe, and briefly shivered.

"Not so bad."

He threw a couple more times, vaguely aware of how timing and a sense of rhythm exacted the precision of each throw. Nikolai watched for a minute and then Armanda came over. Behind them, in the gathering dusk, Evan could hear Yana clattering pots and mumbling over the campfire.

"So, don't I got a whetstone in the truck?" offered Nikolai. "Can't I get that sucker sharp like a razor?"

"Go ahead."

He jerked the knife from the tree and swaggered in lopsided fashion back to the truck.

Evan glanced at Armanda. He was surprised to see a spot of blood on her throat where a piece of bark must have chipped away and sliced her when Nikolai threw the knife. Evan hadn't seen so much as a flinch out of her, and now she was bleeding. Touching her throat with the tips of his fingers to wipe at the blood only brought her face closer, and he knew then she was a dream come alive—or a nightmare.

"It comes from my heart," she whispered, and he couldn't tell from her eyes if she were taunting him or sincere. "I bleed for you, Cowboy. My blood on your hands. I bleed for *papo* and *mamo*. The blood of my race." She laughed at him and flipped her hair. "You're so serious," she said. "But *papo* likes you. I can see that you're a lot alike. You're scared of different things, that's all."

He looked at her. "Scared? What am I scared of?"

"You know."

"?"

She held his gaze and didn't even wince. " You're a virgin— both you and your little cheerleader. The both of you." She laughed. "And haunted by the past. Papa's afraid of ghosts and the dead. He's afraid of losing position with himself. He's afraid for me." Then, as if to make him forget what she'd said, looking into his eyes with the studied movement of her own, she spoke

THE GYPSY LOVER ·161·

earnestly. "Most fathers, I'm told, are in love with their daughters. Mine is. This blood is nothing."

She looked away, toward the trees, then back up the hill. Evan watched her silently, confused, the soft, unblemished side of her jaw, her long blessed hair swept by the breeze, the big lopsided flower minus a petal or two still snared there. He followed her eyes toward the slope where together they gazed for a long time at the dark patch of fresh earth. The sky had flattened out to an agonizing gray and a light wind rattled the maple leaves, laying Armanda's hair in strands across her jaw. She brushed at them and motioned Evan to the campfire where Yana was preparing dinner. Nikolai sat with the door open in the cab of the pickup, fussing with the knife, dragging it across the whetstone then rolling the blade and dragging it back. After a while he shut the knife in the glove compartment and sauntered down by the brook, distracted, lopsided, and alone. He was carrying the bottle of Vodka and about his neck he wore a long red scarf, the trailing halves flung back across his shoulders like a Griffin's wings.

"He don't want to eat right now," said Yana. But she had already prepared five plates, Nikolai's and the extra one side by side on the other side of the fire, growing cold together.

It was falling dusk but Evan could see the cow beyond the fence, moseying back down the hill. A raven swooped beneath the elms, emitted one sharp witchlike cry, and alighted in the branches of a tree—the same tree Armanda had stood with her back against—less than twenty feet from where they sat around the fire. The old woman stopped serving and whispered harshly: "Sonia!"

The bird hopped to a lower branch, fluffed its wings and cocked its head; then with a single flap it was in the air, sweeping between the trees toward the brook.

"She seeks peace, *mamio*."

"You!"

"Evan knows, *mamio*. I told him. Let him be Gypsy, *mamio*— at least *Romany-rye*. He's just a cowboy. He has nothing."

Evan listened to her silly talk, listened to her falling back into her Romany dialect and petitioning in his behalf. The old woman eyed him up close, her face squeezed like a fly's.

"You told him? What do you tell him?"

"I told him some things."

"Ah, yes. Armanda has wisdom like her *mamio*. You watch her, kid. Like a brother you keep your eye out." She glanced in the direction the bird had flown and lowered her voice. "She is Gypsy, not *gaje*. Brother and sister, you hear?"

Evan felt even more foolish with all this talk about ghost-birds and brother-sister stuff, but under the spell of either admiration for the old woman or a confused mystification, he kept his mouth shut.

"Eat, Cowboy Evan." Yana leaned in toward the fire and crossed herself and spat. Even with all her grief and mourning, the old woman was the soul of oddness and good temper. In snippets and snatches, here an anecdote, there, Evan's mind closed over the web of it.

"*Mamio* was top *drabarni* in the Barvale *kumpania*," Armanda told him, apparently in explanation of something close to her heart. "That's old medicine woman to you."

"'Twas nothing," said Yana.

"She knows incantations and spells, cures that defy all modern reasoning. A little Ghost's Vomit or Devil's Shit will set you right. But *papo*, there's no remedy for his complaint."

"Not of this world, there ain't."

"'Tis the *muli*, I fear."

She looked at her granddaughter, uncertain, half in alarm.

"The sway of the spirit, the influence, so to speak. *Mamo*, the blessed. The cursed."

"Be careful, my darling."

"There is but the sad and joyful exchange, and even that could go awry."

Evan watched as the old woman buried her head and sat in front of the fire slurping her stew, a greasy interesting slop seasoned with many herbs and spices. It smelled of mushrooms and fish and tasted of clams. "Here." She pointed to the bread and jabbed a fingernail between her teeth, scraping at something stuck there. She looked at her granddaughter to hush her and then looked away. She was the oldest looking person Evan had ever seen. Her skin was the color of coffee and cream, with a network of fine lines criss-crossing it everywhere, not wrinkles so much as lines like filigree lace. Her shoulders hunched forward and on her head, draped loosely above a high bumpy forehead, she wore something that appeared to be a cross between a hood, a bonnet, and a headscarf. Usually somber, she sometimes laughed with little jerks, jutting forward her neck in that disgusting way and showing what remained of her small teeth.

"O, *mamio*, hasn't this cowboy come to play his hand for us?"

The old woman picked at her stew and mumbled insensibly beneath her breath, and then her voice rose and the incomprehensible syllables became words that developed meaning by degrees. Although she spoke to no one in particular, the overall impression touched Evan and called forth memories familiar and vague.

" . . . when I was a young girl, before we come to America, I went out in the woods and fasted so that I would see the future. Back then young girls who'd seen the sun or wind believed they'd find happiness, they'd get a good husband. But in my dream that night, the wind was pressing like a hand against my back, pushing me faster and faster along a road until I was almost skimming. I turned my head and seen a tall dark shape, but I couldn't make out any feature except the eyes—they was different colors, one so black it was green and the other purple as blue ice, but at the same time they burned. For all I knew, it might have been grandpa or some far gone ancestor who bled with the moon for antiquity's sake. And I give him a parcel I was carrying that had my mother's and some other unfortunate's name on it. He hadn't come for me, but for the parcel, and to this day I wisht I hadn't

·164· Roger Ladd Memmott

give it him. I told your great grandmama, whose time was nigh to birthing, *Pale bajba pelem, mamo*—I'm in trouble again. O, maybe this was a day or so before the soldiers come." She looked at Armanda. "When they come and took us into the forest . . . you know—them soldiers, like you see in films, except more of a rag-tag bunch, just boys, some, and set us up in rows, sitting and kneeling and standing behind—and, afterward, after it was all said and done, their duty and the sorrowful part, not one but me left standing, all for the stained, messy flower of my youth, how they took it one by one, then give it back to me in the form of a spade to dig my mama's and her newborn's grave, me and a boyish soldier or two, to dig, and the ground so hard with ice and snow, *Pale bajba pelem, mamo*—but that's another story. Though soon after I took up with your grandpapa, we married and I never knew but what one seed mixed with the other to produce the heartache and confusion of him who sits yonder, both uncherished and loved by the absence of dreams. But that's another story, didn't I say? Though I have it that an Aryan bride awaited one of those boys, the very cameraman with stripes on his sleeve, she who carried his child within, he who took from me and then witlessly give in return, who after it all lay in his own blood as the Russians advanced. 'Twas all after in the glass and the stars and a throw of the cards, each time I looked." She paused and looked at Evan. "I can tell you this much and no more, how she with child on learning the fate of her man went off to America and give birth there and how that child in time took up with a railroad boy and had a boy of her own. But that's another story." She paused and realigned her train of thought. "Well, I told my mother about the dream and she said I had seen the Wandering Man, a spirit who never rests but goes round and round the earth, sometimes taking peculiar things away from them who see him—burdens and such, if not loved ones, too. He often comes in the guise of them we know, and the sight of him brings either death or change—sometimes both. Like I told you, when just two days later the soldiers come. Sad or joyful it may be called, you'd think twice afore giving the Wandering Man any part of you, burdens or otherwise. Either parcels or gifts. He wears two faces, like the fool, and can give or take. Even still, you're forever doomed to wander. There ain't no rest once you've seen the Wandering Man…."

Together with her words, the uncanny flash of dreams pried a chip of bone from Evan's skull, and the old woman peered inside. It was all so familiar, so vague. Evan could nearly *feel*— more than *see*—what she meant, and knew that she had seen clearly, perhaps beyond understanding, but somehow couldn't get it right in his head.

She continued speaking, but now in fragments, softly chiding her granddaughter and lamenting the days about which she could only dream. O, hadn't they lived the easy life, the good life, upon first coming to America? The threat of city living, of mingling with *gaje*, had been only a vague fear—something even to joke about. In those days, the Gypsies had gone south with the flocks, at peace with the Wandering Man. They had lived by their wits and their cunning. The *bujo* and fortune telling and the miraculous healing powers of a *drabarni's* herb concoctions were everything. And the Gypsy bands with their concertina's and violins, the carnivals and fairs, and the fast dances of the young Gypsy girls that brought showers of coins from the hands of the *gajos.* Now it was difficult for Gypsies to pick up odd jobs. *Gaje* women had stopped hiring tinkers to mend copper pots and pans and replaced them with inexpensive aluminum and plastic stuff. The city had become a way of life. For every little ailment they went to *gaje* doctors instead of to the wise old Gypsy women with their commonplace medicines and exotic cures. And, of course, with each succeeding generation, Gypsy blood was running thin. She glanced at her granddaughter and craned her neck and set her teeth. Her own son! Customs, rituals, traditions, were slipping away like the last faint strains of a violin. The hex of civilization, of technology and change, lay upon them like a giant's smothering hand.

"Take heed, my pretty. You snub the old ways too often, *muli* or no, but still you believe. It will all come back around."

She turned her head from the fire and spat; then, as though picking up the bones of some previous picked-over argument, she looked at Evan and hissed in a strangely good-natured fashion: "*Gajo* talks much to avoid saying something?"

"*Gajo* has nothing to say." He blinked back at her a touch of righteous indignation.

"Gypsy listens—"

"—and watches . . ." said Armanda, menacingly.

The old woman turned toward her granddaughter with a heavy countenance. "He is the wise fool who listens little, watches much, and speaks nothing at all."

"Is that another riddle?" He prolonged his moan, halfway tired of the whole affair. Coffins and ghosts and dancing on graves. "First that creepy stuff about the Wandering Man, and now this. You people are your own worst enemies—sad and joyful exchange. You stereotype yourselves with riddles."

"Riddle me, riddle me ree," chanted Armanda, taking the old woman's side. She shook the rose from her hair as though it were time and combed out the bright strands with her fingers. "At her age to say riddles she's earned the right."

"Here, kid. Yana will give you riddles. Armanda, be silent."

" *Si, mamio.*"

"Like Armanda, you snub my tales of the Wandering Man, but deep inside you know, as if in a dream you had wandered yourself. Last night I threw the cards and counted the stars and you were among them, more impression than either flesh and blood or even ghost. So tell me, kid. Why does the old woman speak in riddles?"

He flipped the remainder of his stew toward the flames. He rocked on his haunches against the log and looked away. The cow stood at distance on the other side of the fence, now bathed in starlight, cow-grateful it seemed for the company. "She's earned the right, I suppose."

"Old age gives her the right, sure, but not the reason. Why does Yana speak in riddles? When first she appears she seems mysterious, but when explained she's nothing serious. Come on, kid. Use god's head he give you. Ask in your heart, kid. What you cannot see with your eyes, let your heart believe. You want to be Gypsy? When first she appears, she seems mysterious. Answer the old woman's riddle. Be Gypsy. Answer the old woman's riddle. You like the mystery of Gypsy? Answer this riddle: When explained she's nothing serious."

"It's obvious," he said, standing up, wondering if the flush he felt in his cheeks was visible. But his tongue loosened and humiliation dissolved in his throat. "You can take your silly riddles and bury them in coffins. Feed them to crows. You don't want answers to your riddles anyway. Riddles aren't meant to be answered. Answer the riddle and what do you have? What you want is mystery." He found himself talking with his hands and wondered if he had read some of this stuff somewhere about riddles, in another life perhaps, and was just now dredging it up: the enigma behind the riddle being more important than either the answer to the riddle or the riddle itself. It made sense.

"Fools answer riddles with riddles," warned Armanda, but he couldn't tell if her tone mocked him or her grandmother.

He started to say again how the thought behind the riddle, the enigma required by the riddle, was more important than either the riddle or the answer; instead, he said, with Aunt Missy's disdain: "*Gypsies!* You want to be riddles yourselves, but you're merely unexplained."

"Piddle on the riddle," said Armanda, brushing petals from the rose between her hands.

Yana poked her neck forward and showed her teeth in a grimace. Armanda sort of tittered and opened her big wide eyes as though she had made a discovery.

"He's afraid of us, *mamio*. The last of the cowboys is afraid."

"O, I'm not afraid, but I'll give you your answer in a word. Gypsy." And then he repeated: "Gypsy. Riddles. Armanda. Yana."

It had been there all the time, floating in the mass and fluid and nerve-endings of his brain. "Gypsy, like the riddle. When first she appears, she seems mysterious, but when explained she's nothing serious: Gypsy. You. Armanda. The riddle itself."

The old woman eyed him severely, and then the harshness of her gaze softened. In the firelight her black eyes shone like two polished stones. She took both his and Armanda's hand in hers and looked from one to the other of them, eye to eye, and there was in them, her eyes, a look of both sorrow and joy. "What will be, will be," she said and pressed their hands one upon the other and released her own. "Perhaps your *papo's* right. We cannot forestall it. O, my darlings, we must sort out our destiny even yet, no matter the fortune or fate." She coughed and smiled and sobbed and embarrassed him again, saying, "Come here, my Gypsy boy. My *Romany-rye*. Give us kisses, your *mamio*."

As you know, Gypsies come and go. They tramp along the western edge of dreams, leaving tricks and shadows in their path. But listen to how it is in Gypsy paradise. The fields are deep and wide, the horses gallop down from the slopes beneath a glistening sky; there are running streams, and along the banks in the shade of the willows, spits of roasted calf and frying trout and fruits and pies. Across the stream, when the sky darkens and the wind comes up, they watch the sons and daughters of the *gaje*, how they shiver there with hunger and cold and beg succor from the little ones. Look to the reflection in the stream and ask, how will you remember them? As shadows of the heart, feeding desire and want? Or will you remember only their tales of vampires and ghosts, princes and frogs, beautiful women and animals who speak as well as dance and fly? Will you remember the Wandering Man and their having for supper hearts of the aggrieved? Such are they who are so unkind to themselves that they suffer without cause. The Gypsy knows them, so afflicted by either hunger or hate. Such as they long for the wheel of fortune to come back around, as it does, forever will, in spite of hope or a damaged heart.

~ 11 ~

The Curse

... 'til death do us part.

~ HOUSE OF PRAYERS ~

REVEREND MOTHER SALLOWAY
Spiritual Healer & Advisor–Come See Her in Person
ARE YOU SICK IN ANY PART OF YOUR BODY?
Mother Salloway has a God Given Power to help you
overcome your problems no matter how big or small.
God Sent–All Prayers and Healing to You

Now you can call upon Mother Salloway to make your wish come true. Touch of her hand will heal you. Mother Salloway has the Power and the Sight. Everyone welcome at Mother

Salloway's. What you cannot see with your eyes, your heart will believe. Are you suffering? Do you have bad luck? Has love cheated you? Bring your problems to Mother Salloway now and be rid of them tomorrow. She advises on all affairs of life, will tell you what you want to know about friends, enemies, rivals, and more. Teaches how to control or influence the actions of others even though miles away. Tells your lucky numbers, advises on love, marriage, business, health, divorce, lawsuits, luck, happiness, heartache, death, and spells. There is no problem so great she cannot solve. Rev. Mother Salloway has devoted a lifetime to this work. From the four corners of the earth they have flocked to her—men and women of all races and walks of life. Guaranteed to remove evil influence and bad luck—also warts. One visit will convince you. She gives you lucky days. Cures troubled hearts. Lifts you out of sorrow and gives you joy. Don't fail to see this Gifted Woman who has been sent to help you. Rev. Mother Salloway is here for a limited time. Rev. Mother Salloway invites you to become FREE. Rev. Mother Salloway guarantees to restore your lost Nature.

WHY SUFFER WHEN YOU CAN BE HELPED
AND FREED FROM ALL YOUR TROUBLES?
Half Price With This Handbill.
By Appointment Only.
REV. MOTHER SALLOWAY
—Here For A Limited Time—
Ridgebury Pines—532 Old Ridgebury Rd.
(Cottage #7)—Topeka, KS
Phone 321-8994
Across the Street from
Elmo's Truck Stop

THE glow from the Coleman lantern illuminated the camper and yellowed the printed flyer in Evan's hands. He had stopped sketching long enough to read it, and then he read it again. No comment, no thought, just a simmering incredulity nitpicking his brain. He set the handbill aside, with caution, as if it were sacrosanct or something of the absurd, in either case not to be tampered with, and returned to the reality of his sketchbook. There, he could at least keep an eye on Armanda while penciling the inconspicuous lines of his heart.

Armanda was busy transforming herself, puttering between the cots: hair bound up in a *bujo* woman's scarf, rouged cheeks, red mouth, painted eyes. Evan worked another few angles of her shoulders and head, stroked the curve of her spine, and then, contemplating the lines of her breasts, closed his sketchbook and put it away.

"Turn your head, Cowboy."

She stepped into a blood-red ankle-length skirt with blue-edged accordion pleats, turned her back to him and wiggled out of her jeans. She tucked the white blouse into her skirt and snapped the skirtwaist tight and fastened a chainlink belt about her waist from which hung medallions and trinkets and charms. "Now, then." She decked herself with bracelets and gold swishing chains, earrings that dangled and looped, pinched her feet into gold lamé high-heeled shoes. "How's this?" She opened her blouse an extra button and flounced the lapels. She could have cursed him or loved him and it would have all been the same.

"Let me see." She nodded toward the sketchbook he had just put away.

"I don't think so."

"Be nice and maybe I'll pose for you sometime. You know?" She did something with a lilt of her head and a twist of her hips and gave him a look that shattered the words right in his mouth and brought the blood to his cheeks.

"I like you in those spectacles," she laughed. "Put those spectacles back on."

She meant the old steel-rimmed eyeglasses that had belonged to his father. They were a weak prescription but clarified the type on the handbill he had been reading in the dim light. He put

THE GYPSY LOVER ·173·

them on, rotating his head to fit the wire earpieces over each ear. They softened and gathered the light around her.

"Real brainy," she remarked. "Kinda sexy, too. Read me something out of that book of yours."

He looked at the copy of Wood's *Master's of American Literature* jutting from his gym bag. "I was just reading some stuff by Emerson," he said, "before I found out Mother Salloway has all the answers."

"We're not in Kansas, yet, Toto. Go ahead. This Gypsy girl will tell your fortune in a minute."

"The Reverend Mother herself?"

"All prayers and healing to you. Guaranteed to restore your lost nature. Scoot over. I'm just a Gypsy girl, the last of my breed, like you. How d'you like this perfume?" She sat beside him on the cot and the scent of roses flounced up with the red petallike flounce of her skirt. "What else you got in that bag, anyway?" She craned her neck, peering around him and reaching with a long brown arm into the open backpack. Her breath and the scented musk of her went all through his lungs and up in his head. "Your harmonica? Play me a tune. What's that? A picture of your parents? So that's where you get those eyes." She held the unframed photograph between her hands and examined it closely. "You could have been the father of yourself, except for Time."

He looked at the adult likeness of himself standing next to his mother. "The father of myself?"

"If you'd been born before him and married your mother, I mean, like that Greek King who gouged out his eyes."

"Oedipus?"

"Whatever you say."

He looked at Armanda and felt the unkindness of words seep through his mouth.

"Maybe he'd be sitting here next to me falling in love instead of you." As she said it, he swallowed without knowing. "I mean if your father, you know, son of yourself, if we fell in love and I married him." She looked at him. "Whose kids would I have?" She looked at the picture. "What if I were your mother?"

"Sure. What if you were my sister?"

"O, like *mamio* wants us to act? What if your blood ran in my veins?" She put a hand on his arm and her voice grew tight. "What if I crawled up inside you to look out your eyes?"

"?"

She looked at the photograph and meandered somewhere back in her head. "They aren't riddles," she protested before he could say. "Just questions begging the possibilities of a different world." She looked at him, but not really, somewhere beyond. "Why things are the way they are and how they might otherwise be, I mean if this instead of that." Now she was looking at him, his eyes. "Don't it make a difference to you, the unrealized alternatives of life?" Now he was transparent. "One little slip of the atom and our world anew."

She held the photograph away from him at arm's length and scooted herself closer by degrees. It was warm inside the camper and each time they moved, the cot groaned with their weight.

"I sometimes wonder how I come to be me instead of some other. How another come not to be me." She studied the photograph and held it away from him and looked back at his face. "What if I could see myself from your point of view?"

It was more a statement than a question, but he took the challenge and dug through the backpack and pulled out his journal.

"What's that, a diary or something? You write stuff in there and draw, too?"

He slapped at her hand and thumbed the pages. When he found what he was looking for, he began to read and he read without eloquence or pretense. "*What if we were cave people . . . ?*" He glanced up and saw that she was thinking about it. "*What if we were cave people,*" he read, "*& lived in caves & ate Woolly Mammoth & had no language except signing & pictures on debatable walls?*"

"Is that a poem?" she said. "What if we loved rocks?"

"*What would we think when lightening struck & trees came undone, their limbs swaying like civilized dreams & fire smoothed away the dark?*"

"What if I loved you, would you bring me flowers?"

"*What if we crawled into our TV sets as though they were caves & language meant nothing, except to some young boy, a girl, the stuttering beat of a heart like roots or grafts going deep into the flesh of generations & our emotions were as dull as bread & the only thing left was the curiosity of dogs sniffing among the rubble of another white hot blast deep inside the guts of CNN?*"

"What of our desire for rain?" She swooned toward him.

"*If we were cave people & lived in TV sets & ate the transistors & had no way of communicating except by graffiti on subway walls, would deep thoughts & the language of gypsies keep our children intact?*"

"That's not what it says." She leaned against him and he could feel how soft the surprise and shape of her breast. "You substituted the word 'gypsies' for—look at that—'computers.'" She had her finger on the margin of the page, all doodled and illustrated with images from the poem, and she kept it there.

"*What if there was no way back,*" he continued, aware of her breath on his face, "*& gravity undid itself & the world entire fell away & left us floating in space: TV sets, automobiles, computers, the fancy china of a five-star restaurant, noodles & that sort of thing, a cow floating by good as the nursery rhyme that started it all, a saber-toothed tiger gooey with tar & the little white blink of the world eons toward eternity?*"

"What if there was no way back," she repeated dreamily.

"*What if there was no way back & when we flipped channels reception was bad, even the Flintstones—everything scrolling, ghostly, & a high-pitched buzz.*"

She followed the last lines with the point of her nail, up close and perfectly rigid in the bronze light from the lamp, and when she looked at him, he could see incredulity of a sort simmering in her eyes.

"That's real poetic," she told him and brushed her lips with her tongue, and it made him want to believe she was genuinely impressed. "Did you write that?" She looked again at the poem. "'Everything scrolling, ghostly, and a high-pitched buzz.' I don't know what it means exactly, not with the head anyways, but it gets in the gut and up close to the heart. Tell me, Cowboy, who are you?"

"Who am I?"

"Who am I inside your head?"

He shrugged, turned to another place in his journal and softly read: "*At night in the wind, all dreamscape, your voice untangling close to the woods, simply mist & shivering leaves.*" He paused, but couldn't bring himself to look at her, then continued. "*If they held me against my will to complete an image, I would call your eyes gentle, your voice soft singing. I would say you were the bright bead of this poem, a promise of pearls.*" He closed the journal and put it back in the bag. He didn't have anything more to explain to her and suddenly wished he hadn't read any of it at all, especially these last few lines he had jotted on a whim, and he refused to look at her, and then he looked at her and wondered what had compelled him and was embarrassed for it.

She handed him back the picture of his parents, her eyes soft and luminous as the reflection of twin moons off the black surface of a pond. And then her face poured toward him, one look after another: brazen, dissatisfied, thoughtful, anguished, tender. "You wrote that about me?" Her voice was a hush. "A promise of pearls." It was as though she couldn't hold it inside her, and letting it go with one slow expiring breath, she came full circle, picking tenderly at the remnants of an earlier thread.

"Your father, he was a poet," she said. "Maybe you're him come back in the form of some sad and joyful exchange, either blessing or curse. That's what I meant by 'the father of yourself, except for Time.' Maybe you're him come back."

"What? The seed of myself?"

She was all yellow in the light from the lantern, her face, her arms, her hands, and then he saw that he was too. And she was breathing funny, as though standing on a precipice looking down. And he could feel the weight of her heart beneath his ribs, how it beat there. It was keeping ahead of itself, and she took a breath to catch up. He took a breath.

"'Stone walls do not a prison make—"

"What?"

"—nor iron bars a cage.'"

She looked at him.

"Like riddles," he explained, "the paradox. Father of myself. A child does not a father make," and as he said it, he puzzled over it, "nor fathers childhood."

Her eyes were a study in wonder and awe. "O, yes," she said. "And there's truth in the riddle." She lay her hand over his and damaged his heart with a look. "If we are who we are because of our parents, had our parents been other then who would we be? Brother and sister? Mother and son? Husband and wife? Stone walls," she said. "Even when riddles don't make a bit of sense, they do, and still you can't get them right in your head, like maybe they speak more to the heart than the head."

He watched the strange familiarity of her mouth as she spoke and wondered if Miss Butler had understood something all along, more than he knew, trying to get it inside the numbskulls of her students; something Gypsies, too, had understood for thousands of years, more than any philosopher, understood as a way of life, understood more with the heart than the head.

"Look at me, Cowboy. Your promise of pearls. Look at me if you want to see a paradox. No, I mean *look* at me." She touched his jaw with her hand and brushed her lips with her tongue and there was language in each gesture she made. "You have the eyes of your father and your mother's mouth," she told him. And then, raising an eyebrow and again dipping her tongue between her lips, she lowered her voice and said something that only a

Gypsy might say, and it didn't surprise him at all. "Seek the truth, Cowboy. No matter the contradictions. Remember to seek the truth, whether in the paradox or the riddle, whether in the blessing or the curse, and be prepared to suffer the consequences." As she spoke, she let her eyes wander across his face, from his mouth to his eyes and back to his mouth. She looked at him slowly, and the movement of her eyes over his face was as sensory as touch. She closed and opened her own eyes as the self-conscious subject of a poem might. "Serenade me, Cowboy. Play me a tune with that thing. Bring me back to earth, to the world we live in now. I want to see the music in your eyes. I want to see your mouth caressing that harp."

At first he could hardly play the harmonica, his mouth was so dry. He laughed uneasily.

She laughed, too. "Pucker," she said.

He slipped his tongue back and forth between his closed lips, wetting them good. He tapped the harmonica against the palm of his hand, then riffled out some of "Old Joe Clark" and after that a snatch of "Wildwood Flower."

"You got talent, Cowboy. I wouldn't of dreamed you could play like that, kissing such notes out of that little bar. "What else do you write in your journal? Lemme see that sketchbook." She snaked a hand toward his backpack. "Fanny Who?"

"Give me that."

She held the book away from him and thumbed a page or two, mumbling words to herself while he tried to reach across her, confusing his hands with her breasts. "O, Cowboy." She jammed a shoulder beneath his jaw, fending and holding the book at arm's length toward the light, read. "' . . . sparing no part of me.' O! 'His touches were so exquisitely wanton, so luxuriously diffused and penetrative at times—' now listen, '—that he had made me perfectly rage with titillating fires . . . my breasts hard as apples.'" She glanced down at herself, as did he, and then back up and smack in his eyes and he tried to laugh and then tried not. "O, Cowboy, you write that kind of stuff in your journal? Next to your poems about me?"

"Hardly."

"But you read this stuff and think about that little cheerleader, don't you? Watch your hands, Cowboy."

He ripped the book out of her hands and jammed it back in the pack, and she leaned into him with a red-mouthed pout, stifling a giggle. "Serenade me again," she baby-talked him, "or read me another poem. I like watching you make love to your harmonica. I like watching your lips pucker."

"Doesn't anything embarrass you?"

"That's for me to know and for you to find out. Serenade me or read me something from that big book, Cowboy. Something profound. We'll both be obsolete before we know it. Read me about cowboys and Gypsies and the end of the world."

"I don't know about those things," he said, and then he added, "I was a rocking horse cowboy once, back in the used to be, and then I went to live with Missy and Goose. Now there are no cowboys left." He scrambled to find the place in the anthology where he had been reading earlier, and Armanda leaned over close so that he could smell her lipstick and perfume and follow along.

"See here? One paradox after another. *The sun illuminates only the eye of the man, but shines into the eye and the heart of the child . . . he who has retained the spirit of infancy even into the era of manhood.*"

"Now isn't that the truth?" She leaned back to gather a thought. " . . . into the eye and the heart of the child," she repeated, deliberating, "like our telephone call to the sheriff," and her forehead was at work. "What those two morons need is a curse, and I've got just the one."

Evan puzzled the mental gymnastics required to make the leap from Emerson's comment on the spirit of youth to the crimes of Missy and Goose. But it was clear to Armanda, every apparent irony and nuance. The glow from the Coleman lantern darkened her eyes and deepened the yellow of her face and hands.

She closed the book for him and stood up and gathered her Gypsy garb about her waist and rummaged in the cupboard for paper and pen. She reached over the sink, stretching, so that the skirt hiked up along her calves and her blouse drew taut, and with X-ray vision, he thought he could see the wonders of his heart: those long tapering legs without too much flesh in the calves, that shapely waist, those hips, the very bones of her shaped beneath the hollow of her throat, her jaw, still growing into every cell of herself and snatching his wits along the way. The images were shameful and sullied and tender and chaste. Everything he might long for but nothing he could fathom or grasp. She turned her face to this lover of uncontained and immortal beauty and devoured him with her eyes.

"What? Can't determine whether their Jonathan or Delicious?"

"?"

"You were looking at me, Cowboy."

"Was I?"

"Like Adam about to partake."

"You're pledged, remember?"

"We each got our demons," she said.

"Yeah. And you're mine."

She sat down beside him on the cot, not too close this time. They both laughed and he felt a minnow in his gut. She had a pad of lined paper, an envelope, and a pen. "Tell me their address," she said. "I put this garb on just to tease you, and now you got me all hot and out of breath." He gave her the address and watched her write. Her handwriting looked sensible, a little small but not cramped, easy to read. "This will hurt them better than voodoo," she said, and asked him a couple of questions about dates.

Dear Missy, she wrote,

> *Ask your husband about that Mexican woman who spent the afternoon last week when you were in Farmington to the flower show. Ask him about your sister and how he used to diddle her up in the barn loft before she got ate by the hogs. Ask him about the Minersville Hotel.*

She signed it, *A Friend Who Knows.* Then she folded the note in thirds, put it in the envelope, and sealed the flap with her tongue. "You get to lick the stamp," she said. "That way it'll be ours together. There will be a bond between us. When we think of the consequences of this curse, when we hear it, no matter where, no matter how far apart we are, who we're married to or how long it's been since we've seen each other, even a millennium, we can say, 'That's ours. Armanda's and mine. Evan's and mine.' We won't tell a soul, until death do us part. We'll never tell anyone, ever, we wrote it." She held the stamp up for him to lick and along with it the tips of her fingers. He felt wicked and dangerously mature.

He forgets who snatched him away from the State, who fed and clothed him from the day she croaked and who give him a home. What inheritance? He don't even know and can't touch it anyway until college or his twenty-first. Who'd of thought such insurance dumped in a trust. It was a revelation to us. You work, you slave. Petition this court and that, but nothing, that trust so tight you can't pry it apart with a mallet or a maul, not even for basic human need you can't. Nothing, that's what we get out of it, nary a cent. And who does he think put the shoes on his feet? Us left in the lurch with a kid not our own. What a ingrate. Somebody had to take the time to knock some sense in his head. I remember the day after we got him, first time up to the table he starts to dunk his eggs like any sissy would with a crust of toast, so I cuff him right off. No wimps in this house, says I. You'll eat 'em runny or over hard and cut 'em with a fork. Can't tell me the sting of the strop didn't toughen that hide. Bloodied his nose a few times to learn him everything about boxing I learnt in the Army. And the funny thing, even with them girly eyes of his, he didn't seem to care. I'd wap him, the gloves all smeared with blood, and he'd come back for more, either for spite or for pain. I couldn't tell. I guess he somehow come out on top in the end, me cursed by the devil herself.

~12~

The Fortune

He could see in her eyes a glow of confidence, of trust.

AFTER she sealed and stamped the envelope, she kicked off her shoes and sat down on the cot across from him. He watched as she pulled an ankle up to her knee and massaged her foot, at the same time allowing him to puzzle the shape of her tapering calf and up beneath the hem of her skirt the shape of her that couldn't be seen. She smiled a little groan of satisfaction, and the sound and image together moved him, and moved him toward the vague impression that he was nothing more than a remnant of her silly whim, less the seed of himself than the seed of her Gypsy schemes, even the tiniest blossoming seed. A breeze wafted through the doorscreen and after it the smell of raw earth and honeysuckle. In the narrow light from the lantern, she studied him gravely. He could feel the wire-rimmed spectacles on his face, and he looked at her through them.

"I like the feel of you, Cowboy."

She said it with meaning, in spite of herself, and brushed her lips with her tongue. A slight parting of lips and those merciless eyes, but he was in her head, the image of him, and some notion beyond that, and he wondered at such possibility, what he might be in her mind and her heart and what she had meant.

She released her foot with a sigh and eyed him quizzically and he turned his eyes away and nodded at the old valise—the *bujo* bag, she had called it—where it sagged open beside her. After sealing the envelope, she had rummaged through the bag, produced a pinch of "goat's hair," and without explanation sprinkled it over the address then brushed it away.

He was about to ask her what else was in the thing.

"Ghost's Vomit," she said. "Devil's Shit."

She dug through the bag and tossed him one thing after another: garlic bulbs, goat's hair, tarot cards, black pepper. "You have the ailment and the Reverend Mother Salloway's got the cure. Hemorrhoids, convulsions, fits." She flung toward him a yellowish rock-like substance shot through with streaks of red. "Aromatic as the inside of an outhouse, but Gypsies'll pay a hundred dollars for a chunk of *johai*—Ghost's Vomit. Cures hemorrhages to headaches, impotence to infidelity. And here's one—diarrhea to mental illness." She tossed him a hard black lump, a cinder of some sort, and he fingered it and pinched it toward his nose. "Grind that up and sprinkle it in a hot tea, you're lucid as an archangel and plugged as a nickel."

"Devil's Shit?"

But she was hefting the gazing ball, all shadowy and yellowish in the faint light, and half leaning, dumped it in his lap. He could see his own surprise in the sudden O of her mouth, and then she slouched back, trying not to laugh, but did—in spite of his pain.

"Heavy bugger," she said.

He gritted his teeth and gathered and turned the crystal in his lap, glared back at himself. It looked like a huge snow globe with some yellowish murk stewing inside. To keep it secure on flat surfaces, a thin pedestal had been attached to it. Evan turned it over and held it toward the light, an after-chuckle seizing him from time to time between ripples of pain. When he finally got hold of himself, he peered into the wintry depths, saw his own bespectacled face centered there, holographic, tiny, elongated and squashed. Beyond that, it was difficult to focus on anything in particular; though, beneath his own reflection, dark shadows seemed to swim in and out of view. Study the ball and its depths long and hard enough and you might be able to convince yourself of anything . . . images of either desire or dread.

"See something?"

He rotated the crystal and scooped it back in his lap. "What do you want me to see?"

He could tell a thing ran through her mind, and she muttered as though to the spirits and tittered self-consciously. She came over and sat down beside him and took his hands in her lap and rolled open his fingers. The wound on the underside of his wrist was scabbed over now, since she'd kept it dressed with some dank goo.

"Soon be a scar," she said. "Scars assure us that our pasts are true, that each man's past is his and his alone. We recall forever the things that caused them, don't we? Scars. Especially the unhealing ones deep inside, them invisible to the eye that no salve can cure."

She set her eye on him until he blinked. When he blinked, she smiled and turned each of his hands palm down, letting them rest in her lap. She studied the fingers of each hand, their shape, flexibility, form. Then, with only the tips of her fingers beneath his, she elevated his hands, studying again in detail, it seemed, the shape of hands and fingers, rugosity of flesh, the knottiness or smoothness of knuckles, spread of the fingers, relative size and spread of the thumbs and webbing in relation to the hands as a whole. Again, she turned the hands over. Relaxed and extended before him, they seemed detached, palms up, fingers curling a bit.

"Tell me I'm going to take a journey and I'll use them to strangle you."

She gave him an odd, heartfelt look, so brief he couldn't be sure—a self-betrayal of sorts—and gestured him silent. With eyes downcast, she went on with her examination, commenting on the color, the clarity of lines, the relative hollowness of the palms, the similarities and differences of the two. She rolled the fingers of the right hand into a fist and gave it back to him. With an index finger she caressed the left palm, probing for firmness, touching lightly the ball of the thumb. His stomach rose and sank with each caress. The light from the lantern poured upon their hands together, her own fingers so slender and long and brown with chewed, tapering nails a brooding red, and when she touched the palm of his hand, her touch was cold.

"I make fun," she said, rueful, "of the old woman's stories, of Gypsy ways and traditions. But, like *mamio* says, there's much to respect . . . and believe." And then she whispered something about how it always amazed her "how much we are our hands."

With the tip of her fingernail she traced the path of his lifeline, showing him where it began just beneath the knuckle of his index finger—"the Mount of Jupiter," she called it—and swooped down around the base of his thumb. Unbroken, she explained, except for a small cross intersecting the upper third.

"O, yes. Here's the possibility of it. Look here. How our lives intersect. What *mamio* saw in your palm the first night we met. See it here in mine?" But what he saw without explanation was the ridge of a scar ever so faint drawn across her palm, the runnel of it cresting at the sides and red as a brand. "And here, how the wisdom of perfection is within each of us to be as good as we will." She was intent on the comparison for a moment and then withdrew her hand from his. "Whether destiny or fate or nothing but chance, herein lies all that might be."

She touched again the tiny, nearly indistinguishable, square containing the point of intersection and it seemed to reassure her. If danger could be expected so could protection.

"What about a month from now? Next year?"

"That's hard to read," she admitted. "With this line there's some confusion. But I'll say this much. You can put aside your feelings of guilt and expect a number of beginnings, if nothing else—false starts, and other possibilities. And look. If given enough

THE GYPSY LOVER ·187·

time, you're bound to struggle through to your own capabilities, to what, in fact, you are—regardless of any obstacles."

"To what in fact I am?"

"I've already named it," she said.

She grew quiet, seeing something in a crease. She began to say, then hesitated, but when he urged her without a word, without a look, spoke to her with the tick of his thumb, she went on. Just as there had been one separation by death in his life, another appeared close at hand, though she couldn't be sure. She puzzled for a time, her forehead pinched, her touch disturbed; then she traced her nail across his palm in the shape of an X.

"Ominous," he joked. But she didn't look up.

"Now this is your head line. Look at mine. See how it sweeps between the thumb and index finger, just above the start of the lifeline, and travels more or less horizontally across the middle of the palm. There, how it slopes toward the Mount of the Moon? Curiosity. Imagination. Intelligence, say. And here, where it curves down toward the heel of the hand, toward the Mount of the Moon—" He thought she hesitated. A shadow crossed her brow and her throat got low with words. "—an ability to see beyond this world. To mark the unseen from the seen. To understand more with the heart than the head."

"You're nuts."

She said that was beside the point, that regardless of what he thought about her or this world, he was bound to agonize more over the seeing of a thing than over the thing seen and that agony would serve him well. He hadn't the slightest idea what she meant by that, but his heart line, aside from all the grief and trouble in his life, whether she knew it or not, was in her hands.

Her face was painfully close, and he was staring at a fascinating little pockmark set among the freckles between her eyebrows. Below the border of the headscarf he could see the minute down over the surface of her forehead. He could also see that her eyes were black, really black, like ink or a raven's wing or a black pearl, and so soft, so luminous they seemed to melt all over her face. She muttered a sort of lovelorn warning, but it was belated: he had already given his heart away without much thought.

In the end, since his fate line was so weak and hard to find, she supposed he would triumph over destiny. "Regardless of any obstacles," she repeated. "And something *mamio* may have missed."

"You could say this stuff about anybody," he complained.

She raised an eyebrow and with an irritating grin held him with her eyes for a moment longer than necessary, and though the reading was over, continued to hold his hand. He felt liquid, like oil, as if his shoulders were sliding down into his arms. She opened and closed the fingers, lacing them with her own, and he wondered if she could feel the pulse of his heart in her hand.

"Feel that?" She looked at him again. "That's my heartbeat in the palm of your hand. I can feel yours in mine." She spoke to him earnestly, and he could see the image of his face in her eyes. She eased her grip and he could feel her heartbeat, quick, like breath. "That's why I like you, Cowboy. Your face shows everything you feel. The way you look at me . . . the bright bead of your poem. I know what's happening," she said. "It's dangerous, but I have feelings too. I love *papo* that way . . . and *mamio*. And *papo*, he loves me . . . sometimes thinking I'm *mamo* come back from the dead. Blood is nothing between us, he is so in love with me. I could love another, I'm sure . . . with a sort of unattached devotion, maybe."

Evan hesitated and then it was too much and he took a chance, working inward from an angle, and all the time she continued to hold his hand even though their breathing was out of synch.

"Discovery," he muttered, contemplating the ragged edge to his voice. "Like when I dropped my bag and had to climb down from the rafters, the whole world opening up, like that, or maybe one of your riddles undone. All of you—you're *papo* and *mamio* and you—you're like the Grand Canyon, and I'm standing on the brink."

It came out every bit as stupid as he was afraid it would, but

Armanda didn't laugh. The little they knew of each other they had discovered so quickly; there were worlds still to discover, worlds that lay within their hands and their hearts that he felt she, like he, longed to explore. Yet in the world of worlds he knew there were those beyond their grasp and better afar than within reach, because a mislaid touch, a careless hand, would shatter them like glass.

"Don't worry over it," she said, plucking thoughts from his brain, and she yawned a yawn of dismissal. "It's a matter of fate more than any discovery or choice, both of us doomed by some commonplace spell. Here, Cowboy, scoot back."

She nudged him back against the wall. The crystal rolled between his legs, and a world between them came pouring out. In that world, their own world, the world they had fashioned through sarcasm and simple-minded quips, the world fabricated to mask their suspicions and fears, the still-developing world of longing that she had so casually dismissed, in this world of re-definition and possibility and hope, he longed for the way she had called him "Cowboy," as though it were truly his name, identifying him in a sense far broader than the flesh attached to his bones, including even more than the mechanism that made it all hang together and gave him both substance and form. In this world, a gesture as simple as her dropping his hand for a mo-ment to brush at an errant twig of hair then taking it up again was a gesture that made him feel complete. Her fingers were so long and thin, and he could feel the edges of her fingernails where she bit them. So difficult to imagine her biting her nails. In this world. So difficult to imagine her growing tired just then, such energy. Her eyes remained bright and black as olives and the lamplight only added to the luster of her skin. If that other world, the world she held before him, not their world together, a world with all the clarity of the vacant crystal, but that separate one, hers, was filled with beasts, he could not see them. If there was black language on the airwaves, he could not hear it. Blind, deaf, and speechless, he traced the contour of her hand and ran a finger lightly across the lines of her palm, pausing to flick that nearly invisible ridge of a scar.

"You telling my fortune, now?" She whispered sleepily, clasping his hand between hers and holding it in her lap. "Tell me about devotion, Cowboy Evan. The love of it. I know the heartache. Tell me about tomorrow and the next day and the day after that." She whimpered something indistinguishable and seemed a little embarrassed for it and sort of braced herself against him and tipped her head toward his face.

He could smell the winsome, slightly bitter odor of her hair and feel her own warm hands about his where she laced his fingers in the pocket of her lap. Alta Mae came to him with a rush and he could feel her slippery mouth softening his behind the gym. And then he saw something and tried to turn away and his head was suddenly light and he hadn't the strength to turn his head or even shut his eyes. Armanda's blouse lay open, pushed to one side by the heavy jewelry, revealing the partial sphere of her breast. This was no fantasy now. As she breathed, it rose and quivered minutely for all its firmness. He looked at her daringly, a promising view of the dark areola and its tightening bud. It surprised him, too, how unprotected, vulnerable, innocent, she had suddenly become. His surprise diminished the desire he felt, filled him with shame, and moved him to such tenderness toward her he felt his heart would break.

She moved her head against his arm, at first tentatively, then to the crook of his neck, and sang wistfully in that taunting voice:

My mother said I never should . . .

She said his name, softly, not "Cowboy" this time, but *Evan*, and it brought him around to the narrowness of that other world. It brought him around to the world she stood in apart from his, from theirs. "I've never told anyone this before," she confided. "So you have to promise, because maybe I'm crazy somehow, so you have to promise me because you've probably never had such a demented notion, never wanted to get outside of yourself?"

His mouth was against her hair, and he watched as her breast rose and fell and he watched as she breathed. After a while, she held her face up to his, and even in the subdued light from the lantern, he could see it in her eyes, such knowing and pain, and he felt drawn toward her and, for the moment, very much older than she and even a little protective and thankful that she had allowed him this wistful and harmonious trust.

"Outside of yourself?"

"Demented. What did I say?" Her voice rose a pitch. "Crawl right up inside you, through blood and guts and bone, right up inside you to see out your eyes."

He listened to the silence, broken only by the spitting of the lantern and a waver in the light and tried again to see.

"I have wishes," she said.

"Wishes?" He acknowledged her with a press of his mouth against her hair, no more the world of a lighthearted curse.

"What I wish I'd never said. What I wish I'd never seen. What I wish I'd never done. What I wish I'd never wished."

The light of the lantern hissed on, more a torment than a blessing to the dark.

"Sometimes," her voice softened and she was thinking about it as she spoke, "I feel as if someone has taken an ax and cleft me in two."

The lantern light dimmed. Outside, a coyote yelped.

"Sometimes I'd like to get out of this world for a while and then come back and start all over again." She looked at him.

"Me too."

"There's an old Gypsy saying that goes, 'I did not come to you to beg for bread, I came to you to demand respect.'"

He heard somewhere in the loose hanging night a bell that tolled and ceased where no bell should be and knew there was none, wondered if she, too, had heard this ghostly knell. But she gave no evidence of it. It tolled but once, and he listened for a moment for another, but his listening was vain. As he listened, she drew her legs up and swung them to one side, tucking her feet beneath her, sitting against him now like an S. She spoke and as she spoke from time to time she raised her face to see his expression or to make sure he was listening.

"A parallel universe, that's what I hope for. Some window to step through, maybe at death, like stepping through a mirror and meeting my image half way. And *mamo*, she goes on among my other without looking back, loving me the way I long for, loving *papo* who's there as well, and even *mamio* and why not you—"

"Everyone's doppelganger among the goblins and ghosts of your own hopeful wit?"

"Call it what you will, but you know as do I from where the longing comes."

"O, yes."

"I just hope I'm existing even now, my other self, among those I love and the possibility of you."

"In a world other than this?"

"We must forgive them," she said.

The moon was up and Evan could see it through the port-hole window above her cot, where it iced the tops of trees in the distance and whitened the night. He listened to her and as he listened he wondered if he should tell her about his dream of her coming down out of the mountains astride that golden mare, the lightening, the river, the rain. And what of the belabored dreams of his childhood: the darkeyed rivergirl, his mother, and the man on the curb? She was such a wiz at palmistry, maybe her interpretation of dreams would center everything, bring it all together, position the past and the present in the larger scheme of his expectations and clarify every last riddle she posed.

Forgive who? he wanted to ask.

But Armanda's voice had grown tired and the lantern spit. Evan pitied her for who knows what and felt at the same time he hadn't the right. She could have talked for hours and left him with little more than a stupefied soul. As now, for instance, this eerie *deja vu*, his mind orbiting the sudden clarity of her unchecked words. All caught up in the intermingling of dreams, some not his own. And what matter his dreams? A sense of dread filled him, both familiar and dull.

"I lied to you, Cowboy."

Just like that, out of the blue. The other world was not half so frightening, nor so dangerous, as the one from which he drew his daily breath.

"She was small and so much alone, my *mamo,* lost beneath the Gypsy stars, composed of nothing more than seconds and minutes all rolled up into flesh, her every breath a pulse of blood from the heart."

She struggled for a moment, trying, and then let it go.

"Until that scarf all noosed about her neck. O, yes. There was no tumor. She just gave up."

If he was standing on the rim of the Grand Canyon looking for discoveries a thousand feet down, she had just given him a shove toward one. Each word she spoke gathered inside him with the same icy clarity of the moon in the trees beyond the window of the truck. The reality of death was one thing, and the sorrow had been hers; chasing phantoms and spooks about the country was another. It was all so fantastic, deliberately fantastic, for the sake of avoiding anything real.

Evan wanted to touch her, to touch her hair, to touch her face, to touch her breast, but, wanting, he said instead, "Were you close to her?"

Armanda pressed against him and sobbed in a hollow sort of way. "Like you're close to a graveyard. But I understood her. *Papo, mamio*—they didn't understand. They're Gypsy. Can't. She was lonely and frightened, and I don't mean of your everyday horrors, either, like whether life has any meaning, or whether some terrorist lobs a missile toward New York, or whether there's a truckers' strike and we become a bunch of savages pillaging for food. I don't mean of boogeymen lurking in old houses or things that go bump in the night or even the goblins of dreams. No. She was just alone, her stars scattered all around, so out of place in our world and dragging *papo* more and more into hers." Her voice got low and the whisper harsh. Her words painted a vague impression and his mind grew dense with the breadth of emotions she must have felt. "Her ax was blunt. Grief is the blunt ax that takes you from behind." She allowed him the desperation in her voice and in the clutch of her hand. "O, Cowboy, I don't want to be *gaji*. I don't want to be Gypsy. I want to be me."

A glance in the mirror and the reflecting surface gives back the immediate room—the sofa, the table, the overstuffed chair and antique organ, a corner of soiled carpet, your aunt and uncle's portrait, like stiff, unloving Victorian folk—but not so much as a hint of human presence.

Why did he think of that?

He didn't want to think of anything other than this soft, luminous creature whose body folded lightly into his, her hair slightly damp, and tiny beads of perspiration sparkling her brow. Missy, Goose, and the rest could evaporate and he would still never unhitch himself from the unaccountable longing he felt in his soul. He placed a hand on her head and smoothed back her hair, and she allowed him, even closing her eyes and nuzzling her face toward his hand. And then she was still. Her murmuring ceased as the cool trill of crickets rose. Leaning against him she was soon asleep. He measured the climate of her breathing, his eyes tired, his arm growing numb with the weight of her. He had difficulty focusing, then remembered he was still wearing his father's spectacles. Although the lantern had dimmed to a steady irritating glow, he could not reach to extinguish it without disturbing her. He looked, but the swell of her breast was lost in the shadows and folds of her blouse.

With his free hand, he nudged the crystal, still in his lap, toward the light. Vision blurred. Something within the murky depths stirred and rose to the surface, and it was the image of a dead woman's face. The small hooded lids of her eyes rested lightly shut; her hair rose and fanned and fell like dark swaying fronds of seaweed—or so it seemed in the roiling, gathering, evaporating mist of the crystal. The ball slipped sideways in his hand and the face appeared to recede. He realized he had shut his eyes to let a convulsion shake him. His heart pumped sludge and he felt the hair stand up on the back of his neck. When he looked again, the image was gone—until he rolled the crystal back toward the light.

The face heaved up at him, openeyed.

"Cowboy?"

He jerked his hand from Armanda's lap and swallowed the slop in his throat.

"Did you see something?"

They gazed in the crystal together.

"A woman?"

Evan stood up and pumped up the lantern a little. It must have been the angle of shadows and light, a flaw in the glass struck at the wrong time by pieces of light. He took off the eyeglasses, fogged them with his breath, and using the coverlet of the cot, wiped them clean. He cleared his throat.

Armanda was fussing with the pedestal on the bottom of the globe. He saw what she was doing and knelt in front of her, keeping the light between them until she managed to get a grip on the pedestal as he held the ball between his hands.

"I told you." She pried at the pedestal with her fingernails. She picked up one of her shoes and using the stiletto heel tapped around the edge.

"A flaw in the glass," he said. "I must have dozed."

"Call it what you want, Cowboy. A flaw. A dream. A ghost. It all amounts to the same thing, don't it? Your head line, where it curves down to the heel of your hand . . . that ability to see more than most." The pedestal came unstuck from the bottom of the globe and she pried out a wallet-size photograph.

"The thing's a trick, then?"

"Is this what you saw?" She handed him the black and white

photo, and he raised it to the light. It was the face of a man with cropped hair, a stubby mustache, and eyes that looked back at him like watery grapes.

"The thing's a sham," he said. "Done with little mirrors and photographs. A magnifying lens."

"I thought you said it was the face of a woman you saw."

He handed the photograph back to her. A finger of sweat slipped from beneath his armpit and chilled his ribs. He described for her in detail the image that had risen from the depths, hair floating and receding as if in a tumultuous sea. It could have been the face of his own mother, he realized.

"Or the face of mine."

The lantern hissed for a moment, brightened, then sputtered and dimmed. Armanda screwed the pedestal back on the bottom of the globe while Evan pumped up the lamp, the last few drops of kerosene sustaining a meager glow. He went to the back of the camper, threw open the screen door, and put his head out to spit. Something roosted in the shadows of a tree, dark and indiscernible but there. He closed the door and locked it.

"Sit over here, Cowboy. I feel spooky."

He went to her and put his arm around her and pulled her back beside him on the cot, and as he did the lantern flickered.

"What was that?"

"Somebody crying it sounds like."

"You hear it then?"

"O, I hear it. A coyote, maybe. Or some kind of bird."

They looked around the cramped interior of the camper, and began a meaningless vigil of childish, inadmissible fright. He said nothing of the shadow he had seen in the tree. What she had produced from the *bujo* bag was enough; it crawled within both of them now, and Evan knew she felt lighter for it, and even as uncomfortable as he felt having discovered the face in the crystal, he was nevertheless glad.

I could see from the beginning that he was a boy after something deeper than even I could give, and I have the knack of giving more than most. *Mamio* says his is the unrevealing temperament of an artist, but I know that, like me, it is only the hope of surviving desire. The way he looked at me, so literate and puppy-eyed, I couldn't but choose to write that note. Take the source of evil, *mamio* would say, and reshape it for good in the palm of your hands. Figuratively speaking. She would say we are each the recipients of one another's blessings and the victims of one another's sin. But there was no curse I laid on them they hadn't already laid on themselves. He who sows ill reaps ill, or something to that effect. Live by the sword, die by the sword, doesn't the Bible say? Although from experience I know a sprinkling of goat's hair can't hurt, together with a few muttered charms. And who wouldn't fling a curse for the sake of the beguiled or ill-used? Every line in his palm told me more than I wanted to know, how ours is a passion play, begun long before we met in this world, and will forever be. I tell you, when the final curtain rings down, the play will go on.

~13~

Her Champion

The dark knight folded . . . his guts a quaking moil.

THE next day Evan found himself on a street corner selling paper flowers. Though, in truth, he knew he was chasing Armanda's soul for something wise and substantial to cling to, something preferable to the unrealized victim of himself, and the paper flowers were but a ruse. He had changed into a pair of Levis and a blue work shirt and further defined himself by rolling up his sleeves, so tan and sinewed in the biceps. Armanda, she was the epitome of his imagination, a stereotype of her own worst dreams, betrayed by everything from the long pleated skirt and dime-store jewelry to the painted face, from the wedge of bandanna to the hair that fell in a long plaited braid to the middle of her back with all the force of an exclamation point. But it was her blouse that argued fact: a sheer, boat-necked silky thing with blood-red flowers. The material clung to her in a petting way and billowed around the nearly perfect shape of her indefatigable breasts.

"Car-stoppers," she explained, shameless.

Above them, the aluminum sky flattened out with an odd, soundless clang. An odor of burning leaves and bus exhaust draped the caged trees along the sidewalk and hugged the buildings and hung in the alleyways like a tangible rag. It was downtown rush hour and traffic was growing heavy. Men in striped suits and women wearing skirts and jackets appeared and disappeared in frazzled droves. On both sides of the street and in the adjacent square pigeons strutted and cooed, some hopping with a disgruntled flap as weary feet advanced.

Earlier, Nikolai had checked his little band into a sleazy motel. He had gone briefly into the dark office and emerged with cabin key #7, a sturdy brass skeleton. The cabin was situated between scrubby oak trees, past the shed of an office with its ugly green trim, and he handed Evan the key, as though conferring upon him some right of passage, and said, "Open her up."

Evan looked at Armanda.

"He means the door, stupid."

He put the key in the lock, but Armanda reached out and stilled his hand. "Mother Salloway's *ofisa*," she said. "If only you knew what you were in for."

"Open her up. The goddamn door," said Nikolai.

Evan felt the pressure of Armanda's hand and the whisper of her breath, and together, they turned the key in the lock.

"Same dump as last year," she griped, entering. She sucked her teeth and unloaded her handbag to the coffee table and flopped facedown on the unmade bed. "No A/C."

Evan's eyes went to the wall next to the bed, where, beneath a ballooning cobweb, a big rust-colored stain was all streaked from scrubbing. It stood out like a patch of blood someone had labored over to remove without success. Stilled in time and with unaccountable memories, the little room had stories to tell.

"Bring in that big trunk," Yana told him. "You know the one."

"And my suitcase," said Armanda.

"Lemme give a hand," offered Nikolai. But the mad Gypsy was already slouched on the sofa and made no attempt at getting up.

"What time is it?" asked Evan, but if he'd spoken, they had

all gone deaf. Lackey, toady, slave. He turned to open the door, and space wallowed back on itself, got dense. Outside, beyond the oaks, the sun struck the camper and blurred the images in a sordid glare. Evan had to think to put one foot in front of the other and to step around the weeping paint. It was all over the road, in puddles and rivulets and diluted smears. At least so it appeared beneath the blathering sun and gloom from the oaks. A needle of light touched the back of his eye, and he worked to remember why he was here. He hopscotched his way around this blotch and that, looked back to see the crow on an overhead branch. It watched him but hadn't made a sound. The suitcase and trunk, he told himself. Twice, he had to dance back over the shadows and beneath the roosting bird. When he returned with the last piece of luggage, the bird wasn't there, and he glanced back at the camper to find a big ravenlike shadow splattered on the side of it then washed white by the sun. He rattled his head with a shake and yanked open the door to find Yana on the telephone.

"Setting up the *bujo*," Armanda explained. "She's calling a number of last spring's clientele."

Evan shrugged, even as she mocked the word "clientele"; he felt how futile the gesture in throwing off a weight.

"What time is it?" he asked.

"Time? Why, it's time to get rich."

Yana put her hand over the mouthpiece and whispered, "You'll know him when you see him, dear. I took a gander in the ball last night. Striped suit and walks like a duck."

Armanda tucked her hair up in the bandana and straightened her skirt while Evan tinkered with the three-channel television. "Time for *Jeopardy*," the announcer announced, but it was a re-run and Evan turned the sound down low. He used the bathroom to change his shirt then plopped himself in the overstuffed chair, inattentive and dazed by the flickering screen, bemoaning to himself both the loss and discoveries of the last few days. He refused to worry about the palette of colors awash on the back of the truck or the bird on the branch. For to think about such was like wandering into some endless night where he found only himself and thus found, found himself slipping further away, until even the dark grew empty and shrill. Even his refusal to fret was in vain, and just when a notion eased him, Yana set the phone in its cradle and Armanda said, "Cowboy?"

He flicked off the television and followed her out the door.

Overhead, the sun cropped the afternoon with absentminded finesse. Inside the truck was worse. The bug-speckled windshield made it difficult to determine the source of light and thickened the possibility of thought. Nikolai complained, but it wasn't about the light. It wasn't about the heat. He muttered a few words and drove the three of them downtown and dropped them off next to the square. He said something about driving to the suburbs to panhandle seeds or find handy work, "maybe a car with a dent to fix." Armanda argued with him, said he didn't need to go. She begged him to stay with them downtown or nap at the motel. But it was no use. He kissed her and patted her on the rump, and finally, the least she could do was get him to promise he would stay away from the bars.

"Sure, my darling. You know me."

He drove off with a flourish and a wave.

Yana grimaced and dabbed a hanky against her chin. "Walks like a duck," she said. "Striped suit." She went across the street to a Kinko's copy center to order a new batch of handbills for Mother Salloway. She came out after a while and disappeared into another store. In the course of the afternoon, Evan saw her across the street every now and then, moving with the crowds, in and out of the department stores and boutiques. Once, he saw her on the other side of the street emerging from Woolworth's, and even from that distance he could see the harried look on her wrinkled, wizened face. About her neck she hefted more gold than an Aztec god, and the pockets of her skirt grew increasingly heavy. She stepped briskly along the sidewalk, weaving between the shoppers and glancing from time to time over her shoulder. Before he knew it, she had ducked into the next shop.

"If you see a cop," Armanda warned, "pack it in."

"Is this illegal?"

She shrugged and scooted the tube of flowers toward the curb, away from a gang of punks who lallygagged beneath an awning. When she stooped to prop the tube against the wrought iron fence caging a withering tree, one of the boys waved to her. He waved, and beneath her blouse the shadow and shape of her breasts rose and fell.

"A dollar apiece," she said, her voice recognizably flat.

Evan plucked one, purple as a bruise wilting in the heat and slathered with glue, the stem twined in green tissue leaves. She reached in the tube and produced a bouquet already wrapped in a cone of green waxed paper. In reaching, the neck of her blouse ballooned like a sail catching the wind. "Now pay attention."

"I am. I am."

She gathered the flowers up and swept the braid back across her shoulder, as if sweeping away the moment, though her eyes had tales to tell, as if to torment, and he could see in the dark of those eyes that there was nothing that couldn't wait—and something else, cheerless and blue.

She said, "Now watch, Rodeo Boy," and swung around and nearly jabbed the ugly blooms up the nose of a young executive type. "For the Missus?"

The man leapt back, pigeon-toed. He slapped at the bouquet and hurried down the sidewalk, a scowl wrenching his jaw. His shoulders were hunched against the evil of it, the backs of his ears as inflamed as something private and obscene.

Armanda shrugged, and the sky rained down an uneven light that clung to her in beads of sweat. Evan could see evidence of it on her upper lip and crawling along her throat in shifts. She wiped at herself and shut her eyes from him and turned her face toward the street. There, she opened her eyes and waved to a carload of school children who sat waiting for the light to change.

"How much?" A spidery girl wearing a baggy sweatshirt detached herself from the gang of punks where they dawdled beneath the awning. They were all leather and chains, one preening an orange Mohawk, spikes glazed with gel. In the window at their backs a ribbon of neon had been molded into a steaming cup of coffee lettered "Grounds for Love." The girl edged along the curb, eyeing the blooms. "How much?" she asked. The neck of her sweatshirt, all torn, sagged over her shoulder like a hoop and bared the upper part of her arm, and on her arm a spider tattoo. She was purple-haired, wearing a biker's glove and smoking a butt. Evan could see a stud in her nose and a ring in her lip. He looked at the sky for some hint of the time and looked at the kid with the Mohawk who then looked away.

"You tell my fortune?" She thought she was being funny, with snot in her voice.

"Do I look like a Gypsy?"

"You're not from around here."

"I'm not?"

"License plate," she said. "On that calamity on wheels that barfed you and this here heartthrob up. Now, don't get all spooky with doodads and such, just tell me if Pauly be the one." She indicated the kid with the Mohawk. "We destined?"

"I wouldn't lose my head over it."

She flipped the cigarette in the gutter, flicked an eyebrow, and had a cone of flowers in her hand before Evan could react. She and her gang were falling all over themselves to get across the street in one piece. And then Armanda did something with her hands. Didn't she do something weird with her hands? Grasp and let loose the air in tangible gobs? Two handed, she flung molecules all over the street, her arms waving as though leading a band. Spider Girl saw. Spider Girl ran. She needed another few legs, scurrying across. Almost on the other side of the street, she stumbled, did a half-pirouette, and got lost in the squeal and grill of a truck. When she emerged, she flopped like a hen with its head lopped off. Purple hair ablaze, her head came spinning over the asphalt, bounced once, and thunked against the curb. At least, Evan thought it did. Not a head but a soccer ball dropped from a car. He could see them now, the truck passing between, no horn, no squeal, no bloodied grill. She took one of the flowers and stuck it in the lapel of her boyfriend's black leather jacket, like a boutonniere.

Armanda laughed, but like something you'd hear at the witching hour. *"De kurva! Jai!"* She cursed. "Little whore!" She had finished with her hands, and now tucked her blouse in her skirtwaist, pulling it taut to her breasts, and Mohawk stared while Spider Girl whapped him on the arm, for certain about to lose her head over one thing or another.

It went like that, in a sort of timeless fashion, this and that and nothing much.

A man in overalls swatted another bouquet from Armanda's hand.

"If we keep this up, we'll have to open a boutique in the downtown Mall."

She was beyond annoyed, tucked up inside herself like a blur, though still posing and jamming her finger on occasion at the punks across the street. And then Evan watched it happen as if in a dream. A car honked and a bronze Mustang came gliding out of nowhere and sleeked to a stop next to the curb. The driver, a flush-faced man with cratered nose, leaned across the passenger's seat and rolled down the window.

Armanda laid her hand on the door with all the confidence of a mesmerist. She leaned toward the window, clutching the bouquet in her fist.

"O," he sang. "Been down so long it looks like up to me."

"I don't have change," she apologized, poking the bouquet through the window, but he didn't give her the money.

"You alone?" he said, revving the engine. "That kid with you?"

She stooped and put her head and shoulders through the window to give him an extra flower. Evan saw in the gesture an absence of meaning gone astray, all in the attempt to make discoveries about love. When she pulled her head back out, he shoved the car into first and popped the clutch. She flashed him the wave of her hand, middle finger in flight. She patted and straightened her blouse, untucked it to get at the twenty, and tucked it back in, face flat as the deadpan sky.

"Ain't I your picture of woe and confusion?"

"With the face to go with it, all down in my guts."

His backhanded compliment brought the blood to her cheeks, and it surprised him when she looked away and lowered her eyes.

Three or four more cars stopped, and Evan hung back, slouching against the wrought iron spikes beneath the shade of that caged and withering tree. A skinny brunette wasted more time than any of the men, even with Armanda shaking her head to the contrary. She was pretty in a pimply sort of way and animated in the use of her hands, and she stretched toward the window of the passenger side, as if such emphasis might validate a sorrowful need. After a while, she took the flowers and paid up, a sheepish repentant look awash in her eyes. Each time, Armanda came back to show him the take, and he could see she was miserable in the doing of it except to keep self-loathing in hand.

When the sky grew dull and refused to announce itself, when traffic started to thin and the number of pedestrians grew increasingly sparse, Evan told her he thought it was time to pack it in. Even the punks across the street were gone, now banished like a troublesome thought, but she ignored him and gathered up another cone of the disgusting blooms.

"See that guy coming toward us? How his feet turn out?"

Evan glanced around as Armanda waltzed her way toward the center of the sidewalk. A lady shuffled her feet and side-stepped, gathering her shoulders against the otherwise unnoticeable chill. A man, walking fast, changed course like a robot, his mind floating somewhere in the bosom of eternity. Evan was still watching for cops when out of the corner of his eye he saw Armanda doing the plod and stomp. He knew that dance. Her partner, a staid grandfatherly type, worked overtime to follow her lead. An expensive looking attaché case swivelled and flopped in his hand. She bumped and rubbed and groped and swung him around. He tottered and clung to her for balance.

"I beg your pardon," he said when she released him. "You seem to be a pleasant enough young lady, but I'm happily married."

She was beside herself with apologies, the raunchy bouquet now trampled beneath their feet. She spoke to him in breathless nuggets and brushed at him. "O, the flowers." When she stooped to gather them up, her blouse set sail and he was in the crow's nest. Next, she was tugging him by the sleeve from the middle of the sidewalk to safer ground. His face reflected the glory of a setting sun, and she touched and pawed and cooed at him.

"Now listen, young lady." He was getting his tongue back. "No harm done. That was quite a dance." He seemed to think this wittily put and took a moment to chuckle at himself. "Here, let me—" He nodded toward the broken flowers, touching and brushing Armanda here and there, rattling off apologies to kill the time, and touching her again. He reached toward the breast pocket of his coat, but she slapped away his hand and jerked a fresh bouquet from the box, this one ugly as the rest. He reached again for his wallet, drew back a gnarled fist and accepted instead the paper flowers.

"But, dear girl—"

She shook her head emphatically, at the same time pressing his fingers around the stems—patted his lapels and brushed at his coat. She leaned toward him and gave him a peck then shooed at him, a lingering expression of encouragement, faith, and love— a wave of the hand—her middle finger up straight as a shaft, while the old man waddled into the crosswalk, feet splayed to the sides, unlike a Chairman of the Board might walk, the back of his head bewildered as the front, a raised hand clutching in simple-minded grateful fashion the horrible flowers.

"We better get."

Armanda began stabbing flowers in the carton, heedless of

any arrangement, when a longhaired drifter wearing an army jacket and rags that harked back to some forgotten time wandered up. He glanced at Evan, scrubbed the stubble of his chin, and turned to Armanda with a contemplative gaze. His eyes batted sleepily while she pretended to worry over the artificial blooms. Evan caught the stench of him, urine and B.O. mixed, the final days of living etched around his eyes. The lines and pores of his skin deeply grimed with journeys unknown except perhaps to the far side of hell. He leaned forward, rocking on the balls of his feet, stumbled over nothing, regained his balance.

"Man." He grasped a wrought iron picket and swung toward her stiff-armed and childlike. "I been around the world, from Bangladesh to Amsterdam, and never yet seen such pros."

Armanda plucked at the blooms.

"I'm talking, man." He took a final drag on the cigarette pinched between forefinger and thumb and let the stub of it fall in the gutter. He let go of the picket and swayed and chuckled and put his face up close like a curious friend. Evan could see that his eyes were different colors, the aberration giving him an imbalanced, sinister air. "Right in the middle of the street, God and his angels looking down." He spit when he spoke, the belabored words slogging up and around the lump of his tongue.

"Beat it," hissed Armanda. "Before I call a cop."

"You and what cop?" He glanced up and down the street. "I won't call no cop. He held out his hand and rubbed two of his fingers against his thumb. "Fifty-fifty and Jack Sprat keeps his mouth zipped tight."

"What the hell you talking about?" Evan sized him up, maybe forty/fifty years old, hundred and ninety pounds, though aptly named; the man swayed toward the curb and pawed himself, batted his eyes.

"We'd like to stay and chat," said Armanda. "But you got enough company with yourself there."

Evan hefted the carton to a shoulder, and together they moved up the street and crossed over to the next block. Traffic was thinning and the bustle of the afternoon had diminished; people were drifting casually between offices and stores. "*Mamio*'ll be waiting," she said, cutting down an ally. "The park's about six blocks up. *Papo* should be there, too." Her hand brushed his, and Evan looked back to see if Jack-the-Wild-Man was following. He was, sauntering behind them in a consumptive slouch, hands clasped behind his back, searching the gutter, and once, passing beneath a fire escape, he jammed himself between two ash cans, opened his fly, and took a leak.

"An image of modern times," groaned Armanda.

"If he had any more sense, he'd be a half-wit."

She giggled and frowned and lengthened her stride; they were walking fast, and she was a little out of breath.

"Tell me," he thought she said. She looked at him and the failing light spread through the lens of her eye like a wince. "Tell me about that little cheerleader you sucked face with behind the gym."

"You're the palm reader."

She looked at him and took his hand and raised and pressed the back of it against her breast. He considered putting his arm around her but didn't.

"He still there?"

"Like a rash that won't go away." He re-balanced the carton on his shoulder and tugged at her. "You tell me," he said. "Tell me about that little dance in the street." He was about to look at her, then changed his mind, then he looked at her, and her wide skirt rasped his jeans. She said nothing, and he watched her walk and her walk was a phenomenon; she slid along the pavement close to him, only her legs below the knees passing each other. A breeze caught her hair and lay naked the entire side of her face. An enormous artificial pearl hung from her left ear; in a glimpse he caught the hard delicate lobe of her ear—an object strange and perfect, as if wrought, like an artifact, by cautious, astonishing skill.

"The trouble with being a con artist," she told him at last, "is that you all too often con yourself," and she looked at him and smiled just the whisper of a smile. "But I'm a Gypsy, remember? Your Virgin Bandit. Where's that asshole now?"

They moved into the next block, the light growing anxious, a little weary, and spreading like water against the sky. Armanda turned once to say something when Evan heard the shuffle behind. The back of his head came up and clapped against his eyes. Going down he knew he had been hit and that it was a sucker punch and he tried to keep the light in his head but the world sunk around him and light collapsed. A mad black thing, either in his head or out, sucked at the light and began to shriek, and the whole sky dissolved into something fumbling along, and he hit the pavement and came back up but kneeling, on the brink of a swoon. He started to cough when flowers bloomed from his chest, so ugly and such beauty to cry for. And then he heard the sound of it even before he saw—the legs, the fists, both hammer and claw. There was a head there, wallowing back against itself, burrowing into throat and breasts and gut. Evan looked again at the sky; he had his feet now. He had the roar of the crowd, far off, in distant bleachers, on tops of buildings, in trees, all beneath the uninspired sky, he a single knight without armor, his broadsword a box . . . a roundhouse swing and the paper flowers burst in a shower of confetti against the sniveling head—for truth and honor. The dark knight folded, crouched, his guts a quaking moil. He re-inflated like a raft.

"I know a thousand ways to ruin men—"

Evan had him in agility, though Jack outweighed him.

"—I seen them flogged, burned, buried, shot, hanged, and loved—" The long arms of the doper came back at Evan, and the man whacked him good alongside the jaw. "—I seen them hacked, pierced with bayonets, blown to smithereens—"

Evan danced back, and when Mr. Sprat came at him, ducked inside and hit him three good ones in the mouth, *wap*, *wap*, *wap*, thanks to Uncle Goose. The man got hold of Evan's ear and nearly wrenched it off. He spluttered and spit.

"—dragged behind a turnip truck, shamed, trounced by fate—"

Evan saw the web of blood, like filigree, along his chin. Jack feinted left and tried to dance, but the legs weren't there. All in the same motion, he bobbed toward Evan, stumbled back, and tripped. That did more for them than an upper cut. Before the man could reclaim himself, Armanda cursed him in Romany and kicked him between his legs, hard, so that the impact of her foot lifted him off the ground. She grabbed Evan by the arm, and they went staggering then galloping up the street.

"—rent by fear, drowned in a cesspool of guilt, cursed—"

"Don't look back," said Armanda.

But they did.

The man grunted and clawed and screamed his way to his feet. He lunged after them spraddle-legged, holding on to himself, then stopped and hurled an empty fist at their backs as if flinging a volley of oaths.

Inside Evan's head a little man with a jackhammer was opening nerves. His arms ached and his knuckles throbbed. His mouth tasted metallic, like dirt and acid mixed. To his ears came a hissing and every running step jarred his lungs. Beside him, Armanda lapped air in explosive gasps. Her chest heaved in time with his. Her blouse was ripped at the neck and she held the flap of it in place. He couldn't tell if she was bleeding or if it was just the blood-red material of her blouse.

"Did he hurt you?"

She shook her head. Her voice was a hoarse and breathy mutter. "There's Grandma."

They jogged toward the barbecue pits where, wizened and grinning her yellow, small-toothed grin, poking her head toward them like some obscene bird, Yana dawdled in front of a green picnic table surrounded by junipers. Their feet sloughed up the grass still wet from watering.

"Evan?" The old woman had eyes like an owl. She started up.

"O, Grandma, you said you glimpsed in the ball. Now look."

THE GYPSY LOVER ·211·

Armanda started to cry, each breath a childish, uncontrollable gulp. She wiped at herself and batted against shadow and sun. "Where's Papa?"

They exchanged a worried glance, Armanda the betrayed. Evan could see in those eyes and in the fallen mouth the accumulation of hysteria and anger and the moment of transition to a grief worse than death.

"We shouldn't of let him go, *mamio*. It's past time now, and you said you saw it in the ball. Didn't you see more than the man who walked like a duck?" Her chest rose and fell. Something old rattled her breath. "He's probably drunk and run off the road somewhere. O, *mamio*, didn't you see?"

"Honey, honey, cover yourself. Nikki, he's got the soul of god. Though it's true, some things can't be foreseen."

As she spoke, the old lady reached a hand toward the raw and bloody side of Evan's head, but his own pain grew shallow against that in Armanda's eyes. The three of them stood beside the empty picnic table, blinking at one another like horrified spectators blinking at their own witless sleep. Evan's vision blurred and he felt as though he were looking back at the world from under the sea. From the murky fathoms, he watched the pickup rise to the surface, come sluing into the park, leap the curb with a clatter, and barrel across the grass with suicidal intent. Behind the windshield, demons twitched in Nikolai's eyes, the knuckles of his hands white upon the wheel. He hunched forward, his drunken face against the glass. He was gunning it toward the three of them, toward the picnic table around which they stood, and then he wrenched the wheel as though throwing a steer. The grass came apart in clumps and spit a fine mist as the truck skidded sideways and groaned to a stop.

Nikolai was down from the cab, shouting and fighting the air with his arms, about his neck that cherry colored fascinator like some ancient's treasured silk. "Why? Ain't I begging her to stay—"

"Nikki. Nikki."

"But ain't she gone?" And then a cry rose out of him, from deep in his heart, a cry that Evan had seen in the eyes of his daughter but never yet heard, a cry and a howl that went beyond sorrow and pain and anguish, throbbing from his very soul as blood must throb from a wound. He screamed, running away tilted to one side, flailing his arms, and words came back without sense or form. Evan watched him hump across the grass, between magnolia trees that fringed the park and stood like monsters, ragged and overgrown, a smell of ozone and burning leaves on the evening air, the delicate scarf clutched about his throat and wafting in the breeze. He limped from the curb into the street, and when he got to the middle of the street he stood and pulled at the heavens with his uplifted hands until a hard light rained down. He damned the *Kuneshti*, cursed the names of Knobby and Groucho. He fell to his knees and scrambled back to his feet, blathering all the time. A car in passing slowed and he pounded on the hood. The driver gaped and snapped his doorlock down and sped up while Nikolai screamed at him. "Get the ambulance. What? What? Tell her to breathe—"

"Papa!"

Armanda followed her father into the street and Evan chased after her. There, he saw her father for what he was: deceptively huge chest, meaty fists and plethoric face with eyes so belligerently popping, possessed by demons beyond even a daughter's love.

"Daddy. Daddy. *Oj dile! Mure dile!* My crazy one. My crazy one. What did you do? What have you done?"

"Sonia, Sonia. Come to Nikki, my lovely bride."

Nikolai had Armanda in a tender embrace, smothering her neck and hair with little kisses. Before Evan got to him, Nikolai kissed her on the mouth, running his hands up along her back. Armanda struggled and then went limp in her father's arms.

"It's me, Papa."

Evan collared him, winced, challenged by the pain in his head, not from his damaged ear but from that age-old question: how do such fathers have such daughters? He swung the mad Gypsy around as if swinging some unfortunate or disastrous mishap of the cosmos, some progenerative quark turned inside out, that thing called fate, as if swinging in his own slippery grasp the uneasy and ongoing dread that he was moving among dangerous lives.

"Be careful, Cowboy."

He danced Nikolai around, the Gypsy's body pliable, fatigued, and wrestled him back to the truck. Nikolai reached out for the bumper to steady himself and puked up everything but a lung. He tottered this way and that, sucking breath and wiping his mouth on a sleeve, and then smearing that scarf, and heaved again. Armanda stood over him, her jaw like a knot. She massaged the back of his neck with her fingers, all the time petting him with her other hand and cooing in a motherless way, the mad face gone red, him struggling there for breath. She had the scarf wrapped in her fist tight as an assassin's garrote to do the work, and Evan thought she twisted it ever so much and twisted again, that face the redder still. With a curse and a coax, and together with Evan, she got him to the back of the camper, and he crawled through the door and onto a cot where he collapsed in a stupor.

Armanda hoisted herself through the door with Evan right behind, and then he turned to help Yana up, but it was a spiritless reunion. The old woman reached her neck forward, probing the air with her snout, and Evan could see Armanda's relief mixed with an overwhelming violence struck in her eyes. They all stood for a moment, shoulder to shoulder, watching Nikolai sleep, and still there was movement to his flesh; the lids of his eyes were about to get up and jump off his face.

"He dreams of Sonia," the old woman cackled.

"He dreams of blackbirds and the way back from hell."

"Your *papo*, he won't last till the moon turns." She looked at Evan and the look was one that forgave the world to its very end, and then to her granddaughter, "And you, my darling, who can tell?"

Armanda cursed and tore the scarf from around his neck and balled it with her hands and when Evan looked the thing was gone, a rivulet of smoke, he thought, ghosted in its place. She lifted Nikolai's head, none too gently, and stuffed a pillow beneath it, and Evan pulled off his boots and swung his legs onto the cot. He wanted to say something to comfort or lull, in spite of the pain in his head. When Armanda saw it, she turned on him, came up at him from someplace deep where only the possessed reside.

"Take your pity and go away, Cowboy. We don't want your tears. We don't want your poems. We don't want your songs."

More than words, it was the absence of truth in her eyes that slurred his guts around. She opened and closed her mouth so that spittle formed on her lips, but all he could hear was the hissing in his ears, and with a perverse and self-abusive relief, he felt the knot inside him come undone.

"I got no tears for either you or the demons in your blackened heart." The heaviness of air in his lungs felt like a drug, and his voice when he spoke had a crust to it. The whole left side of his head was killing him. He heaved a boot on the floor and bolted from the camper. "Goddamn Gypsy witch!"

She threw herself after him, toward the door. "Hey, *gajo!* I think you spent your fifty bucks worth of space from there to here. With the scent of my bosom on it, too—"

He turned around and saw her leaning out the camper door. Her blouse was torn, exposing most of one breast and half the other. He was walking backward, trying to get away from her, trying to get away from himself, from everything, not knowing which way to turn. And as he backed away, those wretched images on the side of the camper began to crawl around themselves, in and out, swallowing and absorbing and morphing the paint, lines and contours and shades shivering anew across the surface, changing shapes and scenes even as he watched. It was as if the entire world—the world he knew, at least—came swimming back at him for all the mischief he had caused. She watched him, an artist's rendition herself, all distorted in the watery confusion and melee of shifting shapes, and the huge cold cinders of her eyes began to glow. The whole side and back of the truck had become a palette of mounting images, and she was atremble at the center, as colors dissolved and splashed around her. Whether it was happening as he watched, whether the developing scenes on the side and at the back of the camper were formed by the magical strokes of an unseen brush, or whether it was all taking shape in his mind, hardly mattered at all, for he watched as the future unfurled, watched as she tore off her bandanna and swung down from the stoop, literally throwing herself toward him, like a wild thing, and then in his arms.

She kissed him on the mouth.

"Like siblings," the old woman cried, climbing down from the truck. "Brother/sister-german, you hear?"

Some things need great study, much learning, key repetition in pursuit of memory. Evan knew this but could not speak it—even living at the center of himself like one of those vague images of shadow and light painted on the surface of a wall. The very idea eluded him like a blue spark amid the flame and failed examination even in the most minute detail. All about him wafted a sense of his own inescapable ambiguity. He held her and she him, his face pressed against the scent of her hair, even a light odor of perspiration, realizing with an odd sense of gratitude that the pieces, the mystery, of her that so racked him now and again would never fall into a neat pattern or place with the kind of natural inevitability for which, in his own ignorance, he had so desperately hoped. In just two days and two nights she had become, and would forever be, the grief and distress of his soul. She would forever be his joy.

She took him into the camper to fix his face, first telling her grandmother to drive slowly back to the motel. When Yana objected, she said, "Just do it, goddamn."

From one of the cupboards she took a foul smelling antiseptic and from the *bujo* bag a splinter of Ghost's Vomit. Hemorrhoids to headaches. She pinned her blouse shut and eyed him wickedly, filled a porcelain basin from the tap. Nikolai snorted, choked, as the truck leapt into gear. Evan grabbed for the open antiseptic bottle and water slopped in the basin. Walls shifted, groaned. The inside of the camper became liquid until the truck was out of the park and onto the open road. Armanda came up against him in the see-sawing of the truck, and poked the chip of *johai* between his lips and past his teeth, her slender brown finger following it to the middle of his tongue. She told him to swallow.

They were wedged back against the wall, between the cabinets and a stack of luggage. She pushed his baseball cap to the back of his head and twisted it backwards and looked at him; then she took it off and held it by the bill and looked at him and put it backwards on her own head and, smiling, scrubbed out his hair and not once did she look away. She soaked a rag with water and dabbed around his ear, sloughing off the blood and shredded skin. She doused a cotton ball with antiseptic and applied it gingerly to his mangled face. He jerked away.

"Good," she said. "The more it hurts, the better. Won't nothing heal without pain."

It annoyed him to think there was innuendo in her tone, then annoyed him to think there was not. The truck rocked, and he placed his hands on her hips to steady himself, surprised at how tiny she was, her waist, her hips. The scent of her, so musky and faint, again so familiar that for a fleeting moment he could almost tell what was going to happen next. She touched him and he winced and pulled away. She rose on her toes, pressing him back against the luggage, and puckered her mouth in mock-concern, clucked her tongue. The antiseptic began to dry, leaving that side of his face numb; he could feel the warmth of her breath against his throat. She kissed him on the cheek and he kept his hands on her hips. He felt dizzy. He looked at her and her eyes gave back an image of himself. It didn't surprise him when she told him in that same throaty whisper as though she were out of breath that she could see herself in his. She called him her cowboy, the last of the cowboys. She called him her gentle knight and told him to beware; she told him, without an iota of sense, that there's no greater monster than reason, then explained herself by saying, " . . . so try not to fathom me, my gentle knight." She called him her champion. She pressed up against him, raising her face, offering the prize. Behind them they could hear the inexhaustible gurgle of Nikolai's snore. And then her face came up and she opened her mouth to him.

Her champion.

He kissed her and ran his hands over the length of her body. He remembered something and as quickly forgot and put his hand on her breast; she didn't resist and he felt her breasts beneath the silky blouse. She put her hand on top of his and looked up at him and undid the pin from her blouse and let it fall open and he put his hand beneath the material and touched her softly as she kissed him with her soft open mouth. She made a sound way down in her throat, like a whimper, and he felt her excitement and in every caress her warmth as she breathed softly into his mouth, then softly inhaling drew breath from deep in his lungs.

*   *   *

In the drab little cottage, she stood on one side of the bed, and he, with a tempest in his heart, on the other. When she clawed the bandana from her hair and gave him a look, he went all hollow inside. Then she was beside him and he wondered about another lost moment in time.

"Unfasten my braid, Cowboy."

She turned her back to him, never unloosening her eyes from his face, and he grappled for the barrette that held the rope of her braid at the bottom. He worked the cords free from their mates and felt the weight of her hair in his hands.

"That's right. Now comb it out with your fingers. Yes."

"That's enough," said Yana.

"You keep it up, Cowboy. I'll tell you when enough's enough. From the top of my head all the way down to my waist. O, yes."

"Think of your *papo*," the old woman warned.

"You don't know the half of what I think of my *papo*. Yes, Cowboy, all the way to my waist. From the top of my head to my waist with your fingers a comb."

Yana stood at the foot of the bed, digging through the pockets in her skirt. She started to say something, then must have thought better of it. Still asleep in the camper outside, Nikolai surely dreamt of his daughter and ghosts. The blinds were drawn, the room lighted by the dim bulb of a table lamp and the flicker of an inaudible program on TV. Through an open window of the cottage next door came the voice of a woman, shrill and contemptible as Aunt Missy's. Evan thought he heard his name called and his heart went chill . . . *steal you away and cut yore heart out to eat it cold.*

"Nice," said Armanda, expressing her appreciation more with her eyes than a word. She drew her hair like water and silk through his hands.

Yana rummaged through her many pockets, emptying the contents on the bed. The *lovoro*: show and tell, dividing the loot. The assortment of shoplifted items made a nice little pile: lipsticks, cosmetics, perfume; nylons, petticoats, panties and bras; jewelry: rings, earrings, necklaces, bracelets, a watch; a blouse—

"For you, my darling."

—a pair of white satin slippers, a comb, a shawl, scarves . . .

Armanda plucked the blouse from the heap, held it up, turned it over and spread it out on the bed. She turned away, and stretching, shucked off the torn blouse in a single agonizing gesture. Her dark hair splashed across her brown shoulders and untangled to her waist. Body averted, she took up the new blouse and shrugged it on, olive breasts flashing in the quick transition. She turned around, fingers nibbling buttons, brushing at the sleeves.

"Pretty," said Yana, and continued adding to her pile.

"Look here, *mamio*." The eighty or ninety dollars from the

man in the bronze Mustang and other curbside suitors fluttered to the bed. Then the wallet, long and thin, and Evan found himself relieved that Jack, the doper, hadn't gotten it. Armanda unfolded the expensive leather as Yana leaned forward; she pinched out two, three, five fifty-dollar bills and dropped them on the bed . . . *the virgin bandit.* From a second compartment, she pinched one, two, four hundreds, two twenties, a ten, a five, and three singles. She dropped each, slowly, one at a time, onto the bedspread . . . *liars and thieves.*

Yana clapped her hands to her cheeks, her eyes like bruised and bulging eggs, her mouth a cartoonish hole. "Didn't I tell you I seen it in the ball? Such wealth!"

What could he expect? What would he find? Mad Nikolai chasing wisps, his daughter and wife all mixed up in his head. Sonia . . . from cancer to suicide . . . all at a whim. Armanda, the end of her race, struggling—as far as Evan could see—to keep her father from some weird state of spontaneous combustion. Who could know the Gypsy whose face changed like water? Lies and deceit. Madness and murder. Anger and hate. Kindness and love. Her champion . . . would he die for her? He would die without her . . . brown fingers fondling the billfold, caressing its secret parts, examining the soft pliable leather with her soft brown hands. Her eyes moved serenely with her hands, those beautiful, childlike hands, and Evan grew suddenly critical of the regard in which she seemed to hold herself, her eyes, her nose, her throat, her breasts, her hips, her legs—even her feet and their charming little glories to extol as she slipped them into the white satin shoes.

Her eyes met his across the bed and in that moment he told her in no uncertain terms of truth and desire and promises to forgive, but her eyes told him the very idea of forgiveness was a joke. She batted those damnable eyes and raised her shoulders in the same deliberate gesture he had seen time after time, so feminine, so boyish, so attractively, beguilingly, corrupt.

"Your Gypsy-witch," she said, his own disappointment reflected in the tone of her voice.

"Not Gypsy," Evan told her, anxious and expectant, while Yana looked on with a puzzled expression. "Not *gaje*. Remember? But you."

She turned her back on him, sliding away toward the bathroom, untucking the blouse, her head lowered and shaking solemnly.

"Gypsy," he thought he heard her say.

I knew when I called him over that day at Alta Mae's swimming party to show Thomas those scabs on the backs of his legs that I should have called Child Protective Services or at least the cops. Half a dozen years later when he finally runs off—or is driven—how can you be surprised? We never know the suffering of one another's hearts, but those legs blistered like that. I could kick myself. He's been a good kid in spite of such brutes, just ask my little girl who's had her heart in her throat since she was nine. Who knows? I've tired, Thomas has, to instill the best values we can, provide every opportunity, and hide or own mistakes behind a door. It's a kind of natural beauty that plagues her, and still she goes to early-morning seminary and Sunday School, reads the scriptures and says her prayers. But "the natural man is an enemy to god and must be proven in all things." And that's the trouble. They've got minds of their own, with every prospect of agency at hand. Correct principles, that's what you teach, and then you close your eyes and give them the long end of the leash. Comes a time you have to hope and pray they've developed a brain in her heads.

~14~

Gates of Midnight

Beneath the sorrowful light, shapes moved in a fury.

IN his journal, Evan wrote:

> *Gypsies dwell in a different time than the rest of us. They wander without amazement through yesterday and tomorrow; we thrive on the present. They navigate perilous cliffs with hurricanes in their hair.*

And he had come to know those winds in a matter of days, standing atop the cliffs. He knew the taste of tempest on Gypsy lips, and he yearned for the bitter taste of tempest on those lips, for the dress red as blood to stain his hands. And he had touched that dress. Why shouldn't he, too, see faces in glass balls and chase ravens about as the fearsome incarnation of ghosts? Would he, in time, carry about snapshots of his own coffin and wander cemeteries for entertainment? If for them a little "Devil's Shit" could cure the most horrendous disease, why not for him? O, he would dance the Devil's Shit Dance and smear himself with angelic rage to get inside Armanda's head, knowing all the time that if he did, he would find the noodles askew, like his own insides every time he raised his face and saw those big sloe eyes.

"Your *papo* will be so pleased!" Yana rushed over, intercepting Armanda at the bathroom door. The old woman kissed her and gently squeezed her breasts.

"Yes, Grandma, but what about Mama?"

The old woman turned back to the bed to finger the crisp hundred dollar bills, ignoring the inflection in her granddaughter's voice.

Evan watched her in the bathroom, brushing her hair, looking at herself in the mirror. The mirror was gilded, the light on it dim, and the face that looked back was not a happy one. She looked at herself and brushed her hair for a long time, then she leaned back and turned on the shower and closed the door. Evan sat on the bed and watched a sitcom on TV without the sound turned up. The TV was from another time as was the programming, and the picture rippled and zagged and flecked in a rhythm that worried his eyes. His head hurt. Little flecks blistered midair, and he wondered if putting on his father's spectacles would help. They didn't. The left side of his face was too tender for even the weight of the earpiece. Yana muttered something to him. She rummaged through her plunder and muttered something about getting a sleeping bag out of the camper.

So thoughtful. So kind.

Armanda poked her head out of the bathroom door, her hair slicked back and glistening, beads of water dripping from her eyelashes, nose, and chin. She asked Evan would he please order pizza and soft drinks for dinner and have it delivered. She closed the door, leaving a plume of steam to evaporate in the hallway, but her image lingered—her scrubbed face and wet shining eyes, a brown shoulder and naked arm as she held open the door and leaned toward him.

Evan got out the phone book and ordered the pizza. Her lackey. Her toady. Her slave. He went outside and looked up at the sky to consider his stars, whether lucky or ill. O, yes, the sleeping bag, and he found himself hurrying beneath the oak to get to the camper where he knew he would find Nikolai still passed out cold. A wind had come up and there wasn't a sign of the raven in either of the oak trees. The moon hung like a lantern in the branches of one, and the truck sat beneath in the wash of its light. There, on the side of the camper, images raced about with their shadows amid the shadows of wavering limbs, some muted, some distinct, but nothing to temper fear nor to put one's mind at ease. What appeared to be a bride in her wedding veil and tiara stood with her hand on a gate. It was impossible to tell whether she was coming or going. What appeared to be an assassin with a patch over one eye stole forward with a gun. It was impossible to tell at whom he was aiming. What appeared to be a raven sat in the moon-lighted branches of a monstrous oak. It was impossible to tell whether the bird was asleep or awake. Evan looked again to be sure. When he saw the thing on the side of the truck, his heart went to his throat like a fist and he glanced back at the swaying branches of the empty oak. But it was there, on the side of the truck, barely visible in the hesitant light, that the bird was fixed like a dread. To his credit, Evan looked away, though he noticed the magic of his own shadow and how, with each step, it leapt beneath his feet as though struggling to flee.

He touched his hand to the knob of the door at the back of the camper when he heard the voices within. They rose in whispers like the wind itself among a thousand stuttering leaves. There was weeping, he thought, a consummate sigh. He was about to force the knob when a wail arose and he let loose his grip. When he came back in without the sleeping bag, now out of the wind, he felt as if his skin had shrunken a size and was too tight for his bones. Yana looked at him and then looked at him again but kept to herself.

"An extra blanket will be fine," he offered, and that was enough.

The shower was off, and the door to the bathroom wide open. Armanda stood there, hazed in the steam, dressed in a pair of panties and a half-buttoned pajama top. Everything he wanted to make of her, she had suddenly become. She leaned for him over the sink, now toweling her hair, and he sat down in the chair by the TV and held the spectacles up to his eyes and looked at her through them. He considered sketching her like that but abhorred the notion of effort it would take, though he could feel his skin begin to loosen. She looked old; she looked young. How could you grasp the essence of a thing never quite true, a thing constantly redefining and proving itself? As if to prove his point, she toweled the steam from the mirror and spoke to herself and the mirror replied. Or so it seemed. Actually, she was talking to Yana as the old woman cleared the bed, packing away the stolen items. She was running a comb through her hair and looking in the mirror, talking about Evan as though he were the subject of an unremarkable dream. He listened with irritation and a sense of betrayal. She told the old woman about his experience of the night before with the crystal ball. Without missing a detail, she described the face he had seen in the glass. Yana sat down heavily on the bed and Evan closed up the eyeglasses and returned them to their case. The old woman screwed up her face and jutted her head toward him. Without ceremony, she produced a dog-eared photograph, in sepia. She looked at it for a minute then offered it up.

"What's this?"

Armanda stepped into a pair of mis-matching pajama bottoms and came out of the bathroom. She put the comb to her hair and sat down on the bed next to her grandmother and looked at Evan while she combed her hair.

"What is this?"

The old woman pinched her lips and tugged at her chin. The gesture gave her a reptilian look. "Ain't we children still," she grieved, "who, even at the gates of midnight, dream of sunrise?" And then she whispered to Armanda, "You're cowboy has seen, but does he know what he sees?"

"Am I supposed to take this seriously?"

"You study that for a while," she said. "The imagination is a land of many spirits. It sometimes deceives, it sometimes conceals, it sometimes tricks or creates illusions of the heart. It can lead us in either positive or negative ways. It allows us to experience more than we know. And if the source from within is pure, it can foster a greater enlightenment, the imagination can. But you know that."

"I know what?"

"Children," she said, "who mourn the loss of innocence and long for a world of order know more than they think."

"?"

"Look," she said, "you seen something. It's as simple as that. You seen even more than you know, and your seeing gives me a hint. Now let me tell you a thing or two while you study that photo and you can give it some thought."

"What? How the Gypsy's plight is filled with misery and pain?"

"O, ain't that the truth? Now listen."

"Yes, listen Cowboy, and get ready to be amazed."

"You," said the old woman to her granddaughter with a sorrowful gaze, and then she looked at Evan. "Ain't we moving between yesterday and tomorrow at the speed of light, 186,000 miles per second, plus? There's nothing more than the past bumping up against the future and us in the middle. Just molecules and light. Or, if you maybe want to look at it like this, you could say the past and the future is only bookends to now, bracketing all that ever was or will ever be, the whole universe squeezed together in a word or a glance or a frown. All squeezed together in a single moment of time. Whatever you know, I am, and whatever I am, you know—not with the head but with the heart, just whimsy and dreams. And to get down to the bottom of it, imagine the merits of being itself, if there is such a thing. Both the quest for truth and the discovery of it, ain't they confined to what you know, to what you see?"

Armanda gave him a wink and ran the comb through her hair.

"But for argument's sake, let's say there's a realm beyond this, another dimension where spirits reside, then either our very existence in this world is beside the point—or it means more than we know."

"That's all double talk," he said and handed her back the photo.

"Well, believe me, like Socrates said, every pleasure or pain has a sort of rivet fastening the soul to the body and pins it down and makes it flesh, accepting as true whatever the body allows. Beyond that, we're just a bundle of nerves, some would say consciousness, making sure the planets stay in their orbit around the sun."

"O, *mamio's* right, damn her to death. Don't you see? Here, Cowboy, come sit by me on the bed, here, next to *mamio* and run this comb through my hair." She gave him a look he hadn't quite seen, both dreamy and intense, and scooted up on the bed to where he could get at her hair. She dropped a hand to his knee. "It's a torment if you put your mind to it, like where do we come from and why are we here, like where do we go, that's what *mamio's* trying to say. It's all a matter of perception, the nature of reality. It's all a matter of choice." She yanked her head back fighting the drag of the comb. "Watch the snags, there. Maybe you know something of it, more than you know. How we're either reduced to nothing and sorrow, how the world is nothing, and us in it, or at the same time, like one of your whatchamadoxes, how this flesh is everything, like a comb through the hair and soft lips, just kisses and bliss, and us standing firm." She gave him a backward glance and then tilted her head forward to straighten the fall of her hair. Yana attempted to cut in, but Armanda's voice rose. "Tell me if I'm wrong, but none of us has ever been any place that we weren't. I've never been to a movie when I wasn't there. You've never been to a museum when you weren't there. You never spent yesterday with me except we were there together. Think back. You never laid in your bed when you didn't. So if we've never been any place except where we were, where we are even now, how can any place exist where we're not? That's what *mamio's* trying to say. Without me in your head, I'm nothing. Without you in my head, you're nothing. Until you dreamt me coming down out of the mountains astride that galloping mare, I'd never ridden a horse in my life. And what about you in the thickest part of my dreams? So look around you, grab hold of my hair and my heart, you might feel it in your hand but it only exists in your head. Whether I do this or do that is nothing at all."

He combed on, wadding her hair in his hand and letting it fall as he combed. "Riddle me, riddle me ree."

"You listen to my granddaughter, *romany-rye*. My darling, she's right, though I don't like the way she tells it. And let me tell you, my darling, my own, there are more than you know who have been to places they weren't. I've told you before, and I'll tell you again, how we each roll through an awareness of time, and by that I mean time's awareness, so—true—not having been where we weren't, through others we find that we nevertheless were. I had an aunt who walked through a mirror and seen the future in a hundred years past. She come back to tell it in snippets and snatches, just enough to tantalize and dispirit the mind."

"O, yes, *mamio*. Like me. Didn't I say I'd never ridden a horse in my life until he dreamt it? This cowgirl, his."

Yana waved her aside. "In less than a year's time, this same aunt become pregnant with herself and died giving birth to the soul."

"O, yeah." Armanda was in a reverie, her face soft and agonized in the dim light of the room as if in the throes of some wretched bliss. "That's the spirit and blood of it, giving birth to the soul. And shouldn't we all?"

The old woman touched Evan on the point of his shoulder as he combed, as if to make a point. "Here's something. Let's say your great-great, double-great granddaddy was a knight in shining armor and his double-great granddaddy twice removed was touched by the Savior himself and even his cousin or brother

THE GYPSY LOVER ·229·

maybe stood by at Gethsemane. Ain't this all in the consciousness of the seed that come down to you? How it meandered through time and generations from one soul to another, carrying the seed of your own being at some point in time? Ain't we a little of them who went before, like a bridge to the ones yet to come? Ain't a spot of my blood in your veins or some common ancestor but six times removed? Ain't you a little of me? And you might consider the molecules of space you pass through as you go before or after the beauty of my Armanda or some cancerous dolt or even generals and kings from ages gone by. We can't escape either the biology or the physics of the world at large, nor do they escape us."

"But it don't mean nothing unless one sees for hisself," said Armanda. "Like maybe he has."

"In that case, he better look around to see what he sees. Look around at this and at that and at what's in your hand and maybe discover some kind of truth. Me? I wouldn't believe nothing I saw in this world. Not even where dinosaurs come from according to the brightest bone-man on earth or whether a black hole in the middle of our galaxy is sucking us in. The truth is that humankind survived ignorance down through the ages, but it's our scientific genius will do us in. Thus and thus is so, says Mr. Bone Man, from tadpole to treefrog to monkey to me. They like to count galaxies and stars as if there's a number to be reckoned with. Thus and thus is so and matter so dense the weight of a billion suns can be drained to a pinprick and you want me to believe a tree's as solid as its trunk? Thus and thus is so, so says them who think they know, for now at least, and next week it ain't—not in a world that changes like water, it ain't. And me? I wouldn't believe half the ten o'clock news or an iota about how the pyramids in Egypt come to be or whether the earth was created in seven days flat—or, for that matter, even UFOs or the slant of politicians back east. Give me the world beyond. And without explanation. A glance in a mirror from this side or that. Spirits and divinity and the wondrous unknown." Yana stilled his obedient hand and gave him a look. "Now then, tell me about you. Tell me if you find meaning in the seen or in the unseen alone."

"Comb," said Armanda.

"You're saying the earth and the stars and the sky and you and this chair and raven's roosting in trees and that old photograph, even Aunt Missy and Uncle Goose and you and this chair and the universe at large, don't exist except in my head?"

"That's magical thinking of sorts."

"And when I die—"

"Didn't I mention to you earlier that one of the things I found most difficult to learn when I went into the forest to fast was to learn not to try to understand more than I could? You can't understand everything. We're all ignorant, only on different subjects, didn't someone once say?"

"You can't understand everything, Rodeo Boy. Life is a mystery."

"But like I says, you can learn to experience more than you know. After all, ain't it better to travel hopefully than to arrive?"

"Robert Louis Stevenson said that."

"Yes he did. I know the saying. But what does it mean? Ain't the solution less satisfying than the problem itself? Didn't you say? Like answers to riddles and riddles no more. Something like that. And what does it matter?" She handed him back the photograph. "Go on. You study that picture for a while and learn something new."

"Yeah, and I'll fix my hair and my face and get ready for the nightmares of sleep."

"Button your top." The old woman frowned.

Armanda snatched the comb from his hand and got up with a jounce. She spun to the bathroom, her pajama top slipped from her shoulder, clinging, the tails making like wings. She looked back and laughed her grandmother's laugh—without a note of joy.

"If it's all a matter of perception, *mamio*, why do you care?"

Yana, in the meantime, wizened witch that she was, cast up her eyes and left Evan to study the photograph while she finished sorting her loot. He gazed on each wistful face glaring back at him from some far off wintry day, wondering what each had seen at that moment in time. After a while Armanda came out of the bathroom, her face scrubbed to a shine and hair pinned back and she stood beside him and put her hand on his arm and together they stared at the somber troupe. When the pizza arrived, she took a slice out of the box and ate it in gobs while the boy counted back change and Yana nibbled away. Evan closed the door and watched with fascination, alarmed at the familiarity of everything he saw, as if seeing at once from their point of view. He took a cheesy wedge from the box and sat between them, and as he did they cast their eyes about in turn, like jackals at feast, and so looking silently caught him up so that he could see there in each brief gaze that among them nothing was his to rightfully claim, neither his heart nor his soul nor the quest for even a lonesome most thought.

When they had finished eating, the old woman lit candles all around and set them about and turned down the light. She took the crystal ball from the *bujo* bag and set it on the end table by the chair. She motioned to each of them in turn, and it wasn't a moment before they were huddled over the glass, restless and expectant, as if awaiting some sad and joyful exchange. He looked and already beneath the sorrowful light shapes moved in a fury. Some leapt like little flames, others twisted and spun. It was a shadow dance challenging his wits. Yana passed her hands over the glass dome and Evan watched until his eyes acquired a dull, throbbing ache. Once, the ball clouded, gave back a glint, and turned as black as some moonless night absent of stars. Like India ink, black. The whole room drew a breath and exhaled a long whispering sigh. Evan felt that spot of pain, like a migraine, pounding in his eye, and saw the inky haze draw back with mats and clouds of form and something like a raven's head, saw it with the clarity of a blind man who sees the unseen, and then what looked like the top of a skull take shape. He acknowledged, more than saw, flesh and bone peel back, and in the crystal, as the haze dissolved around it, what appeared to be the lumpy cortex of a brain, like cauliflower. Breathing gathered throughout the room and settled with a diminishing sob next to the table . . . something feminine, troubled, alone.

"Nightmares and sleep," the old woman whispered, closing her eyes. "What does a young girl astraddle a horse mean to a boy?"

Before she had finished speaking, he could hear the animal blow and the pounding of hooves upon earth. And now in the murk, he could see the head, far distant, like a pinprick, then closer by degrees, driving toward the surface of glass. She was coming down out of the mountain hell bent for leather it appeared, riding less toward than away, and the horse beneath white with froth. Its neck stretched forward, a confusion of mane and her hair all tangled and whipping the wind. O, Cowgirl, she. And though she rode and rode, like some castaway riding the absolute, the dark clouds threatening behind, the horse steaming and blowing and striding the earth, she got no closer than a child across the dining room rocking its way through the years.

"Yes, what? What does she mean?"

"Nothing," the old woman said, leaning above the crystal and gobbling air with her hands. "Nothing at all. And yet maybe the world. Look close. Now tell me, what do you see?"

And looking, he saw. A Cadillac. Blue. The one-eyed man.

"See how he longs for my darling yet to be born, whose mother he holds in his hand? That's the spirit and blood of it. Now look."

A gun. Nickel plated. Pearl handled. Automatic. Small. In the tight, meaty fist.

"Are they out of the mountains yet? Tell me."

He touched the surface of the glass, as if to point through his own amazement at some bewildering scheme, as if to point out the very images that festered beneath the surface of his skull.

THE GYPSY LOVER ·233·

And each glimpse clung to the remnant of some nightmare better left unsaid. Nevertheless, he said. "There. Limping along the side of the road. No, no. I see . . . H-E-R-T-Z . . . a white Camero. And look at that. He's got the pistol apart and I can see him feeding the clip."

"And all for my darling yet to be born, whose mother is death. Now what do you see? Go on. Perhaps more than you know."

The image in the crystal shimmered, drug itself up and back in a silken waft, and dissolved. Perhaps he blinked or some synapse in his brain misfired, for he found himself looking instead at the photograph Yana had placed in his hand, not at the photograph but at those three dismal rows—one, two, three—faces so bleak and now come to life in the crystal. The children, in the first row, sat legs crossed; the women, in the second row, kneeled; the men, in the last row, stood on their feet. The earth all around was covered with snow and it was lightly snowing; in the background stood a forest of black-trunked trees, their branches webbed dense with snow and daggers of ice. Unsmiling, the little group sat, kneeled, and stood, as though awaiting an unseen photographer's prompt to say "cheese."

Evan peered into the glass past his own reflection and in peering fell into the gaze of an eye. There, he saw the image of himself looking out, as if glancing back from a mirror. Snow fell like the tick of a clock, wetting his shoulders, his face, and he found himself now gazing up from the snow-covered ground at the hag and her dear. Some other time, some other place, caught up in a dream not his own.

What?

He craned his neck upward toward an iron sky, the faces of the crone and his love all distorted and ballooned, just cloud smears, now looking in. And what did they see? Him standing third row, one from the left? He tried not to breathe then breathed with a gulp the same air the man next to him breathed. Above, her face was just a pregnant wash, now gazing less at him than at the man next to him who shifted and stubbed his boot in the snow. The man wore a ragged coat and cap, gaped around with ecumenical eyes. Others had on European-style fur caps and regarded the ground. The women wore wool headscarves and long fur-lined coats. The children, dressed in ill-fitting bulky clothing, wore short-billed caps or scarves, and some were bareheaded. Each row formed a dense, straight, and almost uninterrupted line of the same dark features, strangely familiar and unknown.

Another, boyish, epaulets on the shoulders of his coat, first unslung a canvas pack and then a rifle from his arm. He removed his helmet and unpacked a camera and secured the camera to a tripod, tinkered with the lens. He yelled over his shoulder, and Evan could see now the soldier he yelled to wave back. The one tinkered with the camera lens, and the other signaled and hunkered down, maybe fifteen yards away. He screwed a bipod into the threaded boss on the underside of the barrel and spread the legs of the bipod and mounted the gun on a rise, swiveling the barrel of the gun and releasing and re-adjusting the belt. The cameraman looked through his lens and the man beside Evan began to weep without sound. He glanced again at the iron sky, reflective and pale as glass, and could see his look petitioning there. Armanda gazed back, the hag puckering the air above the dome with her hands.

"You want to know?" she said. She hollered without so much as a sound. "You want to know?"

Whether from above or below, he saw how he stood apart from the group, and a part of it yet, separated by nothing but time and confusion and the semblance of space. He heard the click of the camera, and before the film was advanced, got hold of his throat with a thought and jerked himself back, right up and out and away from that strange and articulated smoldering brew. He heard the click of the gun.

"That's nothing to do with me," he tried. "Where'd they go? Charlie, I mean. Her on the horse. What's this?"

"Look."

A girl, beyond his reflection and caught in the glass, some girl. She knelt, first row, far end, her hair thick and black, the shape of her face, her beauty, like something gone wild. The way she craned her neck forward as though testing the air. Something familiar and unflattering in that. Was she looking at him? He couldn't be sure but thought for a moment it was Armanda, then again not Armanda but the way she poked her neck forward, her lips forming some inexpressible desire, some ineffable plea. One of several in three dark rows, all unfamiliar as the inhabitants of a previous world yet known just the same.

"Look."

The photographer, finishing up, collapsed his tripod and wiped the camera down with a rag. He released the back of the camera box and took out the film. He waved the gunner to wait. When he looked at the girl, she shook her head at him, hard, and he went to her with one hand on his pistol and wrenched her up off her knees. Snow fell like the tick of a clock, wetting her shoulders, her face. He wrenched her up off her knees and her arms were held forth like a supplicant's petitioning for some blessing alien and unknown. When she twisted, he gathered her around the waist and up until her feet peddled air, and the gunner loosened then tightened his grip and re-leveled the gun, said something that sounded like "cheese."

Evan looked back from his own reflection in the glass and then away from that lost generation of eyes so familiar and turned on himself and the world to come.

Yana would have nothing of it.

"Look."

But didn't he know more now than he saw?

"Look."

Pressing through lightheadedness to recovery, he knew, without the necessity to see, how she stole that film with a kiss and the flower of youth. And strangest of all, he knew with a stab what old photographs in an attic might mean, and at the center a riddle—and, too, how it all comes together, if not literally, then in a strange, metaphorical sort of way. What more history than this? When he looked again, images collapsed on themselves, one after another, a scramble of arms and legs and torsos and heads, all in the mutual release of surmounting fatigue.

Now, were he to look, among which would he find himself? First row, third from the left? Third row center, less one? Would he find himself standing, camera in hand, or face down in the reddening snow? He swallowed and worked to get air back in his lungs. He felt as if he had awakened from some potent dream and now awake heard a far off weeping subside, leaving the room dense with an absence of sound. He could feel his legs, his arms, like oil; the top of his skull felt as if it had been ripped away.

When he opened his unclosed eyes, he found he was supporting himself on his elbows propped on the table, drenched in a sweat. As if she had never stopped, the old woman massaged the pocket of air between her hands and the dome of the ball. Evan looked at his own hands. He held them out in front of him and looked at them, at his hands and his arms, how other they seemed. They looked so old. He felt as if he had been transformed; he felt as if his shape had changed. Otherwise, what had he found of himself in a place where he wasn't and never had been? He shuddered like a man trying to throw off chains.

"What are you telling me?" He shoved himself back a little, away from the ball. "There but for fortune? How we're doomed by some ancestral plight?"

"I didn't say that."

"How could I have saved them?"

"I didn't say that, *raklo*."

"We've got this life to worry about, Cowboy."

"I didn't say no such thing, but in truth you know as do I that balance must be maintained. You might say we seek to gain equilibrium through them who've traveled before. Whatever I know, you are. Whatever you know, I am. Like that. All squeezed together in a word or a glance or a frown. Just whimsy and dreams."

He looked at Armanda, the reflection of light in her eye. He looked at Yana who sniffed at the air.

An Aryan bride, she had told him, *awaited one of those boys*—and her voice snapped in his head—*the very cameraman with stripes on his sleeve, she who carried his child within, he who took and then witlessly give in return, who after it all lay in his own blood as the Russians advanced.* Hadn't she said? *'Twas all after in the glass and the stars and a throw of the cards. . . .* He paused ruminatively and looked at the hag; he looked at his beauty and then at the vacant and unweathered ball. *I can tell you this much and no more*—hadn't she said?—*how she with child on learning the fate of her man went off to America and give birth there and how that child in time took up with a railroad boy and had a boy of her own.* Another story? O, yes—a story like ice in the heart, witness now to whom- and whatever he was.

"And the punishment?" she asked. "The doom? Why, the punishment is self-inflicted. Ain't we each our own worst judge—and executioner at times? How could you be responsible for the atrocities, the suffering, or even the joy, of a time and a place you never had been? Or Armanda? Or I? Shan't we leave the past to itself and embrace the moment at hand?"

"O, you mean Charlie," he hoped, thinking about now. "What are you going to do about the one-eyed man bearing down with every turn in the road?"

"What can we do?"

He gazed at the crystal, the shimmering words beneath the surface of glass now nevertheless trembling with anger and pain close to his heart, and everywhere he could see the notices posted on lampposts, walls, in offices, shops, and cafes.

No Jews, Gypsies,
or Dogs Allowed

"That boy you was before, he has no place in you now."

"?"

"And yet, how is it possible to separate the one from the other? That boy is both you and not you, just as you belong to every man's past and your present is mine."

Yana said, and as she said, he closed his eyes and held within the possibility of a genealogy he was afraid to name, a feeling like something in a delicate box, something light sitting next to the place where he breathed, and as he held his breath, she sighed.

"If we reject what we are made of, what more are we left with but half the truth of what passes between yesterday and tomorrow? My life is mine alone and you have no claim to it, nor I to yours, except in the interlinking web of time. Yet whatever you claim is mine is yours; aye, whatever you claim is mine. This is the paradox of it, that what happens to one happens to all and yet rests unclaimed but by the victim himself. If we each are responsible for the world at large who then is responsible for us?"

He opened and closed his eyes and opened them again, and it was as though, by some laborious gaze, he might focus on a specific time or place, so closely bound together were the large and the small, the current and the distant, within some exalted scheme. And in that gaze he had seen, knew he had seen, both the longing and breadth of their struggle, perhaps even something of himself, but was too overwhelmed to get it right in his head.

The old woman cackled and wagged her hands above the glass like a hag.

"See anything?" Armanda whispered.

"He sees."

Something rose upward in the crystal and crawled around the inside surface of the glass; it was an image first of the photographer superimposing his and then of Armanda staring up at him from the obscure depths of the globe and then it was nothing at all. He gazed for more, for something . . . saw nothing but an inky swell, and then Yana's hand fingering the cushion of air.

The old woman muttered something, a spell—but, no—something about what really happened, how it really was, yet something only she knew because she alone had the mind for it and the time all along to shape it into a raspy tangle of breath. She named the towns and the villages. The stone houses. She named the executions that had taken place there, named those who had stood against the walls sprayed with new blood over the dried black of the old, and she spoke of the shards of stone chipped away from the bullets striking the walls and the powdered indentations after the men and women and children had fallen and the slow drift of riflesmoke and the odor of corpses stacked in the lanes or piled onto the wooden horsecarts trundling up the hill and deeper into the forest to the openpit graves.

"O children still . . ." he heard with some uncertainty, ". . . for we are in you, your mother is, the bones of your father, and some forgotten ancestor who bled with the moon for antiquity's sake."

Was she speaking to him? Or to Armanda whose head drooped forward in assent? He looked, but all that remained was the reflection of candlelight in a myriad of oscillating flames that shimmered the room and his own squashed face pulling away.

"He sees," the old woman repeated. "Sees the queerness of the world and how little is known, sees his own ancestry and how difficult to plan for the world to come. Sees that life is little more than a breath and how we are forever in the middle of our journey, no matter how old or how young. He sees that his own desire to shape the world invites all manner of paradox and difficulty. And what he sees is meant that he might forget the pain of his life and become." She stopped and drew an undulant breath. "But you know that. The both of you. The trick is in the willingness to step across and move one step at a time through the darkness and muck without looking back."

He listened and wondered and gazed at the empty crystal and as he wondered, for all her riddles and tangles and knots, the old woman rose in his mind as a specialist in grief and overcoming. She understood things lost to philosophers and fools, and the refrain rang in his ears . . . *children still, who even at the gates of midnight dream of sunrise.*

"There's no way around it," Armanda put in. "You have to fight through a series of demons to get to yourself."

"O? And when you find yourself?"

"Trust me. It's like looking into the eye of a storm, riding a horse down from the mountain and right into the eye of a storm."

* * *

Evan shut the door to the bathroom and turned on the light. He sat on the closed lid of the toilet and opened his journal. It was about two o'clock in the morning and his body felt strangely heavy. Beyond the door, Yana stitched together a cozy sleep that had even Armanda snoring in time. He listened for a moment to the rhythm of the night, thinking of a thousand possibilities and at last selecting the sum of all he had come to know:

> *Gypsies dwell in a different time than the rest of us. They wander without amazement through yesterday and tomorrow; we thrive on the present. They navigate perilous cliffs with hurricanes in their hair . . . restless and expectant, as if awaiting some sad and joyful exchange to right every wrong. I see now the horror and blessing of ancestry unknown and how such seeing tempers the soul. I see, too, the face that plagued me last night in the crystal ball. It rolls before me on the hour, but open-eyed, and the features are unmistakable. It is not the face of my mother, it is not the face of any Gypsy woman already gone to her grave . . .*

> *Across miles of empty sound*
> *I swim from shore to shore.*
> *My dim hands stretch down,*
> *I have you by the hair,*
> *seaweed then—*

If I could talk I would, but dogs can't talk, at least not in the world that was—nor in a world separate from riddles—they can't. If I could talk I would tell a weeping tale of wooden nickels and those without. I would tell of dogs aflame. I would tell of dogs down low, for dogs see at best on the level of children or the misbegotten and mocked. Dogs keep their noses and ears to the ground, searching for scraps. Dogs yip, bark, and howl. To those who listen, dogs talk. Put your ear to my snout and hear the truth of it, then, for dogs never lie. *Who was my master in time and whose ancestral seed stressed the look in his eye, stressed as well the look in the eye of his love?* Remember, the flames of the holocaust singed not the hide of the cat, but the dog's, Gypsy's, and Jew's. Blessed is he who has seen through the flames. Blessed is he who has earned the love of a dog.

~15~

The Bujo

. . . the cursed money did its work.

STRANGE women trekked about the room. Hideous men. Each tromped without a sound, one after the other in single file, and each gaped back from a freakish mask. They came from the open bathroom door and up across the bed and round about the room and disappeared into the shadows of the wall, right through that big irregular stain like a pair of gates left hanging, and as they did the whole wall opened up and he could see the troupe in silhouette marching on, a ghostly band toiling uphill in an unbroken line against the rising sun, the light so intense that it went like a needle through his ear and snaked behind his eyes. The LA-Z-Boy was lumped in all the wrong places. He twisted and fought beneath the quilt, but it was a bad drama.

"Say, bub. How about another trip to the zoo?"

His mother wet her thumb and smudged back an errant hair, and he longed for the scent of her, rose-soap and mint.

"You must promise," she said, but before he could reply, she vanished among the last of the lot, those gates behind them rattling to.

When he put his hand out to open the gates, a dark girl whirled her skirt and chanted his name, and the gates shivered and rattled beneath his fist like a box full of coins. He could see her spinning away among the rest, the red dress and white billowing shirt, and hear the echoing laugh. All the while, he held tight to the latch, at once trying to still the laughter and working to release the gate. Just as the gate started to swing inward, the clamor grew. Darkness came up to meet him, and sleep fell away as he opened his eyes.

It was nearly light. Time gathered him back from the stupor of unclaimed rest, and he realized the door was about to be shaken from its hinges. Yana threw back the covers and flopped her feet to the floor. Armanda lifted her head and blinked at the door in a daze. The moment Yana saw Evan, she hissed:

"*Gajo!* Turn your face."

He realized she was trussed in nothing more than a huge white brassier, and he watched through bleary eyes as she threw on her blouse, stepped into one of her voluminous skirts, and hurried to the door. "Nikki?"

It was a middle-aged, heavy-faced man with thinning hair and a large veined nose, disaster written all over his face. He was carrying one of Mother Salloway's "House of Prayers" handbills and beneath an arm he clasped a goose.

"My Gilman!" Yana clapped her hands to her cheeks and stepped aside so as not to be steamrolled. "We got no appointment till ten."

He wheezed in reverence a score of apologies and ducked his head. Obesity had claimed him long ago. The little tie he wore lay upon his chest and flapped when he spoke. He held his free hand against his heart and struggled for breath. Everything else, except his abnormally short legs, was nose and jowls. You could plant that man's nose and grow tulips, Evan thought. He had no eyes to speak of—daubs of clay smudged rudely in the folds of his face. He held the goose beneath one arm and the handbill, along with the morning edition of the *National Enquirer,* beneath the other. Blubbering, he thrust out the goose.

"O, Reverend Mother, ever since I wasn't married no more . . . that is to say ever since she passed on, things has slid down."

Yana grappled with the bird, smacked it across the bill as it went for her, and wrapped it firm in the bowl of an arm. "You shoulda brang a chicken, I told you. Not this duck."

"Goose," he explained. "It's all I could find."

"Well, come in, then. You got the money, like I told you?"

"O, yes. Thank you, Mother." He noticed Evan and nodded, a wistful smile disturbing the lower part of his face.

"*Mamio!*" Armanda was sitting up now, the bed sheet pulled to her throat.

"It's okay, darling." Then to Evan: "Here, Evan. You're a farm kid. Hold this bird." She flung the frantic thing, honking and flapping and spraying feathers about. "It's the *bujo*, honey," she returned to Armanda. "It's okay."

Evan made a net of the blanket and threw it over the frightened goose, restraining a flap of wings and muffling a squawk.

"Come, Gilman. Turn your face while my granddaughter gets dressed. *You*, Evan!" She led Mr. Gilman behind the coffee table and made him sit down on the couch. Without a word, he wallowed back into himself and rested his left hand on one oversized knee, though with a distinct lack of comfort. Evan pinned the bird with the blanket and wrestled it under control. Armanda fought beneath her tented sheet, apparently freeing herself of whatever demons as well as the mismatched pajamas and struggling into who knew what.

Yana stood puzzling Gilman for a moment, a finger pressed to her lip. "Excuse'm." She hurried to the trunk where Evan had propped it beneath that irregular stain on the wall, while Armanda lumped beneath the sheet. Evan watched Mr. Gilman whose eye was on that flurry, patient for the glimpse of a bare shoulder, an arm, a leg, hopeful for something more. Meantime, Yana rummaged through the contents of the trunk. She hunched over, muttering and obscuring her efforts with her back. This and that came flying out. When she found what she was looking for, she shoved it in one of the pockets of her skirt and stood up. She patted and palmed her hair in place and came back across the room.

"Now then."

Mr. Gilman leaned forward, opened the tabloid with a grunt and slapped it down on the coffee table, flesh atremble and shriveling about his eyes. He pointed to the headline. The paper was upside down, facing Yana, but Evan could read it:

PSYCHIC SAVES BILLIONAIRE
BURNS $65,000 IN CURSED BILLS!

Yana dismissed it. "That's old news, but I told you just the same."

"Yes, you told me, Reverend Mother."

Two smaller headlines:

PRESIDENT SHOT IN HEAD TWICE
SAVED BY ALIENS

And

ELVIS SPOTTED IN TULSA

"Here, Gilman."

Yana sat across from him, ugly as a toad. He laid a meaty hand, palm up, before her, the epitome of agony and anticipation. She gathered up the hem of her skirt and wiped his palm with it. She looked him in the eye until he looked away and then studied his palm, the deep greasy pattern of lines. She traced one or two with the nail of her index finger, and mumbled to herself. She sighed deeply, shook her head, and clucked her tongue. "It's the *muli*, I'm afraid."

"I knew it." Gilman ground his teeth and sat back, his little rat's eyes at work, hacked phlegm. "What the heck's a *mew-oo-ly*?"

"Now, now. Let's try the cards to verify. The *muli*? Why it's the influence, the power, the sway, that has you in its grip. Your dead wife's ghost, so-to-speak." She produced a pack of Tarot cards and sorted them in a variation of the two-hand shuffle, deft as a blackjack dealer. Without moving the newspaper, she dealt ten cards in a pyramid spread on the coffee table. "O, looky here. 'The Lovers.' And here. 'The Moon.'"

"Is that good?"

"Oh-oh." She touched another card: The Hanged Man. Then, The Fool. She quickly gathered them up.

"I knew it. O, doom. That's my middle name."

"You been lighting the candles, like I told you?"

"O, yes. Since March when you was last here."

"And you been to the cemetery on the quarter moon of every month since?"

"O, yes. At the stroke of twelve."

"And the chrysanthemums?"

"The chrysanthemums? Why, I leave the chrysanthemums at her feet, like you said. But it ain't done a piddle's worth of damn. She just won't forgive me. She just won't forget. It's all gone to nightmares and ruin since she crossed over."

"Yes it has. But there may be hope. Give me the dough."

"All of it?"

"Listen, dear—" Yana poked her neck forward and leaned toward him, like a menace. She let him see her teeth. "—I told you last March how these curses work. And there it is in black and white." She pointed to the tabloid. "It ain't a light handed saying that 'Money is the root of all evil.' But see if I care what you do. Believe me, it ain't no skin off my nose. I got nothing to gain and less to lose. I'm guiding you through the spirits, so to speak. Heed my advice and the spirits will undo the curse on the money, and your dead wife will forget all the dirt you done her over the years before she finally got peace, and then she'll leave you alone. Just to make sure it's the money that's cursed we'll give it two more tests. That's why I had you bring the duck."

"Goose."

"Yes, well. But if the tests prove out, you ain't got but two possible solutions to relieve the curse. Like I told you, you don't draw every nickel, it isn't worth a cent, all this. You leave a dime in your pocket and it hangs onto the curse. So you got just two ways to go. You can either bury the cash with your wife—"

"You don't mean take a shovel into the cemetery—"

"I don't? I think I do. At the stroke of twelve, beneath a full moon this time, like leaving the flowers I warned you probably wouldn't work in the first place—"

"You did?"

"And there's one more thing."

Yana looked at him and Gilman looked back as if looking at something horrific, and then he visibly winced like a man anticipating an indefensible blow to the head.

"You got to be naked."

A door slammed before Evan realized Armanda had thrown herself off the bed and into the bathroom. The toilet flushed. The water ran. He, together with Mr. Gilman and Yana, looked at the closed door. Armanda was either sick in there, heaving her insides out, or she had become a lunatic in the blink of an eye, hysterical either with grief or some diabolical bliss.

"You okay in there, darling?"

Evan stilled the bird beneath the blanket where it rested on his knees, damp and slippery with goose crap. The toilet flushed again. Pipes knocked in the wall, shuddered against closing faucet valves. Armanda stepped out of the bathroom, her face blank as a pie taken out of the oven too soon, and sat down on the bed.

Yana gave her a squint and then blanked her own face and looked at Mr. Gilman. Mr. Gilman shifted his eyes around and shook his head. He gazed at the table. Something desperate was happening to his nose and jowls.

"You don't mean bare ass—"

"I don't?" Yana patted the back of his hand and admitted that it was a hard thing to ask of anyone. "Maybe there's a possibility that I would maybe do it for you, if you know what I mean. Take your place, say—like proxy. Or maybe you just burn it, the money, like I said before is the other solution. Or maybe, if you're lucky, it ain't the money at all. But I doubt it. After all, you can no more change the things that happen to you than you can change what you happen to. Armanda," she directed, without turning her head to look at her granddaughter, "bring us a glass of water, dear." Then to Mr. Gilman, "Well?"

He reached into his coat pocket and produced a wad of bills bound by a rubber band. He started to dig in his pants pocket, but Yana waved her hand in dismissal.

"Keep the change."

He plopped the bills on the table. "I ain't had but heartburn, to say nothing of a decent sit-down, since she passed." His eyes wandered to the back of his head and slurred around a bit then crept back out, and he watched as Armanda set a glass of water, three quarters full, on the table and Yana took the money into her hands.

"How much?"

"Seventy-nine hundred forty-three." Gilman swallowed, belched. "There ain't a cent more, but change."

She peeled off a twenty. "Oops." She reached beneath the table where it had fallen, bewitching Gilman with her eyes and groping around in the folds of her skirt, and Gilman smiled and squealed somewhere back in his throat like a hog about to be stuck. In a single, unwasted motion, her hand came from beneath the table, wafted briefly above the glass of water, and with two fingers submerged the twenty-dollar bill.

Evan leaned toward the glass, though hampered by the squirming bird in his lap. The water remained clear at first, then nearly indiscernible filaments of red distended from the bill. The filaments thickened, swirled about the bill in ribbons, and marbled the water a deep blood red. Mr. Gilman's eyes surfaced from the flab of his face.

"This ain't good," warned Yana. "I think I guess we should better try the bird. Armanda, get me a pillowcase, dear."

Armanda shook a pillow out of its case onto the bed, and Evan watched as she did, the moment a refuge from the otherwise surreal gyp taking place. The gesture flounced the crepe material of her new blouse and made her breasts roll beneath. Her face was clean of makeup and she was all the more beautiful for it. She had brushed her dark hair shiny and clasped it on the sides with two wooden combs. Today, she wore an old pair of Levi's, the legs cut to mid-thigh, a little higher perhaps, and ragged with fringe. How brown were those legs against the otherwise faded blue of the jeans and so glossed by the sun. She stood against the edge of the bed, and Evan watched her olive-skinned arms rise and fall to jerk the pillow free. She handed Yana the pillowcase, rolled her eyes at Evan, and tossed her hair across her shoulder and behind an ear, a scornful little grimace condemning the Gilmans of the world. She sat down next to Evan on the arm of the LA-Z-Boy, and the smell of her went to his head. She leaned toward him so that he could feel the brush of her hair and rested an arm on his shoulder and together they watched as Yana looped the rubberband back around the bills, fluffed the case, and tossed them in.

"Now for the goose. Evan?"

He was busy with an impression of Armanda and her grandmother, trying to figure the relationship between last night's drama and this morning's shenanigans. He knew there had to be one, knew it would rise to the surface in time, perhaps rancid and green by association, but for now he couldn't put his finger on it—and, anyway, his curiosity had the best of him.

"Evan?"

He collared the bird and offered it up.

Holding the goose by its neck, Yana made of her arm a wing that came down against the body of the bird, clamping it to her side. This gave her the required grip as she stuck the bird's head inside the pillowcase. The thing struggled and squawked.

Yana wrestled to get a better grip where she held it inside the pillowcase by the neck, and the cursed money did its work. The bird honked, shuddered, and went limp with an audible sigh.

"I knew it!" She threw back from the table and flung the bird to the floor.

Mr. Gilman opened his mouth. His tongue wagged, but nothing was there.

"You decide. But I ain't taking it to the cemetery like I said. That money's cursed." She flung the pillowcase back at him as though she were flinging a snake. It flopped in a spiral, the weight of the bankroll in a corner, and he batted it away.

Evan had never seen a person so anxious to part with his money or so desperate to believe. Gilman must have recognized the bleeding twenty-dollar bill and the dead goose as the cymbal clash to his crescendoing horrors, whatever they might be. Now he wanted the horrors to end, wanted so badly to believe that he carried the *National Enquirer* with him like a priest carries a Bible. What more could a Gypsy ask?

Armanda put her head up close, warming his face with her breath and reading his mind. "Even the most reasonable live by superstitions they're afraid to name."

He breathed in her still sleepy scent and watched with fascination the undoing of this strange and gullible man as though he were watching a great mosaic being taken apart piece by piece, and as he watched it produced in him the same emotion he remembered feeling when he once saw a Charlie Chaplin film. The comedian played the part of a hapless bank janitor who dreamt he had foiled a robbery and was embraced and tenderly kissed by the woman teller he loved, then woke to find himself kissing a mop. He thought the movie was comically sad. It was strange how something could be comically sad, but then he remembered Miss Butler and her obsession with the "pleasing pains" of poetry, and he thought of himself, the only person he knew, other than perhaps Armanda and this Gilman, who could look at a sunrise and contemplate death.

THE GYPSY LOVER ·251·

"No one thing remains the same thing always," she said close to his ear, and Yana gave her a sideways glance. "Victims of ourselves, we grow ecstatic on the little murders that keep us alive."

Gilman looked at her and his look argued against a speck of recognition in what she said, for he had murdered his reason, if ever he had any, in the attempt to destroy this plague on his heart—this curse—and survive. The only thing the man lacked was the conical cap of a fool with its drooping bells.

Evan puzzled over his guiltless, waning sympathy for the man. He looked at the goose on the other side of the table, it's neck doubled back on itself, a reddened bead of saliva extending in a line the length of its bill.

"Which is it, then? Bury or burn?"

Eyelids aflutter, Mr. Gilman wagged the lower part of his face by opening his mouth, dug for words with his tongue far back in his throat. Though he couldn't be sure, Evan thought he croaked something akin to, "Set me aflame!"

Yana spilled the money from the pillowcase into a large white handkerchief she had already spread on the table. She folded the money into the hanky and made of it a little bundle by tying two of the corners. It looked like the decapitated head of a bunny without eyes.

"All right." She squinted and craned her neck toward Gilman who by now was all dilapidation and shimmering flab. "You sure you want to go through with it?"

"*Burn it!*"

"Oops."

The bundle dropped with a pat to the floor and Yana rustled her skirt beneath the table searching around. When she found it, the bunny's ears had miraculously grown. She held it in the bowl of her hands, thwarted Gilman with a glance, and muttered a couplet in Romany.

Hogyha nekem sok penzem lesz, felulok a repulore.
Elszallok, mint a fecske fel amagas levegore.

"If one day she's lots of money, she'll climb aboard an airplane and fly off like the swallow up into the airy heights."

Mr. Gilman looked at Armanda and drew down his eyes. He wagged his tongue across his lips and looked at Yana for an explanation.

"My granddaughter, the darling, she's touched." Yana twirled a finger at her temple. "Now then."

She got up and motioned them into the bathroom. Armanda shoved herself up against Evan and whispered something he didn't understand. She pressed and pawed at him and put a hand on his neck and made the face of a moron. When she yanked at him, he pulled her down in the chair and kissed her giggling mouth and wrestled her to the bathroom where Yana splashed the floppy-eared head with nail polish remover, tossed it in the tub, and turned to Mr. Gilman for a match.

"I don't smoke."

"Armanda?"

"Got a lighter, Cowboy?"

Evan shook his head. He dug into a pocket and produced a book of matches. He folded back the foil-stamped cover imprinted with "Ridgebury Pines" and handed it to Armanda. He wondered if he should say something about the magic of hoodwinks and slight-of-hand, jig's up sort of thing; he wondered if he should save Gilman—and maybe himself—for the sake of honor and truth. His tongue lay in his mouth like a worm. Armanda snapped a match across the cover's strike ribbon and flung it with a casual flourish onto the saturated bag. It lay there for a moment, the flame shrinking from orange to blue. Then a flash, like ball lightening smudging the tub, and they each leapt back. It burned hot and quick, reduced the blind hare in a few seconds to ashes, a coiling ribbon of smoke wafting toward the showerhead.

Evan gazed at the ashes. Armanda swayed toward the bathtub and then toward him and next Gilman, exhaling mock relief—tittered a tune.

"Here, now." Yana marshaled them from the bathroom and ran fresh water in the tub, washing the ashes down the drain. Evan sat on the bed next to Armanda and watched Gilman heft himself from one end of the room to the other. The big man's lips moved in a silent soliloquy and he touched his thinning pate and coiled a strand of hair around his finger and yanked it free without a flinch. Armanda said yikes and giggled and squirmed up close to Evan and exhaled on the back of his neck and he felt the silk of her blouse touch his upper arm and beneath it the shape of her breast. She laughed quietly, eyes black as ebony, and up close touched his lips with the tip of her tongue.

"You're a lucky man." Yana emerged from the bathroom drying her hands on a towel.

"O, yes." Mr. Gilman stumbled toward her.

Evan thought Armanda was going to climb inside him.

"I feel better already, I think." He fell with a grunt to his knees, clasping Yana by an ankle, nearly taking her down with him, and kissed her foot, belched. "Pardon." His bowels slipped.

"Gilman!" Her voice demanded he rise, like Lazarus, and he did so with a redemptive grunt. His little pig's eyes poked about, straining and weary within so much flesh. He seemed at a loss for words, chuckled with some embarrassment. A touch of hysteria rose in his throat, for the sound there had no other name, and he pummeled the side of his head with the butt of his hand and yanked again at a few strands of hair. He glanced from Yana to the bathroom and peered at his hands in wonderment and then, with a half-hearted wave, he turned and waddled out.

Armanda laid her weight against Evan as Yana dug through the voluminous swirls of her skirt and produced the short-eared bundle with a clap.

"What a chump," she said, "but maybe he'll rest now. I done my duty for the poor man."

Evan's mind went askew. There was a fourth presence yet among them, and it wasn't the one he had felt the previous night. A figure, darkened by the light behind it splashing through the open door, fumbled into the room. It stood lopsided, features imperceptible, like a block of chiseled stone, but tilted slightly so that its left foot appeared to be standing on higher ground. In its hand dangled Evan's knife, the weight of the bone handle allowing it to swing a little between fingers and thumb, and Evan would have much preferred a ghost.

"Nikki?"

For a split second, half-dazed, Evan mistook the dissolving silhouette of Nikolai and the delayed image of Gilman's departing bulk for Aunt Missy's. She flashed like an orange flame on the flat of his eye, all the time Armanda flooding him with desire, Nikolai standing like an intermediary of the dead, and he could think of nothing else but how appropriately ironic for the fat man to have brought a goose.

I told him to dream of sunrise, even at the gates of midnight. I told him how each of us is a bridge between them who went before and the ones yet to come. I told him not to understand more than he could. I told him how wonder and wisdom are sisters in heart. He come to us out of the night like a sheepish ghost and our destiny was set. Some may think otherwise, but I seen it in the stars and a throw of the cards, I seen it in a fragment of glass. Armanda, she seen it in dreams, though witless herself—the both of them touched by some common seed. And who could forestall it? Each of us links in every man's chain with nary a cause, one link at a time. Some may think otherwise, and think if they want.

~16~

Tunnel of Love

He felt both the perfection of her and a rush of shameful desire . . .

EVAN considered himself at times a dim bulb, but not entirely dark. With one hand on the gates of midnight, the latch thrown back, he knew he wasn't far from the end. But even with that vague notion, he hadn't the power or the strength to hold the gate to. Whether Charlie and his fat wife were out of the mountains, again giving chase, he had no way of knowing—except for his glimpse in the crystal, if in truth he had glimpsed anything at all—though Nikolai's pursuit of some mad wraith seemed certain. Otherwise, why had Nikolai stood in the cottage doorway that morning cursing the dead and his dreams?

"It ain't going to be easy, honey." He waved the knife and it flashed in his fist and his voice went up a notch. "But I ain't forcing you. You want out—"

"Papa. Shush."

"So maybe there's some rough stuff, a little tussle. But don't I take care of that?" He flailed his arms and brandished the knife like a demon enraged. "Or maybe they don't never get there in time. Charlie and his cow has maybe walked their feet to stubs by now, still in the mountains. Maybe they got a tow from the devil hisself. Who knows?"

"Oh, yes," said Yana, and Evan thought maybe she winked. "I think maybe they got a tow, all right—according to the glass, that is. We seen it clear as the moonless night."

"And puny Groucho," Nikolai continued, his own world closing in. "Maybe they don't dare show for what they done to another man's wife." He turned his head from side to side like a ball turret and his eyes were blinking that crazy way again. He leered and smiled grimly, whispering to himself with a sense of wonder. "Or maybe they don't never put it together that we got Knobby and put him in the ground with piss on his grave. Maybe they don't know Nikolai Markovitch. They think maybe they dealing with some shmuck, hunh? Them brothers three, less one. Maybe I stick 'em, they show—." He jabbed the knife gut high into some imaginary foe.

"You shush, Nikolai." Yana went at him and shoved him with both hands so that he stumbled backward out the door.

He blinked at Evan in a stupor. "Who's this?"

"Last of the cowboys, *papo*." Armanda went to Evan and stood beside him and looked at him wearily and then wearily back at her father, an expression that went like a needle to the center of Evan's heart. "Get packed up, Grandma," she told the old woman. "I'm tired of this place. I'm tired of the road. I want to get going and get on with it."

Evan looked at her, but she only shrugged and turned away, and he continued to watch from that gated corridor at the dark edge of the universe these throwbacks to their miserable past: how without sorrow or mirth they thrived on the immitigable scraps of grief and joy. If disaster lay before them, whose hand could stay it? Not theirs. Not his. None that he knew. Caught in the cogs of some great machine, swept along by the shadows in a crystal, bewitched by a wraith, fated by the crease in a palm or a miscast card. Like Armanda, he felt weary with worrying, anxious to get on with it and see the thing through for better or for worse.

They left the dumpy little cabin and drove across the street to Elmo's Truck Stop where they filled up on gasoline, doughnuts, coffee, and milk. Their take in Topeka, not including the soggy red twenty-dollar bill, was just under nine thousand dollars, besides the several hundred dollars in jewelry and clothing that Yana had copped from numerous stores. She gave Evan a hundred dollar bill, a grin, and a pat on the cheek.

"Thanks, I think."

Traveling most of that day, from late morning until mid-evening, his mind was on edge. His face and shoulder hurt from his fight with Jack Sprat, and he was run ragged from his bout with the crystal ball and the LA-Z-Boy and confused by Nikolai's harangue. He felt miserable, and at the same time, with a hundred dollars in his pocket and Armanda beside him, elated. Poor old Gilman, he thought. What a laughable dupe. But he did not laugh.

The truck rattled and hummed and the light got cramped and a little sour as Nikolai blew smoke in the cab. Nevertheless, toward late afternoon Evan felt his mood ease with the changing scenery: through Kansas wheat fields, the country so flat you could stand on a newspaper and see the back of your head. Then gradually, the highway dipped and rose like an unbroken steel band, on either side the vast stretches of green rolling woods. It was hot and Armanda's arms were sticky with sweat. Waves of heat rose above the asphalt, undulating far down the road.

She jounced against him in the cab, every so often taking his hand in hers and lacing their fingers so that it was difficult to tell whose hand was whose. She, too, passed like the scenery between moods of elation and fits of despair. Mad Nikolai hunched over the wheel, quiet for a change, intent on pursuing his ravens and wisps. He frowned at the road and chewed something over in his mind, his jaw muscles moving under leathered cheeks. The hot wind was blowing through the cab, the radio whining Shania

Twain's "Got a Hold on Me." Yana banged the wall of the camper behind the cab every now and again, signaling for Nikolai to slow down. Evan listened to the radio and closed his eyes to those same unsettling images of a sleepless night, dark leaping forms, the inexplicable shriek of an unseen bird . . . it was no use. Armanda teased lightly with the tips of her fingers the down on his arm, and his heart raged like a beast in chains.

When they stopped for gasoline, Armanda scrambled over him and leapt to the pavement before he could get out. She made straight for the restroom. Nikolai got out and pumped gas while Evan checked the oil. The air was pungent with smoked burgers, grease, and diesel fumes. Armanda came out of the restroom and plugged a sequence of coins in the soda machine. She was pushing the Pepsi button with one hand and tugging the inside legs of her cutoffs away from her crotch with the other, when Evan came up. The frosted can *ka-lumped* down the chute.

"Want one?" She popped the tab, broke a fingernail, cursed. She held the can to her forehead, cold and beading with moisture, as she chewed her nail. She tipped her head back, closing her eyes against the hot sun, and chug-a-lugged half the soda.

"Here." She licked the rim of the can with the tip of her tongue, laughed. He took the can from her, but it was the sun, the sun alone, that filled his thoughts—a thick orange light on her slender legs, her arms, her throat. She became for him at that moment like a rumor he had heard long ago or a page he had read in a book or perhaps a thing he had always known, steeped in the back of his mind, just the whisper of possibility and thought. She put a hand aloft to shade the sun, and their eyes locked as he drank, and he saw that there was movement in the curve of her throat and that the sun had saturated her eyes and throat where it hollowed beneath the windstirred collar of her blouse. She looked as if she had been seared on a spit, roasted, now luminescent with heat, as if the sun had gotten in her, and her black eyes were a little bloodshot as though the whites had been burned. All around them the hot light seemed to fall like rain, drenching her forehead in glistening beads. He did not know whether he was smelling the mixed enticements of woods, smoke, and burger grease in the heat that now shot round them or the scent of her body. Whether he could smell it or not he could see how her body churned in her clothes—and the two buttonlike projections suddenly taut in the thin stuff over her breasts. A breeze-caught strand of her hair sent an open look of amusement flickering across her face; the glare of light shot and wavered on the pavement around them. Her mouth went lopsided, and instead of a smile there appeared a sneering grin that was at once knowing and avid and contemptuous. Her eyes flooded with the old Gypsy conceit.

Evan glanced back at Nikolai who was returning from the telephone booth and at Yana who was filling up the water cans. Then he had her around the side of the building and past the restrooms, their brains addled in the heat of the sun. Evan saw it first, but Armanda was quick to stoop. She picked it up, turned it in her fingers, then pressed it lewdly in the palm of his hand, a perfect heart-shaped stone, dappled and smooth as glass.

"Can you imagine?"

Next thing he knew, her arms were about him and he couldn't get enough of her laughing, hysterical mouth. The smell of gasoline and diesel fumes was all around them, and his hands fumbled their way over the material of her blouse, surprised by the warm familiar shape of her breasts. The sun was in their heads and passion wore him out; he trembled with it. She was shaken too, he could tell. She stopped his hand, pressing it tight against her. Her voice was a hoarse and breathy mutter.

"Cowboy," she said, searching his eyes. "Be my cowboy and I'll be the Gypsy girl of your dreams. Here, where my cold heart beats."

"I can't feel it," he said.

"No. It beats like the pulse in a stone."

There was no mischief this time, no Gypsy conceit, no

contempt or naughty lopsided grin. There was only the quiet mocking despair of her mouth and then Yana calling her name.

Armanda wanted Yana to ride in the cab so she and Evan could ride in back, in the camper, but the old woman was having stomach problems and wanted to lie down. Evan felt disappointed but grateful. For the most part, except for the radio or some soulful tape, they continued the journey in silence.

After a while, Armanda said, "Lemme see it."

"See what?"

"Show it to me, Cowboy. You know. It's between us now."

She touched his hand, and he uncurled his fingers one by one until the stone lay separate and heavy against his palm.

"It's cracked," she said.

"No it's not."

"Look here."

He couldn't see it at first but when he ran his thumb across the contour, he could feel it, the slight imperfection, smooth as a tick. "It's not a crack," he said. "A flaw, maybe, but part of the whole."

"Look close," she insisted. "It's broken, all right."

"You feel it," he said. "How warm."

"Cold, cold, cold."

"What's that?" said Nikolai.

"My stone cold heart," she told him. "Isn't it obvious? Lost, then found. Now, you put it away, Cowboy, and be careful how you handle it from here on out."

"Sure. Your stone-cold heart." He buttoned it in the pocket of his shirt. "Just in case I ever lose mine."

The Midwestern landscape unraveled before them, giving way to greening foothills and a broad winding highway. Nikolai said, "enough of this heart stuff" and asked Armanda to tap him a cigarette from the pack in the glove compartment. He popped a wooden match with the nail of his thumb and lit the cigarette and blew out the match. He smoked with the window down, cursing the bad taste left in his mouth. Armanda reminded him to turn on the lights as they entered a three-lane tunnel. A shadow fell over the windshield, and he said something that stirred inside Evan like a sleeping worm.

"Your *mamo* tells me eighty-two hundred—"

"*Papo.*"

"—and it ain't but a few months at the most."

The worm inside Evan slept while he agonized over the gathering light at the end of the tunnel and Armanda leaned toward Nikolai with menace in her voice. She scolded in a low hiss. Evan thought she was going to smack him. Instead, she shifted toward Evan, hip against hip, and whispered, "There's another tunnel after this one." He wasn't sure what she meant, but they came out of the first tunnel and she reached over and put her left hand on the inside of his leg and untucked her blouse with the other, right with her father sitting there, driving. Evan thought Nikolai glanced toward them as they entered the second tunnel. It grew dark quickly, except for the headlights, and the end was not in sight. With the movement of her hand, Armanda spoke volumes, and Evan put his own hand beneath her blouse where he felt the warm flesh of her stomach. He struggled to see if Nikolai was watching, but Armanda whispered loudly, "Do it, Cowboy," and he said, "No," and moved his hand up and over her breast as she twisted his face around and kissed him hot and hard and deep on the mouth. He felt both the perfection of her and a rush of shameful desire and then the hex of it, and the only thing he could think of was apples and the size of his hand and how her heart, not so cold as she thought, thumped madly beneath. She kissed him softly now and moved her hand on his leg, whispering into his wet mouth and shivering against him, and he thought he was going to die or that something inside him would burst if she didn't stop. She was still kissing him when they came out of the tunnel, though she had removed first her hand and then his. The sun struck the windshield, and she looked over at her father and her look was a dare. Nikolai didn't look back, he kept his gaze hard on the road. Evan sat against the door, shaking, beyond understanding. He could see the aftermath of his handiwork beneath the thin stuff of her blouse. He couldn't believe what she had done, or what he had.

"Believe it," Armanda said to him. "Isn't my blood pumping like mad?"

Nikolai was on another planet, Armanda was reading Evan's mind, and Evan's own heart beat with the passion of shameful desire. She gave him a little more room, still breathing heavy, and he thought she was going to say something to either him or her father. Instead, she turned up the radio, and not another word was spoken until they found themselves on the St. Louis exchange. Yana banged on the wall behind the cab, once, yelling for Nikolai to take it easy on the curves. Together with the failing light and Yana's distress, Armanda's mood slipped into some dark abyss. She stuffed her hair up inside her baseball cap and yanked it down on her head. "Let's give the old lady a ride," she said, and Nikolai had to fight her foot back from the accelerator.

When he got the chance, Evan leaned up close to her and whispered in her ear with as much meaning as he could inflect, "O, Gypsy girl." He watched with little amazement as she sulked away from him and kissed her father on the cheek and nuzzled him with her hair, and he heard her say something babyish to him in Romany. He couldn't help puzzling over this strange father-daughter thing, the two of them, both, under some ordinal spell. He noticed that her blouse was still untucked, and she reached over and put her hand on his knee and leaned into him and made a kiss of her lips without touching his and said in Romany, *De babam, muri gajo, de numa kadi ratji.*

"Tell me in English," he whispered, and he thought maybe she blushed, even now.

"Give me courage, Cowboy. Dare me."

"Tell me in English. I dare you."

She put her lips to his ear. "O, baby, my *gajo*, for this one night alone."

"Yeah."

He watched the broken centerline come daggering toward the truck and felt the lilt of the road beneath the wheels and the press of her breath and her hand on his knee. It was getting late and he felt tired enough to die. Some voice on the radio he couldn't quite name softened the light and nagged at the sound. When he undozed, she had him cramped beneath her weight against the door, his nerves wearing thin. It occurred to him that Nikolai had exited the freeway sometime before, and now they were pulling into a restricted camping area, the little pickup trolling among a fleet of RVs. Armanda awoke and sat up and turned off the radio and looked out the window.

"Right here," she said.

Each yard was divided from its neighbor by a coppice of sycamores and pines, offering the illusion of privacy. Nikolai pulled next to a big Winnebago with all the trappings of home, Bruce Springsteen blaring into the warm night air. While they were setting up camp, the ranger came by to check them out then proceeded next door to cite the neighbors for disturbing the peace. With the camper so garishly painted, it was obvious they were vagabonds or weirdoes from afar, but the ranger didn't seem to give it a second thought. He was more concerned with the music next door, which grew quieter but continued to throb between the trees, rhythmic and unsettling as the pulse of a heart.

Armanda went about various personal tasks, humming absently, for the moment it seemed to Evan happy again. Eventually, she settled into helping Yana prepare supper, dutifully setting aside that fifth plate in anticipation of the unlikely guest. Afterward, as they cleared and washed the dishes, Nikolai motioned Evan into the darkness a few yards from the stone grill. Evan expected Nikolai to bring up the incident in the tunnel, if he had, in fact, been aware of it, but nothing was mentioned about the tunnel. They didn't even talk about Armanda, at first. Instead, they spread a blanket over the cushion of needles beneath the overhanging limbs of a spruce and sat, exchanging idle

THE GYPSY LOVER ·265·

conversation while Nikolai smoked. The knife handler never let the cigarette dangle from his lips but held it between his teeth and talked around it like a preoccupied father might talk to a son. He asked Evan a number of questions, his mind flitting elsewhere, among the trees, the stars, a remnant of the past. Did he smoke? Drink? Take drugs? Had he a girl friend? Was she a sweet thing or hard as nails like his Armanda? He chuckled at something inside his head. Had he a girl friend, he asked again. Was he willing to take responsibility for the choices he made? He took the cigarette from his teeth and blew a stream of smoke thoughtfully into the night. He spoke in snippets and catchphrases that hardly made sense. He doused his cigarette in the pine needles and again complained about the taste it left in his mouth. Was he a church going boy? Was he truly running away from home, or maybe . . . from himself? What did he know about Gypsies?

"Are you threatened by my Armanda?"

"Threatened?"

"Ain't she the devil, though? A night and a day plus three and got you all twisted up in yourself hard as a knot. Does she make you weep perhaps for the absence of knowledge and truth?"

"I don't understand."

"You maybe want to do something foolish with my Armanda?"

"No, I—"

"To draw and paint her, my Armanda. So she tells me."

"I've dabbled some."

"Yes you have. Do you paint her in the altogether, maybe?"

"No, I—"

"But you know the shape of her, like you know the shape of your hand. You see it here, up in here. You sculpt it from your head with your hands."

"Nikolai, I—"

"Ain't it a shame, the muddle between fancy and fact?" He looked at the sky, his lips uttering an ineffable tangle of words. "This maybe would give you a sense of yourself, your own attributes, your own origin and seed." He looked at Evan, his eyes dense as the sky overhead. "Perhaps that is why Mosaic Law forbade all graven images of the Israelite God, for wouldn't those ancient Hebrews then worship what they themselves had wrought rather than Him who made them?"

"I don't understand."

"You come to worship my Armanda maybe."

"No, I—"

"You maybe want to enshrine her in gobs of paint and ink. This is not my Armanda. She is more spirit than flesh, and if you mistake her spirit for flesh, if you mistake her spirit for image, it is because you have failed to plumb the depths her."

"?"

"Your dreams of her need no flesh to be real, Rodeo Boy. Even some enigmatic portrait you strive to scrawl cannot conceal the truth of my Armanda, nor anything else close at hand, including the possibility of you." He picked up a twig and snapped it an inch at a time, at first halting and aphasiac in both hand and speech and then as if measuring per snap an assortment of words he had long since read and yet in whole were central to some cosmic intellect kindred to common thought and, under the circumstances and now his loosening tongue, worthy to restate. "Overlook the mistake of it," he groaned, at once summoning the assurance of such words with a twist of his hand and a snap of the twig. "Binding her to the tethers of your imagination will keep her chained to a world in which neither she nor you know the way. Look for her not in a portrait nor in the flesh but in the serenity of the mind."

He tossed away the pieces of stick and brushed his hands of them.

"You speak of her in abstract terms, Nikolai, like Yana sometimes does, as if she were something other than real. As if she were a ghost."

"O, she's real, my Armanda. Like you, the two of you together." Nikolai reached out to touch him, as if to be sure.

"Though I sometimes wonder how long for the world. And me? I'm not fit for it. That makes us a sorry twosome, don't it? But *mamo*, she'll live till the end of the earth, her and her destiny."

"Her destiny?"

"She speaks of blind destiny, such as without scheme or intent." He looked again at the sky and spoke as if to a smattering of stars. "But what manner of destiny is that?" He looked again at Evan. "Don't our very deeds in this world have each before them another, and those each yet another before that? All a never-ending chain from which retreat holds no sway. Fools might even suppose that they have influence over the choices they make, that the choices they make are theirs alone." He dug around in the pocket of his shirt, took out a cigarette and then put it back. His eyes, to Evan, looked like moist peeled-back grapes, and the chiaroscuro delineating his features in the lessoning light was startling and neural as touch. "But ain't we given to choose only what is?" He looked from Evan to the sky and then back as if his words were taken from a source not his own, some universal cognate belonging to the central consciousness of man. "Choice is lost in the flux of generations and every act negates every alternative and chains us one link at a time to the life that is ours. Even what's given holds fast to a future unknown and yet that future is as intimate as the lines in our palm, as familiar and reassuring as the foreseeable course of stars in the sky. Or so the old woman thinks." And he looked away from the stars and opened his fist and clawed the fingers of his other hand there and leaned forward and lowered his voice. "But I would tell you, if I could, that the future takes its cue from both decisions made and the lack of them and while we may seek to argue every cause perceived, we have only the link before and the link behind holding us fast. The world is without order and the order in the events of our lives is that which we have put there, like breadcrumbs dropped in a forest so we won't lose our way. So write and paint what you will, Rodeo Boy. Create the artifice you might. The fact of the matter is wedged between what was and will be though far from what is." He took off his hat and scrubbed at his head and glanced again at the sky. "What then of the Almighty's word and such wisdom to follow it at will?"

He replaced his hat with obvious care and looked as if he were going to take a puff of some phantom cigarette, but realizing his hand was empty, he scrubbed the palm of it across his face and down his chin instead.

"So speak to me honestly now. Children, the both of you. So real, though otherwise still. Ain't she my salvation? Ain't she my doom? In her is the blood of my Sonia together with my own. You may be a nice boy with pleasant eyes, consumed by your nature, foolish and alone. You may yet be desired and amorous yourself for the touch of her, but be forewarned, while she resides in your heart, she remains flesh of my flesh and blood of my blood."

"Amorous for the touch of her?'"

"Let me tell you, Rodeo Boy. In most people's lives, high drama ain't an asteroid heading for earth or a battle for some piece of dirt. It's the agony and suspense in an intimate conversation. Do you love me? Have you betrayed me? Will you leave me? The answers to those questions make the heart sink or soar; they leave lasting marks on the soul, like a trophy or a gravestone. Months later, even years, we look back and think—from that moment, everything was different. Armanda, she don't like it in particular when I take a swig."

"? No, that's for sure."

"Watch for the defining moment of your life, Rodeo Boy. And better not blink. Each happening to each is each's alone. Ain't she but her mother two times out?"

He ducked back inside his head and pulled out another curious comment about that hall they had rented in the basement of an Episcopalian church. Evan blinked his eyes and a lamp flickered, but before Nikolai could finish, it was extinguished in the singsong notes of "riddle me, riddle me ree," and Armanda, in silhouette and shadow, the essence of some larger metamorphosis, came sauntering up.

Nikolai hesitated.

"Sonia?"

"It's me, Papa." She jammed her fingers in the hip pockets of her jeans and showed Evan that lopsided smile, the tip of her tongue brushing her teeth. She had tied a red scarf in her hair, and though she was essence, Evan could see she was substance as well. How could he think to possess just the thought of her as Nikolai urged and deny himself touch? "*Mamio* wants the camper tonight," she told Nikolai, but she was looking at Evan. She threw her head toward the subdued throb coming from the Winnebago as though to explain. "Me and the cowboy will rough it." In the near darkness, her black eyes glistened. She hadn't blinked. "Say, Cowboy?" She prodded his ankle with a bare foot, slipping her toes beneath his pantleg and against his shin, jerked her head for him to follow her.

Nikolai was far away now, as if her presence had banished him to some distant domain, his head cocked, arms roping his hiked-up knees, listening as it were, contemplating voices that rose beyond the airwaves and fell upon his ears alone. Armanda extended Evan her hand, which he clasped and pulled against, lifting himself toward the moon in her hair and that selfsame scarf so vibrantly red and the stars. In all foolishness, he might have pulled her down beside him on the blanket, except for Nikolai and the confusion of his admonitions together with those unsettling dreams.

They walked a short distance toward the thickening trees, away from the light of the moon and the sky, when a patrol Jeep came idling past, the ranger announcing over its P.A. system ten minutes to curfew. He poked his head out the window as they strolled beneath a shadow and started into the trees, and there was tone in his voice.

"Don't get lost, kids."

Armanda nodded and smiled and waved at him in acknowledgment and they watched the tail lights recede into the darkness along the lane. Evan thought of how the darkness of the lane with its overhanging nave of trees was so much like a tunnel, but without a hint of light at the end. And he knew that this was a moment in time that may not come again. In that darkness, he touched Armanda on the point of her shoulder, and she stretched herself up against him, raising her jaw, and he could feel her breath on his throat.

"Where?" she whispered.

And he knew her meaning.

I remember the first time I paid him any mind. It was at a swimming party for my ninth birthday and he was standing there at the edge of the pool, teetering toward the water, when mama called him over. It was the scabs and scars on the backs of his legs that troubled her, but he just sloughed it off and looked at mama and then at me with a worry and a wish. I know that look myself, and it undid me so that I've never to this day got back quite right. But it's not only his eyes. Sometimes I can't get it out of my head that time he kissed me behind the gym and how I could hardly hold back. He tipped my face up, and I thought I might melt right then and there into his flesh. After Mason Talbot's double-handed gropes I never knew a touch could be so tender. We knew then, the both of us, a little bit about heaven and songs the angels sing. Although I think of it as the first time, it was more like a renewal between us of something before this world was. And I could see it there in his eyes, his looking back, and knew he could see it in mine. We're only sixteen, I know, and I don't believe in fate, but it wouldn't surprise me if ten years from now I've got a ring on my finger and his seed taking hold. Some things are just meant to be.

~17~

The Revelation

She gave nightmares a new name.

THE nightsky fell down all around them like a whimpering bell.

It was a bright, calm, hot night, occasionally interrupted by the trill of crickets, a muffled voice, or the rustle of wings. Evan knelt on the blanket to unroll the sleeping bags while Armanda slipped the scarf from her hair. Beneath the blanket the ground was soft with pine needles and mulch, and it was as though they were about to lie like some renaissance two in their bed of posies awaiting earth's shroud to wrap them in dew. For a moment Evan could hear nothing but their own breathing, and then the night itself exhaled a breath of fragrant pine-scented air.

"Such pleasing pains," said Armanda with a hush in her throat, and he knew she was making fun of him. She leaned toward him on an elbow, and he told her again of Miss Butler, how she stood before the class, draped in her flimsy spinster's dress, her hair pulled back and her eyeglasses slipped to the point of her nose, open book in hand, quoting Dickinson or Donne.

"Sad joy."

And there was truth in that, for all the noisy silence that passed between the two of them as they lay beneath the bright night sky. She closed her eyes for him and he took her inside his head for a while. He turned her this way and that, studying the likes of her as one might study the effects of light through a prism, wondering how a thing so fractured with contradictions could be so true.

O, heavenly hurt!

Armanda was saying something, speaking softly. She called him Cowboy in a whisper, muttered something he couldn't understand. He leaned toward her, straining, and saw the impish shape of her mouth. Her face floated toward him, so open now and out of the dark, and he felt her breath and the breathy touch of her lips and her lips were warm. She nibbled at him. So childish. He melted into her lips, her mouth, the fingers of her hand touching his face, and her head fell back and her mouth opened wider, biting and swallowing at him. He fell over on top of her, ready to wipe that impish grin from her enraging mouth. He could not think for the clutter in his head, suddenly yanked back to the irony and despair of the afternoon, announcing in the trembling strength of his embrace that she was his.

And as if she had felt the ownership in that embrace, the struggle of it, she wrenched their mouths apart and forced his head back, holding his head between her hands and searching wildly his face. He said something stupid about how she was going to be his undoing, but if she heard, it meant nothing to her.

She wanted to see herself in him, in his eyes, and told him so. She wanted to crawl up inside him and see out his eyes. She told him to look at her. "Look at me," she said. "I can't see myself. Am I in your eyes? I can't see myself, Cowboy." She told him how she wanted to get down inside of him, in his eyes, in his head, in his heart, and how she wanted him in her. "Look at me, Cowboy. I want you all up inside until you know and can't turn away, until you know what it's like, how it feels to be me."

She was all desperation and desire, and though he had seen them before, they startled him—these duel emotions of elation and despair. She stretched her legs and made a small move with her hips, solid and female, and he did not know how to go on.

"What is it?"

Her chest started to go in and out. Her hips rose against him and he felt her beneath him and she looked back at him, smoldering.

"Hurt me, Cowboy. Hurt me—"

And in that moment he wanted to hurt her. He wanted to lay his hands about her throat and drive himself against her that she might be utterly his. If only he could crawl up inside her and see through her eyes; if only he could trade places with her, as she so desperately wished, so she could see through his. He, too, wanted to see himself in her, to be her, the both of them so bewitchingly possessed. And when he looked, the possibilities were endless. He was in her, all right, but too deep to be certain, like crystal gazing all over again. It was there, beneath the surface of her eye, that he saw an image of himself, not himself but an image of his father, and he watched until it moved away just a little. When it moved, he moved, his desire to tear her apart diminishing. At the same time, an odd sense of triumph and delight coursed through him, dim as some promise of old. He looked again, saw himself smiling now at the pretty blouse, rucked, jammed up in a bundle from armpit to armpit. He watched his own hand touch her with a sense of privilege and caress her in admiration. And when he stilled his hand upon her stomach, she lay quiet beneath it, watching back at him through the shadows of the moonlit night. With a single caress he subdued in her a low animal sound, at the same time pondering where she breathed, more quickly than he, so that the two smooth segments of spheres, with their shadowy tips, bounced and trembled minutely, for all their firmness. He bent quickly and kissed the nearer dark tip, and she shivered from head to foot.

"Don't tease, Cowboy. I bet you hate me, now. Don't you hate me?"

THE GYPSY LOVER ·275·

"Hate you?" He whispered it, mocking. He was about to ask her what she had done to him, what she was doing.

"What have I done? Not me. There's no power holds sway we haven't done to ourselves. It comes from within, whatever you see, whatever you think, whatever you feel."

"More like one of your spells," he told her. "A curse on us both."

She smiled without mirth, a hint of the lopsided grimace that so irritated him at times. He touched her and moved his hand over her breast and she let him hold it and feel it for a moment as though it were a thing that belonged to him. It gave him a sense of power to touch her, and he felt huge in the darkness beside her. At the same time a current of desire sapped his strength and made him feel weak. It was the moment of promise, like a memory, and that moment gripped him and then slid away and was nothing akin to a paragraph in *Fanny Hill,* nothing akin to his fantasies of "Sindy" all locked up in the darkness of Goose's bureau drawer and shadowed in his mind.

She gently removed his hand.

"You promised," she said. "Didn't you?"

"Promised?"

She told him and in the telling her eyes were but a glimmer of something he saw in himself.

"You promised," she said. "I should have known."

"?"

"In struggling through to what, in fact, you are—your own capabilities, like I seen in your palm. Remember? Promise to your mother, you hold so dear. You'll make of me what you will, but you could have, you know that. This moment in time. I wanted you to in spite of it."

She sat up and pulled at her blouse so that it stretched down like a concertina.

He wanted to say, but she looked at him, not glinting or provocative, but as a human being might look at an object. It was odd how bright those dark eyes could be in the moonlight, though he could see nothing of himself in them at the moment. She opened her mouth to say something, but shut it again and went on smoothing and patting her blouse.

"Armanda." He listened to the sound of her name on his tongue and reached out and brushed something, pine needles, from her hair. "Look at me," he said, but she wouldn't look. "I've known you for less than a week, you've known me, but I feel like you've been inside me forever. Down deep where I couldn't get to but knowing all the same and now the way you've come to the surface . . . how I can touch you and feel. I used to have dreams," he told her, "and I've carried you around in here and in here for as long as I can remember."

She looked at him.

"It's not so much my becoming, or any oddness you might have read in my palm, or even a promise."

She looked at him and he heard his voice go soft.

" . . . or even a promise."

And then he struggled, and she let him and watched him now with some menacing charm. He wanted to go on, but instead he reached toward her, so filled with himself, as if to reshape her very form like some master craftsman, and the gesture was as though reaching into the past. "When I put my hand on you, when I touch you . . ." He wanted to tell her, and perhaps did, how when he felt the touch of her mouth against his, the wash of her hair, her breath, how she got all inside him like a blessing. "But you know that . . . both blessing and curse, as if—"

"As if what?"

"—as if—"

"What? We're flesh and blood?"

He didn't know how to go on or what to say.

She said nothing but stared darkly through his chest. And in that moment he knew that she knew . . . *something* . . . though he didn't know what. And the knowing that she knew—was aware at least—of some truth between them, or between their own separate lives, touched him, and he took her by the shoulders and pulled her against him and put his face in her hair and hugged her and held on. She was a sullen and passive lump in his arms. He brushed back her hair and smelt it, the faint, thin smell of the pine needles and the scent of the earth. She drooped a little in his arms and swallowed so that it growled in her throat.

"You make me feel complete," she said, but there was something resentful and odd in the tone. Above, the sharp, clear points of stars came out, and the moon shone down like highly polished marble. "I'm older," she admitted and turned her face on his arm and blinked up at him. "But you make me feel complete, like your blood in my veins." She was silent for a moment, then in a voice so low he wasn't quite sure, uttered in the fashion of a spell, "O, my soul, let me be in you now."

"What?"

He could feel the breathing of her against his chest.

"What did you say?"

"Look, Evan, you could stay with us. We could be together, like it makes me feel when you put your hand on me. Just you and nobody else and find me inside you. Like Adam found Eve. I feel like that, like I've known you since I was a girl, in tales and dreams, and it scares me to think it, your blood in my heart." She drew his eyes casually to hers. "If only you'd been born a Gypsy."

"Or you a cowgirl."

"Considering your life with Missy and Goose, there wouldn't be much you could complain about, would there? Regardless of Gypsy madness, regardless of coffins and the whispering dead."

It was true and the very notion plagued him with a sense of what life might be. He tried to find her in the dark to thwart the inadequacy of speech, but she had turned her face away and went on reading his mind, in a torment.

"Don't think we'll ever be together," she said. "We'll never be complete. Even if you made love to me."

She choked a little, and when he looked, her jaw appeared

fixed, but her mouth trembled at the edges. She sagged in his arms, and when she spoke he felt his face ablaze. At first he couldn't understand what she was telling him. When at last he understood, he couldn't believe. She gave nightmares a new name. Everything with these people was after the fashion of a riddle, and now, with each word she spoke, he felt the terrible flush of adrenaline and clarity of thought that by degrees lifted a veil from his brain. How could he look for her, as Nikolai urged, in the serenity of his mind when she arose there in truth like a tempest? She pressed her head against him, whispering, and he felt her shoulders convulse, and as she told him her face came apart like he had never seen before and, in spite of all her bluster, in spite of that hard exterior shell, she wept.

"Tell me," he insisted, and he gave her a shake. "But make sense of it." He wanted to loose the bands around his heart once and for all.

He waited and the word *betrothed* rose like something bitter from the back of her throat. She called the boy a half-wit and spoke of her virginity in terms of a prize. She would rather it for someone she felt deeply. "For you, Cowboy. Just give me a look." But she said it without meaning or desire, even as she took his hand and pressed it with her own over her breast. Evan took that hand and held it and listened to all her Gypsy-wrought reasons that made no sense at all.

"You're only sixteen," he said.

Her face went gray in the sudden absence of light, and she emitted a delicate laugh, all the more wretched for its lack of expression. "O, Cowboy, you're so precious in your heart. Sweet sixteen. So confused and unrehearsed in the fundamentals of love." She turned his face with her hand and her eyes were intense. "But if he gets me pregnant, I'll kill it with a coat hanger, don't think I won't."

The moon lay dark behind a cloud, and he felt himself in the swoon of it, except light—in the figurative sense—shone all around. He pushed away from her, staring at her, but not seeing her, seeing only the image of himself up to his waist in some swampy muck. A quagmire of possibilities sucked at him. Then a gob for consideration rose to the surface and he scooped it up; he examined the watery thing before it drained away, understood, thought he understood, why even the mad Gypsy couldn't keep his daughter and wife straight in his head. In the sheen of the goop, Evan could see, thought he could see, the extent of the man's loneliness—even as his daughter stretched and shuddered against him. He palmed another gob and gave it a look. Ah, yes, in the grime of it, couldn't he see? Unlike Sonia and Nikolai, Armanda was not to be strung between the worlds of *gaje* and Gypsy. It was her father's duty, he saw it as his duty, to lock her in a single uncomplicated world with a single window on life. No, no. The murk of it confused him, gave back less than he thought—but that blood in her veins, and in his, the flesh of her, just as she had stood with her back to the tree, poised for the knife, for Nikolai didn't care who took her beneath the moon and the stars, in all the foolishness of youth. She had fashioned herself out of thin air, was simply the daughter of herself. Evan tried to make sense of a world where reality served as only a sham. But the muck deepened, rose around him, and remained unclear. Only the surface light of that damnable riddle gave back a vague reflection of truth.

Evan looked at her, unseeing. He knew about arranged marriages and laughed inwardly at that. Blood of whose blood? Type "A" for "Armanda," a singular strain. It was all a joke, a grim, miserable joke.

"Look," she said, "we must forgive them," and she sat up a little and kneeled on all fours, now forming words with her quick Gypsy tongue. "Let bygones be bygones." Your father—unlike the possibility of our grandfather—he resides more in your heart than your bones. This is part of it, the dictates of your head. You remain true to your image of him, to his love for your *mamo*."

"What are you talking about?"

"The only thing that matters," she said. "That's what we're

talking about. Your promise. The commitment to love."

"No, we're talking about you pissing your life to the wind."

"Let me tell you," she said, her voice still a hush, and she rocked toward him and kissed his mouth. "This is the truth of the blessing between us. Why you hold me so dear. All in the notion that your parents may have failed something so deep in your soul, in spite of the common blood in our veins. Now, remember," she said, "the heart of your mother and how you've loved both her and your father with a sadness unmatched."

"O, my Gypsy," he said, and he looked above at the watery stars. "O, my Gypsy," he said. He put his fingers in her hair, and she pulled him down and stretched the length of her up close and nuzzled her face in the pod of his neck. Should he have strangled her when he had it in him and saved them both the grief?

She trembled up through his arms and spoke softly, with reluctance, into the hollow of his throat. "Unless you belong to someone or something or yourself and taste and hear and smell and see and feel as someone or something or yourself, you don't exist. That's why I want to crawl up inside you and see through your eyes. That's why I want you inside me. It's you who makes me feel complete."

"Sure," he muttered, and he lay listening to the breath in her, to the timing and rhythm of their breathing together, and he heard the wind in the emptiness and saw stars trace the lower arc of the hemisphere and dwindle in darkness at the edge of the world, and as he lay there the agony and aging in his heart was like the blade of a knife.

"I couldn't have told you before about this marriage," she tried. "If I'd told you there'd been nothing between us . . . no possibility . . . but now I'll go into this thing with my virtue intact and still letting blood, the both of us struggling through."

Evan said nothing, and she raised her head and looked at him. "Draw me," she whispered. She pulled away a little and sat up and opened the throat of her blouse. He watched as her

THE GYPSY LOVER ·281·

fingers plucked and nibbled the remaining buttons undone. "Like this." She parted the blouse with her fingers and looked away as she did. And then she began softly to weep. "Draw me, like this."

He touched her. He closed the blouse back around her and threaded a button or two. They were a sorry twosome, and he saw very clearly how the sum of all he had known and come to believe led only to this moment and wondered where all after might lead if lead it would anywhere at all. He was about to watch her go, and letting her, letting her as if he himself were in some dream. He touched her, and the full import of what Nikolai had told him lay in the essence of stars and the night. "Someday," he whispered, pulling her down. "For now you're more spirit than flesh."

She shivered and a tremor of fear sagged in his breast as her arms urged him close. Her teeth nicked softly his throat. "Whatever happens, Evan, you can't blame yourself. You come to us unaware but for a purpose. You've always been with me, inside here, where my heart beats. There." She touched his shirt pocket where inside the stone lay cold. "Remember me," she said. "My heart in your hand, there, there, how it beats in your hand. And the smell of my hair and the taste of my mouth. Remember the bright bead of your poem . . . your promise of pearls."

She put her face up and he felt her dissolve like a wish, right into him, so there wasn't an iota of strength or a sensible thought left beneath the moon. Yet there in the firmament above he saw through both confusion and despair first the handle and then the upper side of the cup of the Big Dipper and how that simple and familiar constellation pointed toward the most constant of stars even as it followed the pattern of earth through the void, the most constant and unchanging of stars and a witness to all that should be. He felt beneath his hand the beat of her heart and it may have been truly not her heartbeat alone. She put her face up and touched with her fingers the shape of his mouth. Though far from the embrace of intimacy, their bodies nevertheless trembled as one. There had been something warm in her voice, was something warm in her breath, something real, trustworthy, honest, something innocent, sincere, and, lying so close, as if she were inside him, he inside her, their breathing in time, she lulled him, and he felt warm and strangely at peace. She kissed him and kissed him and moved into him and he kissed her back and it was a good deep kiss, and he felt eager and at peace; he felt blameless and yet inexplicably filled with shame.

Somewhere a dog barked and above them a warm breeze rustled the branches of overhanging trees. She was satisfied now just to lie with him, free of demands. He made no demands. Armanda made no demands and he felt none. Together they lay for the longest time, until there was no moon, and Evan debated what to do, but he couldn't think of what he should do or what had to be done. Fatigue spread across him like a blanket and he moved gladly into the dark embracing folds of sleep when it occurred to him that today had been the first day of school— and as sleep rose beneath him, a curious pang of homesickness hollowed out his breast.

*   *   *

Through a snare of overhanging limbs, the sky shone sterling except for a blotch of white here and there. Against him, she stirred without weight, coughed and swallowed phlegm. Her hands clung to his shoulders as if in sleep she were bound to slip away and rapt on holding fast. He could see the crown of her head below his chin and how her hair shone bright as filaments of black light sprayed across her shoulders and back. Something, a rose petal, had found its way there in the night and he plucked it free. He palmed her there and down to the base of her long neck and looked away from her to the painted truck where it shimmered in sun. The rest of the yard was flecked in shade and bleached to an almost colorless lavender, and quiet. In the morning light, the camper seemed remarkably bright and colorful and clean, and there was the fragment of an illustration he had never noticed before, just the blemish of a woman caught in a watery vortex, her face contorted in the horror of the moment as a dismembered hand reached down from the clouds. Her hair floated like kelp together with scarlet sea fronds gathered and drifting about her throat, and her eyes burned with the specter of loss, the whites cold and inflamed as one left with the insoluble grief of a lover's last kiss. But if there was meaning in it, it was but a fragment in the greater panorama, adrift in one of the riddle parts. When he looked again, the woman's face was lost in a watery blur, and the reaching fist grasped seaweed.

He yawned with uncertainty and carefully stretched, still groggy from sleep. In the distance an engine ground and revved. A pall of yellow smoke rose behind the trees and scented the air with pancakes and bacon. He lay with her upon him beneath the dappled foliage of overhanging limbs and listened to the sounds of all that waking commerce, so alien in the world beyond.

They made so little movement, so little noise, that a blackbird came picking over the loam. It had a damaged leg but was making do by hopping on the alternate, flitting its tail sideways to keep its balance. It came within arm's length, stopped, and put its head up like some advance guard. Evan wondered if it was half blind as well. Though from the side of its head, from a single brown and motionless eye, it appeared to look at him and hopped even closer. They had a staring contest—and then it pecked once at the ground, hopped, and flitted away.

Evan blinked and when he looked again, morning spread like bits of mercury or something organic crawling among the trees and he gazed for the hundredth time at the tangles in his head, like the snarls of foliage against the blue empty sky. He thought about his life and how little of it he could ever have foreseen, and he wondered for all his will and intent how much of it was his own doing. He searched his head, expecting to find something that wasn't there. Although unable to determine what lay before him, he nevertheless knew what lay behind. How could he fault the present when so little had been claimed of the future and so much refused of the past?

He looked down at the crown of her head, her hair eclipsing her face at the cheekbone and gauzing her mouth. O, the way it fell across her jaw and eddied back. It was not so much her hair or the angle of her head, and then again it was, perhaps, her hair. Something vulnerable in the way her hair spread across his chest washed over him and he smoothed a strand of it back from that perfectly wrought ear and thought of her own delicate nature that she refused even herself. How like some telepathic dream she had gotten inside him and slurred things around.

He touched a patch of flesh where the hair divided on the back of her neck the way he would touch a specimen in a laboratory, trying to be objective but not able to deny or still the churning in his blood. And with every pulse, a blur. Now when he looked, the diminishing light on the side of the camper made even less sense, how it sullied the images, obscured the details, and thinned the meaning. Where, say, was the girl in the watery vortex with her seaweed hair? And why now the soldier-boy photographer whose features looked suspiciously akin to what he'd seen in his own? He wanted to hang on to something for his next journal entry and repeated it to himself half a dozen times for the sake of memorization, how nothing stays the same way always, neither love nor hate, neither shadows nor light, neither innocence nor guilt.

O, he could rattle his way back to the farm and apologize in a gloomy breath. Missy would buy him a pair of new Levis and a couple of shirts to start school—a pair of new shoes, maybe. She would slap him and squawk. He considered the evil of it and touched his wrist, still tender and inflamed somewhat around the healing scab.

But where was the scar so deep inside it couldn't be seen?

Armanda thought him childish, the way she tended to his wounds, he knew that, a little guilt-ridden, perhaps, but certainly not bad, a victim of the cards and the glass, of some misplaced hour long since past, the victim of a railway explosion with no apparent cause, of a mother's absentmindedness in gardening without gloves. How real, not this scar, but that, the two of them altogether fictional, his stories of them, and stories to come, just accounts intended to give meaning and purpose to an otherwise purposeless pair.

He searched the landscape of his head, lulled by the distant strains of some tune he could not name. The melody was heavy and when he opened his eyes, clouds piled up like trembling white dunes, the very shape of them rising up to wrestle his soul back to peace.

Armanda stirred in his arms. Her hair seemed to absorb light, contain it, and give back an empty sheen. The angle of her head mashed her lips to a pout, and she absently brushed drool from her mouth across his shirt and then swallowed. She opened her eyes then shut them again, and he drew a breath and wiped his eyes, quick, as though wiping away nightsand.

"Aba detehara?"

"What?"

"It's morning already?"

She blinked and screwed up her neck to look at him; her eyes were flat and distant and her brow knitted.

"What is it?"

"I seen him," she said at length, affecting her grandmother's drawl. "He was the image of Jack Sprat, and he come to me with kindness and apologies and I give him a thing from out of my mouth." She was quiet for a moment, contemplating, as though conscious in herself but unaware of her surroundings. "Whereas before he wanted but got nothing and I give nothing for all of his want. But now in my dream I give him from out of my mouth, just secrets and truth." She seemed to notice Evan for the first time, all at once bright-eyed and stretching, and pulled herself upward like an invalid toward his face, her strangely sweet breath in his mouth. "Do you think I'm doomed now, having seen the Wandering Man?" She pecked him on the lips.

He wanted to say, but instead he wrapped his fingers in her hair, so painfully tender toward her he felt, and pulled until she winced. When that wasn't enough, he wrapped a strand of her long hair around her throat like a noose.

"Murder me," she whimpered. And as Yana banged the door to the camper and stepped with a sullen tread to the ground, she made a small desperate sound in her throat and put her mouth over his.

Sometimes you just know, you know? I mean you can tell. When you look to verify, you see it in the throw of the cards or in the stars, and if you wanted, you couldn't do otherwise than what you know in your heart. You might try, of course, to do otherwise, but the trying gets down inside and shreds you like claws. I knew right off when I seen him there in the pits, a repeat of my dreams, and then in the lines of his palm. And *mamio* knew, at least she come to a knowing in time. Him the brother I might have had in a world apart. You get born now instead of then or to this parent instead of that and the heavens would have to realign to sort things out. In another world perhaps they do. Otherwise, what's to stop the father from becoming the son? The sister from becoming the wife? This universe and none else, that's what. Change a whit and cast the universe anew. It maybe was selfish and odd to some in the thinking of it, but I longed, truly yearned in my bones and my flesh, for his boyish and brotherly seed to catch hold inside me and turn the world around. I longed for the product of us. Completion. Some would declare "shame," others "disgrace," but how could that possibly be, our histories so separate in time?

~18~

The Wedding

A raven . . . was frantically batting itself against the walls.

"EVAN?"

A hand stole across his lap and found his fingers and laced them and pressed with meaning, all less defiant than heedless of the pie-faced woman hulked against the opposite door.

"Cowboy?"

Houses slid away on either side: brick, stone, stucco facades; sharply pitched roofs and wide open porches; rolling, fenceless turf; the pine trees, the oaks. His ghost-face peered back at him from tinted glass. And hers. He looked away from the slippery world beyond the window to a beer can looping between his feet. LeeAnn Rimes finished up "Hurt Me!" and segued into "I'll Get Even With You," singing the transition acappella.

He pulled at the collar of his shirt to loosen the tie and puzzled the small-time thug behind the wheel, how the man's neck rose from his shoulders like a tube and pinched the flesh in a roll at the back of his bulletshaped head. If this was the brother to the groom, how then the groom? The man reached over and punched a news station. Beyond the windshield, the light withered to a peculiar green and the radio warned "tornado watch."

"Evan?"

"Look at that, wouldja?" The driver uncurled a finger from the steering wheel and pointed up ahead. "House afire. Bad omen, if ever I knew."

Up the street a cruiser sparked its lights and firemen scurried between their yellow flashing trucks. A cop stepped into the street and stuck out his hand to slow them and then waved them on. Two firemen in yellow slickers hefted a ladder and others dragged hoses across the lawn and flushed the fire from one window to another and then right out the roof.

Evan glanced toward the stingy sky.

"Cowboy?"

He felt the nudge of her hand in his but looked past her to the burning house and saw there the remnants of dismay. It was a Saturday morning and a small boy stood near the curb huddled in a blanket. A girl, still dressed in her nightgown, clung to his hand. A woman knelt before them like some penitent trying to explain, her face a wicked display of impossibility and loss. Where, O, where, he wondered, was the father in all of this? And who could save them now?

Armanda squeezed his hand until he had to look at her and acknowledge there a reflection of his own despair. She let loose of his hand and touched an earring and adjusted the diamond-encrusted tiara pinned to the bandana she wore. She flopped the weight of the gold chains around her neck and took up his hand again and looked at him. A carnival, a wedding, a wake, her face all painted like a teenage whore's. He tugged at the ill-fitting suit, something Armanda's aunt had pulled from a trunk the night before. It smelled of mothballs and a hint of something sour he was afraid to name. Then in a fit of self-condemnation he named it aloud. Mothballs, he had said to himself in the mirror that morning with Armanda looking over his shoulder, and piss.

"It ain't required," she told him, with a pained and impatient twist of her head. "You don't have to go."

But he only looked at her in the mirror and choked back the

anguish and rage and looked at her and looked at her and looked at her and then again at himself. And now everything slipping away in that dusky green light. And that house afire. Just ashes and embers of all before. Even last night, so tired and hungry, when they had pulled into the *kumpania* outside of Cincinnati, the hour so late, just ashes and embers, and still there was no end to the gladhanding and hugs, the squeezing of breasts.

"Who's this towhead?" someone laughed, and they had introduced him with a wave of the hand—Yana, Armanda, Nikolai. It was as though some advance word had circulated among them and they were satisfied to greet him and treat him as if he were a distant and not very interesting relative.

With but the hint of movement to her lips, Armanda had told him she was sorry and left him to wander aimlessly from room to room, from face to face, straining now and then to catch a glimpse of her. The house was hot and cramped and in the course of two or three hours, a dozen families came and wept and laughed and ate and went. Most of the women looked like God's mistake, the men gnarled and jovial, and one young couple, cousins, both to Armanda and in marriage, made a spectacle of themselves by necking in doorways, in the kitchen, on the sofa—anywhere to goad the elders and keep the children giggling. Once, when the heat and hubbub were at their peak, Armanda found him and took him behind a door. She put her hand to his mouth and he kissed the palm of it, and she took it away and kissed it herself, there, along the ridge of that unmentionable scar, such design therein and the possibility of everything it held. She put her hands on his belt buckle, grabbed it with her fingers, and gave him an odd little jostle. She searched his face, her own so wild, and muttered something about giving her courage, whispering hoarsely his name. And then she was gone, and in her place a thin Gypsy woman with bad teeth and wistful eyes put a hand on his wrist. Her garb was all poetry and art and the filigreed network and expression in her leathered face like some hieroglyphic closed to all but the most gifted interpreter now lost to the world. She invited him into the kitchen with a number of children where she fed them sandwiches and soup.

"How about a side of slaw with that?"

"Slaw?"

She flopped it on his plate with a serving spoon and wet her lips with her tongue and grinned and told him Nikolai Markovitch was the epitome of doom.

"Let me tell you." Her tongue slid across her teeth and she whispered through a leer. "He thinks the Kozinski brothers will leave it alone, them that remain, he's got more thinking to do than either you or I in this life or the next. It's all over the communities from the west to the east, him stealing that corpse and Blind Charlie's vow. Some curses you can't foreswear and hatred is but a sin. But I suppose you know more than I think and maybe something clever about my darling niece's heart." She eyed him softly and pressed his cheek with the bony fingers of her hand, as if in benediction, and he thought in doing so she might begin to weep or pray. "You wear it in the expression of your eyes and in the shape of your mouth, she has touched you so. Such is a torment to the end of your days having taken up with the doomed."

And then she told him to get along. "And don't bother me again with such heartfelt eyes and an innocence of the world to come."

He swung back through the door to the living room and found a shadowed corner and sat on the floor against the wall and tried not to breathe and looked at his sandwich and then ate it in spite.

Now, as they climbed away from the river and above the skyline, the sky itself a watery green reflection of the gray Ohio waters, Evan felt her turning his hand in her lap. She touched it, once again the palmist, and drew her nail along his lifeline and pressed that little window of fate, and it was as though everything they had together become was in her touch and the press of their hands. He held and studied hers, palm up, and fingered there that ghostly brand, and as he did he sought her eyes but she just widened them and shook the query from her head as though shaking free of dread and rolled her fist around his hand and held him tight. He glanced across her at the jawless, pie-faced woman soon to be her mother-in-law, whose owlish eyes were fixed askance upon their hands. The woman had arms like freshly stuffed bladders, wore huge gold hoops in her ears and a bright red babushka tied in a knot at the back of her head. Evan tugged his fingers free, wishing at the moment he hadn't, and gave Armanda's thumb a brotherly squeeze.

The road hooked and flattened out. A stone belfry and then the stone columns of a cathedral loomed into view. A few pine trees rose above the multicolored slate of the roof, and red and yellow roses, dulled by the light, struggled against the bank at the foot of the church lawn. Already, Cadillacs, Lincolns, a vintage Mercedes or two, old battered trucks, and station wagons were lined up in the curved driveway and along the curb. A few people were milling about on the stone walkway and others stood in the shelter of a portico, some leaning across the stone balustrade observing the sky. The sky floated on top of the city like the underside of a fish. And the city skyline swam in the murky liquid of air as though looked at through the watery green depths of the sea. There was not a breath to be taken, the view both surreal and enough to stop the heart—from highrise office buildings, steeples, chimneys, radio towers, and skyscrapers to the wheel of Riverfront Stadium and a trio of bridges spanning the somnambulant waters of the Ohio. The bridges reached across to Kentucky woods or toward the low-roofed residences of Covington which rose among leafy trees between absolutely flat streets.

The chauffeur nosed the big Lincoln up the drive, past the other automobiles and in front of the steps. He shut off the engine and looked at Evan in the rearview mirror and Evan looked back and sat for a moment and Armanda let him. The pie-faced woman got out of the car with a grunt and labored around to his door and stood with folded arms and tapped her foot. Evan looked at her through the tinted glass and waited until she opened the door and then got out and Armanda after him, ducking her head and putting her foot to the curb—all with the poise of a ballerina. She took his hand and looked at him flatly, then casually inspecting the panorama before them, said: "Makes you want to jump, don't it?"

He looked at her and then looked at the river below.

"That's what I mean," she said. "And sink like a stone."

"Come now." The woman gave her a nudge with an elbow.

"You go ahead," said Armanda, and there was an edge to her voice. "I'll be along."

Evan watched the big woman sidle away. He studied her miserably then glanced without hope at the exterior of the stained glass nave. He watched the people beneath the shelter of the portico who gazed at the sky, and whatever power she had over him forced his eyes back to her face.

"O, Cowboy, I know what you're thinking. I know what's in your heart."

He himself gazed at the sky, wishing a tornado would sponge down and suck the two of them off the face of the earth. At the same time, he counted in his heart the minutes until her wedding, and in so many words told her again that if she would pledge her trust in him he would never forsake or abandon her, and she said that she believed him. He started to say, but before he could choke another word from the knot in his throat, she was lost in a flurry of voices and arms. All the women squeezed each other's breasts all around, like some damnable ritual to ward off vampires, he thought. They put their mouths up against Armanda's ears and jabbered incomplete sentences and senseless things. And he could only watch the machinery of powdered flesh and swirling skirts, her at the center of a cog being ground slowly and effortlessly toward the interior gloom of the church. Just as she was about to be swallowed up, he saw her head rise above the others and, even though there was a smile on her face, her eyes glanced back at him in a pained and poignant way.

They didn't go into the chapel, but beneath the shelter of the portico digressed to a stairwell leading to the basement. Evan looked again at the sky and thought back on his days spent in the potato fields next to such vagabonds and how different and otherworldly they then somehow seemed. Dark clouds stood banked in a high wall to the south and a thin and soundless wire of lightening appeared there and quivered and vanished again. He clopped up and down, listening to, and enjoying without satisfaction, the sound his bootheels made on the cobblestones, at the same time growing annoyed by the few birds hopping around on the lawn. Jays, he thought, and magpies, and he looked again from the cathedral to the sky and then to the hideous waters below. When he heard the pickup come groaning up the drive, he felt as if his moment had passed. Nikolai lunged from the cab like a man robbed of his wits. He bolted toward the steps when he saw Evan.

"Hey, Evan." He was red-faced but sober. "You seen my *daro*—the brideprice—my eighty-two hundred dollars?"

Yana labored down from the cab. "Why would he see it, you stupid? They got to pay or nothing's on. Come on, Nikki. It's your darling to think about, and we're here now. Come, Evan." She beckoned him with a grotesque wave of her arm and grunted. "Let us go and meet the groom." And then he thought he heard her say, though her back was to him, "Destiny awaits."

"What? You go meet him," he said. "I think I'll hang around out here." He felt out of touch with even himself.

"Hey, come on now." Nikolai limped over and urged him gently with a hand on his arm. "This is only a temporary thing," he said.

"Temporary?"

Nikolai brushed at his brown polyester knit suit. He touched the collar of his pink shirt and screwed his chin around and

THE GYPSY LOVER ·295·

adjusted the wide wool tie. He chuckled. "Ain't we two of a kind? Don't that little devil run us around though?"

"Yana, wait. What does he mean . . . ?"

But the old woman had already entered the portico and was descending the stairwell. Evan looked at Nikolai.

"You think I let those sonsabitches take my Armanda for life?"

They stood on the grass, Evan clogged with stupidity. Across the river and eastward, lightening flicked the sky and he waited for the grumble to follow. He watched Nikolai limp toward the church, one limp at a time, and felt a renewed sense of hope opening like a fist from around his heart. Why hadn't it occurred to him? Why hadn't Armanda told him? Now the sky grumbled like a distant chide. It was all so perfect, so pat, so Nikolai. Nikolai the thief. Eight grand, a fertility rite, and divorce.

He could see it in the roiling clouds, another illuminating spark given voice. The mad Gypsy didn't care which way Armanda's life went, as long as she was happy in the end. No, no. All he cared for was his *daro*—the brideprice. He gazed at the clouds and considered the possibilities, sorting them around in his mind. O, he could wait for her, bang around the country with Nikolai and Yana for a month, until she came back to them. He wanted to feel happy, but there were still too many things that didn't jibe. Why hadn't she told him? Why had she denied herself as well as him the possibility of hope?

He put his hand in his pocket and felt around for the stone and took it out. It was a thing of beauty, so white and flecked with red, not like the symmetry and perfection of a Valentine's heart but full and tapered and cleft like the real thing, and if he held it tight in the palm of his hand he could imagine the pulse of it, whether from within or from without was beside the point. It had been hers at first and then his and now together their own. He closed his hand around it and ducked his head and let the shiver run its course and started for the church.

At that moment, lightening snapped behind the cathedral

spire. Evan saw it and then saw the few birds start with a scream and reign about scolding in fits and loops as the raven glided in and alighted, folding its wings with a hop. It sort of teetered around and sidestepped toward him, blinked. Evan felt something unpleasant get down inside him and nudge aside that meager sense of hope he fought to claim. He glanced back at the impudent bird and, plugging his fist in his pocket, went up the steps.

He felt weightless, mysteriously separate from the stone walls and the dark oak doors before him. As he passed beneath the portico he noticed the stained glass windows, lead mullions solid as earth, the rich colors dulled by heavy, gathering light. At the base of one window a series of archaic letters:

All Is Well

Lightening popped again and broke around the cathedral like an unloosening of the sky, but not a drop of rain. He let go of the stone in his pocket and followed Nikolai down the narrow stairwell where together they entered a large multipurpose hall. Just inside the doorway, he took out his father's spectacles and put them on. They made him feel less conspicuous—invisible, almost. He stood next to Nikolai who surveyed their surroundings in a glance. Evan too gazed around the room: the high ceilings, the walls windowless and banked, the decor a verdant-gray with navy trim, woodwork a mixture of mahogany and oak.

A man came up to Nikolai and handed him an unsealed envelope.

"My *daro*, then?" But he seemed no less upset. "Here, Evan." Nikolai turned around and handed Evan the envelope. "For safekeeping, the sonsabitches. Put it in your coat." The man who handed Nikolai the envelope frowned and squinted at Evan. Evan turned aside and squeezed open the envelope. Inside he could see a thick stash of bills in fifties and hundreds, at least eighty-two

THE GYPSY LOVER ·297·

hundred dollars from the look of it. He jabbed the envelope in the breast pocket of his coat and glanced around the hall.

A bobbing sea of at least a hundred guests, and there she stood, among a gaggle of women who fussed with her makeup and plucked at her hair. She nodded patiently and giggled and answered each of them in turn and then rolled her eyes when they turned their heads. Beyond her, at the far end of the hall, a curly-haired jovial sort wearing a little red vest and baggy pants and boots, stood on a dais beneath a picture of Jesus praying in Gethsemane, and fiddled to his heart's content. He played tight and wild like Evan had never before heard notes squeezed from a violin, and as he played, brown and weathered men in cummerbunds, three or four in tandem, atotter with trays of food, worked their way through the hubbub toward the laden tables. Both men and women were swigging longnecked bottles of ale or sipping gin-and-tonic and vodka on the rocks from plastic cups; some, along with children, were picking at plates of food. How like a bunch of hens in an overturned truck. Blur your eyes a little and the throng looked just that, multi-colored poultry navigating a barnyard in search of the nearest pile of feed.

He adjusted the frames of his glasses and looked again to find her so far across the hall, and as he looked, the room grew thick with bluster and smoke, and she began to fade away right before his eyes, and as she began to fade, the fiddler's strains ached and whimpered, sometimes overriding, sometimes mingling with, the otherwise shuffling feet and irreverent jabber.

"Who's this?" someone said in passing.

Evan looked at the woman and the gawkish entourage that surrounded her, and his look gave apparent and misconstrued offense.

"Have you ever—?"

" . . . said how the both of them, doomed offspring of war."

"—and you expect me to believe . . . ?"

"O, yes, and the truth cleverly told—"

" . . . said how some far gone ancestor's to blame."

"—is the worst lie of all."

"Some spread for a poor Gypsy man, that Markovitch."

"You're eating it."

"Who was that?"

"Have you ever—?"

Evan closed his hand around the stone in his pocket and time got slow. He found himself moving among the bodies, both perspiring and perfumed, working toward the long tables obscene with food and drink: platters of lamb, veal, beef, and ham, dark and light turkey meat, plates of delicate, greasy-looking hors d'oeuvres, pickled vegetables, shrimp-stuffed cabbage, a variety of salads (potato, macaroni, Caesar, tossed garden, fruit) in wooden, glass, and stainless steel bowls; crystal punch bowls of red, yellow, and green liquid from which both children and adults were given ladlefuls to drink. At the end of the table, a man in gaitered sleeves with a black mustache and yellow teeth poured wine from a two-gallon raffia-jacketed bottle.

"Don't be afraid to eat," he said with a mottled grin, nodding to a stack of plates.

Aunt Missy would have killed to get within sniffing distance of this spread. And there was Yana, busy preparing two plates as usual, hers and the other one to be set aside and grow cold in anticipation.

Evan leaned against the table and gathered up a plate along with a set of napkin-wrapped utensils. Fluorescent light flooded the laps and plates and hands of guests who sat against the walls in wooden folding chairs, and shone harshly upon the glass panes of the pictures of *Jesus and Lazarus, Jesus and the Children, Jesus Healing the Lame and Blind.* Across the table Evan could see his own gilded portrait superimposed upon the glass of some apparently ancient scrollwork:

- *Have ye walked, keeping thyself blameless before God?*
- *Could ye say, if ye were called to die at this time, within thyself, that ye have been sufficiently humble?*

*• Have thy garments been cleansed and made white through
the blood of Christ?*
• Behold, are ye stripped of pride?

Someone scraped back in a chair and laughed and the sting of the violin took on a wild note. A second musician flared and squashed and warped his concertina in time, the glory and abandon sliding like water among the steady murmur of sound that seemed to come from all directions like the sound of a waterfall heard from up close but not loud. Next, a guitar and mandolin joined in, and the music couldn't do but flush each heart listening full and pure. He stuffed a wad of turkey and deviled egg in his mouth, sloshed it down with a pineapple/banana something or other. He gawked around for Armanda but instead found a little dark-eyed beauty who tugged at his sleeve. It might have been Armanda ten years ago. Certainly a Markovitch, if ever he'd met one, and he thought maybe he had seen her last night at the reunion. If not at the reunion at least in dreams, for she presented herself as the possibility of any number of things. She offered her hand, each finger and thumb wearing a large black olive.

"Want one?"

She was missing her two front teeth.

"Been kissing the boys, I see."

"O, no. Except papa sometimes. They just wiggled out one day. Want one?"

"Thank you." He showed her his plate.

"O."

"What's your name, little sister?"

"You know," she said. She stuck an olive in her ear.

"O?"

"Ask them to play a lullaby," she said. "I'm quite sleepy."

"A lullaby?"

She shrugged and skipped away, her long double braids flopping behind.

"Look at that," someone cried.

A fat Gypsy woman came waddling among the throng. She hefted a huge loaf of bread with holes gouged out, many of which already contained coins and bills of various denominations—gift to the bride and groom.

Evan dabbed a gob of tuna pâté between the turkey and pickled cauliflower on his plate and searched around for the little dark-eyed mystery, and as he searched, he tried to think. Instead of the dancing pigtails, he found Armanda on the other side of the hall. And she found him, the pain in those dark, shining eyes a terrible plea.

All Is Well . . .

The fat woman lifted the bread loaf and spirited it around, bobbing it above heads. As it passed before her, Armanda put on a face and humored the crowd by snatching a handful of money with mock-thievery from the mangled dough, and as she did, a roar of approving laughter rose and fell, some applause. Evan watched and saw again the awful sheen in those eyes and a little piece of something down in his gut hollowed him out and rose to his throat. The kid came up and laid a hand on her waist and pulled her against him, off balance and surprised. He was a tall loose-jointed kid, maybe fourteen, whose forehead boiled with pimples. Hair greased back like a homeboy's, the bridge of his nose scooped down from the bottom of his forehead and terminated in a knob. Weak-jawed and fuzzed along the jowls. He wore a mismatched suit and an open-collar shirt, and around his neck, a heavy sterling chain. When he opened his mouth, the teeth were flecked and the grin as idiotic as the look in his eyes.

Armanda twisted herself out of the circle of his arm and stepped away from him, and as she did a hush fell upon the room. She closed her eyes and her voice fell upon the guests with a dreadful sigh. Words to a tune he had heard her hum more than once during their time together, and even now she sang without accompaniment and he was both moved and hurt that her voice, the song, should contain such plaintive grace. The words spoke ironically of the contradictions of Gypsy life, of a young bride crying out to her mother that she had been sold like a slave into marriage, that she would rather die instead, and her voice fell to a lower husky pitch on the final verse, a sorrowful plea of what she should do.

Evan put aside his plate and cup as the guests fell back to the walls, created space. He thought of the world and his place in it at this very moment in time, the setting of the cup, the setting of the plate, each separate gesture, and how every choice defined the future at large, and thinking of such he had an impression of what he must do. The room was hot, and the spectacles had slipped on the bridge of his nose. With a forefinger he nudged them back in place as if restoring sight to the blind. He could see clearly now, and what other choice did he have? Even the ghost's portion had been picked over, the plate Yana had set aside, on the other side of the table; at least it had been nibbled at here and there, as if there were meaning in that. Remnants of vegetables and shreds of meat swam in a sickly liquid or oozed their own greasy gel at the bottom of the plate. But there was an image there, something to be seen, and he could feel the decision of it tremble his limbs even as time got away from itself and space narrowed his view. A remnant of the closing lines of her song, that plea, her expression, and other such heart-mangling trifles were now coming fast at him, both the mystery and the pain and a strange yearning sense of possibility, almost as if heartbreak were a thing to be sought and moved toward.

He looked at the cups and the plates and at the picked-over food and from the plates to a hag, and as he did, a hush, and without ceremony he was listening to the professional simper of the preacher, solidly real, as heavy and solid as the iron chains at the gates of midnight and as heavy as the golden burning bodies and faces of real guests hurling their attention toward the couple who nodded before him. He kicked at a cigarette butt on the floor, tearing the paper and spilling the tobacco, unimpressed by the half-dozen heads that suddenly turned . . . *gathered here . . . 'til death do you.* It was all far away and gauzed, as though he were witnessing the ceremony from a separate world . . . *with this ring.* He closed his eyes and before he opened them, some applause.

Polite chatter.

The violinist plinked at the instrument's strings, retuned, and drew down the bow. He labored through a long melancholy note, followed by the concertina, and Evan forced himself to watch, and as he did he felt the locomotion of his legs, step by step, and Armanda looked back at him, across the groom's shoulder where her face was pressed, and each time he swung her around, another step closer, she caught Evan's eye, he knew she did. He watched, and as he watched, they danced, and as they danced, he moved, the very muscles in his back growing taut, moving among this dancer and that, his arms like stone, and all at once above the violin a weeping, at first far off and then closer, a weeping and finally a wail. Out of the wail rose a commotion, and together with the weeping, the sound of it gnashed in his ears all heated and red, and then he heard what it was and, except for the weeping, it was a voice and the voice rose in a wail above the violin and out of the wail came a confusion of bent and twisted words.

"It's not going to happen," he heard himself say.

"Evan?"

"It's not going to happen," he said, and he was yelling it, and the upper part of her arm was in his hand.

"What are you doing?"

"Say, buddy."

Beyond the open door a blaze of lightening saturated the air and washed the room in shadows of green. It stuttered and sparked and as an afterthought assaulted the building in a climactic bolt. Lights flickered, went out, blinked back on. The concertina stopped playing, then the violin peeled off together with mandolin and guitar, each of them grinding down raggedylike and out of tune. The chatter got out of synch, conversations terminated in a question, and the dancing stopped.

"Daddy?"

Rain began to fall.

"C'mon," he said.

"The unrested dead will have its due."

The kid looked at her. "You say?"

Somehow, a raven had gotten into the hall and was batting itself against the walls. Heads ducked and someone brought out a broom to swat it while others tried to shoo it toward the door. It flew into the face of a screeching girl, and Evan stood with his hand on her arm and pulled her against him, and then it flew up to the ceiling, out of reach, and hovered there above the dais beating its wings. Every face in the hall turned from Evan to the bird and a strange and general lull washed through the room. There was a moment when the only sound was the beating of wings.

"What are you doing?" she said, and her saying was a whisper, all the time her eye on the bird, and taking one deep breath after another, and then her hand was on the hand gripping her arm, and he felt the unloosening of his grip beneath her hand and her moving close. The kid tugged at her.

"Look, buddy."

"It's not going to happen," he said, and shoved at the kid.

"God damn it."

"Shush."

The thing sprung an aura, a halo, that shone throughout the hall, and beat steadily its wings, and then a face all at once where the beak and below the face a torso and then legs, now clad in the most diaphanous of gowns. The image hovered where the bird had been, morphing to complete itself, and a slight breeze seemed to catch the gown. It had the face of a woman, but gaunt, and the thing was potbellied, squatting a little as if about to give birth. Hair stood up on the hoary head as though it had been charged with electricity, and from the translucent folds of the gown jutted a thorny hand. Noosed about the neck a scarf of some crazed material streaming red as blood. Evan thought maybe he was aware of something, some realization, when the hall was filled with sudden and indistinguishable voice, though so quiet it could have come from inside his own head.

The unrested dead will have its due . . .

"Nor can the living forestall it," whispered Armanda hoarsely in reply.

Evan looked as though by command and saw Nikolai locked in argument with a man whose face caved in on itself around a wolfish snout. He saw at once that it was either the man in the coffin come out of his grave, or a twin, and as he looked, the thing moaned and seethed in its grief and grunted in some agonizing labor of both pleasure and pain. There was an agony of joy about it. Evan looked from wraith to Nikolai and back, and when he looked again the thing was gone. Dissolved. Vanished. A puff of dust lingered above the dais below, and, lo, there stood the little pigtailed girl. She had a finger in her nose, her face as pink as a newborn babe's. A general clamor rose throughout the hall, and above the din, the faint strains of music. The little darling did a quickstep in the fashion of a jig, thieving looks all around, that index spelunking a nostril. With her free hand, she slapped a tambourine against her hip and twirled and shivered it aloft, and her skirt lifted and flared like a parachute and her pigtails flopped. A man with a broom was laughing. In one hand he held the broom and in the other, by the tip of its outstretched wing, an apparently dead bird. It wasn't a raven—a sparrow or a starling, a magpie, perhaps.

Outside, the storm raged on. The little girl danced.

"Evan," she said, "what are you doing? Daddy?"

He looked at her and put a trembling hand on her arm and

pinched the spectacles from his face. The pimply groom was about to take a swing when someone put a hand on his shoulder and said, "What the hell?"

"It's not going to happen," he said, and the three of them looked at him, Armanda with her eyes gone shallow and the kid and the mustachioed fellow with his hand on the arm of the kid, and then Armanda said quietly, at the same time looking away, "Then what is going to happen, Cowboy?"

He held her but lightly and watched her in silence and looked for the child and glanced at the kid.

"Answer me," she said, turning. "You and none other but you who shaped so many events along our calamitous course. Tell me."

Evan tugged at her, and as he did the future unraveled somber and aggrieved as the nucleus of a truncated thought and from that core Nikolai's voice rose above the commotion and in that voice a wail, repeating even as he hauled again at her something about the "unrested dead" and all after that was but image and loss. With a meaty finger, the mad Gypsy was prodding the flatfaced man in the chest. The man grinned foolishly, his head tipped and drawn back, like a dog's head quizzically cocked, his knees bent some as if to sturdy himself against anything Nikolai might hurl. Nikolai sprayed the man in a bleat, his eyes twitching double time, his fists clenched.

"Here, now, Markovitch. It wasn't nothing. She was a lover of Gypsies, and you know it."

"A lover of Gypsies?"

"Let it rest, Markovitch."

"Let it rest? Sure, Groucho. I let it rest. Like your Knobby, he rests blowing his big nose where you won't never find him to pray for over his grave. He rests like a salamander."

"You—"

"Yes. Me. Markovitch. Didn't Charlie get to you? Him and Carla on their stubs back in the Rockies—"

The man looked bewildered.

"—back in the Rockies where I bashed their car? And don't your Knobby rest beneath a dung heap with piss on his grave?"

"My brother! You didn't—"

"Didn't I? You don't know Markovitch. With piss on his grave."

The wolfish man stepped back, patting his hands on a cushion of air in front of Nikolai's chest. "The dead will come to you in dreams," he cursed beneath his breath.

"They already do," bellowed Nikolai, at the same time shoving past the guests and raging up the stairs. A flash of lightening brightened his image against the doorway, fixed him in time, and was followed by a thunderous clap.

The man, Groucho, identical twin to a corpse, looked back at the faces that came away from Nikolai as he disappeared through the door. He screwed up the flesh of his jowls and shrugged, displaying open palms in a gesture of righteous indignation.

"Now," said Evan, giving her a tug.

The kid looked at him and then looked at the mustachioed man who looked from Groucho to Armanda at a loss, and the four of them stood there, as if in a dimension apart, the rest of the congregation seeming to bang on some invisible wall that kept them at bay. What now passed between Evan and Armanda was after the fact, though the electricity of it gathered his wits and charged the air about them with wonder and dread.

The violinist struck a chord, and they all turned like supplicants at some religious rite to watch the dark child jiggle her hips and beat a tattoo. And as she jangled and clogged and rose to the beat, as if taking some measure of the space about her, her own being, say, and distance and time, Evan felt the sway of the dance, and Armanda against him, the dancer herself, even before she sensed it, turning wildly on her heel, and Yana, who had already jumped to her feet, even before Nikolai hit the bottom of the stairs. The mad Gypsy stood bare-chested and drenched, having rid himself of his shirt. Gartering his hips was a sash, the fabric both familiar and odd, and now worn red and honorable as a wounded soldier's badge. He threw himself in lopsided fashion to the center of the room, gaped furiously about. The wolfish man drew himself up and back against the wall as the music wound itself down again. Voices trailed off. A cough here. A query there. Nikolai lunged, a little off balance, as if propelled by the winged and fluttering tails of that terrible emblem girding his waist, and Evan saw the blade catch the overhead light as he flung it hard into the man's chest.

"O, my!"

Groucho looked as if he had eaten something sour and he touched the handle of the knife where it protruded from his breastbone and looked down and examined it as one might examine something cherished and rare.

"O, my."

"Here," Nikolai offered. "Let me help you with that." He got a grip on the knife handle and yanked the blade free.

"O, thank you."

"What? Not dead yet?"

He punched the blade hard into the man's gut, leaned with his weight, and sort of twisted and sawed. His elbow jounced, and he punched it again. Groucho thumped back against the wall, toppled chairs in an effort to stand. Wild-eyed, he pawed toward Nikolai, clutched air for support.

"Fiend!"

Nikolai lunged once more, and Evan heard the ugly sound of the blade punch clothing, flesh, strike bone. "You took my Sonia! Raper!"

The man was gasping to get his breath back, and shaking, and trying to hold the blood inside. The handle of the knife jutted from beneath his collarbone. He opened his mouth once more, blood bubbling around his lips, but it was as though all the air in the room had been used up. His eyes puzzled, filled with terror and then tears, and as though a scrim had been drawn across them, went blank. For a moment he was standing there dead. Then he was alive again, gulping down each breath. And then he was dead, carried by some invisible blow back against the wall, clutching now his heart, his lungs, his throat, and like a comedian doing a pratfall, his legs flew out from under him, and he rode the clatter of chairs upon his back to the floor, fighting them all the way.

In the pandemonium of Gypsies shrieking and trampling one another, a powerful looking man wallowed up behind Nikolai and, using his fist like a pile driver, thumped him on the head. A second knife squirted from Nikolai's grip, a carnival knife, and his knees buckled. Yana stood frozen across the room, her hand clutching her throat. Evan made for Armanda who was standing face to the wall, hands pressed to her ears. The kid wrenched at her and Evan hit him in the back of the head with his fist and then hit him again. When the kid started to turn, he hit him square in the jaw and blood and something flew out of his mouth and his eyes rolled back. When Evan called her, there was nothing, so he jerked her around and then had to let loose of her to get his hands back on the kid. This time he shook him and wrestled him down and popped him hard enough to make it stay.

"Cowboy?"

He looked at her, and her eyes were dark and flat and dead.

"Evan, did the man die?"

"I don't know," he said. "Yes. We've got to scram."

"Them that die bad don't stay in the ground," he thought he heard her say.

Next thing, he had her in tow. A cracked voice wailed, a black hand and leg thrust across their path, withdrew. The powerful man had Nikolai in a barrel grip, arching him back against his thick chest so that his feet peddled air. Evan pulled Armanda against him, pressing her face, her head, in the circle of his arm. She struggled and he pulled her back, away from the wide-eyed wolf face, its mouth crazily askew, blood oozing from the still-trembling snout and along the outstretched tongue, puddling chairs and floor. Evan hesitated then reached for the knife handle and the blade came unstuck. In that instant he saw painted there on the surface of an eye like a dark triptych in mirror glass gone cold and already beginning to frost the image of himself paneled to one side and Armanda to the other and between them another, a girlish eidolon, frightening and unknown yet familiar all the same and wondrous as the prospect of some pleasurable dread, and as she looked back from the diminishing luster of that eye, mother sister daughter wife, it was as if he'd awakened to find the heavens all changed and the stars by which he'd traveled gone dim and a new sun casting shadows from the shore of an unknowable void there at the earth's darkening rim, as if his sleep had encompassed whole seasons, and in dreaming he had dreamt not only himself but the world entire, and if he saw more than this or had ever and still had more to see in all his time to come, whether in this world or the next, he would never say but keep the unsaid close to his heart, there among the cilia and the alveoli deep in the pocket of his lungs, like a cherished breath. The eye went glazed, and as he labored to breathe, someone screamed. He had blood on his hand, and a little fountain of blood throbbed from the wound.

Armanda swayed against him, stumbled back, and he let her go and shoved her toward the exit. As they made the door, a world of resolve came clear, bright and vague as the images in a crystal ball, both metaphorical and exact. A blaze of lightening stood the world in green and out of that green like a phantom from sleep, a one-eyed Gypsy came bounding down the steps. So familiar and expected of him who slept, and of the waking as well. He was all wet, his hair matted and dripping and his tattered clothes soaked through; he had three days, perhaps an eon's, growth stubbling his chin, but his timing couldn't have been better. He plowed past Evan, shoving his way into the hall; in his hand he carried a small automatic pistol. He did an about face, flashing the gun toward Evan for a split second, raising his arm, a glint of recognition in his one good eye. Then he lurched to a stop, gaped around the assembly hall, saw Groucho dead in a pool of blood. Saw Nikolai straining against those brawny arms.

Time slid away. Resumed.

On the dais the Andalusian child swayed and tapped her flamenco and spun to some fiery beat and rattled her drum. Evan made for the door, heard a pop, and looked back. There was a dark spot at the base of Nikolai's throat. The burly man relaxed his grip. A second pop. Nikolai sagged in the heavy arms, the sash about his waist gone limp. He was turning his head from side to side as if it had been bound with elastic cord and he an animal, not knowing how he had been caught.

He was a boy after the touch of her and whatever else the world might bring. That was the first thing I think. Then she pokes that pup all rigid and dead and speaks of her dreams, and I had but to look in her face. I been there in the dark place of dreams, and when I seen the look in her face, I know more than *mamo* knew at the time. This is our destiny, this is our fate, fallen like a bat from rafters above. I'm expecting maybe Dracula or some misbegotten ghoul to cross through the light, but it's only a kid. So I ask you: What more is a blackbird than a bird painted black? What more a raven than a stomach with wings? Armanda, she seen the fate of it quick as he steps from the dark, quick as the best *drabarni* around and that would be *mamo* herself. But I think, ain't she flesh of my flesh and blood of my blood? You place all the trust you have in your flesh and your blood. *Mamo*, she don't pay attention to the heart of it but to look in that ball or lay the cards down flat or throw out a riddle to see. Ah, the wonder of youth, the wisdom of age. She'd have the cusp of it maligned in her hand, and there ain't no greater monster than reason, didn't my Sonia once say? She put a finger to the guts of that pup, and I could see then in the dark of her face, for wisdom and wonder and the black rage of fate, that she was a girl after the touch of him and whatever else the world might bring.

~19~

Panic

. . . he knew he was going too fast, but he didn't care.

EVAN dragged Armanda from beneath the portico into a warm green rain. The weight of her yanked him and telegraphed through her loose-jointed arm up into his shoulder and together they reinforced the clasp of their hands. He could see the pickup sitting at the edge of the curb and fixed it in his mind as a goal. Somehow the rain had smeared the images painted on the camper. Or so it seemed. Colors were awhirl, blending to a white and pewter-green. The whole thing appeared fluid as the waters of the Ohio, just one big churning sea.

He ducked his head against the slant and the blur, and she put her face to the rain and cried. By the time they reached the truck both of them were soaked. He triggered the handle and jerked open the door. He yelled at her to get in but she shook loose of him and stood looking back at the church, shoulders shivering and hunched and hands pressed beneath her chin, water sluicing from her temples to her jaw in an overflow of tears. He took her by the shoulders and turned her and laid his hand on her rump and boosted her up in the cab.

"O, *mamo* . . ."

The keys were not under the mat where he had expected but

THE GYPSY LOVER ·313·

in the ignition. Rain spattered the windshield and pinged on the roof. When he shut the door, shoving at Armanda to make room, she gazed back at him without expression. The silky blouse was plastered to her breasts and the white bandanna glued to her head, the tiara askew. In the emerald light of the cab, her eyes were a kind of violet. She didn't say anything, she just looked at him, and he forgot for a moment why they were there. She seemed so small and defenseless he had to remind himself that she could knock a man down and steal his wallet, then end up being apologized to. He touched her face with his fingers, brushing at the waterbeads, and smoothed back a solitary lock of hair that had escaped from beneath her scarf. He grazed her cheek with his lips and groped for something to say. It may have been the weird light, but her moist unfocused eyes mirrored a strange tranquility, some eerie peace, and she said softly his name.

A Gypsy came out and stood beneath the portico and looked at them and pointed and another one came out and after him another and together they started toward the truck waving their hands and yelling. Evan ground the ignition and gave it some gas. He worked the gear into first and turned on the headlights and found the windshield wiper switch and turned it on. He was about to pop the clutch when he remembered the knife. In his left hand, he was still holding the knife. The blade and the back of his hand were splotched and watery with blood. He stared at his hand and the knife for a moment and something sharp screwed its way down in his gut. It was his knife. It had been his father's knife. What right did Nikolai have? He felt the contour of the handle, how it fit his hand like stone. He remembered slugging it hard into his mattress the night he left, the night he had thrown himself over to these kooks. Anguish and disgust surged up from the resentment and washed him clean. He hated Nikolai for what he'd done. He hated his own stupidity for running away from home. He hated his ignorance and confusion over the unimaginable series of events that so mercilessly churned away at his life. He started to wipe the blade against his pantleg then stopped.

He rolled down the window and let the approaching Gypsies see the knife in his hand, but they continued to slosh toward the truck and one showed him a knife of his own. With his left hand he flung the knife that had belonged to his father over the top of the cab and watched through the windshield as it daggered into a hedge on the other side of the driveway. It amazed him how the afternoon had emptied itself right into his lap.

"Cowboy?"

He nudged the pickup along the driveway, forcing the Gypsies to scatter, and lurched into the street, his right leg shaky on the accelerator, the back wheel bumping down over the curb. Thunder clapped in a great splintering of invisible wood and rain came pouring down as if some huge kettle had been overturned in heaven. The road doglegged and dipped and they started back down the hill.

Armanda said something indistinguishable and when he looked there was hardly any movement to her lips and her eyes were fixed on the road ahead.

"So tell me," she whispered."

He had only started to accelerate when something loomed in the side mirror and then got lost behind a curve. They passed the charred skeleton of the house, now smoldering in the rain. Firemen moved about in their yellow slickers, sorting and rolling hoses and gathering equipment and returning it to the fire trucks. Evan looked for the cop car but it wasn't there. A paramedic signaled to slow them by slashing his arm up and down then back and forth and rain slapped against the windshield as the truck picked up speed. Armanda touched Evan's hand on the steering wheel and leaned against him. He could feel the beating of her heart. He took his hand from the wheel and patted her leg, at the same time veering crazily from the path of an oncoming car and again banging the curb. The howl of the engine worried him, and he tapped the brake. The mirror again distracted him and this time he saw the protracted hood of the Lincoln rush up from behind. It dipped and heaved against the road, sponging around curves like a speeding yacht slapping waves.

"So tell me, Cowboy."

Until that moment, Evan had supposed he was at least going toward *something,* had settled on some destination in the back of his head that, with a little effort, he could pry free, hold up to the light, and examine. The police? A doctor? He looked in the side mirror and the idea struck him as stupid. He was moving toward nothing, only away. He had panicked. Even now, soaked with perspiration beneath the wet black suit, the idea of the Lincoln giving chase not only angered but confused him. On second thought, he did have the bride. And the *daro.* A swipe of the wipers across the windshield promised clarity, and he patted the breast of his jacket to feel the envelope beneath—then obscuring rain before another swipe of the blades. He hunched over the wheel and wiped interior fog from the glass with his hand. He hit the accelerator and the trucked lurched and slued to the left.

The Lincoln came up close, so close that he lost it in the side mirror, and gave them a nudge. The back wheels floated free and he turned the steering wheel in the direction of the skid, fought it out. Armanda jounced against him but somewhere far away, her body remarkably slack. Rain washed over the windshield and the wipers cleared it. If they wanted a chase, he would give them one. They weren't getting Armanda back, that was for sure. No love lost here. She could have the marriage annulled in a day or two. Or not.

Sheet lightening flashed and trembled in a series of afterflashes across the Kentucky hills to the south, and mist, like plumes of breath, rose and crawled along the surface of the river. Evan gunned the pickup through a yellow light and swung left onto the parkway, now following the snake of the river. His mind kept going off and on like a light switch. He felt cold and knew he was going too fast, but he didn't care. He wanted to fly.

The Lincoln almost lost itself, yawing behind, its tires spewing water; it skidded broadside into the guardrail then spun free. In the passenger side mirror, as it gained on the pickup, Evan saw the Lincoln's smashed headlight and a shallow indentation along the front fender and the passenger-side door. His adrenaline was boiling when Armanda turned to him and, with a shrug, as though picking up the thread of some previous unfinished conversation, announced: "Gypsy marriages aren't supposed to be happy. You're supposed to struggle together to make a life and fall in love afterwards." Evan looked at her and humored her with a nod. She was corpselike in complexion, her eyes and mouth black as licorice.

"If you want to know the truth," she went on, looking right past him, "I figured he was better off starting a new life somewhere else. Until he goes and steals that corpse." Her voice went to a growl. "I figured the *daro* would take care of it . . . eighty-two hundred dollars on top of our other stash, and he could start again. Maybe he would go and settle down, I thought, for a while anyways . . . stop chasing her ghost." She gave the gist of a laugh that went to the center of his bones. "Then doesn't Groucho come out of the woodwork? Groucho and Charlie? Poor Knobby, with piss on his grave. What'd he know, anyways, *papo*? They'd ought to beat his head between two stones."

Evan looked at her. She tried hard to think, her eyes working back on themselves. She was trying to understand something that appeared to worm just out of reach, and it was as though some elaborate secret she stored touched light then gathered back into the obscure recesses of her head. Evan was glad they were her eyes gazing inward and not his. He wanted only to survive this ridiculous chase.

"Whose?" he asked.

"*Papo,*" she said beneath her breath.

He didn't even look at her. In an attempt to lose the Lincoln, he swerved down an exit leading to a lower level of the parkway—River Road—and in the process nearly clipped the sign at its base. When he looked, the Lincoln was still behind and gaining. It came up fast and gave them another shove. The truck skidded on the wet asphalt and Evan fought for control.

"Another thing," chirped Armanda in curious and casual conversation, and he couldn't tell whether with him or some palaver in her head. "We had got her all strung up, and him with rope burns and still tugging his guts. She could have been anything, a side of beef, a piece of meat." She turned her face toward Evan, her eyes a glowing riddle. "I shut my eyes like this, see?" She put her hand on his arm, like talons the grip. "I shut my eyes and yanked away the sheet and closed the door. Rope burns. See? That's what I get." And she held before him that branded palm. "They'd ought to beat his head, so drunk. It was like hoisting a pig. But he loved her, I tell you, and she him."

Whether she told him more than this or whether by some telepathic glimpse he had seen it in her eyes, or there in the cauterized flesh of her palm, he could see now that wretched and spooling scarf self-twined about the throat and how an older, more mature Armanda sat watching in the vanity, sat watching love betrayed, and felt the rage of it twist then about her throat, could see her Gypsy stars grow dim beneath those weeping hands.

"So bruised with kisses and that longing in her eye, like a woman purged of guilt and forgiving yet."

"What are you telling me?"

"Before *papo* called I hadn't heard a word, him kneeling there when I come at the door and palming back her hair, struggling to get breath back in her lungs. He wouldn't let go until I wound her in a sheet." And as she spoke, she produced with a pass of her hand and twined about her own throat the most red and diaphanous sweep of fabric Evan had ever seen though his wits assured him he had seen it so often before. "And then like a side of beef she's all strung up and I yank away the sheet and close the door. That's when I remember the scarf. I say it, and he gives me a look like maybe he's never heard the word before in his life. So I go back in with my eyes closed and reach up to undo it and she's so cold there around the neck and I can't get it undone like I want so tight's his knot and now caught beneath the noose so I open my eyes just a slit but can't hardly see for the blur and I drop the thing and have to grope around on hands and knees with my eyes shut until I've got it in a wad."

Armanda straight-armed the dashboard to brace herself. The Lincoln smacked them again and lightening crackled around the truck like a loose filament sparking inside an incandescent bulb. Evan worked his way around the thickest part of her babbling and came to the center.

"What're you telling me? What are you telling me?"

She looked at him and blinked, the ghostly fabric noosed about her throat and gathered in frills between her breasts, her eyes already half shut, as if she were about to fall asleep, and the expiration of her breath was like a murmur of doom. "O, *papo*." She turned the word upon her tongue, listening to it, then shook her head as if it were too unfamiliar to place, but kept him in her eye. "When you run your hands down across my breasts," she sighed incoherently, touching herself, "it lights a fire in me."

Evan's lungs grew weak from the bunting of his heart, his throat clogged with breath, and when he glanced at her and then away, the sum of such riddles loomed like the derelict at the side of the road and then dissolved with a sweep of the wiper blades.

"It means nothing, this blood. Papa thought I was *mamo*, come back from the dead . . . his sweethearted love back from the dead."

The rain let up a little, but Evan was having a difficult time because the roar of the storm was still in his head and he could hardly hear her. She was delirious. She was babbling again, sending words like unarmed soldiers into battle. But he had no claim to the words: something about sparing her father the grief of a desperate act, something about childhood in the California *kumpania* and watching her grandfather choke to death on devil's shit because they wouldn't take him to a *gaje* doctor.

"So tell me, Cowboy, what's going to be?"

The truck came out on a tier of highway above the river

whose cool waters steamed up at them from below. Evan's vision slid forward across the pockmarked surface to waves whitecapping around a snag. Armanda looked at him, grinning horribly, and something inside him came apart like a sheet of glass struck by a stone. Deep within he felt the lacerations and a vein of fear began to bleed. If only he could pull over, he thought, he would shake some sense into her.

"What's the matter?" he shouted, because he wanted to get something inside her head. He wanted to tell her how she could do it, start all over again, how together they could. Somehow. But not in a shouting way. No. He shouted at her. He took his hand from the wheel and slapped her hard across the jaw. In that instant something flapped across the windshield and he felt the rear wheels floating again and the Lincoln give them a shove.

The side of the road slid away and they jolted and bumped down an embankment. Even could see Armanda clawing for a grip, and he could see the overhang just ahead and from there the water, and although he kept his hands on the steering wheel, the truck wrenched his arms from left to right as if control had shifted and the thing would have its way. He braced himself and his gut fell away as the wheels of the truck left earth, the hood dipped, and they plunged toward the shallows of the Ohio.

He dreamt suddenly and with the only wits he could claim, and dreaming, he felt the cool breath of morning through his open window as he awoke to the weight of Bozo against his feet at the foot of the bed. All around him rose the smell of freshly turned earth after a hard rain. From below came the odd but familiar sounds of Aunt Missy rasping closed the back door and heaving herself from cupboard to stove. Wasn't that Goose calling from the barn? And, strange, somewhere unbeknownst to the world at large an infant swallowing air. Somewhere lovers quietly snared betwixt sorrow and fear. Somewhere an afflicted heart grown still. Somewhere sun. Somewhere rain. Somewhere now the troubled waters beneath. Somewhere, this. Somewhere, that.

The truck hit the water, went under, then shot to the surface like an unchained log. The engine coughed, gurgled, and spewed. Evan must have banged his head, because details came to him unhurried, one at a time. His hands on the wheel. The current pushing the cab around, back toward shore. Water seeping in around the doors and through the floor. The silence, the water, the rain, a reprieve. The hood, the cab, nosing forward, down. Armanda heaped against the dashboard, the top of her head against the windshield and how it webbed there so beautiful in the diminishing light like a tarnished halo, her body lax as a rag doll.

Evan found himself shouldering the door, but the pressure of the water jammed it shut. His legs were submerged before he had sense enough to roll down the window and worm his way headfirst into the river. The water swirled and tugged him down. The shore lay only yards away. He threw his head and shoulders back inside the cab groping for Armanda, the water like a suction plunging his legs. He almost had her, tore the tiara from her head and with it the bandanna, when the water level reached the bottom of the window, lapped at the edge, then poured across him in gallons. He gulped a breath and rode down, half in, half out, until the truck rested on the bottom, the cab submerged only inches beneath the surface. He reached once more for Armanda, but the force of the water had shoved her all the way across the seat to the passenger door, and he had to worm back out and surface for another breath.

He clawed upward, his face to the rain. The surface of the water wrinkled and chipped away with raindrops all around the white churning circle of the truck. The camper itself was only three-quarters submerged, and he could see its painted corrugated top glistening with rain. Evan glimpsed the Lincoln idling above on the road, and then he felt himself moving away from the truck. Ducking against the current, he struggled back, hand over hand. But suddenly the current had him. He was struggling in every direction, the center of the writhing, kicking knot of his own body. There was no up, no down, no light, no air. He gulped water, painful as stones in the throat. His body let loose its panic and his mouth strained open until the hinges of his jaw were on fire. Turbines screamed behind his eyes and green sparks flew out from the center like struck flint. A wad of darkness gathered in his head. He was dying and knew it, would shed himself and awaken to a separate world where all would seem the same, his own death uncounted but to himself, and the dying of others but phantoms in the world left behind. Whether from this world or that, he reached out to grasp a hand extending from the clouds, saw a glint on the water, heard a call in thin air.

"Don't leave me."

He felt the solid mass of the truck. His lungs heaved, chewing air. When he regained breath, he painstakingly worked his way across the hood to Armanda's side. He went under, groping for the handle, found it, but the door wouldn't give. When he pushed his face against the window, he could see her own face, forehead resting now against the glass, the small hooded lids of her eyes lightly shut—and then they sprang open. Her mouth sagged open in the same lopsided grimace he had seen just before he struck her. Her hair rose and fanned and fell, as did those soft tendrils of fabric she wore so red about her neck, and he knew without question whose face he had seen in the glass ball only a few nights before.

*   *   *

He slept that night inside a culvert that had once drained sludge and byproducts into the river from some bygone factory. Now the inner circumference of the pipe was caked with tiles of dried mud and innocuous growing things. The breath of it wafted from what seemed the bowels of the earth or some torrid remnant of greased machinery and oiled things long since quit. Through the rushes of the twilit river, he could see the stormcalmed waters and the silhouetted mass of a great barge making its way laboriously up stream to some predetermined destination, and he watched it for the better part of an hour with envy and wonder. Across the river the shadowed buildings of Covington rose against the darkening sky like stones of hieroglyph from some ancient order and he wondered what it would take to interpret the meaning of those who came and went beneath the eves and through the sunshadows of the descending night, of those whose lives and histories he knew nothing. Such was like seeing beyond the threshold of another time and place where the unfamiliar was better known and longed for than the familiarity of oneself.

In the night a wind blew out of the south and hissed about the rushes and hollowed out the culvert with a cacophony of voices that could well have been the stuff of dreams. He slept and woke and slept again. Even in sleep he could smell the damp of his clothing intermixed with the breath of waters and the taste of the deep. When he woke again, he got up and sat in the round mouth of the culvert like a ghost in a well tipped on its side and looked out upon the water. To the south, now, with the moon glaring down, he saw what he took for a girl come up out of the water and slog through the rushes and along the bank of the river as though she were searching for the lost or something forgotten or misplaced, but when he studied it again he saw that it was nothing more than a snag bumping and sliding along the shore. Beyond that and partly overcast also in the moonlight, he saw on the surface of the water the reflection of those belonging to the voices in the drain. Or were they but images of himself come up from the river to torment and chide? They rose and skirted like wraiths upon the water and into the weeds, so many he had known and the unknown as well. They appeared to be dressed in robes and some with lanterns swinging and playing in shafts of yellowish light to compete with the moon. He thought they must be laboring toward him across the darkened river and up through the thicket of rushes and weeds and yet they made no progress at all. Someone called to him, his name, and then again, but the shouts were carried away on the wind. After a while he lay again in his niche in the ancient drain and after a while he slept.

In the morning the wind had ceased and when he awoke what he saw looking out through the mouth of the culvert was an inverted V and through the legs of it the brilliance of sunslant upon the water. He heard the barking of dogs and the echo of his name far back in the drain. A hound flopped its head in the opening of the culvert and bayed, and he saw the stooping of the V.

"You in there? Come on out, son. We got you now."

So, it was like that. Just a bright shining lie and the gospel of truth. No choice in the matter at all. In a world of dreams the Wandering Man appears, and what choice do you have, the pulse of his heart in your hand? From a separate world I looked back to see him flailing there. It was all in the screw of his body, so boyish, the remnants of youth sliding away in the foam, how he plunged and thrashed in his drowning, how he raised his face to the sky and snatched at the man. What else could he do? I looked back and could nearly feel the air as it matured in his lungs. He would have saved me if he could. I looked back, lingering I think, and then I was gone. Just a glint, a glint on the water, that's how I went. Just a glint to a boy, a glint to a man, and then I passed in a slur of the light a piece of myself like a breath. It was the very source of me, like an image in glass, the one or the other of us stepping through, though I couldn't tell which. Just a glint and a slur but for that wisp of myself and him and the rest of it contending behind. Now there are other possibilities yet in worlds to come, and I can think of them, possibilities that defy the best imaginations on earth.

~20~

A Sad & Joyful Exchange

"—you got a great past ahead of you," she was saying.

EVERYTHING else he read about in the papers.

MURDER IN THE CATHEDRAL

AP – Cincinnati, Ohio. St. Aloysius Cathedral. A Gypsy wedding turned into havoc here yesterday when the crazed father-of-the-bride revenged a score of infidelity. Nikolai Markovitch, a carnival knife-handler, allegedly stabbed to death one "Groucho" Kozinski. It was reported that Kozinski's recently deceased brother, "Knobby" Kozinski, had been involved with Markovitch's late wife. Immediately following the stabbing, another Kozinski brother, Charles, allegedly shot and killed Markovitch.

The bride, Armanda Walcott, née Markovitch, fled the scene with an unidentified blond-haired Gypsy boy. The two, driving a battered pickup camper, were pursued in a fierce rain by the groom and members of his family. Near Third Avenue and River Road, the truck swerved out of control and plunged into the Ohio River whereupon the bride was killed. Charles Kozinski related a bizarre account of how, only last week, Markovitch had overtaken him in the Rocky Mountains, disabled his car, and left him and his asthmatic wife stranded. (See related story, page 7.)

Kozinski then went on to describe the case of the stolen corpse and possible motives . . . .

It was all there, spread out like a map on page one. For a time reporters were numerous. He was interviewed half a dozen times in the course of an afternoon, amazed at the general accuracy of most of the articles when they appeared the following day, but even as he read, he had trouble imagining the details. How could you get an image of yourself in your head along with the notion of others when everything around you disappeared? Time and the world had passed away from him and also his life as though it were a dream. For a while he thought there was something wrong with his mind. He drew a blank. In one follow-up interview, a reporter asked him a question and nothing was there.

"We're you in love with her? Did you love her?"

It was frightening. It wasn't that he couldn't remember or think straight. Perhaps he remembered too well, like memorizing a speech, reciting it a dozen times before the mirror, then when it came time to speak not being able to come up with the first word. It became his own recurring nightmare, like an actor forgetting his lines and bringing the whole play to an awful embarrassing halt.

Did he love her?

He read the papers obsessively, seeking some clue to unstick his mind. Where were they in all the tabloid yammer? One story, trying to clarify something, used the word "incest." He looked at the word and then for his name superimposing Nikolai's. But nothing. Armanda had remained pure on every account, he knew that. Any violation of her had been more psychological and metaphorical than real. If ever a hand had touched her, it had been the hand of the grief-stricken touching some memory and that touch had never been fulfilled except through a yearning for the dead.

But did he love her?

He wrinkled the paper and looked beyond the black and white of it to find a word about himself. But why talk about the living when so many ghosts were at hand? And yet not a note about the world before it was. Every time he had it figured, thought he had, every time an article forced another piece of the jigsaw, the whole thing came springing apart in a thousand bewildering scraps, another hook, a little subplot, taking him by surprise. And what did it matter? The real story would probably never be known. Journalistic tripe slanting its way into fiction with every retelling an attempt to find meaning. He hadn't a memory that served him correct, and yet every notion of the past lay upon him as inflexible as truth, or at least the wanting of it.

Did he love her?

He sat across the desk from a psychiatrist who shifted a batch of papers and propped his elbows on the desk and leaned forward, making a steeple of his hands. The man had a bead of spittle in the corner of his mouth and one eye aslant. He enunciated his words to the point of madness, though with such kindness in his tone that Evan felt an unloosening in his heart. In the follow-up session, the psychiatrist did nothing but sit in the chair next to Evan, fiddle with a snow globe, and wait.

When his mind finally came unstuck, the images were not his alone, but from another point of view, and he babbled as if assaulted by shadows deep in a Gypsy's ball: how, with nylon cord, the two of them had hoisted the sheet-shrouded victim from the ceiling fan, for surely the victim was she whose final breath dwindled beneath a husband's last kiss; how Armanda had closed her eyes to yank away the sheet and shut the door, how she had gone back in for that wretched scarf—the dismal evidence of a lover's woe. His were the visions and the memories of being inside *her* head, of crawling up inside her to see through *her* eyes, the very exhaustion of wrestling with the body as though it were a slab of beef or a side of venison, hysterical with her own shut-in grief. It was that madness, that hopelessness, that anguish, that he came to feel at the center of her unflowing blood and bones and flesh and in the same despairing breath she had carried in her lungs when she placed her lips against his.

"So tell me."

But it was not the man sitting next to him in the chair with one eye aslant who asked. He looked at her lying there among the satin and frill and sang softly the lines:

Here a sleeping child lies . . .

Now, so perfectly symmetrical in her coffin, hands folded loosely at her breast, and there, in the shape of her mouth, around the eyes, just as she had warned him, the ever so cold remnants of that dark intense relationship left unfulfilled, and just as she had told him he carried in the palm of his hand since birth. These were the fragments to which he laid claim. The drawn forehead, the chalky jaw. The sunken cheeks. He considered touching the loosened flesh on the back of her hand but didn't. He had a great urge to turn her hand over and examine the palm. Instead, he looked at his own, that lifeline she had so confidently read. Was there no end to it? He took a deep breath and gripped the polished brass handle of the casket and squeezed until his hand turned white.

My mother said I never should . . .

Now when he looked, her lips furled slightly at the corners, leering back on themselves. Once an artist's dream and now this, but he had never sketched them well even then, neither the mouth nor the eyes. In the reflecting glass of the still life hanging on the wall above the coffin, he could see nothing but his own emptiness and that filled with such doom.

And then a shadow.

He turned slightly when out of nowhere a woman sidled up next to him, and looking at the corpse but addressing him, said,

"It's a sad state of affairs, ain't it? What the world comes to over time. But she loved you, know this."

Half listening, Evan acknowledged her with a sideslant of his head, and without looking at her directly thought perhaps she was beautiful and ageless.

"O," she mourned, "my poor darling child." And she averted her face.

They stood there together for a moment or two in the somber viewing room of the mortuary, lost in the effulgence of thought and pressed by the odor of flowers, and then all at once Evan realized he was alone. He looked around in the dim light but found only himself and the smiling corpse at his side.

Evan—

The voice rang inside his head, distinctly. Then, again, it wasn't a voice; it was that sneer. He looked at her, and she spoke volumes with those lips, taunting him even in death. No, no. Perhaps he had crossed over into some other world, leaving her behind. Such intimations of her reaching out to him could not be dismissed as mere sentimentality or the after-effects of grief, and the question persisted in spite of the coffined remains as to whether or not she had ever existed except in his mind. The full import of what Nikolai meant when he said to look for her not in a portrait nor in the flesh but in the serenity of the mind now struck him. How could she have died when she had never really lived? She existed in his own heart and mind as surely as the blood coursed through his veins.

He stood looking at her, still gripping the handle of the coffin, and look as he might, he could not get her fixed in his head.

Evan—

Time passed, but it was hard for him to tell how slow or how fast. Social Services held him for a couple of days at Juvenile Hall, next to the County Sheriff's Office. They fingerprinted him as though he stood yet among the living, took a mug shot, and recorded his statement together with Yana's and half a dozen other Gypsies'. Yana sobbed mysteriously, without anger, and held his hand, but then he knew, had come to know, that she, like Armanda, was whatever he wanted to make of her.

"So tell me," he pled, and she stretched her neck to the side and looked at him and clasped his hand and told him he wasn't to blame.

"Not that," he said, "I didn't mean that."

"No, of course not. But did you love her?"

Together, they stood next to a second story window looking out into the street, speaking in hushed voices. From a point of view a little above Yana's head, Evan could see the street and the buildings that lined the opposite side. Except for a young woman in Gypsy garb sitting on the curb, the street was empty. And then the man, of course, sitting himself down next to her. They exchanged a few words and then together looked up at the window, and Evan could see their eyes from that distance. They looked at him only briefly and the woman mouthed something he thought, and then she stood up and after her the man and together they turned away, moving toward the shadows of a tree-lined park across the street and momentarily dissolving into the gloom of the trees. In place of the woman, a raven hopped from the curb into the street, plucked uselessly at some decaying offal, and with a single flap took wing.

So dreamlike, he could hardly imagine.

"The *daro*," she whispered. "Nobody's made mention of it but the Walcotts who say they give it to Nikki. Maybe they did, maybe they didn't. Maybe Nikki, he stashed it in the truck—you think?—and a school of fish is paying for higher education by now."

Evan turned from the window and looked at the old woman, the grid and patchwork of her face. He looked at her and thought for a minute and then he bent to a whisper and told her where she could find the envelope back in the culvert beneath a gob of mud and sticks and leaves.

"Maybe I'll go dig it up," she said, thinking. "Maybe I won't."

The blood of it didn't seem to bother her, or the possibility of any curse.

"Tell me," he begged, and she wept at his honesty and spoke to him about how all things come back around and blessed him and told him to remember that "the place you find when you search for love is your home forever." Or had he read that in a book? "Never you mind," she said, and repeated herself, and pressed the thought to his heart with her hand, and then she pressed his hand and promised to see him off at the airport. She told him she would understand if he didn't come to the funeral. He had already made his peace and enough was enough. "Armanda, she ain't gone so much as she's still here; inside you, I mean—and me—and the gist of them who have returned for want and desire." And he looked at her, lacking, and thought maybe she was onto something when she said, "I knew a boy, when he looked for his darling, a child he found, when he looked for that child his sister come round. All after that was but the birthing of riddles and doom, just a bright shining lie, and all after that—" She paused and looked at him for effect. "But Nikki, that's the irony of it. Things don't always work out like you think." She was about to whisper something in his ear, perhaps the meaning of it all, the final answer, when a matron came and told him to say good-bye and took him down the hall to a detective's office.

The detective was sitting behind his desk with a phone against his ear. "I got Utah on the line," he said importantly. But the newspapers had already beat him to it and put the questions to Evan a couple of hours earlier.

"More bad news." The detective put his hand over the receiver and motioned him to sit. "Your uncle," he said.

Evan could see it clear as a gag in a comic strip, the mouse with a brick, the clown with a rolling pin, the fat lady with a skillet, and now Missy was in the calaboose, the hoosegow, as they say in the funny papers. She had first taken a meat cleaver to him, lopped off an ear. When he came home from the hospital to recuperate, the court released her on her own recognizance, and she finished him off with an iron skillet.

"Damn," said the detective, "gimme the old lady and a kick in the ass. I wouldn't walk in your shoes half an inch let alone a mile."

But to Evan, she and the Goose Man seemed no more than unrealized characters in a bad drama. Perhaps Armanda's call to the sheriff coupled with a sprinkling of goat's hair. *You get to lick the stamp,* she'd said. *There will be a bond between us. That way this curse will be ours, Evan's and mine, until death do us part . . . and we'll never tell a soul.* Or was it Yana's *bujo,* the hexed goose blurting its final squawk the very day of his Uncle's demise? Both Missy and Goose were as far out of his life now as if he had stood in the darkness of their room next to the bed and accomplished the same with that bone-handled knife. What other sad and joyful exchange might such mischief have caused?

Ohio Social Services scrambled around, telephoning, interviewing, and padding his file with a battery of psychiatric and other tests—figuring what to do with a sixteen year old kid without a guardian—then the sheriff came and got him one afternoon and sat him at a desk with a telephone.

"Somebody wants to talk to you."

It was Alta Mae on the other end, and then her father. Her father laid out the parameters, the rules, the guidelines, having first discussed them with an attorney and Social Services. His voice was kind but firm. Then Alta Mae got back on the line.

"It was kind of my idea, Evan. I know the time you've had of it. You'll at least be able to come home and have a place." She paused, as if listening. "Mama wouldn't agree to it, you know, unless you promise to follow some rules and go to church every Sunday. We can go together." She paused. "You know, don't you, that everything you've experienced and might have done is subject to second thought and any wrongs can be righted through him who saves."

Had she said what he thought? Or had he thought what she

said? No matter. The timbre in her voice lulled him, and he listened to her affection, pleased with every phrase, as if she alone could threaten the slight in his heart and the fault in his soul with some hopeful and perfecting design. As he listened, he looked out the window, and there behind the cyclone fence sat the impounded truck, dried river mud up to its axles. As she spoke, he looked for the gay tableau of images on the camper. Splattered with mud and faded from sun, he could see nothing more than a bright blue sky and silverlined clouds, as if every other scene had been washed clean. He listened and puzzled the truck as she spoke, how smallish it seemed, and as she spoke her voice brought back a tenderness in him and he knew she meant well. She spoke of the possibilities, the hope, her words like a snare, and now in the sheen of the sun, there on the camper wall, he could see her face vaguely, looking back at him from a forward pew, and though her look touched the promise in his heart, he wanted desperately to summon the image of their embrace behind the gym. It was as if that voice and the image of her, too, so constant and encouraging, like some cosmic certainty making its way through the void, was the only thing real and as if all else had been but the figment of a miserable thought and he the thinker defied.

The next day, he found himself following an Ohio sheriff through the American Airlines terminal in the Greater Cincinnati Airport. The promise of Alta Mae spread before him like a field of warm alfalfa, and he could feel himself simultaneously moving toward that future he forever refused and backward to the past which rose in his head like a vampire at dusk.

Evan—

Sitting two seats away from the sheriff in the airport terminal, he added the finishing touches to his sketch of her—"a lover's dread," quipped the sheriff with the hint of a shrug. "Looks like something come from beneath." Evan looked at it. He looked at the sheriff, a stocky chisel-faced man who held his cleft chin high, and the sheriff had a grin fixed wide as his jaw, openly betraying himself. He would touch it up for now and then refine and color it one day. He held it at arm's length and frowned and struggled to see what he could not, and then he closed up the sketchbook and wrote quietly in his journal.

> *Ravens pass crowing overhead; blackbirds peck witlessly on a lawn. We glance out of curiosity, expecting to make the final discovery, to find the great secret of life beneath a rock, to feel warmth and numbness and cold. The truth is, we feel nothing at all. Nothing good, nothing bad, not even a sense of discovery.*

The sheriff touched Evan's shoulder and said, "You okay?" He nodded and finished jotting.

> *I looked for my sweetheart and a child I found, when I looked for that child*

No, no. And he drew a line through it, wrote instead,

> *I long now for that day when the past falls mute and old tales instead bring you to light.*

Or had he read that in a book sometime, somewhere?

He closed up the journal and jammed it in his backpack along with the sketchbook and stood up. He placed his hands upon the railing of the waisthigh barrier that stood between him and the glass wall beyond which the 757 taxied for deplaning. It was the first time he had flown, and his stomach worried itself and quietly complained.

"What's that then?" The sheriff pointed as though to a clue.

Evan turned his wrist upright and looked at it. The scab had sloughed off some and the pink of a scar showed through. "A reminder," he said.

"A reminder?"

"Of nothing at all."

The sheriff blew air through his nostrils, annoyed at the prospect of something as cute as a riddle. "Like every other fool," he said, "your heart's desire is to see the mystery and have it counted for aught, but there is none." He pointed to the magazine shop across the terminal, said: "Mints."

Evan shrugged and wiped his face with the butt of his hand and watched as the officer's shoulders, waist, shifting buttocks, and loosely slung .45 moved in a fluid rippling motion. The sheriff had been singing off and on all morning long, and as he walked, he sang off key and without heart:

The Gypsy Rover came over the hill,
down through the valley so sha-a-dy.
He whistled and he sang
till the greenwoods rang,
all for the love of a la-a-dy . . .

Evan took out his father's spectacles and put them on as the sheriff walked away from him. He had put them on to see better, but as usual was never quite sure of what he saw. Was it Yana? She was out of breath and running. At first, Evan thought she was going to bite him, the way she craned her neck, but she took him in her arms and kissed him and held his hand for a moment as she wept and caught her breath. She was a specialist in grief and overcoming, he remembered, who understood things lost to philosophers and fools. He was her *Romany-rye.*

Accompanying her, another woman stood a little ways off. The window was at her back and she stood haloed by the light and Evan thought for an instant that it was Armanda standing there.

"Tell me," was the first thing he said.

"I'll tell you this, my child. It ain't your fault. You're a good kid and don't mean no harm. You come to us unawares, to help us sort out our destiny, and though it is a sad and joyful exchange, all now is made right, and we must accept what is. The best laid plans, you know. The irony of it."

"The irony?"

"Poor Nikki," she started to say, "but he's another story, lost among the damned—" She cut herself off abruptly, then said simply but with a world of meaning, "Things don't always work out like you think, but you can't blame yourself. We meet our fate in the most unlikely places—"

She would know about that, of course. Evan listened sleepily to her hypnotic sobbing voice as she looked up at him and spun her riddles, and once again it occurred to him that somehow it all comes together, if not literally then in a strange metaphorical sort of way. For wasn't it the riddle unanswered, the mystery of the thing, that gave it all sense? Certainly, if he had learned nothing else, he had learned that the riddle is more satisfying than any solution at hand.

"—you got a great past ahead of you," Yana was saying. "It all comes back around, full circle, just like a prophecy in the words of a song. Them fine parents and a little of Armanda in your blood. You'll get along okay because you've seen and learned the ways of surviving. Like Gypsies. You'll make out. Anyways, it ain't the past or the future, it's what's in here that counts." She held a fist against her heart. "We are who we are, nothing more, nothing less, and little pieces of them we meet."

In his pocket he felt and fingered the stone and wrapped it in his palm and it felt warm. The old woman stood on her toes and pulled him down to her and kissed him again. "Here," she said, rummaging in her purse and fingering a number of crisp, wrinkled bills. "Right where you said. *Te del o Del sastipe taj zor!* God bless."

It might have been something Yana whispered to him, together with Armanda's ghostly proddings, or maybe it was just everything closing in on him at once, but for the moment it again seemed to all come together—less riddle than answer— and then it was gone, whatever it was—answer or riddle—Yana's voice still droning in his ear: "We each got our ghosts, Evan. We carry them around in here . . ."

"Wait," he said, and in saying he felt all at once the grip and pulse and tearing away in his breast. "You take this."

He swung the satchel down from his shoulder and zipped it open and took out the sketchbook. He knelt and balanced the sketchbook on his knee and opened it and creased the page and tore it with care and precision away from the binding and rolled the page into a tube and gave it to her.

She watched him without speaking and took the offering and let it unroll in her hand and when she saw what it was, she put her hand to her mouth and pressed it there as if to hush some ungodly stutter of breath and praised him, all with a look and a sigh and the absence of words.

He touched the rim of his spectacles, poked them back on his nose. He was looking at the woman, the girl, standing behind Yana, who looked back at him and said something bold with her eyes. She vanished momentarily in the glare of the sun and then reappeared, smoky and translucent as a reflection in the window behind. There was something familiar about her. Her face was rather beautiful and yet when he looked again seemed gaunt and featureless, and she appeared to be standing above the floor on a cushion of air. She spoke to him with a dark-eyed glance and knowing smile. He looked at her boldly, at her tiny waist and shapely breasts, hair black as a raven's wing. Among other Gypsy garb, she was wearing a flimsy dress that flowered and flowed with the light. There was something about her that, like a riddle, to preserve the mystery of it, he didn't want answered or to understand, as if she were someone who had just entered a room for the first time, crossed a threshold . . . found herself as it were, some possible consequence of the truth.

Dimly, he realized Yana was speaking to him, her droning voice admonishing him, even as she held the artwork close to her breast and took up his hand: "Pray for knowledge, Evan, and truth, and get ready to be amazed . . ."

A wave of misery washed over him. He thought of Alta Mae. His mind raced back to Armanda, and he felt a familiar dread. Telepathy, maybe. He didn't know how else to describe it. It was just there anymore, inside his head, like a ghost.

Evan—

"If I had it in my power," he muttered, "I would forsake all that I know and keep close to my heart all that I don't." Yana at first looked at him with the wisdom of understanding before the wince in her eye betrayed second thought, and he said to her again. For he was in love with far more than Armanda. He knew that. He was in love with the notion of Armanda, and even still he couldn't help but consider the promise and possibilities of Alta Mae, and even so young, the prospect of something closer to commitment and honesty than love.

Yana released his hand, and he looked beyond the glass across the runway where it shimmered beneath a pale and watery sun. *It's what's in here*, she was gesturing and telling him again, *that's what counts.* The sheriff touched his shoulder and nudged him in the direction of the security gate, singing:

All for the love of a la-a-dy . . .

Yana gave a little wave and the girl standing beside her smiled darkly. As Evan looked at her, one last fanciful thought crossed his mind . . . and then it vanished. There was only the enigma. The enigma would remain, forever thwarting his best efforts to define it. He raised his hand to wave, and it was as though his heart had been cut from his breast. There was nothing left to say. He looked at the girl then ahead at the gate. She was the riddle he would take with him.

Or forever leave behind.

During our last session, he leaned forward in the chair and took from my desk a snow globe my daughter had given me the Christmas before. He rubbed his hands over the surface and shook it and contemplated the figures within, and as he did, we had a brief discussion of how the imperative of choice offsets fate. He'd somehow got it in his head that he was responsible for the world at large. For everything that happened. By either his presence, indecisiveness, or fated choice, the world molded itself after the fashion of his heart. There is nothing intellectual in this. It is an emotional response, often the product of trauma in childhood and a legacy of insurmountable guilt. Such magical thinkers think the universe is all in their heads, and although there may be truth in the notion, I have found that by the nature of one's commitment to others such thinking may be tempered and generally put to rest. This boy had formulated such fidelity in a vow and a pledge. He perceived a sort of poetic justice in everything that had transpired, himself at the center of retribution and irony, at the same time confused by whether he was being punished for, or exonerated from, an absence of choice. He seemed not only to understand more than I had assumed but also to appreciate my point of view—in short, that we are each victims or masters of ourselves, extraneous factors aside. This he called the "paradox of truth," and though I hadn't a clue as to what he meant by that, I could see that he was a bright and charming boy with an odd tale to tell, but certainly not hexed. He shook the snow globe one last time and gazed at the world within and then he handed it to me. I wiped my mouth and stood up and released him on his pledge to accept the guidance and care of those given charge.

Lexicon of Romany Words & Phrases
Used Throughout This Account

THOUGH most of the following words and phrases from Romany, the language of the Gypsies, are defined in the body of the novel, they are repeated here for easy reference.

Word	Pronunciation	Meaning
babam	BAY-bam	baby
bori	BOH-ree	bride; daughter-in-law
bujo	BOO-jo	bag; medicine bag; swindle called "switch-the-bag"
chokalee	CHOKE-ah -lee	dried witch's vomit
devia	DAY-vyeh	God
daro	DEH-ro	brideprice

drabarni	drah-BAR-nee	female who has knowledge of medicine; a doctor; a fortune-teller
gaje	GAW-jah	adult non-Gypsy when both sexes are referred to
gaji	GAW-jee	adult non-Gypsy female
gaji romni	GAW-jee RHAM-nee	non-Gypsy wife of a Gypsy
gajo	GAW-jo	non-Gypsy male
johai	JOE-hi	ghost vomit (medicinal concoction)
Kashtare Rom	KASH-tar-AI RHAM	a tribe or nation of Gypsies
kris	KRIS	a Gypsy trial
kumpania	koom-PAN -yah	community of Gypsies, traveling or stationary
Kuneshti	koo-NESH-tee	a tribe or nation of Gypsies, often associated with carnivals
lovoro	lah-VAH-ro	ceremony to divide money, property, possessions among each member of the family
mamo	MAW-mo	mother

THE GYPSY LOVER ·343·

mamio	MAW-mee-o	grandmother
marime	MAR-eh-may	polluted, defiled, rejected or outcast
nav gajikano	NAHV GAW-jee-khan-o	Gypsy's non-Gypsy name
nav ramano	NAHV rah-MAHN-o	a Gypsy's Gypsy name
o DEL	oh DELL	God
ofisa	o-PHIS-eh	fortune-telling establishment
papo	Pop o	father
phuro	PHUR-o	elder or patriarch of a family
raklo	RAWK-lo	young non-Gypsy male
Romany-rye	RHAM-any -rye	non-Gypsy who is liked and accepted by Gypsies
tate	Ta-tee	father
tshatshimo	SHAT-she-mo	the truth
vitsa	VIT-sah	immediate family

Phrase	Meaning
Babam, babam, de babam.	Baby, baby, O baby.
Lungo dromesa zas.	We take a long road.
Na phir pala manda. *Pala ma phiresa, opre potjinesa.*	Don't come after me. If you come after me, you'll pay.
Pale bajba pelem, mamo.	I'm in trouble again, mama.
Hogyha nékem sok pénzem lesz, *felulok a repulore.* *Elszallok, mint a fecske* *fel amagas levegore.*	If one day I've lots of money, I'll climb aboard an airplane. I'll fly off like the swallow Up into the airy heights.
De kurva! Jai!	Hey, whore! Jai!
Oj dile! Mure dile!	My crazy one! My crazy one!
De babam, muri gajo, de numa kadi ratji	Oh, baby, my gajo, oh, for this one night alone.
Aba detehara?	Is it morning already?
Te del o Del sastipe taj zor!	May god give you health and strength!

The Gypsy Lover

Publisher's Questions for Discussion

1. There are a number of parallels in the novel, each in the form of a comparison or contrast, which the author uses to develop an idea or enhance a theme. Consider the following parallels and discuss how each contributes to developing the theme or advancing the plot: Armanda vs. Alta Mae; Nikolai vs. Evan's father and/or Uncle Goose; Evan's dead sister vs. Armanda's dead brother; Bozo vs. Alta Mae's Black Lab; Evan's father's dalliance vs. Evan's mother's dalliance; Sonia's infidelity vs. Evan's fidelity. Identify at least two motifs from the prologue that find their parallels in the final chapter and discuss authorial intent. Identify one or two other parallels that appear in the novel and discuss them as well; e.g., "the paradox of truth" as mentioned by Alta Mae over fries and again by the psychiatrist at the end. What does Armanda mean when she speaks of a "parallel universe"?

2. Why is Chapter 4 important? In Chapter 4, Evan makes a promise to his mother and dreams a dream within a dream. Discuss the importance of the promise he makes to his mother. Discuss issues of identity as implied in this chapter.

In comparing Evan to his father, his mother tells him, "As the twig is bent, so grows the tree." Is this true? What part does the man who took Evan and his mother to the Zoo play in Evan's mind? Why does Evan refuse to contemplate the man himself? And what of the "dark little vagabond that some might think"? Discuss the dream within the dream in the larger context of the novel.

3. Gazing into the crystal ball, Evan is made to see certain atrocities of the past, and at the center of those atrocities a riddle. What does he gain from his experience? How is it possible that Evan and Armanda may have the same grandfather? Consider the paradox of relationships throughout the novel. Consider the ironies.

4. What is the purpose of the burning house encountered on the way to the wedding?

5. Who is the mysterious child with olives on her fingers that Evan meets at the wedding?

6. The story proper is bookended by the prologue and final chapter, just as Yana tells Evan that the present is bookended by the past and the future, that all things come back around, and that nothing exists except the present moment in time. Compare Yana's exposition on existence to Evan and Alta Mae's discussion about how a thing comes to mean over French Fries at the Hong Kong Café.

7. The title of the novel has an ambiguous ring to it. Who is the Gypsy lover? Is it Evan or is it Armanda or is it both of them? Could it be Nikolai? Or Sonia? In the end, what does Evan learn about love? What are his possibilities for love in the future? What is meant when he contemplates the notion that the commitment to love should be greater and is more

important than love itself? Relate Evan's notion of love at the end of the novel to his perception of love between his mother and father and the absence of love he experienced living with Missy and Goose. Compare his notion of love at the end of the novel to his earlier feelings for Alta Mae. How does his notion of love at the end of the novel predict a future relationship with Alta Mae?

8. Who is the Wandering Man? The mystical creature in Yana's tale? The big-eyed man in Evan's dream? The hippie-ish mugger Evan and Armanda meet on the streets of Topeka? Evan himself? If Evan, who, then, is responsible for the tragic outcome in the story? Really? Why?

9. The theme of the novel has been defined as one of "Christian Existentialism," emphasizing the uniqueness and isolation of individual experience in an alien but providential world (who saves Evan from drowning in the end?); it seeks to explain, or to dismiss the necessity to explain, the unexplainable, suggesting, as the protagonist learns, that, " . . . there will always be that in this world which goes beyond understanding and speaks to the heart in a more meaningful way." While the theme stresses the importance of freedom of choice and responsibility over determinism or predestination, it nevertheless predicts a kind of self-destination in the microcosm of the novel: that the individual, if given enough time, will inevitably struggle through to his own capabilities, to what, in fact, he is, regardless of any obstacles. Has Evan struggled through to what, in fact, he is? Can you imagine Evan, having "proven" himself in both his virtuous response and loyalty to Armanda, ever failing his promise to his mother and now to himself and the possibilities of Alta Mae?

10. The book closes with a moral imperative: that the wisdom of perfection is within each of us, giving us the power to

decide for ourselves who we might ultimately be. Such an imperative is, of course, complicated by our weaknesses and strengths and certain events over which we may or may not exercise complete control. Identify some of the motivating factors that lead to the rather simplistic view that the "wisdom of perfection is within each of us and we can be as good as we will." Do you agree with such a notion?

11. Discuss the "voice vignettes" between chapters? How do they comment on character, enhance theme, and forward plot?

12. How has Evan changed in the end? Consider the novel's final passages together with the paradox that order and redemption is born amid chaos and despair. What has Evan learned?

A Note About the Author

Roger Ladd Memmott is a prize-winning author, whose short stories and poetry have appeared in dozens of academic and literary magazines, including *Confrontation*, *Sou'wester*, and *Cumberland Poetry Review*. He taught English and Creative Writing at the University of Cincinnati for several years, was Editor of *Eureka Review—A Journal of Fiction, Poetry & Art*, and currently works in the motion picture industry. He is working on his next novel as well as a book of poetry and a nonfiction work, *The Divine Paradox*. A collection of his stories is scheduled for publication. He lives on the West Coast with his wife and has two grown children.